IMAGINARY FOE

IMAGINARY FOE

LORI SCOTT

The Book Guild Ltd

First published in Great Britain in 2023 by
The Book Guild Ltd
Unit E2 Airfield Business Park,
Harrison Road, Market Harborough,
Leicestershire. LE16 7UL
Tel: 0116 2792299
www.bookguild.co.uk
Email: info@bookguild.co.uk
Twitter: @bookguild

Typeset in 11pt Adobe Garamond Pro

Printed and bound in the UK by TJ Books LTD, Padstow, Cornwall

ISBN 978 1915603 494

British Library Cataloguing in Publication Data.
A catalogue record for this book is available from the British Library.

To Joan, my amazing mother who inspired me
to begin my story and,

To Paul, my wonderful husband and constant
friend who encouraged me to finish it.

Prologue

The sudden sunlight captures the raindrops on the shattered glass around me, a glittering carpet that crunches underfoot. I make my way to the great hulk of distorted steel that was, till now, an ordered procession of ordinary people going about their business. Bonnets and boots depressed as if some huge infantile hand has been trying to wield them like clay; doorframes wrenched off or turned into grasping fingers reaching out to embrace their sympathetic counterparts in a massive metallic orgy, each wreckage moulding to the shape of the other, their contents, plastic and human spilling out onto the unyielding tarmac and despite the occasional hiss and groan of this unhappy monster, clamouring above it all, the sweet silence of shock.

I pick my way around an upturned handbag, upended baby seat and mangled headlights and wing mirrors, drawn to the compressed Mini, its bright yellow paint defiant in the macabre, metal conundrum. A man inside waves his arms in a dance of panic and confusion. He stops when he sees me coming, his face struggling to express his need over his fear.

I pause at the glassless window and can see he's pinned to his seat through the abdomen by a huge metal pole like a fly to a specimen board, a deep red tutu of his own lifeblood spread over his lap. The frame of the car is bent in and around him, a carriage of death to hold him tight.

"Help me." His lips make the shape of the words but there's not enough breath to carry them.

I smile.

"He… help…" he musters; the fingers on his left hand reaching out towards me are his only movement.

I'm unable to quell my excitement.

"Can you feel it?" I say. "How close you are?"

His eyes dull.

"Mum?" he says.

"You're going to die."

A whimper escapes him and he tries to lift his head.

I want to explain.

"It's too late for anything… all your plans, all your loved ones… too late. You'll always be trying to get home now."

The dying man is watching my lips as I speak. I can see the life dimming in his eyes as it moves out of his body. A gurgling rises in his throat before the blood spills from his lips, but his eyes continue to stare as I turn and walk away – away from the moans of agony and screams for help which are beginning to increase around me.

I climb the slope that runs alongside this part of the motorway, through freshly washed grass twinkling with raindrops. The smell of the earth rises to meet me.

PART ONE

1

Two Weeks Earlier

Steve Campbell cursed as the doorbell rang again, followed this time by shouting through the letterbox.

For Christ's sake! He tied his dressing-gown belt and hurried down the stairs. He recognised his wife's voice in the tuneless singing filtering through from outside; something about being a friend and offering bread and shelter. His face twitched in irritation when the bell rang once more before he could open the door. He yanked at it and a cold blast of wind bearing some opportunistic leaves preceded Amanda as she staggered in supporting his wife who continued to bellow her affection for her friends and the world in general.

"Julia! Please!" Steve said.

"Ooh, sorree!" Amanda took Julia's first finger and placed it on her friend's lips while giggling like a girl. "Shush, babe!" She looked around for somewhere to lay her burden and dragged Julia past the fuming husband.

"She's pretty gone this time," she said as she dumped Julia on the stair. "Not the little goody-goody we remember, eh!"

"I thought you were just going for dinner? It's two thirty!" Steve held the door over to keep the wind out, assessing his wife. "We're moving tomorrow, Amanda."

"We found a lock-in. Julia was celebrating." Amanda fluffed her

3

coppery hair and held his glare. "I kept reminding her about it. She just said that's what removal men are for."

Steve noted her appraisal of his plush dressing gown and designer slippers.

"Celebrating life, she said."

She was laughing at him, Steve realised. He smoothed his hair. In his opinion, single mothers shouldn't be going out drinking as often as Amanda did. He couldn't fathom what Julia craved in her company.

"What happened to her key?"

Amanda shrugged, smiling. She bent down to search through Julia's bag, still attached to its owner.

"It was really important that she be back early tonight."

Amanda retrieved a small bunch of keys with a "Shucks my bad!" and sauntered up to Steve, her lips parted, her green eyes meeting his. Her hand dipped below his waist while she maintained eye contact with him before dropping the keys into his pocket.

"I guess she knew that, Steve… things got out of hand," she said, her smirk returning.

He ignored her usual flirtation and pulled open the door for her. "Thank you for bringing her home."

Amanda tossed her hair again, her eyes shining before she flounced out. "You're welcome. She's been a handful, trying to feed the homeless in the town centre." She laughed. "Saint Julia, that's what one of them called her. Saviour of the Down-and-Outs."

She was still laughing as she strode out to her car, her long hair blowing behind her.

"Bloody hell," Steve said, closing the door and facing his wife. He didn't want to be calling Caroline out to help tomorrow, but Julia might still be drunk when the removal men arrived and he needed someone at the house to direct them. He sighed.

She was mumbling now, curled up against the banister, oblivious to her surroundings. He moved to her, his arm encircling her waist, and smelled cigarettes. His face twitched. She'd given that up a long

4

time ago, but she rebelled every now and then. It was like having a third child.

Julia wrapped him in a Southern Comfort embrace. "Is there justice for th' meek?" she slurred.

"Probably not, Julia," he said, grunting as he lifted her from the stairs. He contemplated taking her up to bed but worried he might put his back out and carried her instead to the sitting room, trying to understand her muttering.

"You want something to eat?"

Julia just smiled in response. She was already slipping into sleep as he settled her on the sofa. He took the throw from the back of it and laid it over her, tucked a strand of mahogany hair behind her ear and stroked her cheek. The drinking had begun to plump out her once-lean jawline he'd noticed, yet there were few deep lines and she was still a good-looking woman. Ten years they'd been married and it had been pretty near perfect, but these weekend jaunts were getting to him. He thought she'd put all that behind her once their firstborn had come along. He frowned, knowing he'd have to have that conversation again.

He moved to the kitchen for a glass of water. She would need that when she woke up.

·

The taxi driver pulled up outside the house behind the removal van. Julia let the kids out who were too noisy to bear while she paid him. Their shouting and whooping increased as they ran about on the front lawn like howling dervishes.

"Thanks for the tip," he said, then nodded to the girls. "I don't think they'll be much help today."

Julia smiled, putting her purse back in her bag. "As long as they're not fighting I'm fine with that."

Through the window she took in the vision that was their new home. Together, she and Steve had overseen its piecing together beam by beam, brick by brick, until the shell was there and then, for Julia, the best part, the interiors. It felt like a miracle that it was finally finished, though in fact it had only taken eight months from the go-ahead.

"Thanks again," she said, leaving the car. She took a sip of the coffee she'd brought with her before calling the girls to come inside. At the door she had to steady herself as the children pushed past and a wave of nausea hit her. It had been a good idea to use a taxi this morning, she reasoned, while cursing herself for the night's indulgence. Obviously she hadn't meant to drink so much. She just hadn't noticed the point where she was supposed to stop, that's all. She took a breath and willed the brain fog to clear. She'd worked hard this morning persuading Steve she was capable enough for the job and she didn't want that interfering harridan in her new place on their first day.

She was more irritated with her stepmother than usual as it had been Caroline's grand suggestion that Julia be the one to clear Annie's house this coming week. Julia had complained but Steve had argued his Parlour Princess would not have much to do in their new place because that's what removals people were for; Carrick House, on the other hand, needed to be gone through to sort anything of value from the tat, and Steve wouldn't leave that to strangers. She exhaled. All she wanted was to enjoy her new home, not spend the week in her grandmother's dirty mausoleum. Steve had intended to clean up the old place in the new year, but Annie, found using the dining room as a toilet, had forced their hand and her subsequent removal to an expensive retirement home meant the old house had to go on the market before Christmas to cover the costs. And so Caroline had volunteered Julia for the job. Thanks, bitch.

Her head cleared. Hell, it would take a few days max. She could dimly hear her children exclaiming in delight and the removal men bantering behind her. She took a couple more deep breaths and went inside.

The sudden breeze she felt over the polished grey marble floor as she stepped in told her the children had opened the back door into the garden. They were excited to see their playhouse, no doubt. Steve had insisted on installing a low-level, wooden den for the girls at the side of the lawn. Why shouldn't the girls have a new gaff too, he'd joked?

Her heels clicked like castanets through the lofty white entrance hall to the kitchen, a study in monochrome of black granite worktops and Italian steel units alongside white walls and black wood-framed sliding doors. She poured the last of her coffee down the sink and leaned against the counter for a moment, watching the girls play outside. This house was the culmination of years of imagining: the big spaces, walls of glass and tons of daylight pouring through, revealing everything.

"Good." She nodded to herself.

Seeing Grace coming down the playhouse ladder the wrong way, she opened the window.

"Grace, not that way, honey! Mattie, show your sister how to come down."

Mattie stood behind her youngest, who, realising her mistake, was starting to get upset.

"What?" Mattie shouted.

"Help her! She's stuck!"

Julia watched as Mattie helped her sibling turn round onto her tummy and proceed the right way till she was safely down the two rungs. She took a breath in relief. She could do without accidents or trauma today. Steve liked everything to run tickety-boo, and so far, so good.

•

By the time Steve arrived it was beginning to look like a home: a messy one, but welcoming all the same. Mattie and Grace hijacked him in the hallway and Julia heard both of them pleading with him to come and see their room first.

Julia smiled, listening to the argument.

"I tell you what," Steve said, "I'll see the bedroom nearest the bathroom first because I need the bog before I do anything else."

Julia heard Mattie's characteristic whining. "Aw, Daddy, that's not fair! You know that's Grace's room. And you're not allowed to say bog. Mummy said—"

"I'll race you up!" Steve said. Then there was giggling and a herd of elephants running up the stairs.

Julia put a teabag in a mug and filled the kettle. She hoped he would be happy with how she'd arranged the furniture. He'd cursed when he'd found out he couldn't be home during the move, but a client from Newcastle had insisted on visiting the site and Steve had wanted to be there.

She handed him his tea when he came into the kitchen. "See!" She gestured. "The palm looks good out there. I knew it would."

"Mmm," he said, kissing her on the cheek. "You smell delicious!"

Julia laughed. "I don't know how. I was working up a sweat earlier moving those boxes and plants."

She watched him position his tea on the sill in the corner before slumping into the billowy sofa with a sigh. Grace jumped onto his lap and Mattie sat on his slippered feet.

"Can we paint our playhouse tomorrow, Daddy?" Grace asked, putting her arm around his neck and menacing him with her hypnotic stare.

Steve smoothed his three-year-old's hair, smiling at his daughter's artful tactics. "Not tomorrow, we're going to Grandma's for lunch."

"What?" Julia said, glass halfway to her lips. "Caroline's tomorrow? Why?"

"She thought it would help us out if she cooked for us… Julia, it's only three o'clock."

She sat down next to him. "Steve, I wanted to spend this first weekend in our own home. Just us. Together."

"We always have Sunday lunch at hers. Can't you have a Coke or something?"

Julia pursed her lips but couldn't stop herself. "I don't see why we have to share all of our family milestones with her."

"She's spent this last month wiping your grandmother's arse."

"Steve!" Julia said as the girls burst into giggles.

Steve smiled. "...which couldn't have been easy... and I didn't ask you once, did I?"

"Is that why I have to pack up Carrick House tomorrow? Because you think we owe her? She knows where everything is – more than me."

"If you'd spent more time with Annie you would know too—"

"I've done my time in that place."

"Yes, and Caroline's looked after her all these years without complaint."

Julia looked him in the eye, half smiling. "They like each other!"

"She's busy as hell this week," he retorted, staring her down. "I want Carrick sold."

Julia sat back and looked out the window.

"Look," Steve continued, "she's not coming here. Not interfering in our first weekend together – she just wants to help by doing her usual Sunday thing for us."

Julia took a swig of her wine then put down her glass. He'd perhaps had a stressful afternoon and she didn't want to antagonise him, but he always brought up her obligation to her stepmother at times like these. Of course he thought the sun shone out of Caroline's Botoxed bottom because she ran the admin side of the property development business they'd inherited from her father and the two of them were doing extremely well. Her gaze settled back on her beautiful new kitchen. Her father would have approved of the perfectionist approach that Steve brought to every home he built or renovated, and he always said Caroline could sell sand to the Egyptians. Julia knew she'd lost this argument.

She watched now as her husband picked up the puppet on Grace's knee and harassed Mattie with it. Their eldest giggled and tried to grab it.

"Mr Loco says get off his feet – he can't feel them anymore," Steve said in a falsetto voice.

It reminded Julia of when she'd seen him at the student rally at Embankment in the nineties, dressed as a drag queen, all lashes and Lycra, handing out leaflets to bemused drivers stuck in the traffic jam. She'd watched him from Luke's car thinking she would never see him again. She believed in that moment, she'd left her hometown for good. Yet here she was, two decades later, a respected member of the Wynchstead community—

"Isn't that right, Mummy?" The puppet leered up at her. She gently batted it away.

"Hmm?"

"Family comes first, no matter what." The puppet's grotesque head inclined to one side, waiting for an answer.

Julia shook her head, looking at Steve, a smile playing about her lips. She was too happy in her new home to continue this. "Yes, OK. Caroline's for lunch tomorrow."

"Good girl," the puppet screeched.

2

It was a bad way to spend a Monday morning, Julia mused, sitting in her car looking at the monstrosity she'd been forced to call home as a child but which she hadn't crossed the threshold of since her father's death in eighty-eight.

Carrick House had no doubt been wonderful once with its imposing, double-gabled façade and the massive chimneys like sentinels at each end of the building, but now the red brick was chipped and faded on the south side of the house, and half covered in ivy on the west end, giving it a distinctly lopsided look. She saw the barge boards along the roof top had rotted this side and one had been blown off in the storms last year. While the main roof had been overhauled decades ago, thanks to her father, the sunken porch roof had been missed. It was covered in moss and the bones of the wisteria which threatened to take over the entire frontage in the summertime. Overall it was filthy, and the dark, green-framed windows added to its dreariness.

It hadn't looked so decrepit when Julia was a girl, but over the years, the old lady had refused to allow Steve to fix anything. Thankfully there were no guests to see its decline. Caroline was the only visitor that Julia could remember, at least going back as far as her wedding with Steve. The family were not happy that Julia didn't want the reception at the family home, but it was in such a state even then that they really couldn't argue. Since then Julia only saw her grandmother when Caroline could persuade her out, but the visits of Nana Annie, as her kids called her, had become more and more infrequent, which suited Julia fine.

Annie Allbright had become a most repulsive pensioner – no fairy cakes and home-knitted cardigans from this one. She'd stank of whisky and cigarettes as far back as Julia could remember and she swore like a dockyard worker. She felt justified to loathe the house of such a person.

Her gaze moved to the swing stirred by the breeze under the big horse chestnut at the far end of the house.

Can I have my own swing if I come live with you, Daddy?

She could almost hear her father laughing at her own squeals of delight as he pushed her too high on it all those years ago.

A knock on the glass made her jump. Tom Batson's weatherworn face beamed and he inclined the rake he held towards her.

She smiled, pressing the button for the window. "Hello, Tom."

"Hello, Mrs Campbell. I just wanted you to know I've started on the back lawn and I'm clearing out the beds by the kitchen."

"That's fine." Julia smiled at him. "Steve asked me to tell you, though, not to cut back too much, please – so it doesn't look too bare. He just wants it tidy."

"I know what he means. The season'll strip it down enough without me adding to it. Don't worry, I won't overdo it. And how're you keeping, Mrs Campbell? You're looking well."

"Thanks, I am well, though… not really relishing the job at hand."

"Ah, these things have to be done," he said, staring up at the Old Edwardian house. "How's Mrs Allbright?"

"She's physically strong, Tom, but she can't remember anything or anybody now – she's become a danger to herself." Julia didn't know why she was defending her family's decisions. The truth was, nobody wanted to look after the old cow anymore. "Mad as a bloody hatter, in fact."

Julia just caught Tom's disapproval before he looked away.

"Sorry, did I say that out loud?" she said.

Tom continued to look away as he answered, "Such a shame folk have to go that way. She was a tour de force, your grandmother, in her day. Well respected. And generous."

Julia knew she was being told off.

He nodded to the east of the house. "I remember she let us village kids come and take apples from her orchard. And sometimes she gave us conkers. Or cigarettes."

"Cigarettes?" Julia was shocked. "How old were you?"

Tom chuckled. "Oh, round about ten, I think… no, perhaps eleven. It was the year your dad married Mrs Allbright. The second Mrs Allbright, of course."

Tom looked sheepish and Julia nodded.

"I remember it well…" he said, "the wedding party in the garden, most of the village were invited. We were all wanting to meet the lady he'd brought down from up north. Northern crumpet, we called her – no disrespect, of course!" He looked for Julia's consent of the pet name then continued, embarrassed. "I would do odd jobs for your grandmother after that day and she'd invite me in for a cup of tea and a ciggie." He smiled again at Julia's indignation. "It wasn't considered a dangerous habit back then. It was even advertised on TV when I was a boy. Me and my mates definitely didn't want sweets or apples!" He paused. "She was a nice lady. It's funny I'm back here now after all these years."

"Mmm." Julia tried to imagine a time when her grandmother had been a nice lady. Perhaps she'd only become bitter and twisted after Granddad died? He'd passed away soon after that wedding and by the time Julia had come to live there she'd become a shrivelled, mean old—

"Well, I'd best get on with it!" Tom made to leave but turned back, adding, "My son and nephew will be joining me in the middle of the week and we'll be thinning out the trees and bushes and getting stuck in. It should take us about two weeks. Will I be seeing you around, Mrs Campbell?"

"Oh yes. I'll be at the house most of this week. Just knock at the door, or you have my mobile number if you need me."

"Thank you!"

Tom nodded to her as he strode off, raising his rake in a salute.

Julia took hold of her bag and hauled herself from the car to the gloomy façade. She hesitated at the wide green door under the cobweb-encrusted porch. Using her forefinger, she wiped away some of the murk on the Art Nouveau glass panes, thinking they'd look quite nice cleaned up.

The door creaked on opening and the neglect surged to greet her as she stepped inside, pulling her coat closer to her body. She tried the light switch. Nothing. Only the gloom of the November morning would illumine this dusty atrium today.

"Great."

The grand hallway was meant to intimidate and had done just that when she'd arrived there as a frightened eight-year-old, Julia remembered. It was an extravagant waste of space, being the length of the front parlour and sitting room combined and almost the same width. A bold assertion of rank by the Carricks, who'd built it in 1902, she assumed, though not much of a showcase now thanks to her grandmother's fear of cleaners and visitors in general. Cobwebs wrapped the light fittings and stretched between the carved spindles ascending the stairs. The old-fashioned wallpaper was yellow with grease and age and a fine layer of dust lay over every surface. It looked like Miss Havisham's. Julia was surprised Caroline had let Annie get away with such neglect. The old grandfather clock still ticked, she noted, marking the time you had to serve there. Big ugly thing! She roused herself. The sooner she got on with the job, the better.

Julia picked up two flat-pack boxes and an armful of bubble wrap from the pile Steve had left there and headed into the kitchen. She was thankful the light came on when she flicked the greasy switch, but it was so damn cold! She remembered too late that the central heating had broken down three weeks earlier and Annie had been her usual stubborn self about having workmen in to fix it. She shivered and looked round for any source of heat. The Aga dominating the right-hand wall didn't look like it had been used in years and Annie had flat-out refused to have a modern cooker put in. Perhaps the old biddy had used the microwave then for most of her dinners? Judging by the splatters of food and grease on the outside of it, she knew she'd got that right. She put her bag and boxes down then noticed an electric heater in the corner. Ah, this was how Annie had kept warm – along with copious amounts of whiskey, of course. She plugged it in near the biggest cupboard.

The kettle, as expected, was filthy. After washing it inside and out and using her own cup and ingredients brought from home, she prepared a cup of tea. The clinking of the teaspoon against the ceramic echoed around the room as if she was in a vast hall. She turned to the task at hand and began to hum to herself while she assembled one of the boxes.

The large cupboards above the counters were all full. Grandma Annie may have been a dirty old crone, but she did have an eye for valuable trinkets. Caroline had taken her to numerous antique fairs and boot sales over the years where she'd enjoyed spending her money. Julia's eye was drawn first to the Art Deco, chrome-cover coffee pot, which appeared to be in great condition. Might bring a few pounds, she mused, as she lifted it down and ran her hand over the metal. She buffed it with an old cloth she'd found under the sink then wrapped it and placed it in the box she'd marked 'Auction'. She reached for a garish-looking salt and pepper pot in a ceramic cruet dish. What on earth? Japanese. It looked like something from the fifties, covered in crudely represented, colourful fruits. Julia decided it was tat and placed it on the side. Another chrome teapot on the top shelf caught her eye. It looked almost identical to the first but was smaller. Perhaps it would be good to sell the two pieces together? Something fell gently against the inside of it as she lifted it down, and opening it up she found a coloured daisy chain curled up inside. The twelve embroidered flowers were sewn onto an elastic band which was too big to be a bracelet and too small to be a belt.

It's a hair band, you divvie.

Lovely! She didn't recognise it as one of her own. Must have been Caroline's. The thought of her stepmother wearing such a hippy accessory made her smile. Perhaps Mattie would like it. She popped it in her pocket.

As the pile of worthless bits and bobs grew, so did the idea that the charity shop could benefit from them. Steve had said to throw them into the skip at the front of the house, but Julia knew from her few hours' voluntary work at the shop every week that people buy the unlikeliest things and the shop needed more income to stay open. She would need a box to transport them. Maybe she would pop a few nice pieces in too from the auction box – yes, the chrome teapots for one and the brass candlesticks she could see at the back.

Julia returned to the hall to pick up a couple more boxes. As she leaned over to grasp one, a loud bang on the floor above made her jump.

The tick-ticking of the clock punctured the silence.

"Is that you, Tom?" she said, straightening.

She looked towards the midway landing where the intrepid daylight held tiny dust motes in its grasp. That was stupid. What would Tom be doing in the house?

She climbed the first set of stairs and looked out over the back lawns. She couldn't see Tom out there. She peered upstairs towards the dim landing, the light from the window spreading a little past the top step. The stairs' creaking broke the silence as she mounted them, the grey threads of abandoned spiders' homes ensnaring her fingers from the greasy banister beneath her palm.

She paused at the top, listening, before moving to the guest bedroom. At the doorway she scanned the area: double bed, wardrobe, no window open – nothing lying toppled onto the floor. Satisfied there was nothing amiss, she eased the door shut. Her father's old room which he'd shared with Caroline also looked undisturbed. The bed had been stripped some time ago and all the ornaments cleared, the walls left empty. Julia looked again for Tom through the window, as this room afforded a better view of the back garden. She angled herself to see past the warp in the old original panes down to the far side where the orchard began. Perhaps he was taking a break.

There were two more bedrooms. At Annie's Julia paused at the open doorway, her nose wrinkling from the stale smell of thousands of chain-smoked cigarettes which emanated from every surface in the house but which intensified here. How had the woman slept in here, she wondered. She took a quick look around for anything fallen from the wall, or for a book that may have slipped, but saw nothing. She was relieved to close the door.

Julia paused at the threshold of the room she'd been given on arrival all those years ago. It was empty, but the familiarity of the dusky wallpaper and dark pink curtains beset her. She was aware, while she crossed the faded rose carpet to the window, of pervading gloom and couldn't quite account for the sense of many tears shed in this room. But what young child that had just lost its mother wouldn't have been traumatised, she reasoned?

She peered out at the drive at Tom's big white van and was trying to discern if he was inside when she became conscious of a smell. She looked around and, seeing nothing, resumed her search for the gardener. Suddenly her ears filled up, as if there was a change in air pressure. She put her fingers to both and pressed hard, as much to block out the high-pitched ringing in them as to restore balance. The smell was increasing, absorbing the available air. It was pungent, like incense. The ringing in her ears seemed to have transferred to her head like a migraine. The room had darkened somehow while heat spread across her chest and she struggled to breathe. She fumbled with the window latch to gain some fresh air, but it was stuck. As she turned around, she had the impression of the swish of a full skirt as someone hurried out and a small hand as it pulled the door shut with a bang. Somewhere far away in the darkened, now-spinning room, she heard herself exclaim, "Hey!" but her head felt it would burst and she was going to throw up. She ran to the door. Grasping the handle, she wrenched it down, but the door held fast. Her chest tightened, her thoughts scrambling as she wrenched at the handle again. The door opened, almost throwing her off balance, and Julia lurched out of the bedroom with relief.

In the hall she slumped against the wall in the cooler air, drawing deep, shuddering breaths while beads of sweat trickled down her chest. What just happened? Everything was fuzzy and for a moment she thought she'd passed out in there.

She moved to the bathroom. The mirror in the dirty old closet showed her hair clinging to her temples, her face flushed. She shook her head a little. She had not lost consciousness but had been on her feet the whole time. She had felt dizzy, though – and there was that smell? Was she ill? Her heart thumped as the possibility of pregnancy dawned. Smells always got to you when you were knocked up. Oh God. She didn't want another child and Steve would go mad. She rolled her shoulders and eased her neck from side to side, telling herself to calm down. Stupid to assume the worst. Could it be the menopause come early? Hot flush? Yes, that was it – her first hot flush and she'd panicked. She sighed in relief at her obvious overreaction.

Nevertheless, she'd buy a test kit to rule out pregnancy, because it had to be negative. Had to be. It was as she splashed her red face with cold water and used the arm of her fleece to dry it a little that she remembered the fleeting impression of a child closing her bedroom door. The swish of a skirt. A chill shook her and she thought of the warmth of the heater downstairs.

Her bemused reflection stared back at her. Hallucination?

"For goodness' sake, get on with it," she said.

3

Caroline Allbright walked into Carrick House kitchen noting three full boxes and one half-full on the floor, a counter full of trinkets, plates with uneaten bits of sandwich and used teabags, and a stepdaughter staring out of the window.

"Anything interesting?" she asked. God, what had the woman been doing all day?

Julia jumped. "Oh, Caroline, I didn't hear you… I was just…"

"Were you on the phone? I heard talking."

"I didn't know you were coming over. You said you were busy."

"Mmm!" Caroline looked around. "Well, I have a lunch hour to spare and thought I would pop by to see how you were getting on. We can't afford to linger, you know, with the cleaners coming next week. Have you done any other rooms, dear?"

This was not a ridiculous question in Caroline's eyes as she herself was capable of managing two or three projects simultaneously, churning out huge amounts of work whether in the house or office in a small space of time.

"Er no…" Julia said, half gesturing to the boxes she had done.

"Seems like you need my help then!"

Caroline was used to taking over wherever she went and quite often in her stepdaughter's company. She picked up a plate and began to wrap it. "I've just got back from the home. Annie is reasonably comfortable but agitated."

"Did she recognise you?" Julia asked, turning to the dresser next to the window and selecting a plate.

"No. I think we've seen the last of her making any sense, I'm afraid." Caroline stopped, noting the glass of wine on the windowsill. "Isn't it a bit unnecessary to be drinking?"

Julia took a breath but didn't look up as she put her plate into one of the boxes.

"Actually I needed a little pick-me-up as I felt a bit… down earlier on. I found it in the pantry. It's quite a good one." Julia selected a teacup from the shelf.

Caroline tutted. "I thought you looked pale, but drinking won't pick you up, you know. It's more likely to make you depressed."

"You're so lucky, Caroline. You never seem to need anything."

Caroline looked at her stepdaughter's back, the old struggle ensuing. Sure, it couldn't have been easy losing her mother so young and blah blah blah, but life was tough and that was that. Caroline herself had been forced to rely on her own judgement as her own mother had been absent for much of her young years. She couldn't see why Julia couldn't get a grip. Ever since the child had come to stay she'd wanted to take a firmer hand with her than John had allowed. He'd spoiled her rotten in Caroline's opinion. Still, the child was now Steve's wife and she chose her words.

"We all have our weaknesses, Julia. We all used to drink – mostly whiskey when we played cards here. It was fun but I was acutely aware of staying in control."

Julia turned to the job at hand and tried to force the cup into a small space in the box. "What did you have to lose? You already had my dad."

Caroline raised her eyebrows. "Careful with that cup, dear!" She flicked the switch on the kettle. "I'll make us some coffee, shall I?"

She found a mug and placed it next to Julia's cup on the counter before squatting down to search the lower cupboard. "Did you see the little cafetière while you were sorting… or have you packed it? Oh, here it is." She pulled it out from the back.

Julia stood with her back against the counter, arms folded across her chest.

"I can't stress enough how fortunate I felt that your father wanted to marry me. Annie didn't take to me straightaway, but I knew I could win her round and in time we became great friends." She glanced at Julia. "Ah! The disdain of the privileged. I am sorry to bore you."

Caroline loaded the pot with coffee from the jar and added the water, a smile on her face. "You will never know what it's like growing up hand to mouth on a council estate and then to be brought here to live in this beautiful house – I know I've told you this before, but I want to stress that I wouldn't risk all of that by drinking too much. Who would?" She looked pointedly at Julia before rinsing their mugs under the tap. "It's all about gratitude, dear. Pass me a clean tea towel, would you? In the drawer behind you, third one down. Thank you." She caught the tea towel thrown to her and dried the mugs.

As she leaned over and depressed the plunger Caroline looked at Julia. "Steve told me about Friday night. I think he's concerned about you."

After a breath, her stepdaughter recovered. "Oh, that! He knows my nights out are just a bit of fun… but anyway, I won't be going out much in the near future. I might be pregnant."

Caroline flinched. After the smallest hesitation her mouth stretched into a smile. "Steve doesn't want any more children, Julia, which I am sure you know. Let's hope the test is negative. Why do you think you might be?"

"Oh, you know, tired all the time… nauseous."

"It's probably something else. Stress, perhaps. The doctor will probably suggest exercise – expending energy makes more energy, you know. If you need me to help with the children so you can do more of that it shouldn't be a problem."

She knew Julia would rather boil her own fingers in oil than ask for help with the kids. Caroline's time with the children was restricted to her visits to their home, or whenever Steve had them alone, she would join them, unknown to Julia. Once, Mattie had let slip that Grandma had met them at the local fair. Julia had been furious apparently. The situation was ridiculous, but Julia continued citing various reasons for why she couldn't have the children: either a dentist's appointment or Grace was tired or under the weather – any excuse, there was always one.

Julia would never forgive her for stealing John from her mother. As Julia saw it, her parents had been in love and Caroline had ruined it all. It was so far from the truth, of course, but her stepdaughter would never believe anything different, especially not from her.

"How do you have your coffee again? Black? With one sugar? I hope it's not too strong!" She placed the steaming mug on the counter towards Julia then added milk to her own. She rinsed the spoon under the tap and dried it with the tea towel before placing it in the drawer, much to Julia's obvious irritation. She caught sight of the overflowing box marked 'Charity Shop'.

"Don't feel obliged to give them so much, dear."

"I don't."

Caroline glanced around once more then took her coffee in both hands close to her impeccably made-up, plumped-up face and smelled the aroma, eyes closed in bliss.

"Mmm, so good! My only vice!" She laughed her best little-girl laugh as she turned and moved out of the kitchen. "I'll just take this with me while I have a scout around and estimate how much time it will take to pack up."

.

And report back to Steve, no doubt! Within minutes, the woman had undone any composure Julia had gained since the strange incident that morning. She grabbed another cup to wrap from the upper shelf. The handle knocked against the edge of the counter on the way down and snapped clean off.

"Shit!"

You broke it.

. "I know." Julia scooped the handle from the floor and chucked both pieces into the bin. It was going to be a long lunch hour.

.

That night, in an agitated sleep, Julia dreamt she was swinging to and fro under the big horse-chestnut tree. Her children were there too, playing on the Carrick lawn. They were all laughing. Julia was eight years old again, but her girls didn't seem to notice. She leaned back as she always did to stare up at the sun-drenched canopy shimmering with gilded leaves, the familiar shushing of the big tree above and around her. All of a sudden, the giggles of the girls were lost in the gust of wind that tore through the branches, taking all the leaves with it. Julia looked up to see that Mattie and Grace had gone and the trees had transformed into black, fossilised twisted trunks, stark and menacing.

She was standing now, looking at the house. The wind whipped her hair and the rain lashed her face as she began to run, knowing something was coming for her. She was at the door, but the handle was upside down. She knew she had to move it the right way to make it open or she would be left outside for the unseen terror behind her. The sky was darkening and a howling gale clawed at her dress, her hair. The door wouldn't budge. She yelled, yanking on the handle. Then she realised she'd been doing it wrong all along and that all she had to do was push the door. It swung open and she plunged inside to safety. Her relief was short-lived when she found she was in the pantry. She knew she shouldn't be in there. Time and again she'd been told to stay out. She had to get out before they caught her. It was so dark in there and she couldn't find the light. Her hands searched for the switch in the confined, airless space which seemed to be getting smaller. Someone else was in there with her. She could feel them almost touching her… their breath against her skin…

She woke knowing there was someone standing over her. She blinked to clear her eyes trying to focus on the figure by the bed.

"Mattie?" Her hands grasped at the lamp and knocked it over. She righted it and switched it on, scattering the shadows and the silhouette with them.

Steve stirred, complaining a little before turning over and resuming his sleep. She exhaled and fell back onto the pillows. It had been years since she'd had that dream. In the pantry, with someone, or something.

She waited till the throbbing in her chest stopped and leaned over to switch off the light. After a second's pause she decided to leave it on.

4

"The FSH test," Doctor Jarman said, leaning back in his chair.

Julia didn't know this doctor. He was small, balding with a double chin, precise in his mannerisms, fingernails spotless and well-manicured, rounded at the tips. He didn't look like he would entertain stories of strange smells and doors that were jammed shut by elusive child spirits flitting about the house. She decided to keep her account of things brief and uncomplicated. She wanted to get back to Carrick as soon as possible.

"Mrs Campbell, why do you think you may have started the menopause? Forty-one is a little early – although some women do exhibit signs at your age."

"Well, I had an... incident where I came over all hot and I nearly passed out," Julia said.

"Are you depressed?"

Julia wondered why he'd ask such a question.

"No. But I felt well, panicky, which is unlike me. I had a hot... flush, I think."

Her brain was like fudge, doubtless because she hadn't slept much after that dream last night.

"What were you doing at the time?"

"I was, er, it was while I was packing up my grandmother's house. I was just looking out of the window." She laughed, embarrassed.

"Could it have been from earlier over-exertion?"

"No, I was taking things easy enough and it just came on all at once."

"Has this happened before?"

Julia pondered this. "No."

"And what did you feel exactly?"

"Er, well, hot, nauseous – and dizzy, like I might faint."

Doctor Jarman looked at his screen. "So you've had what? One episode of this?"

Christ, sorry to be wasting your time, Doc. "I just wondered if you could do the test, that's all."

"Are you pregnant?" He arched his eyebrow at her like an omniscient father.

Julia shook her head. "I did a test this morning, it was negative."

Jarman turned back to his computer screen. "Drugs?"

"Pardon?"

"Have you been indulging in recreational drugs? Or are you on prescribed medication?"

"No, to both." Julia frowned as the doctor tapped on his keyboard.

"Still having your periods?" Tap tap. "Are they less than usual, more than usual or just the same?" Tap tap. "Night sweats, vaginal dryness?" Tap.

He swivelled back round to her and Julia caught his glance at her chest as he picked up his stethoscope.

"Let's have a listen, shall we?"

Jarman averted his eyes from hers and fixed them on her cleavage as he put the cold instrument to her chest.

"The test is not conclusive, Mrs Campbell. Breathe in… and out, and in… and out. It will show if there are raised levels of FSH – a follicle-stimulating hormone in your blood which may indicate the onset of menopause or… it may indicate a disorder. And in, and out, in and… out. Now I just want to listen from the back. Can you sit forward, please?"

Julia moved forward in her seat as Jarman, rather than moving behind her, moved closer to reach around her with the disk, keeping his head down. She felt his hot breath on the top of her breast, his lips inches away from her skin as he repeated, "Breathe in and out… in and out… in and out."

She heard a ringing in her ears and his voice became muffled. She felt herself blushing in anger and paralysing embarrassment, and averted her eyes from the top of his shiny pink head with the few thin black hairs at the crown. It was like he was feeding from her: a big, slimy, middle-aged baby at her breast. She thought she would be sick.

"In and out, thank you, and again, in… and out."

He still hadn't pulled away and Julia was sure she could feel his lips touching her burning skin. She was on the verge of pushing away from him when mercifully he was retreating and picking up a cuff to measure her blood pressure. He wrapped the cuff round her upper arm.

"How are your energy levels day to day? Do you smoke?"

"I… I stopped smoking." Her voice cracked as the words came out, her skin still aflame and thoughts racing. What just happened?

"And when was that?" He released the pressure from the inflatable cuff.

"When I was pregnant with my eldest, eight years ago."

"Very good!" he said, teacher-like, noting the reading then unstrapping the cuff. He returned to his keyboard. "How about alcohol? How much are you drinking per week, would you say?"

Damn, she should have seen that question coming. "I, er, about a glass of wine an evening and a couple more on a Friday – or Saturday."

"How many more on the weekend? Would you say you binge on these days?"

"No, definitely not. But if I'm going out with the girls I'll have a few."

"Four or five? Six or seven?"

"No. I can't remember… about four." She knew she sounded guilty.

"Is that every Friday or Saturday or both?" He smiled.

"Usually every Friday."

"And sometimes a Saturday as well?"

"Sometimes," Julia said, wanting to be out of there.

There was a short pause as he entered his incriminating feedback while Julia shoved her arms into her coat.

He turned to her. "Mrs Campbell, I've listened to your heart and taken your blood pressure. There are no irregularities there. As your periods are still regular we can rule out the menopause for now. The symptoms you describe could be caused by binge-drinking, which causes fluctuations in your sugar levels, and this may lead to symptoms of the kind you describe." He smiled in a concerned way, taking in a last look at her cleavage. "I suggest you withdraw from your weekend celebrations for the time being while we monitor the situation."

He turned back to his screen, searching. "Obviously if you find that too difficult we can put you in touch with a local AA group to help you. In the meantime, if such an episode happens again come back to see me and we can arrange to send you for some tests."

The smarmy bastard! Julia stood up, too incensed to speak. She felt tears stinging the back of her eyes but would be damned if she would let him see them.

Jarman glanced at her and gestured as if to stop her. "I'm just looking up the number for—"

"I won't need that, thank you," Julia declared before hastening from the room. Jarman didn't answer but continued tapping into his desktop. No doubt inputting his assessment of the clearly alcoholic but big-breasted Mrs Campbell, she raged.

She had to wait for a young mother with a pram to manoeuvre her way out of the door of the surgery before she could reach the fresh air and allow her anger and shame to spill. That bastard. How did that just happen? Why the hell hadn't she stopped it? And now he had her self-confessing on record as well… She realised how damming a report like that could look, how words could be twisted; as an ex-journalist, she knew that very well.

She thought of her dream last night. It was so real and unnerving.

Now this little chat with the doctor had left her feeling unstable – that would be the word people would use – or unhinged. She hated Jarman for his control, his clarity and his sordid manipulation of her. Locating a tissue from her pocket, with a shaking hand she blew her nose. Why had she started drinking so much again? She had everything a woman could want. Oh, what the hell! She enjoyed a glass of vino. It helped everything along: stressful social events, boring days, boring evenings. Did she feel the nights with her friends were boring then? Could she do them without a drink? Julia didn't know the answer to that. What about nights with Steve? With the kids? Were they boring her?

Now she needed a cigarette. She moved away from the surgery window, fishing in her bag, and hauled out a packet. It was empty. She was sure she'd had one left. She looked up the street towards the nearest newsagents, her eyes catching sight of a bird lying on the pavement not ten feet from her. It was such an unusual thing to see in the high street. She moved closer. It was dead. The poor thing was on its back and perhaps had been pecked at by a larger bird, or maybe gnawed at by a rat as a globule of red jelly lay on its chest, fresh and glistening in the sunlight. Her eyes widened as she realised it was the heart that lay there nestling on the soft feathers and, oh God, it moved! She drew closer, fascinated such a tiny organ could still be pulsating in the open air, on a busy thoroughfare in the town. As she stared, a beetle moved out from under the tiny organ, marking a slick, dark trail in its wake, making her feel nauseous.

A crow cawed from a branch above her, rousing her. Embarrassed now, she looked about to see if anyone had seen her hovering over the little corpse, but there was nobody near. She shivered. An urgent need to get back to Carrick assailed her. With a last glance at the macabre scene, she headed quickly to her car, forgetting the cigarettes.

5

Julia parked across the road from the charity shop. She wanted to get rid of her box of goodies before Steve or Caroline had a chance to sift through them. There was a couple of hundred pounds' worth of stuff in there, she estimated, and she wanted the shop to have it.

She pitched her weight against the shop door, resting the overflowing box on her knee while she pushed the handle. The door gave way and she almost fell into the shop, regaining her balance in time.

Staggering through, she was helped by her friend Row, a sixty-something landscape gardener who'd befriended her all those years ago on her return to the village. They'd met at Little Wynchstead tennis club and both had an immediate liking for each other. Not least, Julia found out that Row had known her real mother many years before and she couldn't help equating her friend with the mother she struggled to remember. Steve tolerated the friendship, though he certainly didn't know how much Julia and Row bitched about Caroline on the quiet.

The thing was, many women disliked Caroline in the village, but Row had a good reason for her feelings due to being short-changed on a job she'd done for the company many years before. Caroline had maintained that Row had messed up and they therefore were justified in not paying her the full amount agreed. She'd refused to talk to Julia about it further when her stepdaughter had pushed the issue. Now

Julia got her own back by allowing Row first access to her children and blocking Caroline at every turn.

"You're not normally on today," Julia said to her, huffing a little as they set the box down on the floor.

"I'm just helping out while Margaret's off, love." Row looked at the box. "You said just a few things in your text – this is exciting! Gill, come and help," she called to the young girl at the till.

Row looked at Julia, a smile playing around her mouth. "Tell Steve we are very grateful!"

"What he doesn't know won't hurt him," said Julia, rubbing the blood back into her hands.

"You look a bit peaky, are you alright?"

At the touch of Row's hand on her shoulder and the concern in her voice, Julia felt a surge of self-pity and her eyes stung with tears. Row pulled her close.

After wallowing in the hug a few moments, Julia pulled away. "I'm a bit stressed, Row, that's all."

"Really?" Row peered into her face. "So nothing serious…?"

"I'm OK. It's just emotional stuff coming up with all this unpacking and packing up." Julia laughed. "Look, I must shoot – I have to get back there and find you more treasure!"

"Will I see you at the tennis club this week?" Row asked.

"Not this week, but I'll call you… Good luck, by the way – I heard you were playing Eadie instead of me…" Julia made a long face then a little smile as she opened the door.

"Am I? That will be a barrel of laughs! Take care, my love."

Julia held up her hand and waved as she left but she didn't turn back around. The fresh air jolted her back to common sense after almost falling to pieces in front of her friend. A bit over-sensitive, wasn't it? Just because a seedy little prick had gotten his end away at her expense this morning! She breathed deep, checked the road to her right to cross to her car before noticing the honey-coloured hair spilling against the passenger window – her window, in her car; long hair, well past the shoulder, the sun catching the tawny hues in it. But was it her car? She looked to her right again, then left, thinking she'd forgotten where she'd parked. Because how could that be her Audi with someone relaxing against her window? There were no other cars on the right as it was a loading zone and on the left there were roadworks. She looked back. That was her car. That was where she'd left it. Her neck prickled as the tiny hairs there stiffened. What the hell?

In the shop, Row paused, seeing Julia standing on the nearside kerb staring across the road, unmoving. There was no traffic going past – not till lunchtime did it get busy. Row approached the glass to get a better view of the road.

Julia was transfixed, her mind full of possibilities and yet non-feasible. As she stared, the occupant began to turn her head. Julia felt her throat dry up and a cold sweat engulf her. The hair of the occupant seemed to take on a life of its own as it flew up and wrapped around the face, then, just as suddenly, the entire vision crumbled and Julia was left gawping at an empty vehicle. She blinked.

Row's hand rose as if to knock on the window.

"What's wrong, Mrs Silver?" asked Gill from behind her.

"Nothing, I…" Row's hand lowered as she continued to stare at her immobile friend, who then jerked her head as if she'd just come back to life and stepped forward straight into the path of a blue saloon which screamed to a halt inches from her. Row smothered her gasp of shock with her hand. She was about to run outside, but she saw Julia hold up her hand to the vehicle as an apology and make her way over to her car, looking inside it first before climbing in at the driver's side. Row watched till she drove away.

6

Things had improved since the pathetic abuse from Jarman. The steam from the bath rose through the candlelight, covering the mirrors and curling her hair around her forehead. The bubbles fizzed against her skin and she took a sip of wine before placing the glass on the corner beside her head. It had actually been a pleasure to hide away in the old house after her awful morning.

Knowing Caroline was not coming round to check on her, she'd been able to take time over the cabinets in the dining room and had found a whole host of long-lost friends in Grandma's collection of Wade Whimsies, the tiny ceramic animals which to the young Julia had their own characters and stories to tell. They weren't worth anything, but since they'd kept Julia quiet for hours on end Annie had let her play with them. Julia had always liked the little brown faun and the grey rabbit. They were at the forefront of most of her stories. The rabbit was the clever one, the faun the follower, timid like Bambi. A vague warning issued from the back of her mind that she hadn't done enough packing today to satisfy Caroline. She yawned and closed her eyes. She would have to make it up tomorrow morning in case the nosy cow chose to do another inspection.

Julie!

The glass smashed onto the tiles, shocking her from her watery cocoon. She peered over the edge of the tub at the glass all over the floor swimming in white wine. How on earth? She could hear Steve calling up the stairs to see if everything was alright.

"Yes!" she shouted. "Can you bring the dustpan and brush?"

How annoying! She would have to watch her feet when she got out. Had she bumped the wine glass with her head? She'd almost been asleep… had been asleep, dreaming of… something…

Another unanswered event of a weird day, she thought, the image of the blonde-haired passenger in her car arising again to disturb her tranquillity. Dammit, what was that about anyway?

She felt so sleepy. And waterlogged. How long had she been soaking?

She reached over and grabbed the bathmat from the rail to sweep the large bits of glass to the side then placed it rubber side down on the cleared floor glistening with tiny shards, so she could step onto it.

.

Julia walked in, fixing her hair into a ponytail. "Do you want a drink?" she asked.

Steve paused the news programme he'd been watching. "Yes, tea, and I want you to have one too." He followed her into the kitchen. "Caroline has been to the house and she says nothing's been done today."

"Does she spy on me voluntarily?" Julia asked, slamming the lid down on the kettle. "Or at your request?"

"How do you think I feel, Julia, seeing you out every weekend with that rowdy crowd of ignorant bitches? Breaking glasses and slurring your way through each evening – I need to be able to count on you—"

"I've only had one! You can count on me…" Julia unfolded her arms and put her hand on his arm in mock concern. "Did you get your dinner tonight? Did I get the kids to bed?" She looked at her watch. "Is it time for a screw?"

Steve's laugh was cheerless. He shrugged her hand away. "Don't be ridiculous. You are clubbing on the reg, there's a drink in your hand at every opportunity – I'm starting to think you're not sober in the daytime."

"You think I would drink and drive with Mattie and Grace in the car? Thanks for your trust, Steve!"

The absolute cheek of him. After Jarman's attack on her today she did not need the Ministry of Exemplary Wifedom on her back.

"You don't need me with Caroline around! Madame Bloody Perfect! I don't know why she doesn't just move in and I'll take the flat!"

She hit you... when you spilled the Coke...

Julia reeled with the sudden memory.

"Leave Caroline out of this!" Steve was shouting. "I won't have it, Julia. I won't have you ruining this family's reputation. Bob Horley saw you making a fool out of yourself outside Finnegans two weeks ago and I had to laugh it off when really I just want to slap some sense into you. Julia, are you listening to me?"

Julia recalled the day in Carrick House less than a month since her mother's funeral. A day her father was away on business, her lap soaking and her glass on its side in a brown fizzing puddle. Caroline had slapped her hard across the face with a, "You stupid little bitch," and hauled her from her seat, continuing to slap her bottom and the back of her legs. Somehow she'd pulled out of her grip and run to the bathroom, where she'd locked the door, hoping to stay there till her father came home. It had been a long wait.

Steve was still shouting. "You are not going to wreck what we have, Julia. You need to get a job and some self-respect. I want order and routine, not this chaos you're generating. Do you actually want your children to see you passed out every weekend on the sofa?"

Julia was about to retort but saw Mattie standing beyond him, crying in the doorway with her thumb in her mouth.

She hurried to her. "Honey, I'm so sorry. Daddy and I are just having a... talk. We were very loud, though, weren't we!" She pulled her daughter close.

"Julia, please..." Steve said, softer now. "I'm sorry I came on strong. I miss you – who we were. It's not our reputation... I love you! I want *you* back."

She looked at her husband and his very earnest face, and a giggle rose in her throat. It was nerves, getting the better of her. She squashed it.

It wasn't fair on him; he was a good father to the girls, she reasoned. If only he didn't champion Caroline so much. Maybe he wouldn't if he knew of her vicious side and maybe she ought to tell him.

Strange that she'd forgotten such an awful day in her life. Caroline had seldom lifted her hand to her – she'd been too afraid of her dad to take such liberties. And why had she remembered it now?

Steve was looking at her, puzzled. She tried to see things from his perspective; was she behaving like a drunk? Of course she didn't want her kids to see her passed out on the weekends, or ever...

She sighed. It couldn't have been easy for Steve to hear Bob's account of her that night in town. Damn him. She'd known, when she remembered the encounter the next morning, that he would blab.

"Look, I'm sorry if you've been embarrassed by me..." She held up her hand to stop his response. "Can we talk later? Let me get Mattie to bed."

Steve reached out to grasp her hand as she passed him, but Julia shook him free. She was still too angry.

As Julia was wiping her daughter's eyes with a tissue in the bedroom, Mattie asked the inevitable question in a quivering voice, "Are you and Daddy going to get divorced, Mummy? Like Sylvia's parents?"

Julia's heart crashed in shame. Staying together: the hardest thing for any parent to guarantee. Since Julia's own childish prayers had been ignored all those years ago, she'd decided to cut God out of the equation and ensure her children had a happy home by marrying someone she felt calm around, removing any chance of disruptive emotions, the kind of emotions she'd left behind – the old Julia. She and Steve were complicit in this marriage-by-numbers game to some extent, she knew that. She'd believed it would work, but despite the successful business and the beautiful new home – evidence of a perfect union, Steve had gloated – according to him, the old Julia was back. She'd sneaked in somehow.

And now she was shocked at how Mattie's words had prompted a vision of a new life, how the word 'freedom' had popped unbidden into her head.

She kissed her daughter's cheek. "Darling, Daddy and I don't argue so much, do we? This is just a little disagreement." Julia gently pulled the daisy-chain hair band from her daughter's head. "This looks nice on you, but it's not safe to wear at bedtime. I'll put it here for you on your table. All mummies and daddies get cross with each other sometimes. Try not to worry, my love."

Mattie looked up at her, her tear-filled eyes seeking comfort. "It's just that on the weekend, when you go out with your friends, I think you won't come back..." Her lip trembled. "I l-lie awake as long as I can, till I hear your voice again in the hallway."

"Oh, my sweetheart!"

Horrified at her own selfishness and feeling defensive in equal measure, Julia smoothed her daughter's dark brown hair from her face. "I will always come back to you, Mattie. I just want to spend some time with my friends – like you do, except Mummy does it at night time, while you're sleeping. Or should be. So you won't miss me."

She tucked the pink and white duvet around her firstborn.

"Mattie, look at me now. I'll never leave you, OK! You can go to sleep when Mummy goes out because you can be sure that when you wake in the morning I'll be here, to make you breakfast and brush your hair. OK? Do you believe me, my love?"

Mattie managed a little smile. "I love you, Mummy."

"I love you too, darling." Julia hugged her tight.

Sort yourself out.

"I know."

"What do you know, Mummy?"

Julia looked at her in surprise. "I know you and Grace are the only thing in my world that makes any sense, my darling."

7

Mattie was in her dream that night. She was calling for Julia from the top of the stairs at Carrick House. Julia was trying to move towards her, but the banisters and steps warped in and out of shape and Julia strained to cross the ever-widening distance to her daughter. Panicking, she tried again to reach her as Mattie began to cry. Julia too was crying in anguish and frustration.

She woke and could still hear her daughter crying. Julia wiped her tears and checked the time: three thirty. She hauled herself out of bed and put on her dressing gown. It was bitter but this was not altogether surprising as the bedroom door was wide open. She glanced back to her empty bed then to the en-suite, which was in darkness. Steve must have gone to check on Mattie, she thought. She ran her hand over the radiator as she passed it. It was on low, as they'd set it at the beginning of the week.

For some reason, the hall nightlight, put in place at Mattie's request, was off and Julia hurried through the dark to her daughter's room. Opening the door, the crying yielded to a sudden eerie silence. Julia paused, taking in her sleeping daughter illuminated by the moonlight. She saw the duvet on the floor. No wonder! She moved to pick it up. The poor thing was likely freezing but too tired to wake up to fix it. Julia reinstated the heavy cover and tucked it under the mattress on either side of Mattie, shivering as she did so. Christ – so cold! Felt like a frost coming – if it wasn't already covering the garden.

She noticed her daughter had slipped the headband on again and she removed it once more. She doubled it up and slipped it around her wrist before comforting Mattie, shushing her back into slumber.

As Julia was easing the bedroom door to a close, a sudden movement in the shadows caught her eye. Her breath caught in her throat and her hand reached out and switched on the lights, but they failed.

Julia felt the hairs rise on the back of her neck. Someone was moving down the stairs. All she could see was a dark, silent shape. Her voice froze in her throat as she tried to speak. It's my imagination, she told herself, as she moved closer to the stairwell – a trick of the light.

Julia's eyes smarted as she strained to define it. It seemed to waver like a curtain in a breeze, the size of a small adult. She inched to the banister to see if it showed up in the thin beam of moonlight cast over the stairs, her eyes watering, breath held. She was dreaming – had to be. There! The shadow had departed from the other side of the window and was gliding down the second flight. Julia was trembling all over as she took the first cautious step to descend the stairs, trying to keep the undulating form in view. She was halfway down when she watched it merge like smoke into the darkness of the hall.

Heart thumping, Julia extended her hand along the wall as she stepped lower and lower into the freezing lobby trying to find the light switch before reaching the bottom stair. Her eyes sought the amorphous shape, her breath issuing in erratic white clouds in front of her. At that moment, she felt, rather than saw, movement in the doorway to the sitting room. Frantic for the light, her hand swept the wall, found the switch and snapped it on without result. She flicked the switch twice more, panic rising in her throat. The idea of a power cut flitted through her mind – or was she dreaming?

Unaffected by Julia's dilemma, the dark mass moved further into the room where a light from the study on the other side cast a faint glow.

Julia held at the doorway, straining to make out some detail where the thing had paused, halfway across the room.

"Who are you?" she called out, terrified yet fascinated. As Julia stared, the thing slowly absorbed the yellow light from the study on its left side like a sponge sucking up water. A million tiny spiders crawled across Julia's scalp and sweat trickled down her spine as it took on definition on one side. It held out its thin arms towards her in supplication. Julia's saliva caught in the back of her throat, causing her to splutter as a wave of even colder air wrapped around her. The one sound was that of her teeth chattering while her mind battled the unthinkable. She was dizzy and her chest was closing in, squeezing her.

The thing in front of her now was a grey yellow and Julia could not make out any features in the jaundiced skin. It took a step towards her yet the next instant it seemed much closer. Julia felt a moroseness fall around her; an overwhelming smell of decay and vomit filled her nostrils and she tried to turn away to breathe but found her chest compressed. The shape began to swim in front of her as her ears buzzed and a pain rose in her chest and then everything was illuminated as Steve switched on the light from the other side of the room. Julia saw only a negative print of someone impress against the light before disappearing as sure as the visitor to her car had vanished yesterday. She staggered and sucked the air back into her lungs with a wheezing, grinding sound, trying to recover but sinking to her knees.

8

Steve rushed to her. "Julia?"

"Did... did you see it...?"

"What?"

"That... thing."

"What thing?" Steve tried to look into Julia's eyes, but her face was obscured as she tried to breathe.

"Mattie, she..."

"Mattie's in bed, Julia."

"...She. Oh my God, Mattie! Grace! Go check on them. Hurry!"

Steve frowned then turned and ran up the stairs, taking two at a time.

Julia's heart rate began to slow as she gulped the air, the pain in her chest easing. She forced herself to calm down and was able to lift her head, which she leaned against the doorframe.

It was a girl, she was sure. Before it evaporated, she'd had the impression of long hair and a dress. The same girl from her car? She shivered, recalling the dread it had evoked as it had lurched nearer to her. Julia had never seen a ghost before and she was still not sure that's what it was, but it was not part of the living. She took some more deep breaths and clasped her hands together to stop them from shaking.

Steve returned. The girls were fine. He helped her to the sofa and asked her if she wanted a cup of tea? No. Water, please. Julia's mind was racing, trying to come to terms with what her eyes had seen but what her brain could not acknowledge. She realised all of the lights were on, including the hall's. How could that be?

"OK what's going on?" Steve had returned with a glass of water. He looked straight at her, daring her to bring more chaos into his world.

Julia took a sip of water, her thoughts racing. She faced her husband's no-nonsense demeanour and countered, "What were you doing in the study, Steve, at three in the morning?"

He seemed surprised. "I was working, of course. On plans."

She looked at him.

"I didn't realise the time until I heard you in the sitting room and checked my watch. It was a bit bloody creepy, Julia, after hours of silence and concentration, suddenly hearing a voice. Then seeing you standing there like a sleepwalker."

She felt mean, suspecting him… of what? She was exhausted.

"I'm sorry, Steve. I… must have been half-asleep or maybe I was sleepwalking. I had a bad dream." She was not ready to discuss this, she realised. She needed to make sense of it all. She sipped the water and, feeling stronger, pulled herself up to go back to bed. She turned, however, and walked to the open study door. "The laptop's off."

"Yes, it is. I was working with hard copies. Julia, what's wrong? Why are you questioning me? You're the one acting weird!"

Julia looked around for the plans and noticed a pile of them on the sofa. "Sorry," she managed. She walked past him while he shook his head in frustration.

"Goodnight," she said.

9

Caroline had chosen a table at the back of the main café at Little Wynchstead where they wouldn't be overheard. The venue had graduated over the last three years, from a greasy spoon to an artisan establishment which prided itself on good coffee, an eclectic menu and catering for various dietary limitations.

"You can get so much gluten-free at this place now," Caroline said, turning the page. "It gets better every time we come here."

Steve muttered, non-committal, tearing at a packet of sugar.

Caroline put the menu down and drew her coffee towards her, moving the complimentary biscuit from her saucer to the centre of the table.

"Look, she doesn't need therapy. She just needs to go back to work, Steve. Women that age have to have a project on the go, to redirect their hormones – otherwise they turn into lunatics."

"I just want things back the way they were before Grace was born. I can't concentrate on the business. I certainly don't need her hanging around the study in the middle of the morning when I'm... busy." He placed his thumb and forefinger on his closed eyelids, took a deep breath then resumed the stirring of his coffee. "Only Julia can make so much out of a bad dream."

"I know, I know. Look, let's get Annie's place sorted and sold and then we can find Julia a job – at the office, maybe... Believe me, once she's stuck in a nine to five everything will settle down."

"No, I don't want her working with us. But I could pull strings at the council. Yes, it's a good idea. Once she's done the house she'll need some new responsibilities... It's just that the decorators are due in a week. Are you going there today?"

"No, I'm having a massage after I finish at the office..."

"Do you have to? Couldn't you postpone?" Steve smirked, changing tack. "I could give you a massage..." He reached over and brushed the back of her hand resting on the table with his own. "I remember your—"

She pulled her hand away. "Remember you have a business to run, Steve, and a big event coming up."

"My annual headache!"

"Oh, stop moaning! All you have to do is be there, do your speech, donate the cheque and leave the rest to me. What's the problem?"

Steve opened the biscuit packet discarded by Caroline. "I know the foundation's good for us. You manage it well. Father thinks so." He grinned. "Not bad for a school dropout."

Now it was Caroline's turn to smirk. "You stuck-up middle-class prick. What do you know about coming from the wrong side of town? With your big house, skiing holidays and every whim catered for? You know! I didn't need your advantages because I had all I needed in here." She tapped her head. "Your kind want people like me to stay at the bottom. But once you see what I can do for you... we're all suddenly best friends." She took a tentative drink and reached for her bag, pulling out her sweetener. "This is too strong."

After stirring her drink and taking a further, satisfactory sip, she resumed. "I knew lots of wealthy people at the beginning. All I had to do was copy their mannerisms, learn about their hierarchies and how to manipulate them all. I think that's why I impressed John."

"John was hard to impress."

"You were always terrified of him... We had the same sense of self-preservation. And he was funny... made me laugh. He knew we'd be good together."

"Wasn't Eve a problem for the two of you back then?"

"He was glad to divorce her... too provincial and way too clingy. He didn't believe in love."

"But he adored Julia when she first came to live with you. I remember him bringing out huge presents at one of the birthday parties and him hugging her all the time. That's love, isn't it?"

"I believe in love, Steve. Love you can direct; otherwise it becomes a destructive force. What John felt for his child when she arrived on our doorstep was curiosity. It was all new for him. He was experimenting with the father role and, to my annoyance, she became his little princess and was untouchable. Got away with murder, she did. She was a defiant little madam to start with."

Steve grimaced and removed a tiny crumb from the tabletop. "And now, I just don't know what's going on. She won't discuss her doctor's appointment with me – although I do know she's not pregnant – thank God! I just wish I hadn't given her the job of the house to do now... enough on my mind without worrying about that. I've a meeting with Shortland tomorrow. I have to let him go."

"The one with the sick wife?"

"Yes. Tell me – why do my staff think they can take the piss like this? Two days out of five he did last week. It's the bloody benefits office he wants to take his sob stories to, not me. Put the ad out again for Monday, will you? I hope we can replace him before the Planet job starts."

He shook his head at the list of commitments scrolling through his mind. "...Then there's Spieler, those units we want fitting in Botchley. I need to get down there before the weekend! I haven't got time to worry about Carrick or how it's dragging! Can you go there tomorrow and hurry it along?" He looked at her, from under fine, groomed eyebrows, a small smile breaking his grumpy demeanour. "Please? It has to be sold."

Caroline looked at him. He was like all males. Happy as long as he could have what he wanted. She'd been annoyed when he'd asked Julia to marry him. Caroline had foreseen trouble and now here it was. Did he love Julia? He probably thought he did. She knew he just wanted a marriage that worked: a perfect lover, mother and wife that would shut up and put out. To Caroline that was reasonable. Marriage was like a business. You did your bit, played your part. She knew what Steve meant about sob stories – who the hell had time to listen to those? Nobody had wanted to hear hers as a kid. You got on with it and sorted it out yourself.

"I…" Caroline stopped and looked at the small flaxen-haired child who'd wandered over from where her mother was sitting with a baby. The child stood looking at her, as still as a statue. Caroline looked over at the mother who, oblivious to her daughter's absence, was trying to feed the sibling. One glance at the numerous tattoos and piercings the woman bore told Caroline all she needed to know about her and her attention shifted back to Steve. "I've got to be at the office for Phil, remember? Look…" She paused, catching the movement of the child in her peripheral vision. She'd raised her arm to point at Caroline.

"I think your mother wants you, dear…" Caroline nodded in the parent's direction, hoping the girl would go away, but the finger did not waver and the blue eyes stared, expressionless.

"What on earth?" Steve murmured.

Caroline cleared her throat and spoke louder. "I think your mummy wants you, my dear…"

The mother, roused from her distraction, looked over and bellowed at the girl, "Chantelle! Get over 'ere! Jeez!" The child did not flinch till the woman yelled again, "Chantelle! Now!"

As the child lowered her arm the mother looked apologetic. "Kids, hey. You never know what they're finkin'."

Caroline's mouth had set in a straight line. She shook her head at Steve before collecting her sweetener and sunglasses off the table and putting them into her bag. "I'll try to get to Carrick after Phillip's appointment." She stood up. "I'm as pissed as you are about this, Steve. The whole idea of Julia doing this packing up was to take the pressure off me. My schedule the rest of this week is a nightmare."

"Are you complaining?" he asked while he helped her with her coat.

"Maybe I am!" She was flirting before she could stop herself.

As they moved towards the exit, Steve's hand brushed Caroline's firm buttocks. Was that an accident? She smiled a little. Let him have a grope – it fed her ego and she was sure nobody had seen it. She didn't work out every day for nothing. She ignored his gesture apart from swinging her hips just a little more – it kept him hungry and hungry people were controllable. She'd learnt that much in her time.

10

Julia sat Mattie down at the big kitchen table at Carrick House with her colouring pencils and some paper.

"Are you alright?" She felt her daughter's forehead. It was warm. She didn't think there was anything very wrong with her, but Mattie had been too tearful this morning to go to school; perhaps a result of the upset from the argument she'd witnessed between her and Steve and the late nights she'd had since, she mused. Or maybe she'd caught a chill that strange night in her freezing room. She felt cold even now thinking about it… and that smell…

She doused the memory. There was work to be done.

"You do some pictures for Mummy while I pack up the kitchen. Alright, sweet?"

"Yes, Mummy. I'm alright."

Julia dropped a kiss on the top of Mattie's head, squeezing her little shoulders. She looked about, feeling reassured by the clutter around her; happy to be at Carrick, among all the familiar artefacts of her childhood? Perhaps she'd been wrong to have stayed away all these years. Unreasonable, even. Part of her felt she should query this new feeling some more, but what the hell! If it helped her to get the job done, what did it matter?

What should she tackle next? Her eye fell on the old scales left out on the countertop.

Julia didn't bake these days and the ready-made cakes she bought at the superstore never tasted as good as those she'd made herself in this kitchen for her school fundraising events. Row usually supplied home-baked goodies for Steve and the girls so Julia didn't have to.

Julia picked up the lightest weight. It was covered in grease. She moved the scales nearer the window so she could have a good look at them, pulling off the cobwebs as she did so, her fingers sticky from the black, tar-like substance covering the metal. Should she clean these up before taking them to auction? She wasn't sure if they were worth anything. Her mind jumped to a warm kitchen long ago and the memory of her finger scraping round and round the bowl then scooping the sweet, floury heaven onto her tongue. She could still recall the sensation of the soft little granules of sugar crunching between her teeth while Grandma Annie scolded in the background. And the aroma as they baked; the best smell in the world, surely... Julia recalled how she would watch the hands on the clock moving to the happy marker when the timer would ring and the cakes would be turned out onto the rack to cool, the divine smell taunting her senses with the anticipation of the warm, sweet sponge between her lips.

She pushed the weights to the back of the counter and placed the scales next to them. They would have to be cleaned even if they went to the charity shop. Or maybe she should keep them?

How pathetic...

"You're pathetic."

"What, Mummy?"

"Sorry?"

"You said something."

"Did I?"

"You said, 'You're pathetic.'"

"I was, er... thinking out loud, Mattie." Julia looked at her daughter and smiled. "I was talking to myself..." But Mattie had already lost interest and was trying to decide on her next colour. Julia tried to trace her thoughts of the last few minutes but could only remember... Wait, had she decided to keep the scales? They were revolting! What was wrong with her? She shook her head. Get a move on or Caroline would have a fit!

Julia picked up the scales and dumped them in the black bin bag. She really had to stop daydreaming or… overthinking. That's what it was.

She began to unload the very dirty pots and pans from the cupboard under the sink while turning the events of that weird night over again. It could have all been a sleepwalker's dream, she reasoned, or perhaps, as she'd begun to suspect, a sinister legacy of the property they'd bought.

Julia had never been convinced on the existence of ghosts. She was a practical person, as her mother had been. Eve wouldn't entertain talk of spirits. It's just a trick of the light or a figment of someone's imagination, she'd assured her five-year-old daughter when it came to answering her fear-filled questions. A trick of the light. She was so convincing that Julia adopted the concept, grateful to counter most of her childish fears with the idea. She even used it to explain difficult situations, like when she'd tried to suggest how a mysterious trick of the light must have removed the last chocolates from her mother's birthday box and that she knew nothing about it. This said while trying to remove the smudges of chocolate from her lips. Eve had assured her the evidence proved to the contrary and pointed to her daughter's chocolate-covered cheeks in front of a mirror, at which point Julia had burst into tears, full of apologies and promises. This time, though, decades later, the concept had failed her. That thing… had seemed so real.

As she started on the other side, dragging pans out towards her, she went over her enquiries with the neighbours yesterday, of whether a young girl had ever lived on the property. Although Steve and she had flattened the existing bungalow, she'd asked about the family who'd lived there. Neither of the neighbours remembered a girl, though, or even one who'd visited. Mrs Blake, who lived on her right side, had told her the old couple had had a son who'd left for Australia in his twenties and never returned. So no lead there, she thought, stretching into the back of the cupboard to retrieve a tiny pastry cutter. Her fingertips plucked at the metal implement, sending it skittering into a corner. Drat! She stretched her arm to its maximum, trying to grasp it. It kept evading her. Her fingers had just found purchase when a sudden heavy downpour of water into the sink above made her jump so much she banged her head on the frame. "Christ!" She rubbed the sore spot as she struggled to her feet.

Mattie was still sitting at the table, but the water was thundering off the cups in the sink like a mini Niagara. Julia reached over and turned the tap off. It was stiff, so she didn't see how it had slipped on. After a moment she turned it back on with some effort then off again. How the hell had that happened? She looked at Mattie, who shrugged and resumed her drawing, humming to herself. She would have to get one of Steve's plumbers to look at it. They couldn't have that happening when there was nobody to turn it off.

Julia roused herself and moved to the next cupboard along. It housed her grandmother's neglected Royal Doulton. She took out the saucers and packed them all together in a sheet of bubble wrap. Shame it had hardly been used when she'd lived there and Annie had become so isolated in her later years there had been no need to get out the china. Julia doubted she was any happier now in the home with all of those people around her.

She looked for the last box begun yesterday of items for auction but couldn't see it. Perhaps she'd moved it to the dining room where she could add pieces to it? She should put all of this in one new box anyway.

"Mattie, I'm just going to get another box, OK?"

"O... kay!" Mattie said as she scribbled.

The old clock marked time as Julia passed by to the dining room. This was her most hated place in the house. The chamber, as she called it, with its oak-panelled walls, topped with white, now yellow, plasterwork of the early 1900s, was dark and dreary, with the large black, cast-iron fireplace brooding over the occupants at one end and monstrous oak dresser at the other. Julia felt the chill of remembered family dinners where she'd been a prisoner to Annie and Caroline's badgering and spitefulness; when she'd gulped down her meals just to escape from their tyranny, giving herself violent hiccups in the process. She hastily looked around now for the box she'd started. She couldn't see it. Never mind, she would start a new one. Hadn't she already decided that?

Returning to the kitchen with a new, flattened box, she stretched out her hand to push the door when it slammed shut with an icy blast, almost catching her fingertips in the jamb. She yelped as she pulled her hand from it just in time. She stood a moment, staring at the brass lever handle, then pushed down on it, pressing her weight against the door. It didn't budge. There was no key for this door, so she knew it couldn't be locked. Julia tried pushing again.

"Mattie?" She paused to listen. "Mattie, the door is jammed, can you hear me?" She rapped on it as hard as she could, though her knuckles made little sound on the solid wood. "Mattie, can you answer me?"

Could Mattie have opened the back door, causing a draft? Unlikely. The bolt lock on the back door was too high for her daughter to reach and these doors were too heavy to slam shut. Plus why would her daughter want to go outside? She held the handle down this time and heaved her whole body against the unyielding thing. Realising it was not going to budge, she set the flattened box down against the wall.

"Mattie! Can you hear me? I can't open the door, come here and speak to me, please."

A muffled reply came back which she couldn't quite make out.

"It's alright. The door's jammed, love. Don't worry, I'll sort it." Julia squatted down to look through the empty keyhole, though why she thought this would help, she didn't know. Peering through, she couldn't see anything, as if the light was out. Then, as if someone had stepped away from the door, Julia could see the corner of a bedstead in a half-lit, dingy room and from which a metallic clanging issued. She gasped and fell back as a soft whisper issued through the keyhole.

"*You know me…*"

An icy trickle traversed Julia's shoulders and settled at the top of her spine.

"Mattie!" Rising, she slammed the handle down and pushed as hard as she could, trying to squash her panic. "Mattie, please speak to me – Mattie! Is there someone there? Oh God!" She knew she could go and call Tom from the garden, but she didn't want to leave her daughter.

From the other side of the door, yet as clear as if it was spoken in her ear, she heard a young girl's voice. "Help me!"

She banged on the door with both fists in frustration and decided to go for Tom. As she made to cross the hall she heard a click and turning back she saw the kitchen door swing open. She ran to the kitchen and stopped short at the doorway, seeing Mattie sitting at the table absorbed in her drawing. She didn't even stir as her mother approached and put her hand on her shoulder.

Julia looked around the room. "Did… you hear Mummy calling you, Mattie?"

"No." Her head was bent right over and her hand moved back and forth with vigour.

"I was sure I heard you calling me. Did you call me… to help you?"

"No, I can do this myself." She didn't look up.

Julia went to the window and looked out. The lawn sparkled in the winter sun with dew unvanquished. Julia could see Tom at the far side tackling one of the bushes with a pair of shears. She eyed the back door. It was closed.

Mattie now had a yellow pencil and was circling it round and round.

Julia went back to the errant door and tried the handle, checking the latch mechanism. It moved with ease.

"Did you shout at all, Mattie? Perhaps to yourself?"

Mattie didn't reply. Julia went over to her again and looked down. Her daughter hadn't seemed to notice the yellow pencil had lost its lead and she was circling the wooden shaft into the paper so hard it was beginning to tear. Julia went to stop her and saw the figure drawn on the swing under the tree: a grey girl with long, lanky hair clinging to her face.

"Mattie, darling." Her hand went to her daughter's, halting the pencil's ravage on the page. Her daughter slumped towards her and Julia knelt to catch her, letting her lean against her chest. Julia felt her forehead. She was burning up.

"Are you feeling bad, sweetheart?"

"I feel tired, Mummy."

"I'm not surprised. You… you've worked so hard on your picture, my love. It looks like this house with the big chimneys. Who is the girl on the swing, Mattie? Is it me when I was little?"

"I want to go home."

"OK, darling. I'll take you home now." Julia kissed her cheek. She looked around the kitchen and hugged Mattie to her. What the hell was going on?

•

Once Mattie was settled on the sofa back at home under a fleecy blanket, Julia checked her temperature. It was not as high as she'd suspected. Mattie had cooled down during the journey home and was slipping into sleep. Probably what she needs, Julia thought, heading for the kitchen.

She poured herself a shot of Smirnoff from a bottle she kept in secret at the back of her spice cupboard. Steve didn't want spirits in the house, but this was for emergencies. She downed the shot then looked again at Mattie's picture. She was sure it was her horse-chestnut tree with the swing below, the house with the green-framed windows drawn next to it. The girl wore a dress that seemed too big. Her hair was long and close to the head, but the eyes, they were the most compelling: narrowed with pinpoint pupils and lots of lines underneath like shadow. The nose was a straight line down, joining a black rectangle for a mouth. The mouth hadn't been coloured in properly, leaving white jagged gaps which looked very much like teeth.

Julia wondered why she felt so unnerved. She was making too much of all of this. It was just a kid's picture. The door had jammed, that's all. But what about the bed she'd seen in the kitchen? Could she have imagined it? And the desperate plea? And if she'd imagined it, had she also imagined seeing a ghost in her house on Tuesday night?

She made a snap decision and hurried up the stairs, taking two at a time. As she reached for the box on the top shelf in her dressing room she was aware of feeling a bit put out that she'd had to leave Carrick House today. She realised with concern that she'd rushed up here with the idea that the sooner she found what she was looking for, the sooner she could return there! It was unrealistic at the least because Mattie couldn't go anywhere and there was no-one to look after her. She was not going back until much later, if at all. She had forgotten that. And why rush back? She hated that house. She set the box down on her bed before noticing how dusty it was. She made a half-hearted attempt to brush the duvet cover around the base as she sat down next to it, catching sight of her wild-eyed, dishevelled reflection in the mirror. Is that how a haunted person looks, she wondered?

Drawing

This morning, when I stepped out into the crisp, clear pre-dawn, it was like I was seeing the stars for the very first time. They shimmered there like diamonds spread on a black velvet jeweller's tray, seeming so close, like I could reach out and touch them. The wintry morning buffeted me with multiple sensations – cold nose and fingers, streaming eyes, smells of sharp pine and pungent earth mingling as I bent down and scooped a handle of snowflakes from the last remaining pockets, feeling them melting in the heat of my hand before throwing them into the sky.

I think I laughed. That was when I hurried away from the house and the security light went off, leaving me in the dark. I wasn't afraid, though. I paused one more time before I left the garden to marvel at the twinkling sky above. No wonder we try to capture such things in paint or in words. I think we're trying to make such fantastical things regular – in our clumsy way. We make them small and 'in deconstruction find a semblance of sanity', my art teacher once told me. I love that idea.

I'm good at it: making little recreations of the beauty, or the horror, of it all. My teacher says I could be an artist. I have a collection of pencils – all nicked, of course. Once I nearly got caught at Brooks in town when I left the shop with a fat drawing pad stuffed down the front of my anorak. The manager realised I hadn't paid and suddenly there he was behind me, yelling.

I'd just stepped outside when he grabbed me, but I wriggled free and ran so fast all the way to the river, past my bus stop and my route home.

I just had to keep running. The good thing was, he didn't know me, so I got away with it, and the bad thing was, I didn't dare go in there ever again, which was torture. I loved that shop, you see – the heady smells of paper and paint excited me far beyond any boutique or the No. 7 counter at Boots.

They gave me paper at the home and I drew cartoons of the carers or of the fat, horrible nurse when she came to check our hair. Of course I made the people I hate look ugly; there were a lot of them. I had a whole book full of cartoons, but Mr Cavendish found it and took it with him one night. He never brought it back. It made him laugh, he said – even though he was in it, looking like a hawk with that beak of his. I think that was the first time I felt I could do something special, something no-one else could. It made me feel good – as much as I could at the time.

My sister is my favourite person to draw because of her round smiley face and curly hair. I showed my pictures to my mum when I lived at home. Sometimes, she'd smile and say I was talented (when she was in a good mood). But if she was coming down, she would hit me and scream – why can't you be more helpful and make some fuckin' money? I hated those days.

I told my nan about Brookes and one year she bought from there a First Artists Kit for my birthday. It was so beautiful – a light-coloured wooden box with fancy gold clasps on it and when you opened the lid it creaked like an old treasure trove. There were so many colours all set out in little squares: deep blues of skies and seas to greens of emeralds and forests; Barbie pinks to strawberry reds, yellows and golds, lilacs and purples – colours of rainbows and bubbles. And the brushes! They were the real thing! Not those rubbishy plastic ones they gave you at school. These had long, slim wooden handles that felt nice in your hand and the softest bristles, almost as soft as my sister's hair. It was my pride and joy. I put it in a secret place so Kas couldn't find it. She would have smashed up the paints and torn out the tips from the brushes in her excitement. It's not her fault – she's just a baby. I kept it in my cupboard at the back, under my T-shirts.

One day I came home and it was gone. I searched and searched,

*hauling out every single piece of clothing from my cupboard. Mum heard
me shouting and came upstairs. She hit me and yelled at me to shut up
and stop being so selfish. There were other people in this house that needed
things, you know, not just me!*

*She'd sold it to one of her slimy friends and the money had been put
to good use. She was slurring her words all the while so I guessed the 'good
use' were the four empty bottles of cider I'd seen on the coffee table.*

*I'd used my treasure trove twice. It wasn't just the loss of the gift itself;
it was the loss of all the worlds such colours, brushes and I could create.
I was inconsolable. I didn't even feel her hands as she tried to beat me to
silence.*

11

Luke Crawford couldn't believe she was calling him. Her voice crashed through his head.

"It's Julia," she repeated.

A rush of emotions assailed him. "Julia? What the hell are you calling me for?"

"I—"

"How did you get my number?"

"I'm sorry, I—"

"I thought we agreed when we split, that would be it – no contact."

"We did agree, I know, but it's been such a long time… Your mum thought you wouldn't mind me… I was hoping you would help me."

His mind whirled as memories flooded his brain.

"Luke?"

"I can't believe this! I can't believe you're calling me… and for help! What about the posh bastard you married? Why can't he help you?" Again he interrupted her when she tried to speak. "You have some nerve calling me now, Julia, after all these years."

"I wouldn't if I didn't feel so desperate, I… please listen to what I have to say. Something is happening to me. And Steve… I can't talk to him about this. He… he thinks I'm unstable… hello? Luke, are you there?"

He reached for his cigarettes. So not much had changed then: volatile, wild, unpredictable, heart-stoppingly beautiful, Julia Allbright. He felt giddy for a moment until he caught himself.

"And are you?" he said.

"Come on. I'm a different person now. This is not a normal situation. I…" She cleared her throat. "Remember what you told me about memory and how it imprints on things and things get left behind… I know I didn't believe you then… and we argued about it for hours. And I remember you justified it all with science, but you couldn't convince me… but… I think I've… seen… there's something in my house."

Luke flipped the lid on his Zippo with his thumb summoning a flame on the down stroke. He drew on his cigarette.

"Luke… you're the only person I can trust who believes in… things like this."

"Oh no! Go to a priest! Why me? Un-fucking real… no thought to my needs or my life."

"I'm sorry, Luke, I really am. I don't have anyone…"

He found it hard to believe that her husband wouldn't dote on her and support her every endeavour or be there for her when she needed it. But he did remember she didn't have family she could trust and she'd been vulnerable when he'd met her. Perhaps her partner didn't care? He'd never considered that.

"Luke?"

"You laughed at me. You said nothing I could say could persuade you."

Julia sighed, "I could be persuaded now, I think."

"What are you seeing?"

"A girl. In my house. It's… it's a new house."

"You were the one out of all of us that would research the origins of a fart in an abattoir. Cover all possibilities as usual."

"I'm trying. I'm the only one seeing her. I think. Mattie drew her in a picture. And I think she'd been there, in her bedroom; I could feel it. God, I sound ridiculous!"

"Who's Mattie?"

Julia hesitated. The lost years between them surged, drowning what they once had. "My daughter."

The offspring. Great. Luke wanted this conversation to end right now. "If she's using the kid it's because she's receptive to her. Sounds like she's trying to tell you something – what's new in your life? What's old? What's been stirred up? Who the hell cares? Now if you don't mind, I have work to do."

"Luke, please don't leave me like this."

"What? The way you bloody left me?" He was furious but lowered his voice. "Don't call this number again, Julia, you selfish bitch. Those days when I dropped everything for you are over."

He was trembling when he put his phone down. He stood up and kicked his waste bin at the foot of his desk, sending screwed-up pieces of paper and the dregs of lunch all over the floor. The self-centred… spoiled… That day.

That day, twelve years ago, she hadn't returned home after one of their many arguments. After two days he'd had a call from her friend to say she wasn't coming back and right there, their ten years of wild nights and exhausting fights were over.

He'd eventually been able to talk to her when she came for her things. She'd said she needed to move on from the constant fighting. She needed a life and she was going back to her hometown to settle down. He'd tried to spark some emotion in her, but she was an ice queen: following her head, she'd explained, not her heart. She was so subdued he'd thought she was ill and wanted to take her in his arms, but she wouldn't let him near her. She'd taken the couple of boxes he'd packed for her and the suitcase of clothes and driven off in her car. He remembered standing in the street wondering why the sun was blazing as his world darkened.

He'd lost two stone in the months that followed and his job as journalist for the town weekly. He just couldn't pull himself out of bed in the mornings, doubtless because he didn't go to bed most nights, and if at all, it was just to catch a couple of hours before sunup. His boss liked him, but after six weeks of Luke rolling in just before lunch unshaven and smelling of stale booze, plus numerous warnings to snap out of it, he'd had to let him go with two months' salary and a friendly suggestion to pull himself together.

Twelve years on, one stupid phone call and he was reduced to mush. He hated her – the selfishness… He pulled on his coat and walked out into the rain, instinct telling him to take a long walk till his anger was spent and his heartbeat returned to normal.

•

Oh God. What had she done? Julia hadn't reckoned on her call exhuming her exact emotional state during their last row ten years before. She stood staring at the phone as if it was responsible for her pulse racing in excitement while her blood boiled at how he'd spoken to her. Arrogant bastard! Her indignation felt familiar. I'm not going through that again. She deleted his number from her phone. I don't need you, Luke Crawford.

She stared at the empty screen, remembering how angry he'd been. Was she selfish? She supposed, after years of silence, the very act of calling him just because she needed help was self-centred. Had she always been that way?

I shouldn't have called him, she realised. Well, she wouldn't have, had she not been desperate. She felt lousy and excited all at the same time. She gulped the remainder of the second shot she'd poured and felt the liquid fire a path down her throat. She recalled what he'd said? What's been stirred up… she recalled the fleeting image of a child in a dress closing the door in her Carrick bedroom. She made a decision.

In the sitting room she checked on Mattie, whose gentle snores indicated she was OK. Her temperature was normal, thank God. That meant she could maybe enlist Sandra to babysit. Their part-time nanny was due soon with Grace from her morning nursery session. If she could persuade her to stay a little longer than usual, Julia could nip down to the home where Annie was. Grandma might know something of the history of Carrick House – if she could get some sense out of her. She hoped they would let her see Annie without prior arrangement.

Julia's thoughts drifted back to Luke. She did feel bad for the upset she'd caused him, but the sound of his voice had sent a buzz all over her body. God, she hadn't expected that. Would she have given it more thought before calling him if she'd known the old feelings would be stirred up? She'd just wanted to hear an ally, she reasoned. Had she been living with enemies all these years then? Amanda would have listened. Julia wondered why she hadn't called her first.

12

The manager was unhappy with Julia's unscheduled visit to the home, pointing out it was outside visiting hours. Julia assured her this was a short visit on behalf of the family as Caroline couldn't make it today and, since she was in the area, Steve had asked her to pop in.

"I'll be quick," she assured her.

Reluctant, the manager asked a slim blonde in a white jacket at the desk to accompany Julia to Annie's room on condition she kept it to fifteen minutes and no more.

Julia followed the woman to a security door and waited while the numbers were punched into a keypad before continuing into a well-lit corridor. Annie's room was past another, smaller reception where a woman sat monitoring a screen. The blonde tapped on the door and directed Julia to be quiet as the old lady might still be napping.

Julia stepped into the sunny room. It was airy and lemon-fresh, the tasteful lilac and white décor reassuring any nervous daughter or son that the Glade at Higher Wynchstead was the best place their money could buy for their ailing parent. Looking at the polished surfaces, however, Julia was sure her grandmother would feel very much out of place here.

She approached the tiny form in the armchair by the window, from where a mucous-laden rattle sounded. She noted the drool running down the old lady's chin over the black stubble presiding there. God, she hated her. From the start, the woman had been mean to her and Julia had never known why, although her adult brain was now able to factor in that Annie had never liked her mother.

Julia recalled visiting Annie with her only once. Why her mum had felt the need to visit Grandma once she'd divorced her dad, Julia could not understand, but perhaps she'd known she was ill and wanted to acquaint her daughter with the family? Julia had never thought about it till now. She'd been five or six at the time of the visit and didn't fully remember it, but she did recall how unsmiling Annie had been and her mum telling a friend afterwards she was sure the old lady had pinched her daughter while she'd sat on her lap as Julia had suddenly jumped down, eyes watering, and almost ran to her mother; either that, or the old bag had whispered something scary. Perhaps that was it, because just two days after her mother's death, when Julia had just arrived at Carrick, desolate and vulnerable, the cow had sat her down and told her such stories of the house that she couldn't sleep at night. She wracked her brains now while watching the old lady, trying to think if any of those stories had featured a ghost of a girl, but all she could recall were tales of slimy goblins under the stairs that came after you in the dark of night, to stick you with their paralysing needles and drag you back to their lair for their breakfast, lunch and dinner.

"You miserable old bitch, Annie," she said.

Annie Allbright's eyes opened and fixed on her. Julia, caught off guard, looked for recognition, but Annie wasn't giving anything away.

"Hello, Annie. It's me, Julia."

Her eyelids did not even flicker.

"Your granddaughter." Julia waited. "I've come to see you, Grandma…" Julia began to feel irritated by the crone's stare. "I need to ask you something. Can you tell me about your house?" Julia studied her reaction. "Is it haunted?"

Annie, silent, continued to focus on her, but Julia perceived a slight shift in her grandmother's attention.

"Was there a young girl staying there?"

"Julia?" Her grandmother's voice was hoarse and dry, as if it hadn't been used in years.

"Yes, it's me. What can you tell me about your house, Nana?" She ground out the affectionate term with resentment.

Annie looked unmoved. "I want a cigarette."

"You know you can't smoke in here."

Annie looked out of the window at the landscaped grounds.

Julia followed her gaze to the lush greenery, bushy rhododendrons and manicured hedges surrounding white benches and ornamental bay trees, all overlooking a central pond and safeguarded by the cluster pines behind them. They were paying a fortune for her to stay here and no doubt Annie wasn't aware of the gesture, but Julia could appreciate Steve's decision to sell the house as soon as possible.

"It's nice here," said Annie.

The wily witch was bargaining. Julia would get nothing out of her unless... She sighed, fishing out a Marlborough Light from her packet. As she lit it and put it between the gnarled, leathery fingers, she looked around for the smoke alarm. She would have to open a window and try to waft the smoke out.

"Come on, Annie, tell me about the house," she said as she struggled with the latch on the top window.

"You were a young girl when you came to us." The old lady coughed and spittle jumped onto her shrivelled lip.

"I'm not talking about me. Did a girl live at the house before me – or before you?"

"He did not enter by means of the blood of goats and calves, but he entered the Most Holy Place once for all by his own blood..."

"What?"

"...his own blood... an eternal redemption."

Annie had another bout of coughing while Julia used a magazine from the table to fan the air away from the smoke alarm.

"Who lived in the house before you, Annie? Was it the Carricks?"

"The Carricks. Two sons... and a daughter."

"They had a daughter? What happened to her?"

Annie stared out of the window again. Julia squashed her irritation at the old woman's evasiveness.

"Did you experience anything strange in the house? Nana?"

Her grandmother's face creased in contempt. "Nothing stranger than angels, stupid girl."

"What?"

"The angels. In a loud voice they sang, 'Worthy is the Lamb, who was slain…'"

"So you've found religion. Good for you." Julia was obviously wasting her time.

"Like your father," the old lady said, beginning to rock herself, the cigarette burning closer to her fingers and dropping a caterpillar of ash onto her lap.

"He wasn't religious."

"He has found Salvation."

Her grandmother was rocking faster now and stared out of the window. She began to mutter. "For you may be sure… that everyone who is sexually immoral or impure, who is covetous… that is an idolater, has no inheritance in the kingdom of Christ and God…"

"Bloody hell," murmured Julia, moving towards the cigarette, now burnt down to Annie's fingers. "Annie, I need to take this now…"

"Repent therefore, and turn again that your sins may be blotted out…"

As Julia reached for the cigarette Annie lifted her hand away and hit out with her other, catching Julia on the face.

"Annie!" Julia grabbed the flailing hand as the old lady spat her scripture at her.

"Depart from me, you who are cursed, into the fire prepared for the devil and his angels."

As Julia wiped Annie's spit from her own mouth, still holding her hand at bay she watched in horror as Annie repeated the words 'You who are cursed, Julia…' and with deliberation ground the cigarette into her own arm.

Julia's gorge rose as the smell of singed hair and burnt flesh assailed her and the old lady started screaming.

As the carer ran into the room, Annie cowered in her seat, holding up both arms against her granddaughter.

"What? No!" Julia stood shaking her head. "I didn't touch her. I was trying to take the cigarette…"

"Cigarette?" The carer pressed the call button on the wall and came over to calm Annie. "You have no right letting her smoke in here… What the…?"

She broke off as she saw the blistering wound on the old lady's arm and the cigarette butt now doused in epidermal tissue on her lap.

"I didn't do that," blustered Julia. "She did it to herself." With a rising sense of doom she realised how pathetic this denial sounded as she towered over the tiny, cringing woman.

"Oh my God! What's your problem?" the woman said as two more white coats came in to help. "Restrain this woman while I call the police."

13

It was raining as Steve drove to Highton police station. There must be some mistake, a misunderstanding. Julia could be unpredictable, but she wasn't malicious or psychotic. He knew there was no love lost between her and the old lady, but she wouldn't have attacked her. Was Annie mad enough to do it to herself, though, as Julia was claiming? Perhaps it was an accident. Still, Julia had never shown the slightest interest in her grandmother, so what on earth was she doing at the home?

The police didn't hold Julia much longer once Steve arrived. His wife was subdued when she came out and Steve felt sorry for her. He put his hand on her shoulder and looked at her a long time. "What happened?"

Tears welled up in her eyes and she shook her head. "Are the girls alright?"

"Yes, they're both fine. Why, Julia? What on earth's gotten into you?"

It was once they were in the car that she started to talk. He listened without comment while she told him everything that had happened in the last week.

When he spoke it was deliberate and slow.

"You're exhausted, Julia." He negotiated the road. "There's no doubt in my mind, during your tussle with Annie she dropped the cigarette and somehow put her arm on it." He held up his hand against her protestations. "Listen to me. You have to drop it. I'll speak to the manager at the Glade and make a donation so no charges will be made and this will all go away. I'm asking you not to go back there again, please – well, I'll be telling them not to let you in anyway." There was silence as Steve drove. He glanced at her. "We're going straight home now and I think you should have an early night."

Steve could feel her stare, begging him to understand. He felt sorry for coming on so strong, but he was trying to stop the conversation from blowing up like it had the other night. He wanted to show he supported her, but he also needed her to get a grip.

He geared down and stopped at a traffic light. "Julia, I tell myself this is just a phase, a bad one! But we'll survive it as long as there's effort from both of us. I need you to agree to join an AA group."

Her voice cracked as she answered, "You think this is all alcohol-induced? An alcoholic's ramblings?"

"I don't know," he said. "But the first step is to get you sober. Then we can look at things clearly."

"I am sober! I'm not imagining all of this! Steve, I know you find ghost stories ridiculous and up till now I never believed in this stuff myself, but I—"

"No, you didn't! You used to be level-headed and responsible, Julia, but now you want me to accept that you're being haunted? Perhaps it was the ghost that burned Annie's arm then? Did you tell the police this ridiculous story? No, I bet you didn't!"

Julia was silent, her eyes brimming with tears.

"Was it the ghost that made you act drunk and disorderly in town last week?" he continued. "It's Mattie's birthday on Saturday and the charity do the following week. How are you going to handle normal life while you're entertaining this bloody nonsense? How are we going to maintain some respectability, Julia? With you going round telling everyone you have a spectre on your back or... you getting smashed out of your mind in the town centre? I think you might find you'll begin to lose friends and that will have an impact on the girls. Think about it."

Julia was silent.

"And I want you to go back to the doctor and ask for some anti-depressants. I'm prepared to stand by you, Julia, but on condition you do as I ask."

She choked back a sob. "Is that more important to you? Having a dazed... Stepford wife that you can parade in public that doesn't give you any trouble?"

Steve geared down for the crossroads, staring at the road ahead.

"Are you giving me an ultimatum, Steve?"

He turned right onto the county road heading south, back to Little Wynchstead. As the car picked up speed he said yes without looking at her. He felt her desperation, but damn it, she had to make an effort. He stifled the urge to relent on this.

.

Julia looked out of the side window through the rain. The landscape was blurred. Like her life. What the hell was happening to her? For a moment Julia hated him. How could he be so unfeeling? Sod him, she'd find support elsewhere. She wiped her nose with a tissue. She was surprised to find herself so soon again considering an alternate life, the possibility of giving up all she'd worked for and valued. But how? She had nothing else. No job, no extended family: an aunt in the Lake District who she didn't know very well and who wasn't interested in her. A couple of friends, single mothers. Did she want their life? Could she adapt to it? Be someone else? Julia realised with a heavy heart she didn't even know who she was, so how could she conceive being someone else?

How did she reach forty-two and not know herself? When she'd been with Luke she'd been an artist, a writer, a lover, a laugh. She'd had a zest for life and now the sole appetite she had was for Friday night and the Pinot, the oblivion. When did she stop painting? Luke had packed her brushes and oils into a box, but it had gone straight into the loft and stayed there. Why didn't she have a job? Grace was three. They had a nanny. No need for her to be at home… She could have been working all this time, even if it was a part-time job. But deep down she had to admit, after being out of the office for all of those years, she didn't have the confidence to go back.

What did she do all day? Tennis sometimes, lunch, coffee, the charity shop – where she pretended she was working and making a difference. She used to contribute with her journalism, but she'd left her job to marry Steve. It didn't make sense. Why did she leave the paper just to be a wife?

She tried to recall whether Steve had put any pressure on her but came up blank. She did remember thinking at her wedding that she could start a family now. Why Steve should inspire such confidence, more than Luke had, she didn't know. Perhaps because it was a less complicated relationship? Or was it because Steve was more in control of himself… or did he control her? No, he just wanted to help her, that's all. Luke was more independent, more inclined to let people look after themselves. Steve only wanted her to be the best mother, or wife, she could be… and she felt safe in his company…

Like a dad then!

Her hand rose to her face. She massaged her forehead, trying to quell the questions. Had she been so desperate for a father, even after all of those years following his death, to take up with someone that would tell her what to do? Why else then? Julia struggled to think of all things she and Steve had in common. School. They'd known each other in school and were allies when the council kids picked on them for being 'posh'. Their families were in business together; they had common history. They liked nice things: designer clothes, gourmet restaurants… art – though not the same artists… music, they both liked classical music, but Steve hated jazz and rock. Still, that didn't matter; she was past concert-going age… wasn't she?

She tried to recall her frame of mind at the time. She had to admit she'd let things just happen between them. He'd been the one pushing all the time and had persuaded her to come and live with him in the village. Why had she agreed to it? She hated her village.

Hated being near to Caroline and Grandma. What had she been thinking? She wished she could remember more.

Up till eight years old she remembered her time living with her mum and how happy she was, but after Eve's sudden death due to an embolism, apart from her arrival at Carrick House, her fearsome grandmother, some happy afternoons on the window seat with the Whimsies or on the swing under the tree, it was all vague. She felt like half of a person.

She realised Steve was waiting for an answer.

She looked at him. His stiff demeanour was her fault. He was uncomfortable with this crazy talk from her and the awful thing that had happened at the Glade. She was glad she hadn't mentioned her call to Luke to him. Steve was her family now. He loved her and he was offering support.

"OK."

She would do as Steve asked – well, she would go to a couple of AA meetings. She was sure she wasn't an alcoholic, but she would show willing. She would even pick up some happy pills, but she wouldn't take them. As long as Steve saw her making the effort it would be alright. She'd find herself a new role at a newspaper or magazine and start to rebuild her image of herself. Maybe with some motivation and direction in her life, the visions and strange happenings would stop. She would make this work for the girls and for her, and Steve.

14

Julia was putting out dinner when Grace wandered into the kitchen, trailing her doll behind her over the polished floor.

"Where's Mattie, hun?"

"She's upstairs! She won't come down. I tol' her and tol' her! I'll get her, Mummy." She ran out before Julia could make her sit down.

"Steve, dinner."

He came in and hugged her. Julia tensed, feeling the embrace was conditional, but she forced herself to relax and dropped her head to his shoulder. She was grateful he was prepared to overlook everything.

He helped deliver the plates, full of food, to the table.

"I'll get the girls." She took to the stairs, but before she reached Mattie's door she heard Grace yell.

In the bedroom Julia was shocked to see her eldest twisting her sister's arm behind her back.

"Mattie!" Julia grabbed Mattie's hands and pulled her off. "How could you?"

"She took my pencil away, Mummy!"

"I don't like her," Grace shouted.

Mattie appeared feverish again to Julia.

"For goodness' sake! That's no way to behave!"

"The girls did it to me at school. They say it's the best punishment," said Mattie.

"Which girls?"

"Debbie and Angela."

Julia's heart sank. Amanda's child, and Sarah's – her two closest friends.

"They did it to me!" Mattie protested.

"That doesn't mean you can bully people like they do, Mattie. It's unacceptable." She tried to turn Mattie towards Grace. "I'll talk to you later about this. Say sorry to your sister."

"I won't!"

"Say…" Julia stopped, noticing for the first time the pile of papers in front of her daughter. On the top sheet she saw the unmistakeable angry gaze of the grey girl with her long hair clinging to her face and the ferocious rectangular mouth.

"Mattie?" She leaned over to lift the paper with trepidation. "Who… is this?"

Grace was clinging to Julia now. "I don't like her, Mummy. She's scary. I tried to stop her…"

Julia put an arm around her youngest and bent to kiss her head. She saw the next page on the top of the pile – the same girl, except next to her was another, almost a twin: the same glare and the black box for a mouth. She reached out and lifted it, and there was another, with three of them drawn this time, each a copy of the other, all hand-drawn by Mattie. She counted eight pages in total with an increase of one girl per page while Grace watched her, tearful, Mattie unapologetic. The one word on each page was the same: 'Angels'.

Nothing stranger than angels.

"Mattie. Who is this girl? Why do you keep drawing her?"

"Because she wants me to."

Julia looked at her daughter for any sign she was joking or making this up. "She looks so… cross?" She didn't like to say scary. "Why is her mouth like that?"

Mattie looked down at her pictures. "Because she can't speak and she's all alone."

Julia shivered in the warm room. She dislodged Grace from her side and urged her to go and tell her father they would be down in a minute.

Once Grace had left the room, she continued, "What is her name, love?"

"I don't know."

"Why have you written this across the top?"

"That's what she says."

"How do you know what she says? Do you hear her? Have you seen her – in this house?" Julia said, thinking of the unearthly thing she'd seen in the light from the study. "Or at Carrick?"

"My head tells me what to do. And I thought of the word when I was drawing."

"Explain to me, darling, what happens just before you draw her. Don't you want to draw pictures of Daddy and I instead, like you used to?"

"I want to and sometimes I'll start, but she stops me and tells me to draw her instead and I have to do that first."

"Why?"

"Because the thoughts come stronger and stronger, and if I don't do it, I can see her."

"Here?" Julia stifled her panic.

Mattie looked confused and looked down.

"Mattie. Do you see her standing in front of you?"

"It's more like, she's in my eyes."

Julia was horrified. She put her arm around her daughter's shoulders and pulled her close. "Mattie, you can call me if it happens again. I'll stop this. You don't have to be afraid."

"No, I have to draw her, Mummy, or…"

"Or what, love?"

"You will be sad."

"Why?"

"Because she said she will hurt Grace and me."

Julia felt an icy shawl descend on her shoulders. She looked round, expecting to see the languid, grey shape pull out of the curtains or the door bang shut.

"Mattie, I… I don't want you to be afraid of this… of her. She cannot hurt you, my love. She just wants to tell me something, I think. And I don't want you to tell your father. It will be our secret."

"OK." Mattie looked again at her pictures. "She wants us to help her."

Julia hugged her. "I know."

She knew nothing. This was crazy, ridiculous. Where to start? As the questions tumbled in her mind, she began to fall back on an old routine. She would start where she always did: at the library, or she would go back to her old workplace, the *Highton Gazette*, and ask to use their resources.

"Let's go and have some dinner, sweetheart."

As she led Mattie out of the room she felt like she was being watched.

Faith

I don't like bullying. Probably because I was victim to it from day one. It makes me so angry!

As I'd crossed the fields in the dark with only the stars for company, I'd replayed the events of my first ten years on this planet and realised I'd been subject to one bully after another, starting with my mum. The only respite I'd ever had was that first home Kas and I were sent to – for our safety, they said.

I was glad to get out of our house and away from Mum's constant badgering, random slaps and punches, but Kas was terrified in the new place. She'd clung to me for dear life. So I'd looked after her. I became mum to her and Faith and Sherri; the two ladies that ran the place became our aunties.

Such amazing women, they were, and it was a real home for all of us. The House of Love, I called it. There was a small group of us, all different ages, each of us encouraged to be their true self but to help others at the same time. We all helped each other. I could tell Faith anything, and she'd talk me out of my worries. For the first time in my life I'd felt safe.

Then before two years were out I was forced back to Hell. That's why I don't believe in God now. Why would God do such a cruel thing? To take Faith away from us, someone who loved us all, only to put us in the hands of such terrible people?

The day they separated Kas and me, I will never forget. I was to go to a home for teenagers. They'd had to tear us apart. Her screams will stay with me forever.

The one thing I can say is that being with Faith has made me stronger. If I paused on that fence this morning it was in anticipation, not fear.

You see, when I make a promise, I keep it!

When my coat caught and ripped as I dropped down into the field, I didn't care. I had a mission and I knew my goal.

My whole being resonated with my mantra, which I used to urge me on, my breath blowing white before me in the frosty air... And it still urges me on.

"Hang on, little sis, I'm coming! Hang on, little sis, I'm coming!"

15

The ground rushed to meet her as she descended. Julia leaned back on the swing as she always did while her feet skimmed the ground and scooped a handful of red and gold leaves into the air; like a flurry of autumnal butterflies, they held for a moment before falling to the sparse turf.

The icy wind, immune to the pale morning sun, scythed through her. She turned over in her mind all that had happened in the last few days: the strange experiences at Carrick House and a visitation in her own home, the drawings, Mattie's strange behaviour and visions. Who was she? The girl from the Carrick family? Or someone abandoned and forgotten? If she disappeared now, would Julia also forget her?

She lay back again, looking up into the shimmering canopy, legs unfolding to propel herself. When she became upright, the girl was standing before her, so close Julia would crash into her. The swing slowed as it moved closer to the wavering, grey, silent spectre which beckoned to her with outstretched arms. Julia was half aware of the dead butterflies rising from the ground all round her, swaying to and fro in unison, a murmuration of russets and golds, intoxicating, but not distracting from the whites of the girl's desolate eyes, the pallor on the skin of her arms which seemed to suck from the meagre sunlight. Closer, the hair seemed not just lank but thick and cloying, like paste, clinging to her face. The girl neither smiled nor frowned but her mouth implored with its unholy gaping. Another shunt towards her and Julia could smell the decay and vomit, the fetid aroma seeping into her mouth, making her want to gag. In seconds she took in that the girl's wrists were swollen and red, as were her lips. Her dress, which she'd thought to be grey, was a faded blue, too big and old-fashioned. Her legs were bare and shoeless. The feet did not touch the ground. She wavered there, an imprint. Her pleading arms her sole expression. As Julia swung the full arc into the stinking immediacy of the spectre, she knew she would never return from it. Letting go of the swing, she held up her hands for protection, crying out. As she fell, the light was sucked into a black vortex which wrenched her out of the wind and into the dark.

She could feel around her the close confines of an unknown prison which muffled her scream and flattened her breath. The heat was intense, and the sweet smell from the bedroom at Carrick House was back and all-consuming. There was a roaring in her ears and the air about her seemed even thinner, like there was little to be had: only a foul exhalation from something close and a wheezing sound which chilled her to the bone. Her heart hammered against her chest and she began to gasp for air, pushing in vain against the sides of the box. Her terror surged and she began to scream.

Julia woke up. She was sitting upright and Steve was trying to calm her down. He put his arm around her trembling body and murmured reassurances. She held on to him until the shaking subsided.

•

Julia went straight to Carrick House the next morning after dropping the kids at school. She was exhausted but today she resolved to get to the bottom of this. She felt the immediate calming effect the house had on her as she pulled up on the drive, knowing she would soon be sheltered within, the mementos of her life around her.

What?

What the hell was she on about? The mementos of her life? She stared up at the fierce façade and the blank windows stared back at her. An overriding urge to turn around and never go back assailed her – make up some excuse to Steve, say she was sick, whatever, and forget about Carrick House. But the memory of Mattie's fearful little face prompted her to continue to the door. She had a job to do today and it wouldn't be the packing. She intended to search every drawer and cupboard for a clue to this apparition, this girl. She shivered. God, it was getting icy out here.

The leaden atmosphere enveloped her as she stepped over the threshold while the clock measured the silence. She refused to be cowed. A hot cup of coffee would get her going... She gasped out loud as she entered the kitchen.

Everything was unpacked: abandoned piles of scrunched-up wrapping paper, bubble wrap, trinkets and china all over the table and counter tops. The boxes on the floor, all empty.

Julia stared in amazement. All the auction stuff, the numerous jugs, plates, cups, commemorative mugs, were all stacked on top of each other. Was this some sort of joke?

"You bitch!" she said, looking at the Royal Doulton tea set and the scales piled into the sink. Clearly this was her stepmother's attempt to undermine her promises to Steve. Rushing to the dining room, she discovered the same reversal of all her hard work. Where she'd packed up at least four boxes, all of them were now empty, the contents back in their cupboards. Her eyes smarted and she closed them. She was so tired. Had Caroline actually done this? She tried to think. Had she herself perhaps decided to re-pack and left it all out like this? Was that possible?

She traced back to yesterday. She'd left Carrick and... taken Mattie home, then after calling Luke she'd gone to the nursing home, hadn't she? Or did she pop back to Carrick first? She couldn't have gone there after the home because she'd been detained, of course... She sucked in a breath. She was so confused. If she'd slept better... But she'd packed these things away, hadn't she? Of course she had!

Caroline had helped with part of the kitchen stuff at the beginning of the week. Wait, she'd taken some boxes to the charity shop, hadn't she? So how much had she done since then? What about the Whimsies? They'd been packed. Julia looked and there they were – in the cabinets. She took her phone out of her pocket. That malicious, conniving... She would ask her outright. She would not be manipulated like this.

You don't want to do that...

Julia paused. No. She had to control her temper. She didn't want to upset Steve. She must stay in his good books. But what about all of this stuff? He'd go mad if he found out. Well, she couldn't fix this now. She had things to do. So when could she do it then? She felt her resolve falter again. Then she strode to the door, kicking balls of wrapping out of the way. The packing would have to wait.

·

She walked, determined, into what Annie had called the front parlour to where the prized Dickens-style writing desk dominated the room.

The mahogany unit held nine large drawers: four either side with a space between them for a chair which slotted under the wide, central drawer. The smaller drawers of the superstructure were joined by a shelved gallery, topped with ten spindles. As a child, Julia would run her hands along the spindles and the beautiful, polished edge framing the inlaid, leather writing surfaces, the middle one raised and sloped, and would ask her grandma every time if she could draw her pictures there. The answer was invariably no until she became a teenager and Annie decided she could be trusted not to scrawl on the leather.

Now this urge to touch was stifled as the entire piece was covered in a thick film of dust. Julia opened the first of the smaller drawers. She wasn't expecting to find anything revealing within the papers stored there as Caroline had kept Annie's papers filed and up to date. Still, she took her time looking at each piece of paper for anything unusual and boxed it up as she went along. At least she would be doing something in line with her husband's wishes today. It had to be emptied anyway because the piece was to be professionally cleaned and transferred to Steve's study in a fortnight. Annie had made it clear she wanted it kept in the family and Caroline loathed it, preferring modern interiors. Julia had struggled to get Steve to agree to it as he too saw it as an old-fashioned relic.

It didn't take her long to go through all the drawers, and as expected, she'd found nothing. The next place to look would be Annie's bedroom.

The old lady's room overlooked the drive at the coldest end of the house and was the gloomiest part of the building. The odour of stale Gauloises cigarettes permeated everything from the heavy linen curtains to the silk-covered ottoman and Persian rug on the floor. The entire room was awash with the sepia stain of nicotine, making it look like a seventies photograph. Even the framed pictures of Christ and the ivory cross on the wall above the bed were yellowy-brown. Julia opened the far window a tad to let some air in, cold as it was.

She shook her head at the numerous smiling, benevolent faces of Jesus and wondered at Annie's sudden shift to religion. The woman had never set foot in a church except for family reasons. She wondered how long this shift to God had been going on for and how someone so immersed in Christianity could still be so deficient in basic human kindness.

She approached the few books in the room which were balanced on top of the chest of drawers by the window. She flicked through as fast as she could. When she picked up the heavy black bible, a ten-pound note fell out and floated to the floor. She knelt and scooped it up, pocketing the money; a fiver each for the girls, she decided. The bible yielded no more surprises and she placed it on top, turning her attention to the drawers. The first had tights, scarves and socks with more clothes in the next two. These clothes must have been the ones Caroline felt Annie didn't need anymore. The third and fourth were empty. Where else would there be papers or journals?

She approached the walk-in closet. The door was sticky at first then gave way, revealing an airless, dark space consisting of a single shelf, spanning all three sides above a rail which stretched across the middle. Shoe boxes and piles of papers filled up the space between the shelf and the ceiling. Julia didn't think her grandmother would have accessed this space in some time, with her bad back and shaky disposition.

God, it stank in here, not just of cigarettes but something more acrid – was it urine? Perhaps Annie had used this as a bathroom too. She needed to get out of here. Using the stool from the dressing table, she lifted her first pile down and took it to the bed, where she began to sift through. She saw that Caroline had sorted through it some time ago. Her writing was on the tops of some of the boxes and piles of papers indicating the contents. Personal letters in one, some of them too long to read now; she put them aside, intending to tackle them later. She skimmed through the shorter ones, though, with barely a nod to her conscience. There were letters from a Michelle Baker, who appeared to be Caroline's mother. These spanned the duration of a year in which she appeared to be begging the old lady to contact her about her daughter, but it was clear from the last one neither Annie nor Caroline had replied back. Old records of John Allbright; his old bank books, death certificate and other personal effects formed a pile of their own. She placed these in the box she'd brought up from the hall to be transferred to her own loft until she could make a decision about them. The main pile was of newspapers, about twenty of them. Julia couldn't imagine Caroline sanctioning a hoard of old tabloids. Perhaps the old lady had insisted, though why these ones in particular? She flicked through a couple, eager to get onto the other boxes. Seeing nothing specific, she put them aside for later.

She found nothing more of interest in the closet, just more bills, some old hats and shoes, and a few photographs of Annie's mother and siblings, now all dead. The photos went into the box to keep and the rest was piled by the door to go into the skip. She looked round for other places where something useful could be stored. The Ottoman yielded musty blankets inside and the dressing-table drawers were empty. On impulse, she searched the pockets of the few coats dangling in the closet, but her search brought nothing. She was just transferring the last of the coats to the bed when she heard a shout from downstairs. She stopped mid-breath, listening. There it was again, though now it sounded like a cry for help. With a slug of dread she walked to the door. The desperation in the plea made her think of Mattie and her strange compulsion to draw. She took a breath, moved to the top landing, trembling at the prospect of another assault on her shredded nerves.

There, again, more muted this time, almost below her. The stairs creaked as she made her way down to the bottom. While she was deliberating, the door to the parlour clicked open. Julia shivered, took a breath and moved to the room she'd been in earlier. It was freezing in there now and her breath was white before her.

She scanned the dreary interior. The black-tiled fireplace, the uncomfortable chintz sofa and chair, sombre faces staring from the framed family photographs on the mantelpiece, landscape prints hanging from the picture rail, the faded flowery wallpaper – all seemed as before, as she'd left it an hour or so ago, apart from the cold. No. Something was not right. Out of the corner of her eye, a tiny movement, a blur. Her eyes darted to the writing table and she blinked to clear her vision. She was jittery, of course, fear playing tricks with her senses. As she began to look away from the table, her attention snapped back to it, to the small object in the centre of the sloped leather panel. She couldn't make out from this distance, but she'd left the table empty and clear.

She advanced towards it, step by step, every nerve on the alert. As she neared the table Julia saw it was one of the Whimsies, the little grey squirrel sitting there.

It's Nutty.

What game was this? Her hand reached out, tentative, feeling the cold air prickling the hairs on her skin. She picked up the tiny ornament. He'd been her favourite bad boy of her animal stories. She'd forgotten him, it was true, but she hadn't come across him till now. She looked closer at the desk. The whole surface of the raised middle panel was clean, revealing the lustrous leather, wiped free of dust while the rest of the table remained covered in a film, smudged where Julia had rested her fingers or piles of papers earlier. The polished silky wood beckoned her fingertips, and as Julia touched the rounded edge, she remembered seeing Annie sitting there with the central part lifted. It was a lid. She'd tried to lift it the next time she'd been alone all those years ago, but it would not budge, and after a while she had forgotten about it.

She tried to lift it now with no success. There must be a release mechanism somewhere. She felt down both sides of the writing slope lip. Finding nothing, she opened the drawer below and ran her hand over all the areas inside and found it: the simple hook on a spring mechanism which could be pulled back to free the lid. The job was messy, she noted. The piece had doubtless been devalued by fifty per cent at least. She was able to pull it now, though it was stiff. Excited, she pushed the lid back, revealing small compartments with various useful things in for writing and accounting, and dull-looking coins in another. There were two small drawers with white porcelain handles.

The first one she opened held men's rings – Granddad's, perhaps? There were also some tie clips and cuff links. She smiled to herself and held up one ring to see if it had a stamp on the inside. It was gold. They'd all have to be valued. She took an envelope from the pile and popped the jewellery inside, placing it in her pocket. The other drawer held a small notebook. In the front pages were shopping lists, jobs to be done. It was perhaps a handbag notebook, she thought. The type you keep handy for day-to-day reminders or calculations in the days before Filofaxes and mobile phones. Sure enough, there were some sums scrawled on one page and some simple bookkeeping notes on another. Annie never kept the accounts. Still, it didn't look like Caroline's scrawl. There were a few torn-out pages and the book seemed empty after that.

"Damn!" She tossed it onto the rubbish pile. It fell open on the last page which had a name written in red. Picking it up, Julia read the name, Micah Wozniak. There was a phone number below it. Julia felt unease at the sight of the name. Micah. As far as she knew, the family had no contact with anyone from Eastern Europe, but this name pulled at the threads of her memory. She looked around the empty room once more. Her breath was no longer visible, but she still felt chilled. She went to the kitchen to find a drink. She would need it before she called this Wozniak person.

16

She'd settled for a coffee and, after a few sips to warm her up, looked at the number again. It was a landline. Perhaps this Micah was long dead. Or had moved. She picked up her phone and dialled, cursing when the annoying automated service piped up: "You've dialled an incorrect number..." After messing about online and a call to an enquiry line, she found out she was missing a digit in the area code and tried again.

At the sound of the voice on the other end of the line Julia knew her mistake. Confused at her urge to slam the receiver down, she took a deep breath.

"Er, er, hello, I... is that Mr Wozniak?"

"Who wants to know?" His Slavic accent and deep voice terrified her for no reason she could fathom.

"My name is... Sharon. I'm a... helper at Carrick House where Mrs Allbright lives... lived."

"Who?"

"Annie Allbright." Julia wished she'd not started this. "Of Little Wynchstead? Your name is in her address book." Julia could hear the tremor in her voice and cursed herself. She struggled to account for it. "I'm sorry, this is rather a delicate matter. It's a bit upsetting."

"I don't know this Annie Allbright." His quiet voice slid under her skin like icy water. "How did you get my number?"

"In her address book. I'm calling everybody she knew to let them know she's very unwell, seriously ill, in fact. And we're not sure how long she'll last…" She was babbling. "It's such a shame. Everyone is very shocked. I am sorry, I know this must be upsetting for you."

"I don't know her. You've got the wrong number."

It seemed he was about to hang up.

"Caroline said you were a friend of the family…" she blurted, "and it was OK to call."

There was a silence and Julia held her breath, wondering if she'd gone too far. She was sure he could hear her stuttered breathing. The silence swung between them like Poe's pendulum. Julia racked her brains, trying to remember this voice, why it infused her with such fear.

When he spoke again his voice was measured and malevolent. "Tell your Caroline I don't know any old lady and I don't want any more phone calls."

The phone clicked on the other end.

You never said she was old.

It was a small detail, but Julia knew the man was lying. She should have prompted him to talk more… yet she had to admit she felt only relief that she didn't have to listen to the oily voice any longer. She replaced the receiver with a trembling hand. She knew she wouldn't call the number again, but she input his name on her phone, feeling it was significant.

Sitting there in the silence she wondered why she'd been so quick to call him. Was she going to ask him if there was a ghost in the house? Ridiculous! It was as if her impulses were not her own. She'd handled it wrong. What information could she have gained with that piss-poor approach? That's what her ex-boss Mike Paton would have called it: piss-poor. It was his favourite insult. She would have pointed out that at least she now knew the man had known Annie and didn't want to talk, and that made him a questionable character. Julia wasn't sure Mike would agree with her conclusion, but she believed it sound. Wozniak. Surely a name like that would stick in your mind, yet she couldn't recall such. How come his voice had that effect on her if he wasn't part of her past?

It was some time later when Julia left the house for her old workplace, the *Highton Gazette*. She was shocked when she noted it was almost two thirty on the dash, leaving herself very little time to research. But of course she'd had to spend at least two hours throwing things into boxes to reverse the mess she'd found in the house that morning. She was getting angry again thinking of it. She rolled her shoulders to ease the stiffness in her neck and forced herself to think of something else.

Mike had sounded so pleased to hear her on the phone. He admitted he'd expected her to call years ago, even saying it would be like she'd never left if she came back to work for them. Julia had been so moved by his warm responses to her after the strangeness of the week and Steve's demands that she'd felt choked and ended the call before Mike picked up on her vulnerability. Even he wouldn't be so generous if he knew what a state she was in. In the meantime, he'd arranged for her to use the library this afternoon, though he himself wouldn't be there. Thinking about her old friend and the normal exchange they'd had over the phone so cheered her she felt ravenous all of a sudden. She eyed the sandwich sticking out of her bag. She'd earned her lunch, that was for sure.

•

Waiting to pay for her packet of ten Vogue, Caroline tapped her fingers on her purse, mulling over the call she'd just received. That was a blast from the past, she thought. One that should stay there! She paid the three pound sixty-five without complaining of the cost but did not thank the assistant. She was ripping open the packet before she reached the shop door. Damn it! She'd long ago believed she was through with this disgusting habit, but after that call she needed a drag right now.

Micah had sounded pissed and no wonder. What the hell was Julia doing calling him? Caroline had no doubt it was her. Where did she get the number? She tried to calm herself. There had been no discussion about letting friends and relatives know about Annie, so why was she calling him? What did she know? She lit up and drew heavily. She had to contain this.

She moved towards her car then stopped as she received the head rush from the nicotine. She took a few deep breaths. At dinner tonight she would wait and see what madam had in mind. If she was going to poke around in the past, Caroline would shut her down right away. And she could count on Steve's support in that, she was sure.

Caroline had worked hard to convince Micah to leave this to her to handle. It shouldn't be a problem, she told herself again, as long as the stupid cow kept drinking herself to sleep at night – who would listen to her? She was no threat to the world Caroline had built for herself. A gust of wind blew ash onto the lapel of her cream jacket and she cursed out loud, brushing it off with her finger. And now she would reek of smoke when she walked into her meeting in ten minutes' time. She couldn't allow the client to think she was anything but in control, and reeking of cigarette smoke showed weakness. Once in the car she pulled her bottle of Number 5 from her bag and sprayed her jacket with it, trying not to choke on the pungent smell in the close confines. Damn it! And damn her!

17

The familiar feeling of anticipation gripped Julia as she entered the cool hallway of Cormorant Publishing from the revolving doors. At the stainless-steel desk she signed in as a visitor to the *Gazette*'s office and was given the pass Mike had organised for her.

"Do you know where to go? Fourth floor, west side," the receptionist said, indicating lifts to the right of her. She was already looking at the next person in line before Julia gave her thanks and made her way to the lifts.

The girl on the *Gazette*'s reception desk was young and cheerful. She called up Simon, one of the features writers whom Mike had told Julia to ask for. Julia sat on one of the seats to the side of the massive open-plan office, absorbing the frenetic atmosphere and feeling a wave of nostalgia for the buzz.

Some older faces she recognised and when they saw her they waved while talking on their headsets. They were busy and motivated, and she envied them. She noticed a young girl, an intern, laden with a tray of coffees, going from one desk to another. Julia smiled. She'd done her own internship with the *Gazette* and straightaway clicked with Mike, her editor. She hadn't minded making him any number of coffees, feeling privileged to be there. Although some of the work, like updating the databases, had been dull at times, the banter in the office was good and she'd loved doing the research for the journalists. She'd worked long, unpaid hours during those first six months and in the end was rewarded with the offer of a job on Mike's team. Julia's throat tightened now to think how confident she'd been compared to how she felt now. She'd let it all slip away.

"Julia?"

She looked round to see a middle-aged version of a young man she once knew.

"Simon! There you are. All grown up…"

"Decomposing actually!" he said, laughing. He gave her a hug as she stood up.

"You look well," she said. "I couldn't believe it when Mike said you were still here."

"For my sins! Remember I was going to leave… then it was at your leaving do when I told you I was going into broadcasting? Well, I couldn't – Jennie fell pregnant."

"You're a dad? So am I." She laughed. "I mean, a parent."

"Funny, isn't it?" he said, leading the way across the main office to the east side of the building. "When we first started out, we were going to do so many things. You wanted to be special features editor, but you met Steve and that was it – you left!"

"I know." She forced a smile and sought a platitude. "You just don't know what life's going to throw at you next."

He seemed to like that comment, she noted, as he smiled and went quiet for a moment. "How's Jennie?" she asked, more to break the silence than out of genuine interest as she didn't care much for his wife.

"She's good, thanks, running her own cake-making business."

"Did the studio not work out then?" she asked, ready to commiserate.

"No, that's going great too, thanks. She runs the cake-making part-time."

Hmm, as perfect as ever, Julia thought, her own position slipping a little more down her competence ladder.

As they neared the far door to take the stairs up to the archives, they were stopped by an imperious, "Julia Allbright! Not someone I expected to return to the fold!"

Turning in the direction of the loathed voice, Julia forced a syrupy smile. "Margie! Well, you know I missed being told what to do…"

The insult was ignored by the tall, overweight, brunette, who smirked. "Well, you should have called me. I'm always ready with good advice, hey, Simon?"

"I'm sure Julia remembers."

"I'm just doing some research actually."

"For real? And can we expect some Pullitzer prize-winning tome next year?"

"Piss off, Margie."

Julia was as surprised as Simon at her own response, but Margie just laughed as she veered off to towards the ladies'.

"As articulate as ever, my dear. See you next Tuesday!"

Julia baulked at the irritating, sing-song farewell. Did she know about her meeting scheduled next week with Mike? Had he told her? That cow always knew everything about everyone in the office. She forced herself to relax. Margie was famous for her off-the-cuff insults; this had to be one of them.

"Just ignore her!" Simon led the way up to the first floor and through a red door into the comfortable library room. "You know what she's like; nothing's changed there." He led her to a bank of two microfiche readers and two PCs. "So what are you researching today?" he asked while checking the first machine was on.

"I'm looking for articles involving Little Wynchstead citizens over the last fifty years or so."

"Oh, any particular topics?" He didn't sound interested, which suited Julia well.

"It's a project I've been working on for a couple of months now. I might use the information in a book later."

"It's all set up for you. In fact, I would start on the PC; it will save you time rather than trawling through all the fiches, although you may need those for the older articles… you remember how to read them?" He held a dark blue plastic sheet between two fingers. "These are updated machines, but it's just a step from the old model;

just place it under the reader." He demonstrated and switched on the light. The screen lit up with condensed pages of the *Highton Gazette*. He showed her where the zoom was and how to move around the page and how to switch to the next one and how to print.

"See, just like before. All the *Gazette* stuff is here," he said, tapping a thick, scrappy-looking file, "and these are the *Herald* records."

"Great, thanks."

"I'll make us a coffee?"

Julia smiled at him. "I'll have mine black with one sugar."

Julia sat at the computer first and did some general searches until Simon had given her her coffee and moved to his own tasks.

She input several word combinations into the search field. Carrick House came up in connection with recent fundraising events or the regular garden parties which her grandmother had held in the eighties. The missing or dead teenagers coming up in the county were well-documented cases linked to the surrounding larger towns, none connected to the village and no links to Carrick House. She stared at the photographs linked to the articles to see if there was the slightest resemblance to the long-haired girl of her nightmare and Mattie's drawings, but the dead children were either the wrong age or race, or looked different to the image Julia had in her head.

Sometime later she moved to the microfiche and began an hour-long stint of scrolling through hundreds of articles, at the end of which she sighed and had to admit she'd perhaps wasted her time. She continued, though half-hearted, to scroll through for a while longer. After going through page after page of petty theft incidents and articles on the residents versus the Wynchstead Bypass Committee, she just felt frustrated and more aware of the time ticking away. She went back to the PC with the search engine and input the Carrick family, Little Wynchstead, and was rewarded with a full article, as she knew there would be.

It appeared Carrick House had been built by a Colonel Matthew Carrick on his premature return from the Second Boer War due to a severe leg injury and infection which left him with a noticeable limp and impaired health. His former contributions in Egypt and the Sudan had earned him military decorations and mentions in the London press at the time. His wealthy mother, happy to have him home safe and sound, had provided him with the capital to build the house in Little Wynchstead on the proviso he marry and settle down. Mrs Elizabeth Carrick had borne him six children, but two of the girls died as infants and one boy was stillborn. The remaining two boys and the girl all survived into adulthood.

Julia moved the cursor down, through information about the boys who'd gone into military service to the part about the daughter, who, it stated, had married a military man and moved to Aldershot in 1921. Nothing else – except a reference to mentions of the family in a book about the influential families of Highton. A photograph accompanied the text and Julia peered at the young girl in the picture to see if there was anything familiar about her, but she was somewhat obscured by the older brother. Mmm. She doubted she would get any more information at the local library, but it was worth a shot. She took a screenshot and walked over to the printer. She was getting nowhere and had the constant feeling she should be back at Carrick, which didn't help her attention span, or her mood.

Back at the PC and, feeling frustrated, on impulse she reached in her bag for the piece of paper torn from Annie's notebook. She input Micah's name, checking the spelling, and was astounded when the screen opened under the headline 'Two Convicted from City Parlour'. After clicking on it and scrolling down through the text, she read that in April 1972, two men, Robert Goodyear, twenty-six, and Micah Wozniak, aged twenty, had been convicted of running a brothel in Manchester centre. A young woman of sixteen, Caroline Baker, had also been convicted in connection with the crime. Baker? Mother, Michelle Baker on her deathbed, writing to Annie Allbright – wanting to say goodbye to her daughter? She sat back, staring at the screen, feeling the familiar quickening in her veins she always had when research paid off.

How did this information fit in with what she already knew of her rival? Caroline herself had told her of her early life in Longsight on the outskirts of Manchester. How she'd escaped an alcoholic stepfather and mother who didn't care, moving to stay with a friend in the city. She'd told Julia she'd taught herself how to type, landed a job with a building firm and learned her skills as she went along. Mmm, she hadn't mentioned skills like these, though. What a past and what classy associates! If Micah was connected to the Allbrights, it was without a doubt through Caroline. Julia scrolled down to read the rest of the article. Caroline was given a twelve-month probation order for her involvement in the management of the brothel, the sentence softened due to her age and it being a first offence. Wozniak was given fifteen months' jail sentence. There was no picture with the article.

"Anything interesting?" Simon stood at the end of the desk, peering over.

Julia started but remembered to drop the screen out of sight. "Oh! You made me jump, Simon. You look like you're going home?"

"Well, it's five to five. You are lost in your own little world, aren't you!"

Julia remembered he could be bloody patronising sometimes. "Yep, I certainly am," she agreed. "I'll do some prints before we finish."

"OK, I'm just going to see a man about a dog and I'll be back to lock up. See you in a minute."

Julia started printing before he'd even reached the door. She planned to be gone before he got back to avoid any discussions about going for a drink to catch up. She wasn't ready for that yet and time was ticking away, anyhow. She packed her stuff up as fast as she could, shoved the microfiches back into the wrong files and left. He would be miffed when he had to sort her mess out, but ultimately he liked it when people proved inefficient; it made him feel so much more superior.

•

Julia struggled to answer her phone as she climbed into her car.

"Hi, Julia?"

"Amanda! I was going to call you when I got home."

"I thought I would have heard from you by now. You've usually texted me at least twice in the week about how you can't wait to get out of the house! I was beginning to think you weren't coming."

Julia dumped her bag and pulled the door to against the biting wind. "Hang on… just getting into my car. God, that wind is vicious."

"Yeah, it's horrible out there. Such a grey, grey day. I can't wait for my hols in Feb."

Julia smiled. Despite being on benefits, Amanda managed Tunisia every year thanks to her many boyfriends who were always earning well and who hung around for at least twelve months at a time.

"You're right, I'm not coming tonight. I'm sorry, hun."

"What? Why not, babe?"

"I…" Julia realised she didn't want to share with her gossipy friend.

"Are you in trouble with Big Daddy?"

Julia laughed. "Well, you could say that. Look, I said to Steve I would put my boogie boots away for a few weeks and be a good little mama and wife."

"A few weeks? Come on!"

"Well, this week… this weekend at least." She could see she'd have to fight this corner on a weekly basis.

"We're going to Prohibs tonight! It's gonna be great! Please come, Ju-Ju."

Julia hated that nickname. It was always used when Amanda was at her most needy. "I can't, Amanda. Let me fix things with Steve and when things have died down we'll celebrate big time, I promise."

"Are things bad then?"

"No… it's just that he wants me to go out less and… I should rein it in a bit. Hey, guess what!"

"He suddenly got a sense of humour?"

"Ha har. No. I'm going back to work. At the *Gazette*. Well, I might be; Mike might take me on part-time."

"Do you want that, Julia? You live the life of Reilly – why go back to the grind now? Most of us would give a child to live your life."

Julia remembered how it had felt in the office today. "You know, I do want it. I was thrilled being there today, by the whole vibe of it. It was great."

"So did you have an interview?" Amanda was unenthusiastic.

"Not yet, I was researching. Yes, I was going to ask you, do you ever recall a teenager or young girl going missing – from the general Highton area or the villages, while we were growing up?"

"No. Nothing like that happens round here." She paused for a moment. "I can ask my mum if you like – she kind of knew everyone's business where she lived. Why this interest?"

"I'm… well, I'm thinking of writing a book along those lines and was just looking for inspiration, but… yes, call me if your mum remembers anything."

"OK. Wow, you're all motivated and raring to go, aren't you! A part-time job *and* a book! You will have to put your hangovers on hold, love!" She laughed.

"Probably," Julia said, a bit harsher than she meant to.

Amanda must have heard the annoyance in Julia's response because she brought the conversation to an end with a cheery, "Well, enjoy your evening with the family," and a, "I'll see you tomorrow at Mattie's party, let you know what you missed out on – ta-ra, babe!"

Julia sat staring at the screen, her reply dead on her lips. Amanda had rung off. Was her friend jealous? Or was it that she just didn't care? She hadn't encouraged her at all or offered support. She just wanted a drinking pal. That's all Julia was to her – a fellow pisshead. Another revelation.

She started the car.

18

"Will you girls be quiet, I can't hear myself think!" Julia moved the hair out of her eyes with one hand while she stirred the cheese sauce with the other. She wanted to have the meal ready before Caroline arrived.

"Haven't you girls turned the TV off?"

Her daughters were oblivious to her, their shrieks growing louder. Grace was hiding behind the palm and Mattie, a scarf over her eyes, was yelling while trying to find her. Julia hurried into the sitting room to put the television off. The reporter's voice blared, "Mark Cavendish, head of Marsden Centre in the mid-seventies, was taken in for questioning today for the alleged abuse of twenty-nine teenagers in his care…"

Julia shook her head. "Another one…" She turned off the set.

As she re-entered the kitchen, the girls were still shouting. It was clear they needed a job. "You two lay the table for me, please."

She poured the sauce over the cauliflower and put it in under the grill. The lamb needed carving. Where was Steve? She looked at her watch again, taking a sip of wine. He'd made Sandra stay late tonight and she'd not been happy when Julia came in. The young woman insisted she was fine with the occasional extra hour babysitting, but she was going out with her friends tonight, and not that she didn't want to help out, but… Julia said she understood and had assured her it was a one-off.

She frowned now, assessing what still needed to be done. She too would rather be out with her friends than preparing dinner for that manipulative cow arriving at any minute; even though she now had the most superb ammunition at her disposal.

She checked herself. Caroline's visit was for Mattie's benefit since it was her birthday tomorrow. There could be no confrontation in front of the children. She would have to save it for a rainy day. Julia took a drink of her wine, warning herself to stay calm. Taking the carving knife, she sliced through the meat and gristle with firm strokes, seeing the flesh peel away from the blade with some satisfaction.

The doorbell chimed like a starter gun. She carried the sliced meat and cauliflower cheese to the table and took off her apron, wiping her forehead while the girls rushed to the hall, greeting Julia's blight to the evening.

"Hello, darlings," Caroline cooed, bending down and planting a kiss on their heads. "Look at you, birthday girl, don't you look splendid in that dress! Let me hang my coat. Are you feeling better, darling? Your daddy said you weren't very well this week? Grace, take this bag for me, dear. There's a little present in there for each of you."

"But it's not her birthday," Mattie protested, running after Grace into the kitchen. "She shouldn't get a present!"

"Mattie, it's not yours either – till tomorrow," Julia said. "Anyway, you know you both have a little something on the other's birthday. Don't be mean." She sipped her wine then caught a look from Caroline over the rim. Some communication passed between them like static electricity. Julia knew it would air itself soon. "Do you know where Steve is, Caroline?"

"Held up at work, dear, I'm sure."

"He golfs on Fridays, but he's usually back by now." For Caroline not to remember Steve played at the Styner Club every week was strange. "So you haven't come from the office?"

"I've been at Carrick since four, Julia. Where were you?"

Here it is, Julia thought. She turned away and refilled her glass. "Would you like some wine?"

"A lemonade, please."

"Mummy, can we have lemonade too, please? 'Cos it's my birthday!" Mattie smiled her biggest smile.

"No, my sweet, there will be plenty of fizzy drink tomorrow at your party. You can have some apple juice with your meal."

Caroline wasn't going to wait for an answer to her question.

"I've been tidying up, Julia." She accepted the glass and said with an expectant smile, "What the hell is going on? The place was an absolute mess, worse than it was on Monday – it looks like you had a party in there—"

"I was going to ask you precisely that, Caroline," Julia said, keeping her voice low. "Is this some sort of game you're playing because I tell you it won't work!"

Caroline was about to retort when Steve walked in. He looked at Caroline. "Ladies!"

"Daddy!" The girls ran to him, wrapping themselves around his checked golf trouser legs.

"Hello, little chicks. Mmm, dinner smells good. Sorry I'm late! You please start while I change. Go and sit down, you two."

Once at the table Caroline resumed her attack in her politest tone. "I do not have to explain myself to you, Julia, but you owe me an explanation. Nothing has been done at all. This whole week has been wasted. Steve's going to be furious."

Julia viewed Caroline through her Pinot haze and felt a simmering rage at the woman's presence in her house. Why did she even exist? It was her fault her mother had died alone and so desperate. She'd stolen her father from her mother, stolen a happy childhood from Julia as sure as she was ruining this evening already.

"I'm not going to be dictated to by you anymore, Caroline. You are in my house and you will treat me with some reshpect." Oops, that came out wrong.

Caroline shook her head. Pursing her lips, she picked up a serving spoon and began to dish out the meal to the girls, who were looking from her to their mother with each exchange.

"Julia, you have to get a grip. You're not going to earn respect in this… state you're in, you… I think we ought to carry this conversation on when the children have gone to bed."

Julia swallowed her words, remembering her daughters' vulnerability sitting at the table between two vipers.

By the time Steve joined them there was only the sound of eating at the table. "It's very quiet," he said, reaching for the salt. "Everything alright?"

"Everything's absolutely fine." Julia's words rolled out as if her mouth were stretching around each syllable. "Where have you been, Steve?"

"The golf club."

"You're very late. Sandra wasn't too pleased."

Steve took a sip of the wine Julia had poured for him. "Sandra receives a larger pay packet when she does overtime and she needs the money so I'm sure she ultimately doesn't mind. What's your problem with it?"

Julia didn't answer right away. She pushed her food around with her fork a little. "I don't mind, I just thought you would be home by five, that's all. I had a busy day and I needed your help with the meal."

Steve scoffed. "A busy day? Doing what? Apparently Carrick House is a mess, Julia. Your busy-ness has certainly not been directed there…"

Julia froze at the insult then took a swig of her drink. Finding it empty, she reached for the bottle and poured herself some more. She was incensed he and Caroline had been talking about her again and that he should be so rude to her now in front of the bitch and in front of the children.

You should tell him about Caroline.

"I'm going to!"

Steve looked on, exasperated. "What? Haven't you had enough?"

She ignored the question and took a gulp. She wanted to lash out at both of the little conspirators. "I've been contacting old friends. Of Annie's."

"Of Annie's? She doesn't have any, well, she used to know some women at the club. But why? She can't remember her own mother's name right now, so what's the point?"

"I told him Annie's taken a nasty turn." The last three words slurred into each other.

"Him? Who? For goodness' sake, Julia, how much have you had to drink?"

"I called him. Micah… Woshniak. You know him, don't you, Caroline!" She tried to focus on Caroline's face, but it was becoming blurry.

"Mmm? Well, let me think…" Caroline drawled, looking at Steve. "I can't say I recall anyone by that name. Sounds Russian." She shrugged and grinned at Mattie, who was staring at her, wild-eyed.

"He's Polish, Caroline. You knew him in Manchester." Julia's brain was fizzing with the effort of trying to articulate. She missed Caroline's glare as she was trying to cut the lamb on her plate. Steve did not, however.

"Who is this guy?" he questioned, but Caroline stopped him with a minute shake of her head.

"Yeah," Julia said, now focused on the blur at the end of the table. "She knew him from th' parlour." Her head swayed like that of a nodding dog on the dashboard of a car. "Give me a chance!" she asserted to an empty space on her left. "*I* will tell him…" She giggled and raised her glass in mock salute. "She's the Parlour Princess – not me! How much for your time, Car… o… line?"

"Julia, that's enough," Steve snapped, livid at the attack on Caroline, who stood up, her cheeks red and her mouth set in a grim line.

"I think I've had enough dinner—" she said.

Steve put out his hand towards her. "Stay, finish your meal."

"No, thank you. Girls, since you've finished, come with me to the kitchen for some ice cream. Then we can watch *The Little Mermaid* together as a treat."

"Oh yes!" The girls scrambled down from their chairs, their mother's strange behaviour forgotten.

"They're not your kids," Julia declared to Caroline's back.

"You are *pathetic!*" With the children having left the room, Steve launched at his wilting wife. "I'm through with this, Julia! Why should I put up with this after a hard day's work? Why should Caroline put up with your insulting insinuations? After all she has done for this family!"

"She is not family!" Julia shouted. "She's a tramp that stole my father from my mother and ruined her life, ruined my life. I don't want her in my house ever again!"

"This is my house, you stupid woman. I paid for it. I say who visits, who stays and who does not. Right now *you* are on my list of unwanted guests. You're frightening the children and pissing me off. I am not participating in this ridiculous conversation while you're so drunk, Julia... You will stay away from the sitting room while the children have their dessert. Once we've put them to bed you can go up and say goodnight in a civilised manner – if you can get up the stairs!"

"So you are the new Mr and Mrs Campbell, are you? The new couple of my house? Is that what you're trying to do, Steve? Force me out? You won't get rid of me that easily." Her words were slurring into one another again and were slowing, as if on elastic. She felt depleted and slumped in her chair.

Steve stood up, holding his plate. "I'll have this in the sitting room." He shook his head. "If you could see yourself..." He walked out.

Julia heard Caroline's voice in the hallway: "She needs professional help, Steve. She's talking to herself again! She was doing it at the house."

She strained to hear Steve's response, but it was short and inaudible. Caroline made an effort to lower her voice, but Julia caught snatches of what she was saying: "Sam... her imaginary friend... heard her in her bedroom often... doctors..."

What ridiculous story was the woman concocting now? The words 'childhood... schizophrenia' drifted in from the hallway, fading out as her husband and his accomplice moved away to the sitting room and closed the door. Julia pulled herself up, defiant and distraught, and made her way to the kitchen to her secret bottle of vodka. She sat at the island submerging her alien world and its strange stories with each gulp.

•

Caroline had just put the children to bed having watched half of the movie and read Mattie a short story. Grace was already fast asleep, but Mattie had to be reassured that she'd see Mummy in the morning because she wasn't very well right now. Caroline had set the door ajar as she left their bedroom and flicked the hall nightlight on.

She and Steve went out to the front of the house now so she could have a cigarette. Steve voiced his disapproval at her new habit, but Caroline was not in the mood to kowtow to him. After her first drag and release she went straight to the point. "It was a bad idea to have her sort Annie's belongings. She must have found Micah's number somewhere, though I never came across it all these years I've been helping with the paperwork. Why she should want to call him, I don't know."

"Who the hell is he? How did she find out about your past?"

Caroline shook her head. "I don't know, research on his name, I guess. I worked for Micah at the parlour I told you about. It was before I met John… Anyway, the police raided, we were sentenced. I was given a probation order and he went to jail. I was devastated because he was my lover at the time. I was so young and alone. I missed him while he was inside. We had a lot in common, you know – sod all upbringing, poverty, forced relocation. He was fresh out of Poland and we both wanted to make some money. When he got out he came to see me, but I'd met John by then."

"Did they get on?"

"There were no hard feelings. They liked each other, did a few jobs together. He kept in touch even after we moved here, though it was understood it was best not to meet in public here. An accent like his and his appearance would have been the talk of the village. He moved to Stoke and into different areas of money-making." She took a drag of her cigarette. "He called me after Ms Busybody rang him today."

"What did he say?"

"Asked me how I was keeping, what the weather was like – what do you think, Steve! He was furious. He was convinced she was a reporter after some dirt. I had to assure him it was probably Julia calling, though he said it was someone called Sharon. Sharon?"

Caroline shook her head. "Anyway, I told him he must have misheard and that if it was her, she was just doing as she'd said: letting friends of Annie's know about her condition. I convinced him that Julia doesn't know anything about him. The last thing we want is Micah coming down here. He's like a rat if cornered, will take out anyone, male, female… or their kids."

"Christ! This is madness. I'll speak to her tomorrow when she's sober. It's more serious than I thought. I've had enough of it all."

"You've got to sort her out, Steve, or I will."

"Caroline?" He hesitated. "You can't bring your old ways into our life."

His partner appraised him as she finished her cigarette. "You're willing to lose everything? We don't need a light on us, Steve. I've worked too hard to let some fucking flake tear it all down. I'll speak to Micah, but you have to stop this mayhem she's creating. If you've any love for the girls or your lifestyle, make sure she sees the light." She threw down the stump of her cigarette and ground it into the step. Steve knelt down to remove the stub, bemoaning her bad habit, but Caroline had already gone inside.

•

By the time Julia made her way to the sitting room it was empty of people, of enemies. She lurched towards the sofa, slopping the contents of her glass over the arm. She muttered something inaudible and made a clumsy attempt to wipe it with her sleeve. She placed the glass down on the coffee table before tottering to the DVD cabinet. Trying to focus on the titles, all of a sudden she had to lunge for the waste-paper bin, into which she vomited half-digested lamb roast and cauliflower cheese. Wiping some vomit from her hair and a splash from her chest with her trusty sleeve, she returned to the movie selection, found her favourite love story and moved back to the sofa for respite from the spinning room. She lay down then realised she hadn't put the television on. She couldn't see the remote anywhere. She had no control over the TV. Over her life! That bitch was taking away her life again. And now she was saying she was mad! A few tears squeezed out from under heavy lids before she passed out, clutching the DVD box to her chest.

19

The gummy edge of her eyelids flickered as Julia stirred, reluctant to wake but assaulted by the blast of white noise emitting from the television. The whole room dazzled from the electric rain on the screen. Squinting, she sought the remote. It was on the floor. She reached out for it, trying not to lift her head too much, the room swimming around her.

If she could just... Jesus, it was cold! She clawed the end of it and dragged it to her, shivering despite the alcohol she'd consumed. She stared at the buttons, waiting for them to come into focus, then turned the offensive thing off.

A foreboding percolated the sudden silence. She tried to think how she'd gotten here on the sofa. What was last night? The dinner. She remembered insulting Caroline and arguing with Steve at the table. She groaned. Oh God, am I in trouble! Remorse surged even as her eyes drooped and she began to sink back to sleep. She shuddered. Reaching a hand to the back of the sofa, she pulled the alpaca throw over her, welcoming its instant warmth. Her mouth was so dry her tongue stuck to the roof of it and her jaws were clamped to stop her teeth from chattering. Just as she was falling back to sleep the television came on again, louder than before.

Julia jolted to attention and half sat up, staring at the screen, the throw falling from her chest. She pulled it up again to her neck and was still holding it when it was wrenched from her grip and tossed aside. The white glare from the television illuminated the pale girl standing at the end of the sofa, her stare boring into Julia with such intensity she felt she would wither from it.

Julia yanked herself up, a strangled cry issuing from her throat of sand. The vodka glass flew off the table before her as she stumbled, all the while keeping the girl in sight. Glowing in the flickering light from the screen, the girl took a step towards Julia. Julia could see the veins on the outstretched arms as she lurched closer and a foul smell enveloped her. The girl's dirty feet spread a black trail as she advanced, her serpentine hair slithering over the shoulders of the tattered dress which looked like it had lain in dark earth for decades, a flickering black and white nightmare. Julia blinked and shook her head. In a macabre dance, Julia took two steps back for every advance of the thing, terror and fascination holding her captive. As it came closer she saw around its neck a tiny silver chain with a snake on it. It seemed to sit embedded in the skin rather than on top of it. Julia felt another surge of nausea rack up in her throat. She trembled violently. She'd backed up to the wall now and could go no further.

The girl's mouth was opening in a deathly gape like a deep, black shadow spreading across her face, yet the sound Julia now heard was not coming from there but seemed to be piercing the clamour from the television, an electrical whine followed by a hiss and popping sound, but the second time Julia thought she could discern the words, same as before in the kitchen: "H… el… p… me…"

Julia's hand flayed about, searching for the light, the door, anything which would allow her freedom from the hideous thing before her. Still hissing and popping, the screen emitted an unearthly wail: "H… el… p… me… J… ul… ie…" Julia pushed back against the wall and turned her face away from the bloodless fingers now only inches away. Her breath exhaled in one long ragged gasp; her chest constricted and appeared to fold in on itself. Tiny wisps of air struggled through to her lungs with short wheezing noises as the obscene thing's face drew closer and robbed her of her last breath. Julia felt the chill of the grave encompass her, cutting off all flow in her veins, severing her connection with the world. The television and the sitting room disappeared from sight and she was once again in the black space, unable to see, to breathe, to move with the plea of 'help me' ringing in her ears as she lost consciousness.

·

When she awoke she was lying on her side, her face pressed against the carpet. The gloom of dawn pervaded the room; the television was dead.

She pulled herself up with care, checking for bruises or any other damage. She seemed alright except for a sore forearm and elbow. She supposed she'd landed on it. She caught a whiff of the vomit she'd expelled into the bin and frowned in disgust. It was evident she'd pushed the boat out this time, considering how sick she felt and how her hands were trembling. Self-loathing enveloped her as she lifted the bin and took it to the kitchen.

The cold blast of air as she opened the back door startled her and she stared at the carpet of white covering the back yard. The snow was as unreal to her as her life had become. She leaned out as far as possible, trying to deposit the bin upright onto the steps. It tipped on a stone and spilled its slimy contents over the pristine white. She would have to clean it up later.

Back inside, she stood for a few moments at the big windows looking out. It was as if her kitchen's colourless theme had infected the garden, bleaching it, removing the life from it. It looked like a fairy tale from the pages of the Brothers Grimm. She expected to see the wicked witch standing in the corner.

Julia flicked the switch on the kettle and brooded on what she'd seen or dreamt. Impossible to know if it had been real, she'd been so drunk, but dream or not, it was still the same girl. What did she want from her?

God, she felt wretched. It was Mattie's birthday and she had to face a wall of screaming children at eleven.

She opened the cupboard and cursed seeing all of the jars and tins within arranged in straight lines with the labels visible. Steve's obsessive urges. She turned a few around and mixed them up before retrieving a jar of instant. She doled out a heaped teaspoon and added some water. Her hand shook as she lifted the sugar bowl and it fell from her fingers, crashing into the mug and knocking it to the floor. The noise reverberated around the kitchen and her head like a siren. "Jesus Christ!" Julia leaned her head against the cupboard. She saw the almost-empty vodka bottle where she'd left it the night before. That was a step she was yet to take in the morning. It didn't have to be a permanent one. She poured a double. After the first sip she was in tears, desperate to pull herself together, wishing she could erase the night before and the sorry scene her girls had witnessed, and underlying it all, the fear she was going insane. She downed the drink: vodka and tears, so common a mix they should name a cocktail after it.

20

By the time Mattie came down for breakfast, Julia was calm and organised, dressed in a luxurious cashmere dress and her hair swept in an elegant chignon. Her daughter exclaimed in delight at the bright banners over the dining table with the nest of presents in the middle, sprinkled with glittery pink, ballet shoes confetti.

"Mummy! It looks lovely!" She threw herself into Julia's arms and hugged her.

Julia felt a surge of guilt. She knew her daughter's tight hold on her was in part due to relief that her mother was acting normal. She hugged her back, breathing in her child's fresh-from-bed smell and feeling grateful for this easy love. For the first time ever she realised that Steve's suggestion to get help about her drinking wasn't such a bad one after all.

"Can I open one now? Please, Mummy?"

"I tell you what, go and wake Grace – gentle, now! And I'll take Daddy a coffee. As soon as they come downstairs you can open them, darling." As Mattie skipped out of the room, Julia gave herself a pep talk before she faced her husband. She didn't know how she would make amends this time.

•

Ordered pink chaos was the best way to describe the party, Julia mused, but it was going well and Mattie was having fun. Julia sipped her wine while she watched the girls playing pass the parcel; the greedier ones taking advantage of the dreamy, slower kids. No different to adult life, she observed. She wondered which category she'd been in at eight years old and supposed it had been the dazed crew. In her scary new world at Carrick, Julia had retreated into her books and make-believe for most of her childhood. She'd woken up once she'd realised her A-levels would be her ticket out of the house, but here she was, twenty years on, still sinking into her dreams, this time helped by anything fermented.

Julia had approached Steve before he'd left the house. He'd been cool in his response and she knew he would have more to say about it tonight. Caroline was ignoring her.

"Hey!" Julia moved to separate Angela and tiny Susan McNulty. Susan ran off crying to her mum on the other side of the community hall. "Angela, you mustn't do that. Look how you've hurt her. That's so mean."

Angela looked away, embarrassed to be pulled up in front of her friends, and Julia made a mental note to speak to her friend about it.

"Julia, you missed such a rave last night!" Amanda said, arriving at her side. "Connie finally snogged some bloke and they went back to her place – together."

God, it was like being back in high school.

"Amanda, did you see that? The girls are physically attacking each other. I expect Susan's mother will be over in a minute."

Amanda laughed. "Whoa, so serious! Girls will be girls, love! Julia? Come on, babe, lighten up. You should have come out with us. You're far too stressed."

Julia glanced over at Susan and her mother. They were leaving the room. She hoped they weren't going home. She faced Amanda. God, she was irritating. Nothing ever seemed to warrant serious thought in that auburn head of hers. Unsurprising, really, since she was on strong anti-depressants and had been for five years. Julia should have expected this response, but the flippant remarks just irked.

Her own reply came out stiffer than intended. "Mattie had this done to her and now is inflicting it on Grace. I'm not happy about it, Amanda. Please can you speak to Debbie about it? If we all stick to together as parents, then the kids will know we're serious and it will stop."

"It?"

"This bullying."

"God, Ju-Ju. You need to drink up, babe."

Julia looked away, seething.

"How long are you going to let Steve keep you in anyway?"

Julia cleared her throat. "It's… my decision too, he… anchors me, you know."

Amanda raised her eyebrow. "To the ship?"

"It's not like that, Mandy…"

"You're afraid."

"Of what?"

"Freedom? Yourself?"

Julia was prevented from answering by her mobile going off. Grateful to get away, she hurried into the adjoining kitchen to take the call where it was quieter. It was an unknown caller but she recognised the slight northern accent as soon as he spoke. Her response was immediate.

"Luke? Hi. How are you?" It was a stupid question but she was so pleased he was calling her after their last talk ended on such a bad note.

"Julia, I was worried about you. I've been thinking about… our last conversation and I was a shithead when you rang—"

"Luke, it's OK. It's just so good to hear your voice and…" she swallowed, gathering herself, "to have your support, however it comes."

"I would like to meet you… don't know how you feel about that? If you don't like the idea we can talk now if you like?"

Julia heard him take a drag of his cigarette and the memory of his pace, the gestures unique to him, came rushing back. "I would like to meet. When?"

He sounded less stressed when he answered. "Can you do Monday morning? I'll come there to Little Wynchstead?"

Julia agreed to Monday at eleven but wasn't keen on the locals seeing her with a strange man. Highton would be a better location. Luke agreed to meet on the east side of the town which was older and less frequented by the business sector.

By the time Julia ended the call she felt light-hearted, dizzy almost – in a good way. She saved his number on her phone and looked up through the serving hatch into the main hall.

She had a sudden impression of another birthday party, a long time ago in a hall lit with round coloured lights and a DJ in the corner. There were teenagers in flared jeans and a disco ball scattering colours all around the room: laughter and music, smiling faces. The strains of 'Fernando' by Abba filtered through along with excited, childish northern voices. Disorientation swept over her and she grasped the counter top, watching a teenage boy and a girl with long fair hair dancing together in the centre of the room.

Fernando

It took me half an hour to reach the village road. In the silent dark, I stood there, waiting for a car, humming that song. It will always remind me of when I danced a slowy with Johnny Peters on my tenth birthday.

Johnny was a resident at The House of Love. A year older than me, he had been there six months by the time Kas and I arrived. He was tall, with dark blond hair that just reached his shoulders. He looked like a surfer – without the tan, of course! (Nobody has a proper tan in England – unless they've just come back from Spain!)

I'd watched him for weeks, stealing quick glances around the pages of the book I was reading, staring at his tawny hair from behind him in the dinner queue and every chance I got I'd watch him play football with the lads during our breaks. He was quiet and didn't show off like some of the others. He was a dream. I never dared to think he'd ever notice me.

I had a silver disco top to go with the necklace Nan had bought me and Faith handed me a pair of skinny pink jeans for my birthday so I'd have something new to wear at the party. I remember begging her to allow me to wear make-up on the night, and like a big sister, she offered to help me put some on. She chose a soft blue eyeshadow and mascara, but she said I didn't need lipstick – and neither did any young girl, in her opinion...

That night, my heart was beating so fast when I saw Johnny heading towards me. Surely he was going to walk past me? I tried to look away but he held my gaze. Then he was talking to me as the pipes of Fernando filled the room and the coloured lights from the disco ball spun around us. He took my hand and I felt I was floating. I knew everyone was looking at us, but I couldn't tear my eyes away from his. He told me how pretty I looked and I tried to laugh it off, but I knew my face was burning and his hands felt hot on my waist. I never wanted the song to end.

Later, in the hallway, I let him kiss me. It was typical that my nan caught us in the act, but she didn't tell me off. She pulled me aside later and warned me that boys weren't to be trusted. Look at her own son, she said, how he'd abandoned us all. She said no matter what rubbish boys or men gave us in life we had to remember who we were – that we were strong and we didn't have to accept what they said or did.

I knew she was wrong about Johnny and that he was not like that. He was kind and honourable, but I was old enough to realise she was just concerned for me. I told her I loved her and I hugged her tight. She felt like a little bird in my arms. I told her that one day when I was grown up and earning money, we could all live together and I would look after her. She sniffed and turned away when I said that, and when I asked her what was wrong, she said she was tired from making so many sandwiches! We laughed at that.

I still have the picture of me and her from that night, somewhere… I wish I had one of Johnny too…

A blue Renault driven by a young blonde woman pulled up for me as the edge of the sky began to turn to pale silver and I jumped in. The car smelled of dog but I was glad to get into the warmth and start my journey to you, Kas.

I'll see you soon.

21

"Where's me mum?"

Julia started and looked down to see the brazen little face of Debbie, Amanda's daughter. She looked back at the hatch and saw the familiar birthday party she'd set up that morning. Taylor Swift's 'Love Story' was playing and the girls were in a circle with the older ones singing and miming to the lyrics with knowing looks at each other while the little ones tried their best to copy and keep up. She looked back at the eight-year-old who was sizing her up. The child looked very much like her mother.

"I don't know, Debbie, but while you're here, I need to let you know something."

"What?"

Julia crouched down till she was at the same level, took the child's hand and looked her in the eye. "Touch or hurt my daughter one more time..." She paused for effect. "And I will tell your mother, the headmistress and the police, and you will have to leave this village and go to a new school. You won't be the main girl anymore – you'll be the new girl, the one to be bullied by people like you, and it won't be sweet. Your life will change for the worse, I warn you!" She moved her face a bit closer. "So leave Mattie and Grace alone, and Susan McNulty too."

Debbie's gaze flickered, then she snatched her hand away. "I never touched her," she said before running out of the room, probably to tell her mother. Julia didn't care. Her house of cards was coming down anyway, so what the hell. She might regret her moves tomorrow, but today she was going with it. She felt strong, energised. She was about to take a sip of her wine but poured it down the sink instead. She looked through the hatch again and locked eyes with Mattie, who gave her a little wave and a thumbs-up. Julia smiled and waved back.

22

Steve lay in bed basking in satisfaction while he waited for his Sunday-morning coffee. It had all gone better than he'd expected. Julia had taken the verbal assault without challenging him and agreed to his conditions of joining an AA group before the week was out. She also consented to attending the doctor's appointment he would set up. He wasn't going to back down on this. He didn't think his wife was crazy as Caroline kept intimating; Julia had been smashed, that's all, too drunk to know who the hell she was talking to. No, she wasn't crazy, but other people might think so if this was allowed to go on. She'd admitted to calling Micah but had explained it was just a stupid impulse to find out more about Caroline. Although she'd told Steve she couldn't accept Caroline for ruining her mother's relationship with her father, she did agree to treat her in a civil manner from now on.

Yes, he was pleased with the outcome. She'd been sorry for the scene she'd caused and was eager to put things right. He'd used her conciliatory mood to his full advantage, of course, persuading her to wear her hair up while they made love and to do things the way he liked it for a change. The thought of it caused a shiver now and he felt the itch stirring in his groin. He allowed himself to remember her on her knees and him slamming into her as she groaned. He wondered if he could coax her into another session this morning and felt himself getting harder. The door swung open and he turned, hopeful. It was his youngest, dashing into the room.

"Daddy! Daddy, can we go to the zoo today?" Grace leaned over the edge of the bed and put her face up close with her little hands clasped together in prayer.

Steve flicked onto his side, laughing at her contrived plea. "No, sweetheart, today we're helping Mummy pack at Nana Annie's house and I'm going to fix a few things. Since the sun is out, you and Mattie can play in the garden for a while."

"Ohwa!" She complained as she climbed onto the bed. She began to jump at the side of him as she chanted, "I… don't… like… going… there… it's scaaaary!"

"It's just because it's old and a bit grubby. Come on now, stop that. You can build a snowman, it will be fun." With a sudden movement he grabbed her wrist and yanked her down. "I said, stop it!"

Grace landed on her bottom and slid off the bed as he released her. "Sorry, Daddy."

"What's up?" Julia asked as she set the tray down, noticing her daughter rubbing her wrist, her head bowed.

"I'm just telling Grace why we can't go to the zoo today."

"You can have fun in the snow while Daddy and I get some work done. Now go and get dressed, darling. If you're very good perhaps we can bake some cakes together this afternoon when we come home."

Her face brightened a little. "OK, Mummy. Mattie!" she called as she ran out.

Julia sat on the edge of the bed, placing the mug on the bedside table. Steve grabbed her and pulled her towards him, his hands going under the elasticated waist of her pyjama bottoms.

"Hey, Mister! Work to do this morning, remember!" She pulled away.

Steve slumped back onto the pillows, irritated, looking at the swing of her hips as she went into the bathroom and thinking again of their lovemaking. It had been years since Julia had let him do that to her. She professed not to like it, but she hadn't complained when he'd started turning her around. He groaned. It was obvious she wasn't up for any this morning, and now he had a raging hard-on.

He picked up yesterday's paper and turned to the business section, hoping a couple of paragraphs of city news would calm him down.

·

Steve hadn't commented on the mess they encountered at Carrick, for which Julia was grateful. She'd felt embarrassed that she hadn't been able to finish her allocated job, but Steve hadn't even looked at her askance. Rather, he'd set to reloading the boxes, whistling in an irritating manner which made everyone exclaim in mock protest. The atmosphere in the old house was different with him there, lighter. Shadows lay where they should and there were no strange incidents or smells. It almost felt like a normal household.

Julia and he finished off the kitchen, then the dining room, taking a break halfway through to join the kids outside for a snowball fight on the back lawn. To any onlooker, they must have appeared the perfect family, she thought, as she watched her husband chasing the girls to deposit them on their bottoms in the soft snow. She scanned the black windows of the old house wondering if there was an onlooker somewhere behind them and caught sight of a red kite soaring close to the roof; its mew-like call to its two companions carried on the wind as the three of them circled overhead. The sight made her anxious and she begged off at that point to sneak upstairs to hide the newspapers in Annie's room until she had a chance to read them alone. She didn't want Steve finding them and throwing them out.

As they drove back home she stared out of the car window. There was still a lot of snow around, but travel had been easy in Steve's four-by-four skirting around the several thwarted, smaller cars which had been abandoned in the lanes over the weekend. The winter sun, twinkling through the sylph-like birch trees, was already dropping its tenuous hold on midday but still strong enough to make the rooftops of the few homes along the way glisten and shimmer.

The snow made Little Wynchstead beautiful and Julia had loved it in the past during the rare winters it fell. But the lack of colour and uncompromising cold was upsetting her this time. For flora and fauna it was death visiting, and death was too much on her mind right now. She saw neighbours talking outside a couple of the houses – hats, coats and mittens, spades in hand – and even while she recognised the opportunity the snow gave for a different perspective, for her today it reduced the usual lush landscape to negatives of a hitherto welcoming, reliable world.

Up ahead a lone figure stood at the bus stop, her back to their approach. Julia's heart jumped into her throat at the familiar grey shape with the long fair hair. As they drove nearer the figure started to turn towards their car. Julia found herself pressing back in her seat, holding her breath as the face came into view. Julia recognised the teenager that worked in the local newsagents. She sighed with relief.

Steve looked at her, sensing the tension, and she smiled at him.

"Are you alright?" he asked.

"Yes." After noting Grace asleep and Mattie with her headphones on, she asked him, "Have you heard me talking to myself before, Steve?"

"Only the once… at the table. You were very drunk."

"It's just that… in the house, Annie's house… I think I might have…"

"Julia, when I'm alone working on something, I often tell myself what to do… out loud. It's no big deal." He smiled at her. "You're fine, princess."

She cringed at his pet name for her, seldom used these days but still irksome. Steve's phone on the central console buzzed. Julia saw Bob's name on the screen.

"It's Bob, should I get it?"

"He always calls at the wrong time," Steve said, frowning.

Julia answered. "Hi, Bob, It's me, Julia. He's driving at the mo."

Bob's voice was faint. "Hey, Julia, no worries, how's my gal?"

"Good, thanks."

"Tell him I'll call him later," Steve muttered.

"Can he call you when he gets home?"

"Yes, no worries, Julia. I just wanted to know where he was last Friday. I had to team up with Freddie – had a crap game."

Julia looked at Steve to see if he'd heard Bob, but her husband was busy beeping his horn at another driver.

"He'll call you soon, I promise," she said. "Cheers, Bob." She replaced the phone.

"Bloody lunatic cut me up…" Steve said.

She smiled and stared out of the window, unseeing, thinking of what Bob had just said.

•

The clothes she chose to wear were loose-fitting and modest, but the colours of dark browns and reds enhanced her pale skin and set up her dark hair. She felt nervous about every little thing; she'd even snapped at the children, which she felt sorry for now.

They'd been so excited to have a day off due to the extra snow which had fallen overnight, but Julia cursed when she received the predictable text from the school office in the morning. Thank God for Row, who was going to mind them for her.

She stood before the mirror now, erasing some of the eyeliner she'd put on. Too heavy. A light touch: just a smudge under the lashes, clear moisturiser on her lips, keep it natural-looking. She sighed at the crow's feet and shadows under her eyes. She looked tired and haggard, she thought. And so? This was just a friendly meet-up, wasn't it? She looked into her eyes in her reflection – so why had she changed her mind three times about her outfit today?

She'd better get a move on or she was going to be late. Should she wear the new boots Steve had bought her? She felt a twinge of guilt as she hauled them out of the cupboard. Because she was acting like this was a date, wasn't she? Her guts twisted – damn her husband. Why was he so cold and precise? She couldn't remember the last time he'd held her close when they made love, always turning her around like he didn't want to look at her – and asking her to wear her hair in a ponytail. Who did he imagine he was with? It was shocking to note how little she cared while she considered this; with each late night spent in his office or each tiny revelation like Bob's call yesterday, Julia felt more and more detached. She collated each little incident, memorised them and used them now to justify her need to look good for Luke. No. Not good. Desirable. Too bad. She refused to feel guilty. She removed the lip moisturiser, replacing it with her favourite red shade. Downstairs she slipped the boots on over her black leggings and took a glance in the hall mirror. The butterflies threatened to rise into a giggle but she squashed them.

"Girls! Get a move on, please!"

Row lived at the end of her road in a spacious bungalow she'd bought with her husband thirty years before. She'd been widowed three years after purchase but couldn't bring herself to leave even though the house was too big for her now and she had to employ help to manage the garden. Julia relished that they'd moved so close to her old friend in the village. Steve hadn't realised yet, or if he had, he hadn't commented on it.

Row opened the door accompanied by energetic barks from Buster, her terrier. The girls were excited to see him and ran inside, hoping he'd chase them, which he duly did.

Row embraced Julia. "You alright, dear? I was worried about you last week…"

"I'm fine, Row. Thanks so much for having them. Bloody schools shut at the mere suggestion of snow these days!"

"It's my pleasure," the older woman said. "You look very nice… It's not the job interview today, is it?"

"Er, no. I, er… I'm doing a bit of research. Meeting a journalist I knew…"

Row smiled, glancing at the black leather boots and noting the red lips. "Good, dear. Well, don't delay. The girls will be fine."

Julia mumbled her thanks while turning away to hide her embarrassment.

"I'll be back at noon, don't worry."

"Enjoy! Life's short, dear!"

Julia smiled to herself at Row's approval as she got into the car and the excitement of the reunion ahead hit her with full force. She took a glance at her eyes in the rear-view mirror – they were sparkling like a teenager's.

23

The Highwayman was a dive. Inside, colourless furnishings and punters merged in a dimly lit, forgotten place, the meagre clientele hunched over their morning pints, immersed in memories and wisps of thoughts. The smell of stale booze and regret was so depressing Luke couldn't stay within for too long, which was why he was outside, leaning against the sign pole bearing the cracked and flaking picture of some horse-borne scoundrel when Julia turned the corner from the car park.

Luke had become a photographer, not because of his journalistic bent but to make sense of the world. After he'd lost his job following the split from Julia, a friend had offered him the chance to make some money helping him take pictures at weddings. Luke learned the basics of setting up the ideal portrait, but along the way he also discovered the pure beauty that could be captured of people when they were unaware of the lens. After framing so many people in the moment, he'd finally been able to perceive himself adrift temporarily, his grief for a lost love but a snapshot of him and his life so far. It had brought him round. Since then he tended to be more philosophical. He saw things, good and bad, more and more as a transition, and he was able to frame it, with him on the outside. As Julia walked into the picture, he saw his past, his present and he wondered about his future.

The slim figure that had rocked his world in one phone call took care walking along the snow-covered pavement in her long coat and black boots, head down checking for ice like the few other people on the street. Her silhouette etched against the backdrop of the old Victorian townhouses and the lanky skeletons of the plane trees. As she neared, he saw the expensive coat and boots, the designer handbag, the shining hair. Within twenty feet it was all about her face: her thick dark hair coiled back, loose wispy strands gently caressing her pale skin, the deep green eyes marking him as she approached and a tentative smile playing about her full lips. Red. The main colour in the frame. He took a breath.

"Hello, Julia."

She stopped just in front of him and her breath, cool white, drifted towards his face on the wintry air.

"You don't look any bloody older, Luke."

"Did you expect me to?"

She smiled. "I've changed. All rolled out, like pastry…" She laughed. "But you look… well, I won't say like a boy, but unaffected somehow…"

He shook his head, smiling. "I'm not that lucky. I'm as sentimental as they come – death, Disney, there's no escape!"

She stared at him a moment longer before turning her attention to the pub. "Shall we go inside?"

"It's pretty gloomy in there – how about that walled garden?" Luke nodded to a gate across the road.

"I don't think it's open."

"Let's go see," he said, taking her arm as they stepped into the road. "Did you get here alright?"

"Yes, Steve made me take the Cayenne out today, it's… it has winter tyres on."

Luke sensed her embarrassment. "Tell him I appreciate it!"

They'd reached the pavement.

"How about you?"

"I took the train," Luke said, letting her go. "I wouldn't chance it in my old banger."

Julia put her hand on his arm. "I'm glad you came."

Luke was caught off guard.

"I treated you very badly, Luke," she continued. "I'm so sorry."

Luke ushered her away from the road, bemused.

"I've been thinking about what happened to us. It was my fault. I was so spoilt when I was young," she continued, her face flushing a little. "Everything I wanted, I just had to ask. But I see now that I didn't have the love I needed. My dad tried but he didn't have the time and could only lavish presents on me. I didn't recognise the love you gave me – in fact, I think it frightened me, I felt unequal to it, battled with it… we battled with it. In the end I… I ran back to what I knew. I failed. You didn't."

Luke didn't know what to say. To his relief, the silence was broken by the town clock chiming in the adjacent building.

"I didn't come here to wring an apology out of you, Julia." He cursed at his brittle response, knowing he sounded defensive.

"I just wanted you to know," she said.

"It's OK." He felt himself smiling but he resented their breakup being addressed so soon and without warning.

She turned away then moved to the gate, pushing it open as the sun came out.

He followed her to the entrance like the bewitched no-hoper he knew he still was, floundering in the sea of emotions her confession had wrought.

"It looks so beautiful."

The pristine garden shimmered in the sunlight. It seemed almost a shame to ruin the flawless scene, but it was so tranquil they couldn't resist. It was quiet enough to hear the snow put-putting beneath their feet as they entered, closing the gate behind them.

"It's gorgeous," Luke said. "Like Narnia."

"It's a memorial garden for the wife of one of the benefactors of the town. The little shelter over there has been dedicated to her. That's why there are so many rose bushes here. Apparently she loved them. She also loved daffodils and you see those little squares of boxwood hedges? In the spring they're just full of them, like boxes of gold."

"Do you still paint?"

"No. I... I put it away, with everything else."

She looked so sad he felt he ought to shift the conversation. "Have you found out who she is? Your ghost?"

"No, but I have found out some things about Caroline. Of course it doesn't take a mastermind to know her background isn't all she'd made it out to be—"

"Do you think this girl is connected to her then?"

Julia shook her head. "When I worked for Mike he used to say, never put the chain away until all the links have been put together. I'm keeping all options open right now."

24

Julia told Luke all that had happened, starting with her first day packing up the kitchen at Carrick House. She finished with the vision she'd had at Mattie's party.

"It's like being drawn into a parallel world. More and more I'm drawn to Carrick and when I'm there, I… I'm just half there. I can't explain it. And what I'm most frightened about, Luke, is how she's using Mattie."

Luke dug his hands deep into his overcoat pockets as they turned the first corner to cross to the middle of the garden. "I think this girl is connected to the old house. All the packing up and moving of furniture, it's woken something up somehow. Perhaps she was a relative you didn't know about? Someone who lived there with Annie before you came?"

Julia felt a shift in her brain; something becoming dislodged and almost slipping into view. She gazed at the fountain ahead but saw instead herself swinging under the tree all those years ago watching her father laying rocks on the back lawn, Caroline coming out with a cup of tea for him and standing there while he drank it. She remembered how he dwarfed her with his massive frame even as he leaned against the wall. Julia hadn't heard what was being said as usual. They'd excluded her most of the time they were together.

"Julia?"

She started, pulled to the present by Luke's gentle nudge. She was embarrassed to see she'd stopped walking and she resumed her route to the centrepiece of the garden. "But how could she show up at the new house then? Are there rules about how ghosts... get about?" She laughed. "I can just about accept the idea that Carrick is haunted, God knows it's creepy enough! But are you saying that both houses are haunted?"

"She's haunting you, not the house."

"So somehow, I summoned her when I started packing up and she accompanied me back to the new house?"

"Well, if she's connected to you in some way, it's possible... or maybe there's something you found that she's associated with?"

"No, I... What about a hair band?"

"Well, maybe – anything connected to her or her past."

"Yes. It's the one thing I brought from the house. I didn't recognise it but it was cute. I... God, I gave it to Mattie!"

"Don't worry. But I would get it back from her and keep it on you. Could you ask Caroline about the history of the house?"

Julia shook her head. "She's not speaking to me. And she thinks I'm schizophrenic. I don't want to give her any more ideas about me being crazy – though I suppose Steve has told her everything. They already have me on happy pills and seeing a therapist."

"They do?" He looked concerned.

Julia sighed. "No, not yet, but that's their plan."

"What do you mean she thinks you're schizophrenic?"

"I think a couple of times she's heard me thinking out loud and now she's making a thing of it. She's trying to say I did it as a child. That I had an imaginary friend or something."

"Perhaps you did, Jules?" He'd lapsed into his old name for her but looked away from her gaze.

They'd come to the large, rearing stallion, once a deep rich brown, now transformed by verdigris due to its many years in the centre of the fountain.

"I love this statue," Julia said. "In the summer when the fountain is full and they turn on the jets it looks like he's playing in the surf..."

"Lovely," he murmured.

She felt the heat of his gaze but didn't dare return it.

"What do you think she's trying to say about the angels, Luke?" She shivered as a frosty breeze sprang up, stirring the dead leaves on top of the ice in the fountain base.

"Angels... they're different things to different people. There's the religious take on it, of course, that angels have different jobs in heaven and all that, but the general, accepted idea is that angels are messengers. Even so, it's a stretch for most people to believe in them; I find people are more ready to believe in ghosts."

"So I'm to receive a message?"

"Could be she's the message."

He seemed to remember something and from his inside pocket retrieved a small silver item the size of his palm. "This might be useful. It's a digital voice recorder. To catch some EVP."

"EVP?" she asked, looking at it.

"Electronic voice phenomena. Your spook's already spoken to you using the energy field from the TV. My guess is she's trying to contact you but you're not always receptive. This is really sensitive. It has four built-in mics with almost three sixty-degree pick-up so it should capture whatever's out there, even at a low level. If it's difficult to hear her, we can play it back through my PC where we can slow it down or amplify it."

"I used to have one for interviews." She slipped off her gloves to take hold of it and turned it over and back. "Not quite so many buttons, though!"

"Don't worry about that, it has the usual record, rewind and play. This is the power on and you have to set the area it will pick up the sound from, here. You can position it upright and point it outwards in front of you so it can pick up sound from more than one direction. Use these arrow keys to set up the mic pattern; see, front and back pick-up. You can ask her questions and this should pick up her responses."

As he pointed out the various buttons his fingers brushed hers and lingered over the back of her hand, causing a shiver to run through her. Did he notice? She chastised herself. She'd no business speculating. She turned her attention back to the device and tried to concentrate.

"You can save your recording under a file name pretty much like on your computer, so it becomes part of your file library, but the main thing is to get the recording."

"How much recording space does it have?"

"The batteries are new so you should get about twenty hours."

"Thanks," she said, putting the device into her bag. "I feel better having a plan, you know, doing something."

He was staring at her again. Her hands rose to fix her hair.

"Were you happy before this all started, Julia?"

She looked down at the snow, moved it about with the toe of her boot. "Is anyone ever happy in the moment? Since this started, I thought at first that I just wanted things back as they were, but lately… I'm not sure. It's like I've been asleep, Luke, and I'm waking up, remembering all I used to be, all I wanted to be. It's like the fog rolling away…"

"I missed you," he said.

She felt guilty for encouraging him, even for agreeing to meet him here.

He must have sensed her discomfort because he burst the bubble with his next question. "Tell me more about your kids."

Julia began to walk towards the small brick pavilion on the far side. She told him about how determined Mattie was and perhaps a little spoiled, and how Grace was a feisty little tomboy always trying to best her sister.

"Motherhood's certainly tougher than I expected – but very rewarding."

She noted everything about him while she talked. How his thick black hair still fell onto his forehead but was streaked now with silver, that the laughter lines around his mouth and eyes had deepened, of course, but not in a way that aged him. Luke was one who'd always attract female attention throughout his life with his high cheekbones, full lips and the determined set of his jaw. The only thing that saved him from looking like the proverbial lady-killer were his soft brown eyes which radiated warmth and empathy. He hadn't put on an ounce of weight, it seemed: still as rangy as ever, all gorgeous six foot two of him. Now she looked at his strong, capable hands as they took the plastic wrapping off his cigarette packet. She wanted to hold that hand.

"And…?" he quizzed.

Julia realised she'd tailed off, distracted – no, consumed by his masculinity. She felt a bit dizzy and foolish. "Where was I?" she said.

"You were telling me about the charity event this weekend."

He smiled at her and she felt her heart leap. Oh God! If she hadn't already revealed herself, she soon would at this rate. She fought for control.

"Yes, the whole charity thing was Annie's idea originally, though Caroline maintains it was hers. It's called the Carrick Foundation and offers financial assistance for homeless shelters for children throughout the county. This event is an annual one and the money raised is used by the shelters and also to raise awareness in the community. Caroline used to say, you have to give back, you can't take all the time; she even seemed the real McCoy when she visited the children's homes with Dad, but I think now she just wanted the positive publicity for the firm.

"Steve and Caroline really don't care about people that have nothing and Annie never did either. I remember one year the company bought up a load of housing association homes in West Highton, then demolished them to make way for luxury flats. The tenants had to move and those that couldn't afford to were evicted. I found out one family had ended up in a hostel. Caroline didn't give a damn. Said it was for the greater good as they would be housing more people in that small area in the blocks they were putting up. At higher rents, of course! To me they were destroying something that was working already for their own profit. It's all a sham. There, what do you think of it?"

She nodded to the building before them.

"It's quite a structure!"

They'd come to the hexagonal arbour built of the same red brick as the surrounding garden walls. Julia smiled. "It is special. He was an architect, which is why it's a bit more than your average garden pavilion."

Luke retrieved a small camera from his inside pocket and took a few shots, capturing the arches on the three front facades and the peaked tiled roof.

"Begs to be sat in, by lovers," he murmured.

Julia said nothing while he crouched down, capturing her in his next photograph. The snow glimmered all around her and the drip drip from the roof and the trees lent a gentle percussion in the background.

Smiling, Julia moved out of shot to check the plaque on the central pillar.

"That's right. Her name was Stella McAdam. 'My darling Stella, life will be intolerable now you're gone. You've taken the sunbeams and stars with you.' Sad, isn't it?"

"Romantic. Bet he had a new wife within two years."

"He did not!"

Luke laughed as he put his camera away. "So what do you have to do at the event this weekend?"

"Not much, just show up, welcome the mayor and the press, pretend to play with the children and pose for photographs with Steve. It gets harder every year!" She shook her head. "The difficult life of a haunted, middle-class housewife!"

There was a silence while they looked at each other, each with their own thoughts.

"I have to go," Julia said. "To pick up the girls."

They turned away from the pavilion and Julia took them up the shorter route back to the gate.

Julia realised with embarrassment they'd only spoken of her the whole time. "How about you?" she asked. "Are you…? Do you live with someone?"

"No. I'm not seeing anyone right now."

The blessed words.

"Your mum said you're freelance now – photographer."

"My mother needs a good talking-to, giving away my details!" he said in mock seriousness. "Yes, I like visuals these days instead of words. I got sick of writing. I still do articles, of course. I've written a couple of 'how-to' books." He smiled. "But next year I'm going to India, in April, to do a travel book, so a bit of writing but photographs mainly."

"Wow! That's great." Julia's words rang hollow in her ears, thinking that he would be away for weeks on end, but how was that her business? She was a married woman.

"Yeah, I'd done one on Israel which I financed with an inheritance from Aunty Belle. You remember her?"

"Of course, I'm sorry. When did she pass away?"

"Just after you left."

There was nothing to say. Luke had loved his father's sister. Julia was aware this would have been one more kick in the teeth after her leaving.

He continued. "Anyway, they liked my Israeli book. They bought it and commissioned me for three others. India's my second one. It's changed my life, Jules."

"I'm glad for you." She could hear her own insincerity. No sooner had he come back into her life, he would be leaving again. But that's fair, isn't it? She had nothing to offer him.

Why had she thrown him away? Steve was right, she was pathetic. And now their time together was over. She felt miserable. It had all gone so fast. But what had she wanted from this meeting? Whatever it was, she hadn't got it. She slipped suddenly on the pathway and he caught hold of her hand. She felt an electric charge through her whole body. He squeezed her hand before letting go.

"Thanks. So, I can call you, if I manage to record something?"

"Call me if you need me, Julia."

She looked at him now and he smiled, but it was not as warm

as she'd expected and his voice was matter-of-fact. She realised with horror that she wanted him to grab her and kiss her, and felt embarrassed, that he might be able to see her desire. She'd felt a heat generating between them earlier, but now his actions were perfunctory. As they neared the gate she struggled to keep the conversation going.

"I'm going there today so I'll set up the recorder. I'll have the girls with me, though, so won't be able to ask questions."

"It's still worth putting it on," he said.

Once through the gate into the street, the wind assailed them, grabbing at Julia's hair and blowing their coats around like washing.

"I'm at the station." He looked apologetic as he indicated the opposite direction.

"Oh, yes." She'd hoped he would walk her to the car park, but he seemed eager to leave. "Well, bye then." She managed a tremulous smile but felt close to tears.

Luke must have seen her vulnerability because he reached out his hand and touched her cheek gently. "Chin up," he said. "We'll speak soon." He turned and walked away.

Julia's eyes blurred on her way back to the car and she was angry with herself. What the hell did she expect? She wasn't being reasonable. Crazy, haunted Julia flitting about from house to house, man to man, like a pinball. She was fed up with her own weakness.

She would take whatever position Mike offered her tomorrow and make herself over. She would find her self-respect and she wouldn't need Steve's support or Luke's arms and she would rebuild her life without their help. She slipped on the unused bit of the car park and righted herself in time. The wind was not helping her keep her balance either and it was a struggle to cross to her car while the sky darkened and tiny droplets of sleet stung her face.

She fumbled with her keys, dropped them in the snow and crouched down to retrieve them, a sob rising in her throat, despite her resolve. As she rose, clutching snow and keys in her freezing hand, she saw a man staring at her through the windscreen of a black four-by-four. Julia would have glanced away but he seemed familiar.

She stood, wiping the tears from her eyes so she could see better. Her vision cleared and she saw he was haggard, around sixty, with thinning, shoulder-length hair, greased back from a receding hairline. A neat black goatie framed a thin-lipped mouth. She shivered under his scrutiny. The man hadn't flinched nor looked away. He started his car now, continuing to stare till he reversed. He looked over at her again before pulling away, leaving Julia feeling exposed somehow, invaded.

She watched the four-by-four till it reached the exit then climbed into her car, throwing her bag on the seat and locking all the doors. She sat back, trying to account for her nerves.

She heard a laugh.

She swung round, grasping the steering wheel and at the same time depressing the car horn by accident, making her jump even more. The back of the car was empty and silent. Her eyes dropped to the footwells, ears strained, senses alert. What the hell? She looked about the car park for anyone going to their car, but there was no-one.

Could the radio be on? She checked it, even depressing it on and off again, but the volume was so low on the setting, it couldn't have been that. Anyway, the voice had come from behind. She looked in her rear-view mirror. Could there be someone in the boot?

For God's sake! She was not going to look. This was ridiculous. She took a deep breath, trying to calm herself. That man had made her edgy, that's all. She looked around the car park again to make sure he'd not returned. She had to pull herself together and get going. She was already late for picking up the children from Row's.

25

Julia led Mattie and Grace to the sitting room, past the uncollected boxes filling the hallway at Carrick House. The removals company, caught up in the wintry mayhem, had left a message saying they couldn't get through and would call to re-schedule at the end of the week. Steve hadn't been happy with this, of course, and had suggested he might send his own guys round later in the afternoon to get every box out of there, so she was here to finish off as they'd planned.

It still felt calm and normal in the house, as it had done yesterday with Steve around. Julia was thankful for that. She'd been reluctant to bring the girls here today, but there was no-one else to look after them.

Mattie's face lit up when she saw the coffee table full of the little ceramic animals. "Mummy, they're cute!"

"They're called Whimsies," said Julia as she put the heater on. "You can play with them while I empty these last two cabinets. Keep your coats on till the room is warm, girls."

"I want the squirrel and the lamb!" said Grace, grabbing at them.

"I want the lamb!" said Mattie.

Julia rolled her eyes. "Now, don't fight. Share them then you can swap over when I come down. I'm just popping upstairs for a minute. Nicely, now!"

On the stairs, Julia paused and looked back at the sitting room. She could hear the girls had settled into some sort of play. They'd be alright.

Annie's room was icy; her breath preceded her in little white puffs as she crossed to the far side of the bed, knelt down and pulled out the yellowing tabloids from underneath. As she stood up, she caught the tagline along the top of the uppermost one, 'Britain's lost Children pg. 5'. She must have missed that before. She skimmed through it and found the full-page story of the same title. It began with the recent disappearance of a young girl in Wales, the fruitless search which ensued and listed five other cold cases of missing children, including one Suzanne Moore, who had disappeared during the seventies. She looked at the date of the paper: March the third, 1988. Feeling a quiver of excitement, she checked the dates of the other papers. They progressed back to 1977, the oldest paper at the bottom. She pulled it out. It was dated September thirteenth; it was the same year her mum had died and Julia had come to the house. The front page was all about the death of Steve Biko, anti-apartheid activist in South Africa. Page two had Brits out at the beach with their tops off catching a last-minute tan, and there was a piece on Elvis following his death the month before.

She turned over to see a photograph of a young girl with long hair who had gone missing from a care home in Stockport. The Midlands? She couldn't make out any distinguishing features of the girl. It was grainy and black and white, so the colour of her hair was unclear, but looking at the text, Julia saw she was described as fair-haired. This was the Suzanne Moore mentioned in the later tabloid. She was thirteen and had been at the Marsden Centre for fourteen months when she'd gone missing on a day trip to Blackpool. Marsden? Wasn't that the care home on the news at the moment? Julia stared at the picture, trying to at least get a feel for the girl: who she was, what had happened to her, whether it jogged any memories. It looked like a school photo and yielded very little. She shivered despite her coat. Her hands were stiff and red with the cold.

She scanned the rest of the paper then, finding nothing more of interest, moved on to the next one. There was an article of the same girl in each of the papers, all carrying the same blurry photograph, and the last three articles had no photographs at all and were very small. The texts all spoke of the investigation into Suzanne's disappearance, but the later ones lapsed into speculation and offered no conclusions. The final article which Julia had first read was about the failure of various investigations into missing child cases and the changes to the missing persons procedures in general which were being put in place as a result; poor consolation for Suzanne Moore who, eleven years later, still had not been found.

The silence pressed around her and she realised the girls had been on their own too long. She tore out five of the larger articles, folded them in quarters and pocketed them. She gathered up the papers and left the room, now empty of everything except the old furniture guarded by a non-judgemental Jesus from the walls.

Confident she'd established the reason for the papers being hoarded and holding the essential details in her pocket, she dumped the papers for recycling by the door and hurried towards the sitting room. Grace and Mattie hadn't missed her and were still playing.

The room was much warmer, but outside the earlier sunshine had been swallowed up by thick dark cloud. It would be as black as night by four. She switched on the light, looking at her watch: nearly two o'clock. God! What had happened to the afternoon? She glanced outside again. If it snowed she might have difficulty getting home. Even with Steve's fully prepped car, she still had to get round other drivers who might not be moving at all. She should maybe leave now, but there were just the two cabinets left in the room to do and she had promised Steve. She could do it in an hour.

"Girls, would you like some hot chocolate?" They didn't answer, so engrossed were they with their game. Julia fished out the flasks and Row's flapjacks she'd brought for a little indoor picnic, pouring each of them a drink and arranging the treats on a paper plate. It was nice and cosy; no need to rush home yet.

She turned her attention to the glass-fronted mahogany cabinet. A beautiful piece; it was late nineteenth century with suggestions of the Arts and Crafts movement in the tracery on the glass doors and the carved wooden posts on the top of it. It was just over four foot with shelves inside down almost to the ground. As lovely as it was, it was too fussy for her house. She was glad Steve intended to sell it and its twin over there in the corner.

Her phone buzzed. A message from Steve. His van was stuck at Highton so wouldn't be coming this afternoon and she should make sure she left Carrick early for home as more snow was forecast. She looked outside, and as if on cue, the wind was whipping up the leaves and flailing the trees bordering the lawn.

She pocketed her phone and knelt in front of the unit. The first figurine was a Capodimonte in greens and blues. As a child she'd looked at it, thinking how handsome the man was. It reminded her now of Luke years ago: a carefree youth, light on his feet and in his heart. The figure was donned in peasant's clothing, his sleeves rolled up, a roguish smile on his face and his dark hair across his eyes. A small dog at his feet was on its hind legs scrabbling for attention.

That's me this morning, Julia sighed, looking at the hapless dog, making a fool of myself. As she wrapped it she thought of Luke: the firm grasp of his warm hand, his easy way of speaking to her, the movement of his mouth – the recorder! Thank goodness she remembered! She walked over to her bag and pulled out the gadget.

"What's that, Mummy?" Grace said.

"It's a… just a thermometer – it gives readings of the temperature in here."

Her answer was designed to stem Grace's interest, which it did. Julia switched it on, pressed record and placed it on the top of the cabinet, smiling; the girls would have wanted to do karaoke if they'd known what it was.

She went back to her place, kneeling at the foot of the cabinet, breathing the musty wood smell and cradling the porcelains before double-wrapping them for their journey to the auctioneers. The girls' animated voices rose over her while she held each piece, looking at the beautiful faces and remembering the family stories linked to some of them. The one she'd just wrapped was bought on a day out in the Cotswolds and this one was given to Annie for her birthday by her father. She recalled the day he'd given it to her, the rare smile it had evoked as her grandma had opened the box. She heard the wind now shaking the windows and howling through the chimney, and her girls' voices rising and falling as they played out their stories, the hallway clock tick-ticking…

Julia looked at the birthday present to Annie in her hands and felt odd. She looked up at the window. It was pitch black outside except for the white flakes being hurled at the panes. The silence prompted alarm and her gaze moved to where the girls had been sitting. They were gone. She looked down at her watch: five o'clock! What the hell? Her hand rose to her face. She'd been crying. Julia tried to stand, but her legs were so stiff and numb that she collapsed on the sofa. She dropped the ornament onto the seat and rubbed frantically at her limbs to bring the blood back into them. As she felt the warmth seeping back into her muscles she was able to hobble to the unlit hallway.

"Mattie? Grace? Where are you?"

The stillness of the house answered her back from the dark stairwell to the upper floors. "Girls?"

Had they gone to the toilet together? They wouldn't want to go alone, that was for sure. Why would they go without the lights on? Mattie was tall enough to reach the switches. What the hell had happened during the last two hours? Julia trembled. Had something happened to make the children run out of the room? Why hadn't she heard them?

"Mattie? Grace? It's Mummy here. I'm alright. I've just… I was sleeping. Come on. It's alright." There was no other way right now to describe it or explain what had happened. Julia must have fallen asleep. Upright? Kneeling in the same position for two hours?

She switched on the hall light and the shadows leapt back just as she heard a muffled cry: not quite above her, not from this floor… stifled. As if from the wall cavities. Her heart raced as she called. "Girls! Mattie? Where are you?"

The cry seemed to emanate from the dining room: "Mummy!"

The dining-room door creaked as Julia pushed it open onto the darkened room. Julia knew at once that the girls were not in there. She listened waiting, trying to control her surging panic. The cry came again, from the vent at the base of the wall: frightened, desperate, just audible.

"Mummy!"

"Mattie! Grace, speak to me!" Julia backed out of the dining room and ran to the kitchen, relieved to see the pantry light emanating under the closed door at the far end. The pantry. Of course! They must've been looking for something more to eat and somehow trapped themselves inside.

She was surprised when the door yielded without effort. The girls weren't there. The pantry was a walk-in cupboard, not very wide but about six foot long. The entire back end had been stacked with boxes and old appliances when she'd come in here a week ago looking for wine, but now the floor space had been cleared. Where had all the boxes gone?

She stared, amazed at what her mind was registering: a clear outline of a trapdoor on the floor with a circular ring at the head of it. Julia didn't know the house had a cellar. Oh God, now she could hear muffled pleas from below. Oh, please don't let them have fallen down there! She sprang to the trapdoor.

26

Julia's hands fumbled with the metal hoop, then she was pulling the heavy door up. Below, the frightened face of Grace peered up from the base of a wooden ladder. Her tear-washed face crumpled anew. "M… Mummy!" She was holding a lit candle in a small flat pewter holder.

"Darling, what are you doing down here?" Julia was already clambering down and was assailed by a thick, putrid smell, intensifying as she descended. "Oh, what is that? Are you alright, my love?"

She dropped down the last two steps and took the wobbling candle from Grace, crouching down to hug her close. Grace's whole body was trembling and Julia smoothed her hair, trying to reassure her.

"It's alright, darling. I'm here now. Are you OK, baby?" She ran her hands down Grace's arms, checking everything was intact. "Sssh, now, you didn't fall down the steps, did you? Why did you come down here, Grace? You could have hurt yourself."

From behind an eerie chant emanated from the shadows. "Make friends, make friends, ne-ver ev-er break friends."

Julia stood and lifted the candle, placing a hand over her own mouth and nose as she did so to try to mask the smell. "Mattie?"

As the circle of candlelight spread further, the unnerving recital from the shadows led her to her eldest daughter: "Make friends, make friends, ne-ver ev-er break friends…"

Mattie was squatting in a corner facing her. She had only her underclothes on. Her arms clasped her knees. She stared straight ahead. "Make friends, make friends, ne-ver ev-er break friends." Her mouth hung open following this, drool dripping from her lower lip.

Julia's heart plummeted seeing her eldest in such a state. She knelt down in front of the child.

"Mummy, can we go now?" pleaded Grace. "She keeps singing that song and I don't like it."

"Make friends, make friends, ne-ver ev-er break friends."

"Mattie? What's wrong, darling? Sweetheart, it's Mummy." She waved her hand in front of her daughter's unseeing eyes.

Mattie started the refrain again, a little louder this time, the only animation from her being the little finger on her right hand which seemed to twitch with each beat of the monotonous chant. Julia searched and saw the pile of clothes to the left. The tuneless singing grew louder as Julia reached for Mattie's arms. Her daughter was freezing.

"Mattie…" She had to raise her voice now to make herself heard over the tuneless chant. "I'm going to dress you now, honey, and we're going home."

"Make friends, make friends, ne-ver ev-er break friends." Julia was pulling a T-shirt over her daughter's head even as Mattie intoned. By now she was not pausing between but chanting non-stop.

"Make friends! Make friends! Never ever break friends!" Each time stronger and louder than the first. Her small body was beginning to jerk with each word, exaggerated and strident now.

"Mattie!" Her own voice rising again, Julia placed a hand on her daughter's chest, trying to calm her and to suppress her own panic.

"Mummy, please!" Grace begged. "I want Daddy."

"Mattie!" Julia shook her. "Mattie!"

Mattie screamed now, "…Never ever break friends. Make friends, make friends…" Suddenly she grasped Julia's little finger in the crook of her own as she finished.

"…Never ever break friends!"

As Julia stared into her daughter's eyes, she remembered.

Her friend, San. Her secret friend who had kept her company all of those scary years at Carrick, the friend she couldn't see but could hear as if she was sitting next to her. The friend that had looked after her – made her laugh, told her what to do when there was trouble. They would sing the song when they were making up, linking their pinky fingers – at least, in Julia's mind, till it was done.

"Make friends! Make friends! Never ever break friends!" Mattie shouted now at the top of her voice, her whole body straining with the exertion.

Grace stood screaming with her hands on her ears. "Mummy, make her stop! Make her stop!"

In a frenzy, Mattie screamed, "Make friends! Make friends! Never ever…"

Julia shook her, yelling. "Mattie! Stop! It's Mummy… Please! Stop now! San! I remember! I remember you."

Mattie slumped against the wall, gasping, and Julia fell back, shocked. Shocked to recall a whole part of her life in an instant and in response to this assault on her daughter. She watched her now for any signs she would begin her song again, then, on hearing Grace's little choked sob behind her, she roused herself, trembling as she pulled Mattie close. She pulled in Grace for the hug too with one hand while she rubbed Mattie's back with her other, trying to revive her daughter a little before releasing them both. She picked up Mattie's tights and began to put them on her unresponsive limbs.

"Grace. Tell me what happened from the beginning."

"I want Daddy, Mummy."

"I know, darling, but I can't take Mattie outside in the cold like this, can I? While I dress your sister you can tell me. Come on, Grace, you're a big girl now and we need your help."

"You started speakin', but it wasn't like you and Mattie said we had to go."

"What do you mean it wasn't like me?" Julia's stomach constricted at the thought of her daughters going through this. She pulled on Mattie's jersey over the T-shirt.

"First you was singing that song that Mattie sung, but not nicely, Mummy… and you sounded like a little girl. Then I heard someone cryin', but it wasn't you and… Mattie went out of the door and I shouted to you, Mummy, to help us but you couldn't hear me. You jus' kep' looking at the orn'ment. I was scared, Mummy, but I had to go with Mattie."

"It's OK, darling, you did right. Don't worry."

"She came here, but I wouldn't go down. It was too dark and Mattie said we could take a candle. She lit it, Mummy, not me!"

"Honey, it's alright," Julia assured her while putting one of Mattie's shoes onto her daughter's icy foot. "Where is her other shoe, Grace?"

Damn it. Julia lifted the candle higher and looked around the walls. She saw a light switch on the wall. She walked over and tried it. The room was revealed in the dim yellow light as she blew out the flame.

It was empty. Four bare brick walls which had been painted over, now a dullish grey colour and a bumpy hard floor under large pieces of dirty lavender carpeting which curled up the walls at the edges. Looking at the carpets, Julia felt intense claustrophobia seize her. She looked up at the hatch. It was still open at the top of the ladder. Why had it been closed when she arrived? After the girls had come down?

She hurried back to Mattie, grabbing the other shoe on the way. She pushed it on while struggling to control her own panic. The smell assailed her nostrils again.

"Oh my God. Doesn't the smell bother you, honey?" She put Mattie's feet into the skirt and lifted her daughter gently to standing and pulled up the tights and skirt. Mattie swayed, staring ahead of her. "Grace, you go up first. Mattie, darling, we're going home." Julia took her hand. "Come on – be careful, Grace!"

Mattie was slow, and although Julia could pull her along, her body hung back. Julia heard a creaking noise above them and a shudder drove through the ladder. Grace screamed halfway up and

Julia watched, helpless, as her terrified daughter clung to the rungs. She eyed the hatch.

"You're alright, Grace – keep going." She steadied her voice.

There was a whining noise like a big heavy door swinging on its hinges as she continued to reassure her youngest. Cold sweat trickled down her back. Please let her through…

"Hurry up, darling." She held her breath as Grace neared the top. The creaking sound was louder now. Another jolt shook the ladder and Grace cried out. Julia tried to make Mattie grasp the ladder rungs, but her hands were clenched and kept falling like heavy weights to her sides. Julia picked her up. Placing her on one hip and holding her with one hand, she used the other to grasp the wooden rungs. It was difficult, but the loud creaking and fear of being trapped gave her strength.

Grace was through.

"Stand back from the edge, darling, we're coming up now."

The ladder vibrated again, a little less this time, as Julia hurried to the top, where she placed Mattie on the trapdoor edge and held her there as she herself climbed out then pulled her daughter away from the gaping hole. In the silence that followed, she looked down into the strange grey room where she'd left the light on. She felt dizzy again as the dirty lilac carpet seemed to rush up and move away again. She wavered. A thought played around the edge of her mind, almost coming into view. Something was familiar… she could almost… if she could just… She felt a tugging on her sleeve; it was Grace, her tears beginning to fall once more.

"Mummy, let's go."

Julia shook her head. God, what was wrong with her? She looked at both daughters, standing so forlorn and bewildered, and pulled them to her. "My babies."

She looked back at the innocuous space behind her, now silent, and wondered if she'd imagined the creaking and shuddering of the ladder? She closed the trapdoor. "Let's go," she said.

Carrying Mattie, Julia ushered Grace into the sitting room and instructed her to put her coat on. As quick as she could, she put Mattie's lifeless arms into her coat and zipped it up, pulling up the hood before dragging her own coat on. She remembered to turn off the heater once they were all ready, and after throwing the recorder into her bag, she picked Mattie up again and hurried Grace outside into the blizzard. Holding Grace's hand, she dragged her through the thick, new snow, immune to Grace's screaming. The car beeped ahead as she released the locks and the lights illuminated the vehicle through the whiteout.

Once she had the girls secure in their seats, she started up the car and grabbed a window scraper. The freezing wind and snow stung her face as she cleared the panes, all the while eyeing the house, lit up like a beacon from the lights she'd left on. Each moment she dreaded seeing somebody looking down at her from the window.

From the boot she grabbed the fleecy blanket she'd put there earlier and hurried back into the car, closing the door behind her to keep in the heat. As she tucked the blanket around the children, she checked Mattie was still strapped in and saw her daughter had closed her mouth and stopped drooling. She seemed to be coming round.

"It's alright, my love," she soothed. "You had an adventure, but Mummy found you. Are you alright, my darling?"

Mattie began to cry and Julia was relieved to see the tears. Grace held out her hand too and Julia put a hand on both girls to calm them. "There, my loves. It's OK. We're going home now."

"Mummy?" Mattie's voice was barely audible. Her frightened blue eyes tugged at Julia's heart. "What's this?"

She opened her small fist to reveal a silver chain blackened with age and neglect with the letter 'S' hanging from it. The 'S' was distorted, stylised in such a way that it might not have been a letter. It looked rather more like a snake.

27

Julia put both girls in the bath when she got home. Neither spoke much while Julia lathered up the sponge and did their backs and arms. She felt like a nurse tending two shell-shocked war victims.

Once in their pyjamas she took them downstairs. Steve was still not home. She'd call him after she and the girls had the soup she'd heated on the hob. Julia watched them as they ate. They were a pinky colour now from the bath but both so listless and exhausted from the stress. It would be best to get them to bed as soon as possible.

·

Just after nine, Julia woke up. She lay there for a few minutes. All she could hear was the gentle breathing of her daughters while they slept. She knew she should give Steve some watered-down version of why they'd gone to bed early. She dragged herself up. The daisy chain lay on the dressing table and she picked it up as she passed and shoved it into her cardigan pocket.

Steve's briefcase was in the hallway. The kitchen was empty but she noted a plate with remnants of a pasta dish left on the central island.

Julia approached the study without making a sound. She listened at the door but all she could hear was the occasional tap on the keyboard. She went in.

Steve looked up from behind the screen and seemed to hesitate before speaking. "Oh, hi," he said.

She moved towards him, but Steve half rose to meet her, clicking the keyboard as he stood up then sat down again. She stopped in front of the desk, noting his discomfort. Had she caught him in contact with a lover?

"The girls had an upset today while we were at the house. I decided the best thing for them would be an early night."

"OK," he said.

She felt he wanted her to leave.

"What are you doing, Steve?"

"Working. Talking of which, are you going for your interview tomorrow?"

"Uh-huh. Can I have the Cayenne again?"

"I'm using the work's van, so yes. I tried to book you the doctor's appointment but they weren't taking any. Some of the GPs can't make it in with the snow. What about the girls tomorrow? They won't be at school, I suppose?"

"No. Too few teachers. I'll drop them at Row's." She noted his frown on hearing her friend's name. She walked behind him to place both hands on his shoulders. "So what job are you working on?" The screensaver was the only thing visible.

Steve stopped her hand as it strayed to the mouse and he swivelled round to face her. "You look nice."

He said it in a way he might compliment old Annie, but his other hand moved to her buttocks and proceeded to explore her firm muscles with his fingers, squeezing and caressing.

Julia stood for a moment, letting him fondle her, and bent over him and kissed his head, her breasts teasing his face. She could tell she'd aroused him enough to leave him irritated as she pulled away and moved to the door.

"Steve, did you move all of the boxes out of the back of the pantry on Sunday?"

"No. I thought you were doing it?"

"It's done, don't worry. Must have been Caroline. I'll finish off tomorrow after I've seen Mike. Tell her not to bother coming down."

So could she assume he didn't know about the cellar then?

She turned and walked away. "I'll sleep with the girls tonight."

"Why? What happened?" he said, annoyed.

"Just the usual: little girls' bickering, y'know. Goodnight, Steve."

·

The packing was done, yet Julia was still there at noon, in the sitting room at Carrick House. She'd warmed up with the hot chocolate she'd brought, sipping it as she stared out of the window.

The blizzard had gone on all night and now the gardens dazzled in Arctic white. According to the forecast, this was the last of the snow, but enough had settled to use it as an excuse to cancel her interview with Mike this morning.

She'd had to come back; the chance to uncover Carrick's secrets was slipping away. Once the snow thawed, the cleaners would be called in and her time here would be done.

She'd researched her on her laptop this morning while she had her breakfast; Suzanne Moore was born in a suburb of Manchester in May 1964. Her mother was a drug addict and she and her younger sister had been in and out of care since ages ten and four. The social services had tried to keep the girls together, but when their care home was closed down the girls were split up. While Suzanne was moved to Marsden her sister Karen went to a foster home outside the city.

Suzanne had lost her one true friend in the world at that point, Julia thought. It must have been heart-breaking for her. Terrible. At times, Julia had felt hard done by as a child, but she could at least say she'd had a mother that loved her and her father had loved her too, in his own way. At least he'd been protective of her.

Suzanne Moore had had no-one, it seemed. She'd tried to run away from the home before and the police couldn't conclude whether she'd run away again that day in Blackpool, 1977, or been abducted.

It appeared to Julia the police had been too quick to close the case, but she knew there were too many cases of the missing for the police to solve; only the higher-profile ones would receive the attention they needed. Of course, the main qualifier for that would be that somebody gave a damn for the victim and was prepared to shout about it.

Julia looked around the room. The question was, did Suzanne Moore end up here in this house, and how? The link had to be Caroline. She would have still had connections to Manchester. Did she use Wozniak then to help her? But what did Caroline want with the child, and did her father and Annie know what she was up to? How could he not know? Perhaps he'd been drawn into something he couldn't extricate himself from?

And when did Suzanne become her friend? Because she knew now Suzanne and San were one and the same – had to be. Was it her first year at Carrick? It was all hazy; the little games in her bedroom with her dolls, tea sets, promises made, laughter shared, San at her side as she entertained with her own stories, keeping herself apart from the adults. She couldn't remember San in her teenage life. She'd later fled to university, grateful to be free of the family – and something malevolent in the house that she'd never fully acknowledged.

She suddenly recalled one night sitting on the stairs with her teddy on her lap in the darkened hall listening to the hum of the adults in the sitting room; quite often Steve's father, Mr Campbell, would join her father, Caroline and Annie. They always started the evening with a game or two of rummy or crib and a bottle or two of whiskey between them. Julia remembered hating the smell of the whiskey. She'd had to endure it as she kissed her father and Grandma goodnight. She wasn't allowed to stay up and was always sent to bed early on those nights. Her breath caught in her throat, her mouth dry. Something almost slipped into view – something from that time. Julia fought the urge to shut the memory down. She felt a surge from her belly to her throat.

"Oh God!"

She stood up, a moan escaping her lips, and leaned against the window frame, afraid of digging further, afraid of what she would find out next. Is this why she'd avoided herself? Her whole life?

28

Caroline was not happy with the current turn of events. For the last three decades, it had been easy maintaining their success and the respectability it prompted. Now this silly bitch was threatening everything.

Micah, like Caroline, hated loose ends, and he was in the village, following that spoilt brat around to find out what she was up to and to stop her doing any more digging than she'd done already. And he would stop her. That's what worried Caroline. Unlike her, Micah didn't know what subtlety meant. He didn't have the patience for persuasion or even careful disposal. His early family history in Eastern Poland was littered with murdered relatives, deportation, poverty. There's not much room for caution in a life like that, she knew, and he just didn't understand or respect Julia's high profile in the village. Any death, natural or otherwise, would attract the national press because the charity had made the tabloids a few years back. She'd spent most of the morning on the phone to Micah trying to make him see things her way, and he'd been his usual prickly self.

She had to concede he was useful, though. He'd just revealed Julia's meeting with a man in the old town on Monday. Very interesting. Micah said there had been some intimacy between the two so she figured it wasn't the newspaper guy. Micah had confirmed they'd held hands – an old friend then or lover? Was she having an affair? Reluctant to admit it, she could see the logic in Micah staying around, even if only to report the bitch's movements. Like today. Why hadn't Julia gone to her interview with Cormorant? What was she up to at Carrick House? Yes, Micah had proved useful – and still could be. If she could just persuade him to do things her way this time.

.

Julia sat staring at the recorder in her hands. She felt she was about to invite someone in as her finger hovered above the play button. She was aware she could leave now and allow the house and all its memories to be sold. She could make the necessary changes to recover her life with Steve and they could raise the girls together. She could take a job, take the pills – for a while, at least until things settled. They could be the happy family she'd always assumed they were. There was no need to discover anything more.

She pressed play.

Her own voice leapt out at her catching her off guard: "…just a thermometer…" She released her breath, remembering now her explanation to the girls as she'd placed the machine on top of the cabinet. She could hear the soft voices of Mattie and Grace in the background as they played out their stories against the sound of bubble wrap being rolled around porcelain. Julia smiled, listening to the girls' characterisations of the little animal figures.

After about five minutes of this, white noise blared from the small speaker. A sudden dip in volume was followed by low fluctuating notes like those played on a flute but muffled and fading, like it was moving down a tunnel. Had the girls stopped talking when the static began? She could no longer hear them. Words flitted among the notes and she stopped the playback, rewound a little and turned up the volume to maximum.

It was a girl's voice, eerie in its isolation, fluctuating in volume: "Get me out." The mournful plea intoned twice and it was as if it was crossing dimensions to be heard; its unearthly resonance caused the hairs on Julia's arm to stiffen.

The static returned, becoming so loud Julia went to turn down the volume but halted at the sound of a child's sob, a gulp of tears with a sharp intake of breath and humming, or was it more crying? A child moaning? The hum wavered back and forth like a vibration. From the speaker issued a rasping whisper which made her blood freeze: "Come on, love, be an angel."

And a laugh: humourless, cruel. It was a man's voice, a London voice, hard and heartless. But Julia remembered this voice could be soft sometimes, when he read a bedtime story or pushed her on the swing. Her mind reeled. Why was her father speaking to her now? Why would he want to be heard? Julia pressed pause with a trembling hand. Was this confirmation that he was connected to the girl? Was he instrumental in her disappearance from the home? He couldn't be… It was because he was part of Carrick House, having died there…

She took a breath and pressed play again. More static flooded the recording, followed by a child's voice singing.

"Make friends, make friends, ne-ver ev-er break friends." The same flat tone Mattie had used yesterday.

She heard Grace: "Mattie? Where are you going?"

There was a scuffling sound and Grace, confused, continued, "Mattie? What's wrong? You knocked the flask over! Mummy!"

Julia could hear sobbing now. Her gut wrenched when she heard Grace ask her, "Why are you cryin', Mummy?" She felt more anguish as Mattie must have walked out of the room while her youngest grew more frantic.

"Mummy! There's something wrong with Mattie. Please, Mummy, I'm scared, stop cryin'… please, Mummy!"

The crying continued, then Grace could be heard following Mattie out of the room. Her voice echoed from the hall, dwindling to silence, absolute, unnatural silence, while Julia apparently knelt, with a porcelain in her lap, neither seeing nor hearing for two and a half hours as her daughters suffered alone in the shadows of the house, ushered to the decrepit cellar with its dark secrets.

Tears rolled down her cheeks. She felt worn out trying to make sense of it all. She wrapped her arms around herself and cried out.

Hearing her father like that... he'd sounded... cruel. When Julia was little he could be strange sometimes, unfamiliar, like when he told adult jokes that made Caroline laugh. At these times, it was as if Julia was not there. Later he would notice her and stroke her cheek, becoming her father again, but if he'd been drinking, it would take till the next day before she felt she could approach him.

She replayed in her mind the appeal she'd heard to 'be an angel'. It was laden with malevolence and sick merriment in the tone. It was the tone now that was familiar, stirring uncomfortable feelings. Her hand shook so much as she reached for her phone she knocked it off the table.

Her words to Luke began with a sob. She hadn't meant to, but it burst out on hearing his voice.

"Julia? Are you alright?"

"Yes. I... I'm sorry Luke... I'm scared."

"What's happened?"

"I have a recording. I want you to listen to it. I think... something's going to happen. Can you come over?"

"Where are you? Are you at Carrick?"

"Yes, I... I know I shouldn't ask you, Luke... and it might be difficult. The snow's thick out here."

"I can get a train if they're running and a taxi from the station. What's the address?"

"I could pick you up from the station..."

"Don't worry, let's see how I get on. I'll call you if needed. It wouldn't be good if you were seen picking me up."

"No, you're right. OK." She sniffed, embarrassed about her tears, and gave him the address.

"Luke?"

"Yeah?"

"Thanks."

"Stay put and don't fret, matey."

The phone clicked off. Julia held it to her chest, comforted by his use of the endearment, which had started in their student days. She contemplated getting a drink for her nerves from the cupboard in the kitchen and remembered it was empty. She'd taken all the alcohol to her own house halfway through last week. Damn.

She would wait for Luke to arrive. Even while she was thinking she couldn't listen to it again, she was already replaying the tape, waiting for the eerie implorations and her father's hoarse whisper.

•

Luke trudged through the snow up the lane. The taxi had dropped him, unwilling to venture onto the untreated road. Silver birch trees shushed above his head and sifted fine snowflakes upon his face and hair. There was a smell of pine in the cold air that cleaned your lungs as you breathed. The road was empty of people, though he could see from tracks in the snow someone had been out walking their dog, perhaps from one of the large neighbouring houses nestled back from the road behind tall trees and high walls.

He came to an empty black Range Rover about fifty feet from the silver gate of Carrick House. It was the sole car abandoned in the road, but not because of the snow, he surmised, peeking inside and seeing a map book and an empty binoculars case on the passenger seat. Probably a twitcher, he thought as he continued on and up the driveway.

He paused halfway, staring at the dreary-looking façade in front of him. He could see how this place could be scary to a young child. Perhaps that's why Julia was here, to exorcise the memory of it.

He'd vowed to himself not to be drawn in after their meeting yesterday. Just give her the recorder, he'd told himself, and leave. No lingering hugs, no reminiscing. Almost achieved. He'd blabbed he'd missed her but had regained control and left, feeling intact. Just. He hadn't intended seeing her again so soon, though, thinking they would've discussed the recordings over the phone, but he'd been helpless against her pleas today. So here he was, steeling his emotions. And there she was, standing in the doorway under the porch, wearing a chunky white jersey and slim black leggings, and the house hunkering over her like a giant spider waiting to wrap her up in a gossamer shroud.

He tried to rationalise when she jumped down the step and hugged him to her. She's afraid. She's not thinking straight; I'm just here to help her. He looked around, feeling uneasy.

Julia must have felt his body stiffen. She pulled back. "Sorry. I feel so shook up, that's all. There's nobody here, not even the gardener." She led the way inside.

He stepped up to the threshold and hesitated after the first step into the hallway. It felt colder in there than out in the open and grimy – sullied, even. Julia stood looking at him but didn't say anything. He noted the desolate interior and the dusty stairs winding up to the shadowy upper floor, expecting to see the spectre of the lost girl looking down on him. A malignity and foreboding brushed the back of his neck. He knew stepping in now meant he couldn't go back. He was re-connecting to Julia by coming here as surely as if he'd returned her hug outside. It was a mistake, but it was too late. He couldn't leave her now.

He sighed as he turned round to close the front door. He didn't see the glint of the binoculars as the sun caught the glass and the reflection exploded like a small star in the bushes.

29

They sat on the window seat. Luke pulled out a flask. "I didn't know if you had anything, so I made us some coffee. We can add a shot of this too." He produced a small bottle of brandy from his pocket with the flourish of a magician. He poured a shot into the black steaming liquid in the flask cup and handed it to her.

The sunlight bounced off the side of his head like a halo and Julia glanced into his dark eyes as she sipped the drink. She looked away, feeling the alcoholic coffee fire a steamy path to her belly. She smiled and nodded to herself. "That's good."

"I also brought your favourite – malt loaf!" He hauled it out from the rucksack. "Survival bread – mmmm!" He tore open the wrapper with exaggerated urgency. "Can you pass the butter, my dear?"

Julia smiled and held out her hand, savouring his clowning around in the sunbeams, the light picking out the silver threads in his thick glossy hair that Julia suddenly wanted to run her hands through. He placed a chunk of the sticky loaf on her palm and after a couple of bites and a few more sips she was feeling much better.

"Do you want to hear it, Luke?"

"Yes, go on. I think I'm ready for it now."

His face remained impassive throughout the playback while Julia explained what was happening to each of them, finishing with how she'd knelt there in a trance, unknowing of her daughters' ordeal.

"Do you remember anything during the time you were in this trance?"

"Nothing specific, but you know when you wake up from a dream and you can remember the feel of it? Well, it was like I was a child again, but... I can't give you any details. You must think I'm crazy!"

"No, listen, she's drawing you back to the past. Think about it. If she has no physical boundaries, why should time have boundaries for her? Reports of ghosts are often of them doing things they did in their lives, the same route between rooms, wearing the same dress, the same cry for help. I think she's dragging you back so you can remember. What happened afterwards?"

She described how she'd come round and, after a worried search, come to the cellar room under the pantry and poor Mattie undressed and freezing in the corner.

"You must have been freaked out by that."

"I was." She shook her head. "Mattie was singing the song – the same one as on the recorder. One I used to sing with my imaginary friend."

"You remember him now?"

"Her name was San. Luke, I think my imaginary friend and this... apparition is one and the same. I think her name is Suzanne Moore. I found newspapers in Annie's cupboard and they all had an article about this girl that disappeared from Manchester. I think Caroline was involved."

"Jeez. And your father?"

"I think it's my father... on the tape." She gulped. "As for San, she was a voice in my head when I was little. One day she was just there. She told me stories, gave me warnings and looked out for me. I don't know how I forgot her... When Mattie was singing that song... it was awful. She wouldn't stop..."

"Why would your father be on the tape, Jules?"

"I don't know."

Luke grasped her hand and squeezed it. "I think you should take me to the cellar."

•

Julia led him through the cold, desolate kitchen. She stopped at the pantry door. The boxes were back, covering the trapdoor. This didn't surprise her. Nothing was normal anymore. Luke helped her to move the boxes to the front hallway then together they stood looking down into the pallid room. The light was still on as she'd left it.

"I'll go first," Luke said, sensing her reluctance.

"I'm not sure I…"

He paused on the third rung down. "Come on, you'll be alright. I'll look after you."

She smirked. "You don't think you're a little overconfident?" Her humour dissipated, though, with each step down into the room. The smell of vomit assailed her once more. Turning from the ladder with her hand over her mouth she was shocked to see Luke standing there at ease. "Can't you smell that?"

"Smell what?"

"The vomit, and… it smells of… fear, shit and fear!" Julia must have gone green or deathly pale as Luke stepped towards her, concerned.

"Where is it strongest?"

"The room is reeking with it!" She felt angry and disoriented. The familiarity of the room was again triggering an unreasonable fear within her. Something about the way the edges of the carpets curled up against the walls…

"I can't stay down here, Luke. There's nothing to see. Mattie was in that corner and Grace at the bottom of the ladder."

"And the trapdoor was closed?" He turned to the carpet and pulled it away from the floor.

"Er… yes… When I got here… I don't know how… I mean, they wouldn't have closed themselves in… couldn't have." But Julia knew as she spoke. Knew that *she* had kept them prisoner until Julia came looking for them. *She* had wanted Julia to find this room.

"Mattie found a necklace here with an 'S' on it. I think it was hers, Suzanne's. What are you doing?"

"I'm just looking for clues – like the necklace." He was pulling the carpet up from the corner, revealing black mould underneath and all along the edges. "This may be the cause of the smell, Julia."

"No, it's not that. I think…" She paused and looked at the yellow bulb. It had started to flicker. "Oh God, don't go out!" Claustrophobia seized her. She looked at the top of the ladder; the hatch was still open.

"It's OK." Luke put a reassuring hand on her arm.

"Luke, we should—"

The bulb flickered faster and began to sway on its cord. Julia watched it, mesmerised, the filament swinging from left to right leaving an arc of light in its path. She heard a clinking of metal on metal and saw in slow motion, like a scene from a movie, a young girl on a bed reaching out to her. The girl was older than Mattie: long matted hair, desperate eyes. Her one hand extended before her. The mascara she wore had run down her face and been smeared across her cheeks, her lips darkened red by a lipstick that had leeched into the skin round her mouth, framed by a black rectangular mark.

Julia heard Luke's voice calling her, but it was like he was in another room. She stared at the girl, who seemed to be saying something. She tried to hear her over the ringing in her own ears and the increased clanging of metal. She leaned towards the girl's desperate grasp. The girl mouthed the words again. Julia leaned closer and closer still.

The scream broke through: "Help me, Julie!" Before Julia could begin to comprehend it, she heard a man's voice bellow, "No!"

The light had stopped swinging. The vision had dissolved. Julia turned slowly to see Luke standing there, white as a sheet.

She wanted to cower and run at the same time. Luke moved to her and put a hand on her shoulder. "We need to ask San some questions…"

"No… I want to leave now. It's not safe. Please, Luke."

"OK, listen, you go and I'll ask her…"

"No, Luke! Please!"

"Don't worry. She can't hurt me."

He walked her to the ladder and she was grateful to see the light of the pantry and the walls of it above, but she didn't want to leave him. She clung to his arm, one hand resting on a rung, and felt a tremor. She glanced at Luke.

"Did you feel that?"

There was a huge bang above their heads. Both ducked on instinct.

"What the hell?" Luke said.

"This is what she does, Luke! Come with me. I'm not going without you."

"Let's go," he said.

The ladder began to shake as she scaled each rung. There was a rushing sound from above like falling pebbles getting louder and louder. Julia looked up, expecting a landscape to cave in on her. At the hatch she saw it was the trapdoor rattling as if lying on a bed of jumping beads. As soon as she was out she leaned on it to try to stop it moving.

"Luke?"

A low rumble issued from the secret room and began to get louder. The trapdoor began to bounce against the floor.

"Hurry, Luke!"

She could see him below her, staring ahead of him, unmoving. Oh God! Would she have to go down there and drag him up? The trapdoor began to heave. Julia feared she would be pitched back into the cloying chamber if she stayed on it.

"Luke!" she screamed.

She anchored her body into a safer position using the walls of the pantry, determined to hold down the door. She looked around for something to throw at him, to wake him out of his stupor.

"Luke! Wake up!" He turned then, like a drugged man, and came up the ladder rung by rung as if climbing out of quicksand. The whole area continued to quake and Julia stared, unbelieving, as the panels of the trapdoor started to work apart beneath her even as she tried to hold it down.

"Come on!" she begged, more to herself as she tried to hold on to what seemed like a raft at sea which bucked and lurched. The thunderous cacophony in her ears seemed to be at a peak as Luke, little by little, emerged through the opening, struggling to hold on. She grabbed him to help him through. As his foot left the top rung the trembling and roaring stopped.

Julia knew he'd been in the same dream-like state she and Mattie had been experiencing in the house. She looked into his eyes.

"Luke… she was…" She laughed then clamped her mouth shut.

Luke seemed to come to life. He pulled her out of the pantry. The two ran back to the sitting room.

"She was a prisoner here." Julia fought to squash the hysteria in her voice. She took a breath.

"Christ, Jules."

She shook her head. "The newspaper said they never found her." Her body trembled. "She was on a bed. She was reaching out to me and…"

"What the hell went on here?" His voice was soft.

"I don't know… I don't want to."

"She needs you."

Julia nodded. She felt weak and guilty. Guilty for wanting to run away from it, to leave this house now and let it be sold with its secrets. She saw now she'd denied her past since she'd left for university. And before that too: years before when she used to immerse herself in her stories away in the dining room or on her swing. Julia had always assumed it was to get away from Caroline, but there was more to it, she realised now. San had spoken to her from the grave, trying to be heard. Why had Julia forgotten her?

She looked at Luke. She was good at forgetting. That was the one thing she did particularly well. She hadn't been able to commit to him because of her past. She'd given him up and closed him off like she'd done with everything else, like closing a book.

She looked at his dark eyes and full lips. His lips red and moist… She met his gaze. She leaned towards him and he bent his head to her. Just once more, she told herself. She had to just taste him once more. It would be enough. Julia's head swam as their lips met and the blood surged in her veins.

She moved up against his chest and he grasped her to him. His lips pulled and pushed against hers, his tongue probing and tasting. Senses reeling, she felt his hands in her hair then touching her face. Her hands felt his soft skin under his jersey and she clasped him closer to her as she felt herself giving in. She pulled away from him and with one rapid gesture pulled her jersey over her head, revealing her black satin camisole, soft skin pushing against the lace. She took his hand and placed it on her breast and leaned to meet his lips again as he caressed her through the silky fabric and she moaned with pleasure. She pressed her body into his chest while her hands loosened his zipper and she pressed him back against the arm of the sofa. His kisses fired a path across her brain and her hips began to push into his. She felt him lower the camisole strap then put it back in place.

Her eyes sought his. She pulled back.

"Jules…"

Her body cooled even while her lips still tingled from his kisses. Her hand pushed back the loose hair from her face. She saw him defenceless. Once deserted and now, tempted again to hurt himself, because of her. From the depths of her reasoning Julia saw he was giving her a chance, to do things the right way – for him and for her. Did she really want to renew their relationship in this sordid way, while she was Steve's wife and while she was not in control of her life? What did that tell Luke? That he was second choice? That he was useful to her, for now?

She fell back against the sofa, grabbing her jersey and holding it against her. Was she destined to stumble through life forever? It was time to grow up and start feeling good about her choices.

"I'm sorry," she said.

"Don't be."

"You're right! I don't want to ruin this again. I love you, Luke."

He grabbed her, pulling her close, breathing in the jasmine fragrance of her hair, kissing the top of her head.

"I've missed you so much." He sounded joyful.

She raised his hand to her still wet cheek and she kissed it, turning her face to look up at him.

He kissed her again, long and gentle, then stared deep into her eyes while he stroked her hair and said, "I love you too, Julia Allbright. What the hell are we going to do?"

She stared at him for a moment before burying her face in the crook of his neck. He hugged her tight and when he felt her shiver he took hold of her jersey.

"Here, put this back on," he said.

He helped her pull her jersey over her head then, reaching down, retrieved his coat from the floor to cover both of them. Julia relaxed against him. She hadn't felt so safe in a long time. She wondered how long the feeling would last.

30

Steve stood in the hallway of Carrick House and listened. It was too quiet. He looked around at all the boxes, still waiting for their collection, and shook his head in annoyance. The sooner this was dealt with, the better. Every delay was costing him.

Caroline had said the estate agent had asked to meet him here. He didn't see why they were insisting on this now as the place hadn't been done up yet, but Caroline was adamant, saying Steve had to talk them through the makeover he intended to carry out. He'd assumed Julia had let the guy in, as that was obviously his Rover parked in the street, but why was it so quiet in here? And what the hell was she doing here anyway? He hoped she'd been for that interview and had good news.

He walked to the sitting room, wondering why he couldn't hear voices, and opened the door. The twilight, filtering in through the dingy windows, revealed the sleeping, intertwined lovers covered partially by a coat. He took in that Julia's hair was all bunched up around her face; her arm lay across the man's chest and her leg draped across his loins. Her lips were swollen like they'd been sucked long and hard. The man's arm encircled her, cushioning her head, his hand resting on his wife's shoulder.

Steve felt the rigid set of his own jaw when he tried to speak.

"Julia?" he croaked. He watched the man stir and his wife snuggle into him, adjusting her body to his. "What the bloody hell!" he managed, louder this time.

"Shit! Julia! Wake up."

Luke's frantic shaking stirred her from the most restful sleep she'd had in some time, to see Steve standing in front of them, grilling her with dead eyes.

"Steve! What are you doing here?" Julia said as she jumped to her feet, smoothing her jersey over her breasts and trying to flatten her hair.

Steve held his hands up to stop her coming any nearer. "What the hell have you done, Julia?" His voice was flat. The sterility of it made her blood cold.

"Steve! I…" She was going to apologise, but deep in her heart she was not sorry and she wasn't going to pretend. "I asked Luke to come here. My family – something happened here Steve, something bad – he was helping me with—"

"With his fly undone?" Steve roared as he leapt towards Luke, knocking Julia to the side.

Luke swerved to the other side of the sofa and dragged himself up out of reach. Steve lunged over and swiped wide towards his face. Luke kicked out with his foot and connected with Steve's arm, knocking him off balance. Steve staggered into the end of the sofa and grasped his way up again.

"You bastard!" he yelled at Luke, lunging towards him again. Luke held up his right arm to deflect the punch and jabbed at Steve with his fist catching him on the cheek under his eye. A spray of blood shot into the air as the skin split. His head was forced to the left by the blow, but it was as if he didn't feel anything. He kept advancing and his left fist came round, catching Luke on his jaw. Luke staggered back a few steps but recovered his balance. He deflected another blow aimed at his face and jabbed out again. Steve dodged it.

"Stop it!" Julia shouted.

"Listen, let's talk about this!" Luke sounded conciliatory. "You prick."

An animal cry escaped from Steve as he lunged again. He looked insane. His face ran with sweat and was bright red. He ran at Luke, who deflected his attack and made a low punch into the stomach and one to the kidneys as Steve doubled over.

"Luke, stop! You'll hurt him!" Julia shrieked.

As Steve fell to his knees he grabbed at Luke's foot and Luke jabbed it back into Steve's face. The heel caught his temple and he keeled over, letting go.

"She's not yours anymore," Luke finished.

Julia ran over to her husband and put her arms round his shoulders.

Luke looked on, a curl to his lips as he did up his zip, dragged his coat on and grabbed his rucksack. "Julia, I'm going."

She looked at him from where she crouched over Steve, shaking her head as if to block out what just happened. "Luke… wait…"

He stared at her. "I *have* been waiting." The silence stretched between them, punctuated by Steve's gasps for air. "Don't let me down again, Julia. I couldn't bear it." Luke turned and walked out the door.

As the front door slammed, Steve seemed to come to life. He roared and pushed Julia away from him. "You bloody whore! I make a life of luxury for you, put up with your drinking and your pathetic performance in bed, and this is how you repay me?"

Julia recoiled. She understood he was upset, but his words were so vicious, and precise. She knew then that Steve hadn't been in love with her for a long time but had been using her. As much as she'd used him? Perhaps. Her life was a lie and she was tired of it. She didn't want to pretend anymore, but her instinct was warning her she had to, for a little bit longer.

"Steve. This was my mistake. I needed help. He was sympathetic. We had a drink together – that's all."

"I can't believe you're using drink as an excuse for this!" Steve gasped, holding his side as he got to his feet. "What about all the promises you made to me, Julia? To see a doctor, the AA? It's all just talk for you, isn't it?"

"I was going to go to the AA, Steve, but…" How could she tell him what brought her back to this house day after day or turned her thoughts to it before bed every night? If Carrick House had an evil history that was connected to Caroline then Steve couldn't know about it until it was out in the open. She simply couldn't confide in him. He just wouldn't believe her and would see it only as an attack on his business partner.

"I have to finish here, Steve. Carrick House is my past. I have to bring it to a close."

"What are you talking about, Julia? It doesn't look like closure with your ex. More like opening things up again – your dirty thighs for one!"

"Steve, we didn't do anything."

"All you whores are the same." He was shouting now. "You open yourselves to the nearest prick available depending on what it is you want. And what a prick I was! It was my money, wasn't it?"

"I didn't want your money! I had a career when I met you. I was on track for promotion. I gave it all up for you. Steve, we had something once… remember?"

"We have *nothing*, Julia! After the charity event I want you to move out. Up till then you will be the model wife and when we split you'll settle for what I give you or I'll fight you for the girls."

Julia closed her mouth, her argument dying on her breath. Sparring with Steve right now was downright dangerous. She stood up and reached for her bag.

"Don't bother!" he snarled. "I don't want you at home tonight."

"Well, I can't stay here!" Julia looked around her and caught sight of the sofa which was still crumpled where she and Luke had lain.

"Stay wherever you like, but you're not coming home tonight. You will toe the line, Julia. You have a lot to lose." He bent down to pick up his keys, which he'd dropped in the struggle, and winced as he stood up again. "And if I ever see that loser's face around here again, I will kill him, Julia."

"You and who's army?" She couldn't resist.

He turned around. "Don't play with me. You don't know who you're dealing with." He slammed the door as he went out.

He was wrong about that. She knew very well the influence Steve had in this town. Her legs felt like they would give way and she had to sit down. Oh God! What had she done? She could lose her children. But no, a judge wouldn't rule in Steve's favour, would he? Unless Steve could prove she was an unfit mother, she thought, panic gripping her. He could be very thorough in his application. He would rope in a lot of witnesses for his case: Caroline, Bob, Doctor Jarman – he would maybe even get Amanda to stand in the witness box for him! What was she saying? He would just pay the judge off – he'd had enough speeding fines squashed and building plans put through with his clout in this town, just like how he'd donated to Annie's home this week to persuade them not to press charges. Oh God! The Glade – they would probably witness for him too. It would all be so easy for him, and getting custody of the kids would be just another game. She wouldn't stand a chance. She shivered.

She poured herself a coffee from the flask. What should she do? She would have to stop drinking altogether and buy some time with Steve. She couldn't go to AA now, though, as that would be a formal admission of her problem, wouldn't it? Or perhaps it would make her look like she was a responsible adult? Would that be better? She needed to speak to a solicitor.

And tonight? Where would she sleep? She couldn't call Luke again. She'd done enough damage and wasn't sure she wanted to hear his plans for her either.

"To hell with them."

She shivered again. What about Row's? She'd give her a bed for the night, no questions asked. She may as well take her time, though, stay a little longer. She looked towards the hearth, thinking she could make a fire. Lucky there was still wood in the basket. It must have been there a few years at least and would be bone dry. Maybe the firelighters would work too. She went out to the hall for the newspapers. Before gathering them up she checked outside to make sure Steve had left. It was dark now and a light rain had fallen and turned some of the snow to slush, but it was slowly re-freezing again across the driveway.

Back in the sitting room she tore pages out of the newspapers and rolled them up before laying them out in the grate. On top she crisscrossed small pieces of tinder, putting small logs over them, and pushed bits of firelighters in between. While she was rummaging in her bag for her lighter she found a lone cigarette which somehow had managed to survive being squashed flat. Good.

She lit the paper pieces and a couple of the firelighters, blowing at them for a while until the fire took hold on the tinder. She sat back watching as the flames licked the edges of the logs and reached for her cigarette and the flask. It was empty. She sipped at the brandy instead as she smoked. She thought of Luke and the touch of his hands on her body. She shuddered with pleasure thinking of it and an involuntary moan escaped her even now. She was amazed he still had such power over her.

Don't let me down, he'd said. Did he want her to move in with him? With the children or without? Did she need him that much? Dammit, she needed to get a grip.

The logs were beginning to catch now and she put the fire guard in its place. She realised she was hungry. She finished her cigarette then broke off a chunk of malt loaf. She would go to Row's, but right now she just wanted to get herself together. She would leave when the fire died down. She lay on the sofa and stared at the flickering flames.

31

Steve winced as Caroline applied TCP to his temple.

"Your friend Micah tell you?"

"You had to know."

"You could have pre-warned me!"

"I thought it would be better if you were surprised so it would have more impact on her."

"Yeah, well, I took the impact, thanks very much." He grimaced, eyeing his grazed shoulder which still stung from the TCP, then pulled his shirt up over it and stood up, tucking the ends back into his trousers.

Caroline put the lid back on the bottle. "Where is she now?"

"At Carrick. I told her to stay there the night. Sandra's looking after the girls, but I'd better get home." He flinched as he put on his jacket.

"I hope this has motivated you enough to make some changes, Steve."

"I'm divorcing the bitch and going for the kids! Is that enough for you?" He grabbed his keys. "Just give me time to work it out." He went out and slammed the door without seeing Caroline's smile of satisfaction.

He paced up and down outside the lift, his stomach in knots. His head was full and he felt the familiar sliding sensation behind his eyes, from one temple to the other. How dare she. After all he'd done for her! His teeth clamped and started to grind. He had to force himself to blow out through his mouth to release the pressure, to stop the feeling that he was going to pass out, but there was only one way he knew to stop this spiral down to gibbering idiot… He looked at his watch and back at Caroline's door.

Her knowing smile when she answered his knock told him she'd expected him to ask her to look after the children.

"I'll be back by eight," he growled.

"Don't worry, I'll go there now so Sandra can get off home. You'll feel better afterwards." It was a statement of fact.

Steve grunted as he left.

Back at the lift he wiped his palms on his trousers. The lift door opened and he hurried in, nodding to an old woman inside who was one of the residents. As the lift began its slow descent he shifted on his feet, feeling the sweat running down his back, and tried to stop the scraping together of his teeth. The woman eyed him nervously. He smiled back but was sure it came out more of a grimace and decided not to try making conversation. He punched the minus one button three times when the lift stopped on the third floor and opened for no-one in particular. He wondered if he should have taken the stairs.

Second floor, first, ground floor, the synthesised version of Queen's 'Don't Stop Me Now' whining in the background. By the time he got down to the garage it took all his strength to hold back and not push the old biddy out of his way. His jaw shuddered and something clicked in his head. This was it – he was going to lose it. He felt faint as he neared his car. His hands fumbled with his key fob, releasing the locks, then he was plunging into the driver's seat and starting it up.

He hoped now he was driving it would subside. Christ, he hated that house so much. God knows he'd been superhuman to have made it through the other day when he'd helped Julia pack up. Course, the Ativan had helped. But now, because of that useless bitch, he'd had to suffer another visit to the hell hole…

He concentrated on breathing out through his mouth while

negotiating the bends out of the parking lot, trying not to think back, when he was ten years old and had been lured there. It felt like it was happening all over again. His erection was pressing uncomfortably against his zip and sweat gathered now around his collar and on his chest. He took the road out of town heading south and focused on his breathing, in and out, in and out, blowing out as if trying to expel bad air. He rubbed the side of his jaw which was cramping and driving pain into his temple. He tried to concentrate on his driving, but there was little traffic around and nothing to distract him from the memory of his persecutor leaning over him, mean as a rabid bitch, inflicting pain, time and again, and then the guilt as her manoeuvres turned his pain to pleasure and release.

And the shame: for the number of times he returned there – for more exquisite torture inflicted by her or him. It rolled over him: the pain, pleasure and confusion, just like when his young mind had tried to make sense of the strange sensations and compulsions it had aroused in him. His panic rose to consume him again and he fought the rigidity taking over his body. He wanted to find a service station and wash his hands. He wiped them on his trousers. Hold on, hold on… He was on the motorway now and he knew it would only be forty minutes… thank God the road was clear. He made himself think of the better times with them, when it was simpler and more normal. It helped.

He could wash his hands at Marshall's, he affirmed, breathing out through gritted teeth. He hoped his favourite, Shaz, was there so he could give her a good fucking. He wanted to hear her scream and he would scream along with her.

32

1977

Julia woke up clutching her Tim Teddy in the pink bedroom at Carrick House. She lay still in the dark. The rain pattered softly against the windowpane. She snuggled her face against her furry toy and her eyes drooped. That's when she heard it: someone crying. A child.

She sat up. She knew her father had visitors tonight, which is why she'd been sent to bed already. If there was another child in the house then she wanted to play. She could show them the Cindy house and all the different clothes she had for her dolls. They could have such fun well… if it was a girl. Not a boy, she didn't much like boys. She heard it again.

The cry seemed to come from the vent above the skirting board. Julia climbed out of bed with her teddy held close.

"Hello?" She tiptoed closer to the dusty grill. She could hear a low humming noise. "Hello?" She was a little louder this time and the humming stopped.

"My name's Julia." She waited and after a long pause some words trickled through, most of them inaudible. She just caught the end.

"…San."

"What did you say?" she asked, putting her ear closer to the vent.

The reply came back stilted and half muffled, but she could hear it.

"Help… me, Julie…"

Julia waited, listening. "Where are you?" This time she spoke louder and strained to hear the muffled voice.

It came back stronger. "I'm down here."

"OK."

Julia put on her white fluffy dressing gown with the pink piping trim and her red slippers, knowing if Daddy caught her wandering about without her slippers on, he would be really cross. She picked up Tim again and went out onto the landing towards the stairwell. From the top of the stairs the hum of adult voices from the parlour droned on. She wondered if the girl was in there. But if she was, she wouldn't be asking for help because she would have her mummy with her. Perhaps she was locked in the toilet up here? That happened to her once and it was very scary.

Julia could see the single toilet next to the bathroom, but the door was open and it was dark inside. Julia listened for more cries as she descended the stairs and made her way to the kitchen. A dim light emanated from there and when she peered in she saw the pantry was all lit up.

Biscuits! Julia had been told time and again by Aunty Caroline to stay out of the pantry, but the night's adventure was making her hungry. Caroline wouldn't know if she took one biscuit, would she? Or two? She turned and looked towards the front parlour. The door was still closed and the adults were enjoying themselves. Her daddy's raucous laughter drowned out all the other voices, then she heard other people laughing. They would be drinking the horrid juice that smelt bad and she hated it when they kissed you goodnight. Especially her nana's kiss – it was all sloppy and wet, ugh!

She made her way to the pantry. Her eyes sought the biscuit tin before she even entered the room. She reached up to it, but the shelf it was on was too high up. She looked to her right to see if there was something she could stand on and was surprised to see a gaping hole with a dim light shining from it. Julia had been in the pantry one other time since her arrival in the summer and there were usually boxes in that part of the room. She crawled to the edge of the hole and looked down into the yellowy void.

A pool of light illuminated the end of a bed and a ladder down to the grey floor.

Julia peered into the room. "Hello?"

She heard the same humming noise which she could now discern as someone moaning.

"San, are you there? It's me, Julia. I've come to help you. I'll get you a biscuit."

She jumped up and, after placing Tim Teddy on the shelf, she moved a wooden step stool into position. Holding on to the lower shelf, she climbed up to reach the tin. It wasn't too heavy. She lowered it to the shelf below and climbed down to the floor. It was hard to prise the lid off, but she managed and her eyes lit up at the selection before her. She chose three of her favourites and put them in her pocket. Picking up her toy again, she approached the trapdoor.

"I'm coming," she called down.

What to do with teddy? She couldn't hold on to the rungs and Tim at the same time. She contemplated throwing him down into the room and following him but discarded the idea as she didn't know what was down there, and anyway, he might be hurt if she did that. She looked at her pockets, but they were too small. She realised she could tuck him into the top of her dressing gown and still see around him. Good. She liked him close.

The ladder wasn't at all wobbly, but the wooden rungs felt slippery, so she took her time descending. At the bottom she turned around in the yellowy light, clasping her arms over her chest, holding on to Tim. It was a big room with the bed just off to the left. The lamp on the floor on her right side illuminated the walls there and there was just enough light to show the double bed was empty. There was a nasty smell like sick and wee, and Julia looked around to see the source. A bucket just behind her looked the likely culprit and she moved away from it. In the corner, there was a black object on three metal legs with black wires going along the ground to a board with lots of plugs in it, and what looked like a white umbrella on a pole and a big light which was turned off. She was engrossed looking at it all and jumped when a clinking noise issued from the shadows on the other side of the bed.

Peering into the gloom, she took a tentative step towards the bed. Her hand fumbled in her pocket for the biscuits.

"San?"

There was no reply. She inched closer to the bed but didn't want to step into the shadowy bit.

"I've… I've brought you some biscuits…"

There was only silence from the dark corner and Julia wanted to go back to her bedroom. She ought to at least leave the biscuits there… She was sure she could hear breathing in the shadows as she climbed onto the bed and reached her hand over to place the food on the waxy linen.

A scrawny yellow hand shot out and grabbed her wrist. Julia yelled, pulling back hard. A creature surfaced from the shadows with seaweed hair and huge black eyes in an infusion of vomit and pee. Julia, stifling a scream, wrenched herself free, leaving a trail of biscuit crumbs over the sheets. The apparition picked up a large, unbroken piece of biscuit from the sheet before stuffing it into her reddened mouth.

Julia clutched her arms around Tim Teddy, her eyes stretching to make sense of this strange, dirty being.

"Are you San? I heard you."

The girl dragged her gaze up while taking more pieces of biscuit from the cover. Her movements were sluggish and her speech slurred.

"Get me out… got to help me."

Julia saw the girl's slimy hair and chafed lips with the faint black lines around them.

"What happened to your mouth?"

The girl mumbled around the biscuit as she chewed, blinking slowly. "From the tape." She looked back at her hand and rattled the handcuffs against the frame. "Find the key. I want to go home."

Julia looked at the small bedside table for keys and could see none. Her eyes darted around the room and, finding nothing, rested back on the girl, on the cuffs. "What are those?"

"I'm a prisoner. Can't you see?"

"Where's your mummy? I could call her."

The girl sneered. "She doesn't care."

Julia didn't know what to say. "How long have you lived here?" she ventured.

"A day. I dunno… am not feeling well. I've been sleeping. You have to help me," she said.

Julia tried to give her a reassuring smile, but the girl's face did not acknowledge her efforts. She seemed to be struggling to keep her eyes open. They shot open again.

"You must tell someone I'm a prisoner," she urged.

"I… can call my dad," Julia blurted.

"Is he the one with th' black spiky hair?"

Julia nodded.

San appeared to liven up. "No, not him… Is there a neighbour? Or call th' police."

"I… don't know how to call the—"

"You have to get me out!"

Julia took a step back. The girl's wild-eyed stare was unnerving. "I can look for the keys up there." She looked up at the ceiling.

"Hurry," the girl pleaded, wiping her mouth as she spoke.

Julia ran to the foot of the ladder and froze when she heard footsteps crossing the wooden kitchen floor. Someone in high heels. She looked around to find somewhere to hide and scrambled under the bed.

She heard Aunty Caroline exclaim, "What the hell?" Then the sound of the tin lid being dragged back over the cookies. She was going to be so angry, Julia thought as she lay, still as a mouse, her stomach churning.

The prisoner girl must have known it was best if she acted normal because she stayed seated on the bed. Julia could see her thin ankles and scrawny, unwashed feet. She lay there holding her breath.

She heard Caroline call for her father before coming down the ladder. Julia saw her feet come towards the bed.

"OK, you little brat, you can come out. I know you're there. I can see your foot." Her mean and cold voice transfixed Julia. She was unable to even move the errant foot and could only stare at how the lilac carpet folded up against the wall where Caroline was standing.

"Jesus, girl! Have you been sick again? It stinks in here."

Julia's father's heavy tread could be heard on the ladder rungs.

"What's up?" he asked.

"Your daughter! That's what! Under the bed."

"What?"

He knelt down and grabbed Julia's arm. He didn't seem to notice her bumping her head on the metal frame as he hauled her out in front of him.

"What the hell are you doing in here?"

Julia clung to Tim Teddy, too afraid to speak.

The girl on the bed was pleading and rattling the handcuffs in protest. "Let me go!"

Julia felt sick. She'd stumbled into a big secret, something she didn't understand.

"What's going on?" Grandma Annie was peering through the trapdoor, trying to make out what was happening.

"Ma, you should have closed the door! Now I've got Julia to deal with." He knelt down till his face was level with his daughter's, breathing the fetid smell of stale cigarettes and whiskey into her face.

Julia tried her hardest to speak but her teeth chattered so much. "Daddy, I d-didn't mean to be… t-trouble, I thought…"

"What did you *think*?" he snarled.

Julia reeled back from him. His eyes weren't looking at her right. It was like he couldn't see her.

"D… Daddy, I…" She felt her teeth sink into her lower lip as he shook her hard and she began to cry.

"What do we tell you, Julia, when you're put to bed early? What?"

he bellowed in her face, and Julia felt fine droplets of spit against her skin.

"To s-st-stay in…"

"Let me go!" The girl wrenched at the handcuffs.

"*In where, Julia?*"

"M-m-my…"

"Help me, somebody!" the girl shouted.

"Do something with her, Caroline!" her father said.

Caroline walked over to the girl, who half cowered as she approached but didn't stop begging for her release. Julia watched, terrified, as her stepmother slapped her with full force across her cheek.

Julia's tears fell all the more, even as the girl did not submit to Caroline but instead struck out at her, pulling her hair and scratching her face.

Caroline stepped back for a moment, screeching and cursing, and balled her fist ready to lay one on the child.

"No!" her father shouted, and pulled Caroline back. "None of that! Ma!" he yelled up the ladder. "Get the needle… And you, you little bugger." He turned to his daughter, grabbing her arm. "I'm going to teach you a lesson in doing what you're told." His hand came down hard on her rump, making her gasp and causing her bladder to give way. He hit her again, this time on her bare legs, again and again, while he shouted, "When I say stay in your room, I mean it!" He hauled her onto his hip and began to climb the ladder, pausing to curse. "Fuck it! She's pissed all over me."

He looked at Julia as if she were dirt. She wanted to hide behind Tim Teddy, but she'd dropped him in the room. As he emerged from the pantry with her, her grandma was approaching with a large needle.

Julia screamed and hid her face in his shoulder. "*No, Daddy, no!*"

"I don't think this is a good idea," Annie said. "I gave her a dose only a few hours ago. I think it was just after dinner—"

"Just do it!" John yelled. "Caroline? Come and get this off Annie and then come and deal with Julia – she needs changing."

He cursed his way up the stairs, trying to hold Julia away from his body until he reached her bedroom and dumped her on the bed. "Get out of those clothes and get some dry ones on or Caroline will do it and you know she won't be gentle. He pulled his now-wet shirt away from his body with disgust and looked at Julia like she was vermin. "I'm going to have a lock put on this door." He went out and banged it shut after him.

Julia lay there, shaking and gulping back her sobs, trying to understand what had just happened then, remembering her father's warning, she jumped up and ran to her chest of drawers. Her fingers shook so much they slipped off the handles. She dragged out a nightgown and a fresh pair of knickers. With trembling hands she took off her wet things and used her dressing gown to dry herself. Even as she was pulling the nightgown over her head she heard Caroline's voice in the hallway. By the time her stepmother arrived in the room Julia was lying in her bed, the covers pulled right up to her neck to hide the shuddering of her small body.

Caroline approached her bedside. An angry red welt was swelling on her cheek where the prisoner had scratched her. She brought her face up close to Julia's.

"Listen to me, you little shit! You've had it too easy since you got here. Daddy's little princess, aren't you! Well, let me tell you that every princess has to pay… there are no exceptions. I don't want you here and I can get rid of you real quick if I choose. You want to go and live in a children's home? No. I'm sure you don't! So you do as you're told. Understand?"

Her hand went under the covers and gripped the soft skin of Julia's arm between her finger and thumb. As she pinched, she twisted the skin. "You'll forget tonight ever happened. Everything you've seen. You never saw it. *Do* you understand?"

Julia squirmed and tears flooded. "That hurts. It hurts—"

"I am not fucking joking, you brat." Caroline's other hand swung round and slapped Julia so hard on her cheek a small explosion of light filled her vision, accompanied by a ringing noise in her head while Caroline pinched harder and her arm burned like it was on fire. "You will forget it happened – *alright?*"

"Ah-ow, owwww!" Julia started to scream, but Caroline silenced her with another blow to her head.

"Shut up, you little bitch! You're not going to ruin things here. You will forget this! Say it!"

Julia's head felt it would explode and her arm had gone numb, but she had the sense to respond. Her own voice sounded tinny and faraway: "Yes, Aunty Caroline… Yes."

"*I said, say it!*" Caroline yelled, her face contorted, her nails now cutting into the soft flesh of Julia's arm like miniature daggers.

The child sucked in her scream and sought for the words. "I n-never saw… i-it. I can't remember… Aunty Caroline. I can't remember anything… please… please!"

Julia gasped in relief as Caroline let go. Her stepmother sat looking at her with loathing for what seemed an eternity before she stood up and walked to the door.

"I don't want to hear one word about it, Julia, and if I hear you mentioning it to anyone else, I'll call the children's home myself!"

She closed the door behind her and Julia dissolved into deep, racking sobs of relief and shock. Her legs and bottom stung where her father had walloped her. Her head was still ringing and her arm was so sore. She clasped the area that was burning and was shocked to feel it was wet. She looked down and saw in the half-light a dark smear where she'd spread the blood which Caroline's nails had drawn. She gulped and wiped it with her sheet, sobbing at the same time. She wanted her mother, but she was gone. Tim Teddy was gone. She had nothing to console her. The tears fell and fell, and the shuddering of her body only subsided when exhaustion stepped in and sleep overcame her.

33

She was lying on the sofa when her eyes opened. The fire had died down, but the embers glowed red. How long had she been asleep? Or was that a vision she'd had rather than a dream? It didn't matter. She remembered it now. The devastating truth that she'd obediently forgotten. She felt a knife slice its way through her heart. Dad! His betrayal was too much to bear. She felt the familiar constriction beginning in her chest and then anger. As the tears fell, she pulled the daisy-chain hair band out of her bag and wrenched at the colourful flowers and tiny stitching.

"I can't. I won't do this!"

Changing tack, she rose, strode to the fire and pulled the guard away. She threw the chain onto the hot coals. A flame ignited on one of the petals and began to lick the length of it. She would end this now and forget it all. She didn't have to go any further. They would sell the house and all of its secrets. If she destroyed the chain, San could not reach her, away from Carrick – there would be nothing to connect them.

A guttural cry wrenched through the silence and an icy breeze charged past her, extinguishing the fire – as easy as blowing out a candle. Julia spun round. She saw no-one but the wind whipped around her, pulling at her hair and tearing at the papers she'd left on the coffee table.

"*What do you want from me?*" Julia screamed above the noise.

The air stopped moving as suddenly as it had begun. The ensuing quiet pulsed around her.

"What more could I do?" she pleaded to the discontented silence. "I was a child!"

The room was freezing now and Julia eyed her bag. She ran to the door, grabbing the bag and her coat, hoping to God the keys were in her pocket.

Julia pulled on the handle, but the door would not budge. She screamed back, "Let me go!"

The voice was behind her: "Make friends, Julie."

She spun round, searching for its source. "Please…"

Her father's laugh echoed round the room, turning her blood cold. His derision fell on her, a thick black cloak of despair. She felt dizzy and the light dimmed till she was in the dark space again, immobile. The air was thick with the cloying sweet smell she'd experienced in her bedroom and was choking her. There was a board pressed against her face, boards all around her, a box entombing her. An overwhelming horror and disgust seeped into her pores and her mouth opened to scream, but the sound came out muffled as though a ghostly hand had covered her lips. Julia's mind reeled as she tried to reason.

She must have swayed on her feet and as she lost her balance the weight on her chest lifted and the room came back into view. She staggered back, clutching her bag, and then lunged for the door, grateful that it now opened with ease. She ran through the hall and cried out with relief as she opened the front door and crossed the threshold to the freezing cold outside. She skidded along the path to her car, rummaging in her bag till she found the keys. She released the locks and hauled the driver's door open.

Once inside she locked all the doors, slammed the car into reverse and put full pressure on the accelerator. She cursed as she heard the low hedge behind her scrape the underside of the bumper, knowing she'd overshot the driveway. Changing into first, she flattened her foot on the accelerator, making the car slip and slide on the partly frozen slush.

Calm down. She didn't want to hit the gate and end up a prisoner here. The car just missed the pillars as she turned onto the road, the seatbelt alert chiming from the dashboard. She braked a little and geared down. By the time she went past the parked black Range Rover she was in control. She had to get to Row's then she could figure out what to do.

"Oh my God!" A sob caught in her throat. She wanted to pull over and call Luke, but she knew that would be a mistake.

"Dad, oh, Dad!" Tears fell and obstructed her vision as she turned onto the main road into the village. His involvement in this disgusting crime was more painful than how he'd treated her that night. She hauled the car over to the right-hand kerb and stalled the motor as she opened the door, leaned out and threw up into the gutter. The loathing and hate welled up in her for the people that had taken her in. No. Not people, animals, no… animals were not cruel and vile like that. Scum. Her own blood. She retched again into the pool of vomit seeping into the grey slush below.

She rested her head against the doorframe, breathing in the clear frosty air while she wiped her mouth with the back of her hand and tried to calm herself. Able to sit up straight, she leaned back against the head rest. Pulling her bag onto her lap to look for a hair elastic, she found the daisy chain sitting on top of her purse. She froze. Her eyes raised up to the dashboard then continued up to the rear-view mirror. That was when she saw the black car behind her, waiting at the turn off to Carrick House from where she'd just fled.

It was similar to the one she'd seen at the parking lot last week in the old town she realised. Could it be the same one? Why had it been outside the house? Was it following her?

After closing and locking the door, she looked in the wing mirror. The car hadn't moved from the crossroads. Perhaps it was stuck in the snow. Unlikely, though, being the car it was. She pulled her seatbelt around her chest and started up. At the bend she was still checking out the black car in her mirror. It was still there. It wasn't following her. She was paranoid, that's all – after the day's events it was understandable.

She felt a little more clearheaded since she'd been sick. Her shaking had stopped and she began to warm up from the heater. She wished she could view this terrible thing as a kidnapping for ransom, but the camera she'd seen in the corner of that prison suggested a crime more perverted. Given Caroline's seedy past it was possible that Micah and her were abusing the girl… and her father allowed it… in his own house. In her grandmother's house!

Julia choked back a sob. What could she do now? No wonder her grandmother was sitting there shouting for redemption! She hadn't had the merciful, quick release her father had with his sudden heart attack. And Caroline? How did she live with herself? How did she… what if she still was… active in that world?

Julia's vision swam for a moment. "Oh God." She could not let Caroline know that she knew, but Steve would have to be told, otherwise they could not protect their girls. How could she make him believe her?

Julia was on the open road now to her home on the county border. She could go to the police, but she would have no proof. They would think her mad; a psychiatrist might be recommended for her, if not a spell at the Priory.

The lights zooming up behind her caused her to raise her hand to the mirror, the glare was so bright. The car swung out and drove next to Julia in the lane for oncoming traffic. Her heart plummeted when she saw it was the black Range Rover. Before she could think, it began to inch over into her lane, forcing her towards the ditch she knew ran alongside. What the hell! She slammed on the brakes on instinct and was able to inch back into the centre of the lane, but the Range Rover also braked and moved towards her car again. A light ahead of the driver caused him to decelerate and pull in behind her. The oncoming car blasted its horn in protest as it passed.

Julia floored it, trying to escape. She was going sixty miles an hour when the car caught up with her again. She dared not go any faster because she knew there was a left bend ahead with a bad camber, but she also knew the bend would come up with short notice. The tormentor moved his car towards her again. She took a breath. She would not be forced off the road. She would wait this out and maybe he would make a mistake on the bend. All she needed to do was hold her position in the lane. She didn't sway off course this time as he drew closer and closer.

You want to ditch me you'll have to push me!

She stole a look into the cab of the black vehicle as the light went on inside it and she recognised the same man from the car park. The dread swept over her again. She waited for the screech of metal to come, but it didn't happen. He seemed reluctant to make physical contact. She held her position in her lane, casting glances into the car. What did he want? She stole a glance from the road to her speedometer and back again. The Range Rover loomed close to within a foot from the car. He was trying to intimidate her. He wants me to drive into the wall, she thought, glancing at the red-brick barrier between the road and the cemetery that lay beyond it. Don't panic. Stay straight. They were approaching the first bend but the sign for it hadn't come up yet.

She glanced again at her tormentor. He grimaced at her. She looked back and hit the brake for the first sweep to the left. She left the four-by-four out front and watched as it too slammed on brakes. He swerved over to the left and into the space left by Julia, handling it with ease.

Julia braked to put some distance between them, wondering where she could drive to. There was no police station out here and no houses on this stretch. There were smaller country lanes going off to the right and left, but they would be iced up and single track. She did not want to be followed onto a deserted country lane by this lunatic.

A car came round the second bend from the opposite direction and Julia saw the black four-by-four speeding up ahead of her, out of the bend and onto the straight. She watched at first, unbelieving, as he sped away, disappearing round the next curve. He must have tired of his little game. She felt her grip on the steering relax a little. Who was he? What if he was looking for a place to turn around and come back for her? She would have considered turning round and driving back to the town and the police station, but she was so close to home now. Had he gone? Would it be safe to drive all the way to her road? She didn't want to lead him there. But how did he know he'd find her at Carrick? Did he also know where she lived?

She neared the bend, still not knowing what to do. She took the bend at forty-five as it was a tighter one. There was one more gentle curve ahead before the road straightened out and the walls gave way to unfenced woods on either side. The tarmac stretched ahead into the darkness and Julia couldn't see any cars ahead at all. He must have gone! Unless he'd put his lights off. She put her foot down.

Julia thought again about the implications of this guy being outside Carrick House. Was he responsible for Steve's unexpected arrival at the house today? So he must have been hired by Steve, she reasoned. A private detective? Hang on! He'd tried to force her off the road. Oh God, was he a hitman? Did Steve want her dead? If Steve had hired him that would mean the guy already knew where she lived, so he might be waiting for her. And dare she go home if Steve had arranged this? This was ridiculous! She thought again of pulling over and phoning the police, but she knew how insane she would look to them, especially after the incident with Annie last week, and she didn't have any proof that Steve had hired this man. She had to stay in charge of things or they would put her away and she would lose the children. Could this guy really have been hired by her husband to kill her? Or could it have been Caroline? Yes, it was more likely to be her. She just couldn't believe her husband would want her dead.

She could see another car approaching on the right-hand lane up ahead round about where the turn off was to her road. Its headlights were on full beam. Her guts tightened as it approached and she flashed the driver to turn it off, slowing a little. At halfway, the car ahead shifted onto her lane and started coming straight at her.

Julia slammed on the brakes, a gasp of fear escaping her lips. The car's headlights drew closer and closer, blinding her. Her mind spun.

Her hands gripped the steering wheel. Chicken. Chicken, chicken. He was not going to hit her. Stay, stay… The car was coming at a speed towards her and the dreaded possibility of her girls caught in Caroline's clutches beset her. Luke… Her guts twisted in anguish.

All of a sudden, between her and the car there was a shift of snow from the ground upwards: not a flurry stirred by the wind, rather the snowflakes thickened and moved upwards into the black sky like white ash from an unseen fire. The sound of screaming brakes brought her attention back to her assailant and she saw between them where the snow was thickest, a figure standing all in white: a snow princess, arms out to the sides; someone, some thing, turning towards the Range Rover, illumined in the headlights. Happening so fast yet Julia observed, in slow motion, the oncoming driver swerving to avoid the white spectre and overshoot the lane. Hitting the black ice at the side, he lost all control. The car careered into a tree, bonnet buckling like paper till the front end folded around the trunk and smoke issued from its crumpled top like steam around a pot lid.

Julia slammed her brakes on now and controlled the skid that ensued. She pulled over and stopped but didn't switch off the engine. She looked for the snowstorm with the ice maid at its heart. There was no sign of her. Now was her chance to drive away, but her legs were like jelly. She twisted round to see if the driver's door was opening…

34

She sat, immobile, focused on the driver's door of the crashed car. Five minutes must have gone by, though it felt like an hour when Julia finally found the courage. She stepped out into the surrounding dark, lit by headlights and the interior light in the crumpled Rover. She glanced up the road; it was clear, all the way back to the bend she'd just sped through.

She approached the wreck one step at a time as the engine hissed and spewed white clouds from its bonnet. In the middle of the road the soft, untouched snow crunched beneath her feet. She paused, watching for movement within. The icy wind blew her hair over her eyes which she brushed away. A screech above her head made her duck and cry out till she saw the barn owl on its spectral flight into the trees. She continued towards the wreck, her eyes now focused on the figure slumped against the window.

She could see the driver's hand was caught between his temple and the glass, like he was thinking about something or merely resting against the pane. Was he pretending? Waiting for her? She paused again, biting her lip. The Rover continued to hiss and creak as she took another step, holding her breath. She could make out a large gold ring with a black central stone on the fourth finger and felt a stir in her memory. A cracking sound and the car shifted. Her heart leapt as the hand dropped away suddenly and the man's glassy eyes turned on her, a single tattooed teardrop below the right one. Julia stifled a scream and lost her balance, falling hard onto the frozen earth.

A voice echoed across the decades: "Hey, Wozza, bring some more rocks."

It was him: the tall, lanky man from her childhood, smoke curling from the cigarette held in his thin lips as he looked down at her from the rockery he was building with her father that day.

That sunny day, she'd watched them from her swing as they barrowed to and fro with rocks her dad had brought in on the back of his truck, Caroline planting little shrubs between each one as they were laid. Curiosity getting the better of her, she'd approached her dad's friend and asked him, "Why do you have a teardrop drawn on your face, Mr Wozniak?"

Squinting against the smoke of his cigarette, he'd offered a lazy smile and replied, "So I don't have to cry any more real ones, little baby."

A car door slammed behind her, jolting her back to the present.

"Are you alright, miss?"

A man with grey hair in a black parka was looking down at her.

"Miss?" he queried.

She looked back at Micah's unseeing eyes. "He's... dead."

"OK now," he said, following her eyes to the Rover. "Take it easy. Have you hurt yourself?"

"No. I'm... OK."

"Let's get you back to your car and off the road."

Julia let the man help her to her feet. The car was still running and she was grateful for the blast of heat from inside as the door opened.

"I'm just going to check on the driver. You stay here." He took out his phone as he approached the crash. While talking, he stared into the interior for a few moments.

Julia felt a bit more relaxed now there was someone else there with her. She scanned the open road before her. Nothing. Her eyes returned to the mirror. Whatever Suzanne had done to help her in the past, she had stuck her neck out tonight. Julia was indebted to her even more now.

The man tapped on her window. Julia lowered it.

"He, er… you were right, he didn't make it. Are you sure you're OK?" He didn't wait for Julia to answer and continued, "I've called an ambulance. They should be here soon. I've got some hot tea in a flask, let me go and get it."

Julia considered Suzanne's last words to her: "Make friends…" What did she mean by that? How could Julia make amends now? Julia shook her head trying to grasp everything. Someone from her past had just tried to kill her and now he was dead. Her father was a criminal, as was Caroline. She went to accept the tea through the window from her rescuer, but her hands were shaking too much. The man pulled the cup back so the hot liquid wouldn't spill.

He opened her door. "Let me put this here," he said, placing it in the cup holder below the dashboard. "Put your hands around the cup and when you're warmed up try to take a sip."

"OK." She nodded at him, but her eyes slid back to the Rover.

"Put your window up and keep the heaters on full." He hung around outside the car, hopping from one foot to the other to stay warm.

When the ambulance arrived she was starting to feel better and had managed to drink some of the sweet tea. The paramedic knocked on her window. She recognised him from her school days. He was as surprised as she was.

"Julia Allbright? It's me, Ted Benson!" He opened her door. "Boy, I am sorry to see you at a scene like this."

Julia managed a smile at the guy who'd been the gawky schoolboy that flicked paper balls at her across the desk and was now wrapping her in a foil blanket and checking her pulse. He asked her if she'd been injured and what had happened.

She told him how the driver had been driving on the other side of the road when he appeared to have lost control and at first was hurtling towards her before veering off onto the verge.

"That must have been terrifying…"

"It was."

Ted's colleague called him over to the wrecked car.

"Give me a moment, Julia."

When he returned she asked him, "What did he die of? I feel I could have helped, perhaps."

"Well, not a hundred per cent sure, but it looks like he took a blow to the head, so it would have been quick. Nothing you could have done."

She looked down so he couldn't see her eyes.

"Julia, I have to ask you, as the police are coming, I… can smell alcohol on your breath. Have you had a lot to drink tonight?" He looked embarrassed.

Julia felt her gut clench at the same time she heard the police sirens and knew this was not going to be good. How many shots had she had? Two, three? But that was since this afternoon and she hadn't finished the double Luke had poured. Please, please, don't be over the limit. Her girls. She could not lose them to Caroline.

35

The police had arrived, and after asking some routine questions and breathalysing her they'd escorted her home. A young female police officer drove the Porsche with Julia in the passenger seat while the police car followed.

Julia had phoned ahead to warn Steve she was coming home. He'd listened as she explained she'd been in a car accident and someone had died. He asked her how much she'd had to drink, but she didn't answer in front of DS Blakely, sitting next to her. Thank God she'd tested just under the limit. Perhaps she would have been dead now if she'd drunk more; she might have panicked and ended up smashing into the ditch. Or been arrested and in danger of losing everything.

A police car pulled up behind them as Blakely manoeuvred the Cayenne on the drive. A tall officer from it waited at the front door as they approached and Steve came out of the house. Her husband looked weary and his eye was almost swollen shut, a livid bruise starting under it. Julia saw steel in his eyes so fleeting she doubted whether Blakely saw it, but he was already mustering a look of concern as he walked towards her.

"Julia, are you alright, my love?" He extended one arm and Julia moved into the curve of it.

"Oh, Steve, it was awful!"

Her head rested on his shoulder and his other arm came round to embrace her. Appearances, Julia knew she could count on him for that.

"Thank you for bringing her home safely, Constable."

"Evening, Mr Campbell." It was the policeman that spoke. "Mrs Campbell doesn't appear to have sustained any injuries and the vehicle seems intact."

"What happened, darling?"

God, he hadn't called her that in years.

"It was awful, Steve. A man driving on the straight just after Prenton Lane... He lost control, I think, and started coming straight for me. He... he swerved into a tree. Perhaps he had a heart attack or something."

Steve looked at her and she wondered if she'd overdone it.

"That's a good old shiner you have developing there, Mr Campbell," DS Blakely said.

Steve smiled. "Yes, unattended rakes on garden lawns are dangerous things."

The policewoman didn't smile back but continued, "It seems to have caught you on the opposite side of your head as well, Mr Campbell."

Steve replied easily, "I think I should leave gardening to Julia, Constable, and stick to building sites. I'm much safer there." He squeezed Julia's arm and mustered a sympathetic, "Let's get you inside, my love."

Julia smiled at DS Blakely. "Thank you so much for bringing me home."

"Well, I'm pleased to see you're alright, Mrs Campbell. If you think of any more details regarding the crash, please call me on this number. We'll be in touch."

"Thank you, Officer."

Julia took the card offered and put it in her jacket pocket. She and Steve walked into the house together and split apart once the door closed.

"Were you drinking?" Steve accused her.

"What do you expect after today, Steve? Of course I'd had a drink, but I'm not drunk. If I had been I would have been arrested! They breathalysed me."

He looked at her as if she was stupid. "How do you know you were below the limit, Julia? I've friends in high places and you'll still be enjoying the benefit of that."

"For goodness' sake." Julia moved to the kitchen to make herself a hot drink.

Steve followed her. "I meant what I said today, Julia. We are over."

"Why did you come to Carrick today, Steve?"

"You would have liked that, wouldn't you – if I hadn't found out! You two-faced bitch! It's irrelevant why I came. How long has it been going on?"

"I only met him once before today. I know it looked bad, but I swear to you we didn't do anything, except kiss."

"And that makes it alright? Imagine if you'd walked in on me, Julia, half dressed, sleeping with some woman! How would you have felt?"

"I know," she sighed. "It's not your fault, Steve. I… my past is catching up with me. I've found out some terrible things which I can't ignore. The thing with Luke is… I never meant for it to happen. Nothing did happen, Steve. I wish you would believe me. I'm so sorry you got hurt." She looked at his swollen face and went towards him, hand outstretched to touch his cheek, but Steve shied away.

"Don't give me that. Your pity is the last thing I want." He went to turn away and stopped. "What's happened to us, Julia? I thought we were strong? What is this crap about your past? You've been living in the past since Grace was born."

"I've been hiding and I didn't know it." She looked at him, searching for some compassion, some hint that he cared. "I'm not sure if we have a future together. But there's something I have to clear up first."

"Can you tell me what it is?" He glared at her.

She nodded. "Soon." She averted her eyes.

"I'm going to bed," he said. When she didn't look at him he raised his voice. "I trust if you're going to see him you will use some discretion."

"I won't be seeing him," Julia said.

36

Luke looked at his watch. It was ten thirty. Her kids would probably be at school by now: a good time to call her. He brought his hand to his forehead, deliberating. Was he about to make a fool of himself?

Last time he hadn't made an effort. He'd just let her go, didn't try to get her back, and he'd lost her, for too long.

He took his phone out and opened the screen, and closed it again. "Damn."

He'd thought of her all night, tearing himself up inside, imagining she'd made it up with Steve and they'd had long conversations about how they were going to work on it and make a go of it for the kids' sake. And he would no doubt admit he still loved her, because how could he not? And she would decide it would be best for the kids if she stayed with their father…

"Shit!" He reached for his sixth cigarette that morning. His throat was raw and he looked a mess. Unshaven, hair unwashed and huge black shadows under his eyes. Was he going to fall apart again? Was he going to give her up again?

Not without a fight this time. He pulled out his phone again and dialled her number.

"Hello, Luke."

She sounded calm. Too calm for his liking. It was mean of him, but he felt he had more chance with her if she needed him.

"Julia. I was worried about you…"

Her voice quivered as she started to speak. She cleared her throat and asserted, "I'm OK. I'm so sorry, Luke."

"I didn't sleep."

"Me neither."

He resisted the urge to ask her outright where she'd slept.

"Did you stay at Carrick on your own? I was worried."

"I did for a while. I know what happened now, Luke. I remember it all."

He wanted to ask her if she'd gone back to him but said instead, "Is it bad – what happened to Suzanne?"

"It's as bad as it can be."

"What are you going to do about her?"

"I have a plan."

"And us?" He cursed himself for sounding pushy.

She hesitated before replying – building up to a gentle let-down for him, he was sure. "I must protect my girls, Luke."

So she was going to stay with Campbell. Luke felt his heart shrivel. He realised if she did this to him again it would end for good. It would be over. He hadn't realised till now that all these years he'd buried his hurt, but hope had lay dormant right next to it. Now that hope was being dashed again yet he couldn't be angry with her this time.

"I'm glad I helped you, Julia. I don't regret seeing you again."

"I... Oh, I have to go. The doctor's reception is calling me back. I have to make an appointment."

"Why? Did he hurt you?" He felt anger rolling over his despair.

"No, no... but I have to... I can't explain right now, but I'm alright, Luke, really, I am. Look, I'll call you later."

He somehow knew she wouldn't. He felt desperate. "I'll call you tomorrow, Julia."

"Bye, Luke."

The phone went dead before he could reply. He stared at the empty screen a long time then he roused himself, squared his shoulders. It wasn't over yet.

Julia felt guilty cutting Luke off like that, but she had to focus on her kids right now. She hadn't lied about the doctor's appointment. She needed an official report from the GP that she was stressed and a prescription for anti-depressants. She was going to be the perfect wife and mother. The charity event loomed ahead – something she had dreaded but was now part of her plan.

The company and the charity – Caroline's babies. The babies her stepmother truly cared about due to the status they afforded her. She would do anything to protect it all, Julia knew – even send out a killer to erase the one threat to her.

She resolved to make sure that monster was held accountable and was never around her children ever again, or anyone else's, for that matter. Julia had even cancelled Sandra's shifts for the rest of the week, deciding she would pick up the children from now on.

The doorbell rang as she made her way through the hall. She reached for the latch to open it and jumped when the door swung open to reveal her stepmother.

The older woman pulled her key from the lock. "Good morning, Julia," she said, her mouth settling into a straight line as she made to enter the house, but Julia stepped in her way.

"I'm busy right now. It's not convenient."

Caroline drew herself up. "You've certainly been busy from what I've heard – wrecking your marriage and smashing up cars. I need to discuss something with you."

Julia cursed herself for not pre-empting this assault. "I don't want you t-to come in." Damn her shaky voice!

"Don't be ridiculous! Steve is very upset with all that's happened and I'm not going to discuss this business on your doorstep. I—"

"And I'm not going to discuss it with you at all!"

Julia had forgotten the woman had a key. She would have to get the locks changed. The arrogant bitch. Julia could see now the evil Caroline had brought into their lives, tainting her family: their name, reputation, their memory – everything was under threat due to her, not to mention the attempt on her life last night. She may not have wanted her dead, but Julia incapacitated would do very nicely, no doubt – so she could push her way into their marriage and control things more.

"You should mind your own business; it's not as secure as you might think, bitch."

Caroline flinched, but her voice was quiet and hard when she replied, "And what business is that, Julia?"

"You'll see, Caroline."

"How dare you threaten me!" Caroline jabbed Julia's arm with her finger. "Have you forgotten who you're talking to?"

Julia swiped her hand away and brought her face closer to her enemy's. "The days when you could bully me into submission are over, Caroline. You are nothing but an evil, conniving, manipulative witch who has had her day. This is *my* life, *my* family and I am not letting this go. The fact that I'm still here this morning proves it."

"I don't know what you're talking about. After all I've done for you and your girls!"

"I never needed you, Caroline. I don't need you." Julia mentally shook herself for her double assertion – it was like she still couldn't throw off her fear of the woman.

Caroline pulled back a little. "Who died last night in that crash, Julia?"

"How should I know?" Julia lied. "What does it matter to you who died – the only one who matters to you is you. Did you even love my father?"

"My relationship with John is none of your fucking business—"

"How did my father die?"

Caroline baulked then recovered. "I told you. It was heart failure."

"Which room was he found in?"

"This is morbid and I don't want to talk about it." Caroline's face was scarlet, her mouth a grim line.

"It was the cellar, wasn't it!"

Caroline had taken out a cigarette and lit it. She exhaled. "We never used the cellar," she said.

"Why would you put a carpet down in a room you didn't use?" Julia watched as Caroline looked away across the lawn, refusing to answer. "So I'm thinking maybe he had his heart attack in there and since he died in there, that's why you never used it again? Or was there another reason for closing it up?"

Caroline turned back and looked her in the eye. "He died in the kitchen like I told you before. I don't see the point in pursuing this. He's gone and there's no point in digging up the past – no good can come of it."

"That's a matter of opinion, Caroline."

Julia decided to end the conversation before she said too much more. She took a step back into the hallway and grabbed the edge of the door like she was going to use it as a weapon. "I'll see you Friday at the manor."

Unless you want to come and try to kill me yourself before then?

For a minute she thought her stepmother would try to stop her closing the door, but to her relief, Caroline turned abruptly and stalked back across the drive.

When she closed the door, she was trembling but felt euphoric. Was it that easy? That simple to stand up to her? Why hadn't she done it sooner? Just after her wedding all those years ago would have been a good time.

Still feeling victorious, Julia pulled out her phone and called Tom, outlining her request to him.

"No problem," he assured her. "Just think, in a few months' time the house will be sold and you can forget all about it."

Julia almost laughed out loud.

37

The bitch remembered. Caroline knew it. She lit another cigarette from the one in her hand now down to the filter. She realised she'd carried the ashtray to the bin and forgotten to empty it; it was still sitting on the shelf next to it. She crossed over the office to retrieve it, cursing as she went. The woman was taunting her. She'd found the cellar and remembered the incident somehow. That's how Caroline regarded the whole thing. The incident.

True, a few people had been removed at her bidding in the past thanks to the faithful thugs that had worked for her, but this was different. This had not been murder. It was an accident. The whole thing had gone wrong. She sat down at the table with the emptied ashtray, pushing it into a space between the un-cleared breakfast dishes and office papers.

The plan had been to keep the girl alive, keep her sedated while John got what he wanted, then release her up north. It had been easy for Micah to lure her away. Once he had her in his car, he drugged her and brought her to John. She barely knew who she was, much less where she was in the end.

The kid had reacted to the drug, or maybe they'd given her too much. The more Caroline had thought about it over the years, the more she realised their plan had been loose and flawed. She'd gone along with John because she was afraid of losing him, losing everything. He'd explained that he just had this need sometimes and had to sate it – that it didn't change how he felt about her, how they were a team and always would be. She'd agreed to it. Never thinking where it would all end.

Caroline wondered why she couldn't get over it. Was it because it was just a kid? Why did she care? Kids born into lives like that never had much of a childhood anyway – she knew that. Why dredge it up all the time? Churning it over in her mind? Was it because this girl had the same persecuted look in her eyes that she herself had borne before she'd run away from home, from her heartless mother and the abusive boyfriend at the age of thirteen? Was it because this girl didn't even have the chances she herself had? They'd preyed upon her before she could make any choices then discovered her dead in the cellar after three days. Looking back now she could see they'd been careless and Caroline's guilt had started there – and the fear. The fear that one day Julia would remember.

She found herself blinking now to clear her vision and wondered at the sudden sentiment – was that for Suzanne or for her own thirteen-year-old self? As one tear fell onto her cheek she suddenly yelled and, with a satisfying sweep of her arm, cleared the dishes from the table to a shattering heap as they hit the wooden floor below.

Year after year Caroline had watched Julia for signs of recollection. She'd dreaded this day, but now it was here she had to admit she felt something like relief. The wait was over. Well, almost. Perhaps that's what the tears were – a release of tension. She could live with that. She just couldn't live in prison. So, she would have to see how Julia wanted to play it. Clearly her stepdaughter was feeling powerful going by her bravado at the house. Had she told Steve about her discovery then? No. She couldn't have because he would have been yelling by now. Micah had been right all along about removing the problem. A pang of dread hit her again at the thought of the car crash that Steve had told her about. Was Micah the deceased driver? She shook her head, discounting the possibility. How could Julia outwit him? No, it couldn't have been him. She was letting her imagination run away with her. This was a random accident.

So why hadn't he answered his phone this morning?

Micah had said he would stay and watch her last night after Steve had stormed out. That whole bust had been well orchestrated even by her standards. Proceed with caution, she'd warned him. Had he forgotten that part? Her gut was churning.

She looked down at the island of smashed crockery on her floor, the dregs of her breakfast and the ash from the ashtray floating in the pool of tea around it.

She lifted the receiver and dialled zero. Lucy answered and Caroline requested her to come to the office with a mop and bucket.

What did Julia know anyway? What could she actually do if she'd remembered it all? Could her story not be written off as the ramblings of an alcoholic woman? Since when did that little nobody have the capacity to plan anything? More likely, Julia would do nothing. She had no proof. And did she understand that in making this public, the scandal would be huge. Did she realise she also stood to lose everything? She hasn't got the nerve, she told herself.

There was a knock at the door. "Come in," Caroline sighed, expecting Lucy. It was Steve.

"My God, Caroline it smells like an ashtray in here." He coughed, stepping around the mess in front of him. "What the hell happened?"

"Oh, you lightweight." Caroline walked over to the window, opening it for a blast of cold air to sweep in like a hasty housemaid. "That is what it looks like – an accident. Why are *you* so stressed? Fretting about your marriage, by any chance?"

"I was thinking how I might go for custody."

"Your wife will show you how; the woman's a mess."

"So all I have to do is prove her instability?"

Caroline raised an eyebrow. "Sounds about right." She closed the window again and sat back at her desk, flicking a speck of ash off her tight skirt.

"If I can make a public show of her…"

"At the Manor?"

"That's right. Any claims I make afterwards, plus the few

witnesses I have to her bad behaviour – Bob, Amanda, the staff at Annie's retirement home – I think it all might work for us…"

Steve had walked around the desk and stood looking down at her, their knees almost touching.

"Did you find out who died in the accident last night?"

"That's why I'm here, Caroline. I'm sorry… It was your friend, Micah. The police are trying to trace his relatives in Poland."

So Micah had timed out. He'd made the wrong move. Caroline felt a pang for her old friend and hate surged towards her stepdaughter. But mixed with the hate was the question again – how? Julia wasn't much of an adversary – how could she have outsmarted him?

There was a knock on the door before it opened, revealing Lucy and her bucket. The girl hesitated when she saw Steve. "Oh, sorry, Caroline! I didn't realise you were having a meeting?"

"It's alright, Lucy," Steve interjected, stepping back a little from Caroline. "I came up the back steps. You weren't to know."

"Come back later, Lucy," Caroline snapped, irritated they'd been talking so loud.

"Did you put him up to it?" Steve asked in a lower voice after Lucy had left.

"Are you asking me did I put a hit on your wife? Are you crazy? Like I said, he did things his own way. He said to me he was just going to keep track of her, follow her movements. I don't know what the hell happened."

"I had to ask, Caroline, OK? It appears it was a head-on approach on Micah's part so it looks like he was challenging her and he must have lost control. It's a wonder the police don't want to press charges against Julia, though, because her alcohol levels were just on the limit. I think they've been lenient because of me. But I'll use that information later if I need to."

"But now we have a problem. He had my number on his phone."

"Shit!"

"Mmm!"

"Is that all you have to say?" Steve's voice cracked in panic.

"There's no texts. I can say he contacted me because of Julia's call about Annie... maybe, we can make this accident look like it was Julia's doing somehow... let me think it through. Has Julia been telling you anything about her past, Steve?"

Steve looked at her. "Last night. She said she'd discovered a terrible thing – something she couldn't ignore."

Caroline's lips drew tight. "Anything else?"

"No. Why?" Steve stepped closer to her and looked down into her upturned face. "We must stick together, you and I, Caroline. I'll need you behind me if I go for custody, so you should tell me what I need to know." His hand dropped to cup her chin and his thumb caressed her lip, smudging her lipstick.

Caroline was not willing to let any man dictate to her, but she realised she would have to play Steve along for a while. Dammit, she wasn't going down! Her hand moved to his crotch and caressed through the fabric.

The look of desire on his face vanished when she dropped her hand and pushed her chair back on its wheels as she laughed.

He scowled at her. "You are going to help. You will make us some coffee at the manor and you make sure hers is going to have the desired effect – you know what to use. By the time the speeches start she'll be falling all over the place. I'll pass it off as a tipple too many, but you'll need to take the kids once the shit hits the fan. I'll take her home once she's humiliated herself and come back to you – the devoted stepmother looking after the neglected children." He leaned against the desk. "If we can discredit her as a mother and her drinking becomes public knowledge, we can make it look like her irrational thinking led to her meeting up with Micah, or at the least, perhaps Micah's family can be persuaded to jump on the bandwagon; a manslaughter charge would keep her out of our hair for a long time. I would get the kids and I wouldn't have to pay her a penny."

"What about the scandal of it all? I didn't think you'd be up for that."

"The scandal will all be Julia's and I'll come out rosy." He smirked.

"I'll put a PI on her, get some photos of her and lover-boy. I'll look like the long-suffering husband, always there to babysit every Friday night she was out on the town."

"Yes. It could work for you," Caroline said, warming to the idea.

Caroline felt a bit better. If they could work together, they could get out of this. Nobody would listen to the claims of a raving bipolic.

She grinned at her partner. "Manslaughter? I like the sound of that."

38

Luke saw Julia's name flash up on the screen and answered before the second ring.

"Hi, are you alright?"

"I'm OK. What about you? How's the jaw?"

"Bloody sore. I bet Steve's eye looks good."

"I'll have to apply some concealer to it tomorrow."

Luke cringed at the intimacy this would create between the two.

"After this weekend, we'll be separating, Luke."

His heart soared. He had to stop himself from whooping out loud. At the same time he told himself to cool it; he knew better than to offer her a place to stay and instead said, "I didn't expect that so soon. So you've talked about it. Will he support you, Julia?"

"I've got a job. Mike at the *Herald* saw me today and offered me a part-time position as features contributor. So I'll look after myself."

"That's fantastic. What about the children?"

"They'll come with me. I'll apply for full custody and Steve can have visiting rights."

"And Caroline? Will you let her see the kids?"

"Never. Children can't go where she's going."

"Be careful, Jules."

"I will, Luke. Things are going to get messy and I wanted to warn you to keep your head down. You might be approached by press. I can imagine Caroline might leak something about us to them. We can't see each other for… a while. Gaining custody, I have to look respectable. Steve will fight me on every level and he'll be looking for anything he can use against me."

"I get it, don't worry."

"Plus, there'll be bad publicity about Carrick and my family, and you'd best steer clear of it all – I don't want you to get hurt by all of this."

"Thanks for the warning, but I'm a big boy, I can handle it. I can still call you, though?"

Her voice softened. "I'm so close to sorting things out, Luke. When it's over, I can make things right between us – if you'll have me? I don't know how bad it's all going to get. If you and I don't work out after all of this, I'll understand."

"It's going to be alright. I love you, Jules. Tell me your plans so I can help you – give me your address."

"No. Luke, you've got to stay away."

"I will, but just let me have it. I'll feel better knowing I can reach you if I'm needed?"

"I don't want you involved, Luke. Just let me do this—"

"Trust me, Julia. Trust me to stay out of your way when you ask me."

There was a pause while Julia considered his request. "It's 5 Sycamore Close, Little Wynchstead."

He scribbled it down. "Don't worry. You won't see me at breakfast!"

"Look, I might not be able to call you tomorrow, but I'll give you a ring on Sunday when it's all over."

"Are you sure I can't help?"

"Yes. I know what to do, Luke."

"Be careful."

"You're my best friend, Luke – do you know that?"

Carrick 1980

Remember how I used to help you, Julie... you and me versus the world and the Controller. Remember that time... you were having a paddy because she'd stopped you going to that party and I just wanted you to stop crying! I told you I'd do anything and all you could say was I hate her, I hate her, I hate her.

Let's play a trick on her, I said.

You were worried that you'd get the blame – like that time I smashed her perfume bottle. Do you remember, she convinced the Brute it was you and you got sent to bed...

I wanted to push her down the stairs, but you said, no way!

Then there were more tears and I couldn't stand it! I promised to you I would sort her out. Then we made friends – linking our pinky fingers. You remember that now, don't you, Julie...

"Make friends, make friends..."

...never ever break friends.

Can you scare her? you asked me.

That was boring. I didn't want to do that. I said, I could move something so she'd look for it, then I'd put it back and she'd be confused. Then I could hide it again and she'd think she was going crazy. You were worried – thought you'd be blamed, but you were smiling too.

Then you were called in to dinner and I knew exactly what to do.

•

Remember, Julie, a door opening, the clink of tableware, chime of cutlery. The dining room, where there is food which doesn't smell and people that don't smile. You sit, looking nervous between the Brute and the Crone. The meals are placed before the abusers and the abused. Light plunges to its death in the surrounding dark wood panels and dark green furnishings. Pale faces look like the dead, except for you, my friend, who still shines, even when you are sad.

As the Controller goes to sit on her seat, I move it just a little and she falls spectacularly to the floor, taking with her her plate of food so its contents take a slow slide like a colourful, lumpy waterfall onto her chest. For a moment there is stunned silence followed by shrieks of pain as the hot food burns. I look at you for approval and you are fit to burst. The Crone unleashes a wheezy guffaw, spraying food onto the white linen tablecloth, before collapsing into uncontrollable cackles. While the Brute stumbles round to help the bitch, I see you laughing silently till your face is red and your eyes are lit up with joy.

You look like Kas when you laugh like that.

39

Julia woke. It was four thirty. She'd been laughing in her sleep. Caroline had missed her chair at the dinner table. Vivid, like it was yesterday – roast potatoes and slimy chicken all over her stepmother's designer clothes, adorned here and there with an array of emerald peas. She remembered Caroline's look of mortification and her father fussing over her, lifting chunks of food off her chest while Annie laughed till she was breathless and she felt a chuckle now rise in her throat. Suzanne had done that for her, and so many other things, all those years ago. She hoped she would remember them all one day.

She wondered if Suzanne approved of her intentions today. As Steve snored beside her, she went over her plan. Was there a flaw? Could Suzanne see it? Could she see the future?

She recalled Tuesday night when Suzanne had stood between the two cars, saving her. The dream was a reminder, of the bond between the two of them. Or was it a reminder of what she owed San? There was no doubt she was beholden to this lost girl. She was doing this because it needed to be done, whatever the reasons and whatever the cost. Although she was sorry for Steve and the problems it would cause his business, she felt sure he would understand that for their daughters' safety alone, Caroline, Annie and John Allbright had to be exposed.

Her thoughts turned to her father, a man she'd never truly known. Feeling the now-familiar crushing of her heart that came with his memory, she traced back in her mind to the man who could be kind and sweet and sometimes funny but could also be a demon, one that sheltered his own daughter while helping to imprison someone else's. Had there been others? Had Caroline's and Micah's influence changed him into this demon? Or had there always been a part of him that was bad?

Julia wondered now if that was the real reason why her father and mother had split up? Had Eve discovered a side of her husband which was not acceptable to her? No, she couldn't have known, for if she had, she would never have left her with him and would have made provision for her with her sister in the event of her death. But who knows they will die at the age of thirty-one? Nobody saw it coming, least of all Eve.

And what would Steve think of this story? It was ironic that his insistence on her packing up the house and Caroline's refusal to do so had led to this revelation. Even as the decorators were appointed to start on Wednesday, to plaster and paint over the old, Julia knew that for her, it would never hide the evil that had been played out there. She was the one person in all of this that would never have true release from it all. She'd paid for being the observer all her life, even when she wasn't conscious of it, and she would continue to pay. She suspected Steve would not see things her way.

Even if they hadn't already been on the verge of separation Julia knew that what she was about to do would end their marriage. In Steve's world you never aired your washing in public. He would tell her to deal with it, have therapy but shut up and carry on as normal. Surely, though, Steve would agree that Caroline should never see their girls again?

It didn't matter what he thought, she told herself now. She was going ahead with her plans. She reached under her pillow and pulled out the necklace with the 'S' on it. She gripped it in her palm and imagined its wearer's terror and fear. This was the only way she could make up for not saving her and forgetting her all those years. She pulled her fist to her chest. It was going to be a hell of a day. She had to get more sleep.

40

Before dawn Julia rose and headed for the warm spray of the shower.

Steve was sitting on the side of the bed frowning at her when she came back into the bedroom.

"Christ, what was wrong with you last night? Tossing and turning, felt like you were packing up your stuff already – will you need help with that, by the way?"

She ignored the jibe and averted her eyes from his enquiring stare. "I didn't sleep well. We'll both need an inch deep of make-up for the photos, I think, I've got terrible dark rings under my eyes."

"That you have," he said, moving to the bathroom.

"Your eye is still a bit swollen," she retorted. "You might have to pass it off as an allergy."

She heard him grumbling as she rubbed her hair with the towel. After a few minutes he came back out and began to slip on his jogging bottoms.

"What are you wearing today?"

It was a question neither of them had gotten round to asking of the other with all that had gone on. As Steve's soon-to-be-ex-wife, she didn't think he had any say in what she wore anymore but she answered him. "The pale blue Hobbs dress with the matching jacket."

He didn't answer her as he pulled on a warm sweatshirt and left the room. He was just making sure she was coming, Julia knew. Of course, she'd no intention of dressing up today because there was no need.

Julia skipped the eggs Benedict, their usual weekend indulgence they'd shared in the last couple of years. She heated some croissants instead to go with their coffee. She mused how strange it was that this might be one of their last breakfasts together, but she felt nothing about leaving him, except a pang as she noted the playhouse, which had still not been painted; guilty as hell for breaking up her children's life.

"What time are you waking the girls?"

"I think I heard them talking but I'll call them down soon."

"And you're coming through for eleven thirty?"

Another confirmation.

"Yes, Steve. I told Caroline yesterday."

He went back to his paper.

Julia felt uneasy at his attention to the schedule. Her feeling of control slipped slightly and she wanted him to leave now so she could put everything into action. "Have you got time for another coffee?"

He looked at his watch. "Yes, but I'll have it in the study. There's something I have to do before I see this client this morning."

Good – that would mean he would be out by eight thirtyish. She poured him his coffee and waited.

.

Steve left the house in his usual calm manner looking the successful businessman he was. Julia had covered up the bruising under his eye which had faded a bit and some of the swelling had gone down. The publicity photographs would not reveal too much today.

As soon as his car left the drive she went upstairs. The excited chatter of the girls could be heard from the landing, about the party and the dresses they would be wearing. It was at their breakfast when Julia could be sure Steve would not return that she explained to the girls they were not going to the party today.

At their horrified faces she was quick to outline the magnificent day out Aunty Row had planned for them which involved going on the train into London, a visit to Hamleys and a special visit to the theatre to see *The Wizard of Oz*. Their disappointment changed to elation till Grace asked, "Are you coming with us, Mummy?"

"I can't today, darling. I have to go to the boring party because it's a business thing and Daddy wants me there. Daddy knows you're not coming and he told me to give you a big kiss and wish you an exciting time, OK? So finish your breakfast, then you can go and get ready. Don't forget you have to brush your teeth and wash your faces first, before putting your dresses on!"

The girls were excited, but Julia's gut churned at the deception she'd started and the fear something would go wrong before she had a chance to get the girls out of the way. She just hoped Steve would forgive her all this at the end.

"Hurry up now!" she said.

Row was waiting for them at the station. Julia had briefed her only that she needed the girls out of the way while she attended to something which may get unpleasant.

"Thanks for doing this, Row. I expect to be back at yours this evening, but I've left their night clothes and a change of wear for them in a rucksack in your porch, in case... in case things go wrong."

Row hugged her. "Don't worry about them at all. We'll have a wonderful time and be waiting for you tonight back at the house. Be careful, my dear."

"I'll see you this evening. You're an angel, Row."

As Julia returned to her car, she recalled Mattie's pictures of 'Angels'. What had Luke said? That angels were messengers? Julia still couldn't fathom this part of the puzzle. What relevance did this have to everything she'd discovered and how did it tie in with what her father had said on the playback? She felt there was some element of it all that she just couldn't pinpoint. The missing jigsaw piece added to her anxiety; it was like going into battle without the full kit.

A fleeting thought of how easy it would be to just forget all about Suzanne and let the past go crossed her mind yet again, but she brushed it away. This is what Suzanne wanted, she was sure, and

Caroline had to be dealt with. The others had all suffered and been silenced. Now it was just her stepmother that walked unscathed, unpunished. Julia wanted justice for Suzanne.

She marvelled that she'd never taken such a definitive step in her life before today. She'd wafted along, being everybody's friend and never rocked the boat, but that was all going to change now. For better or worse, she asserted, checking her determined expression in the rear-view mirror.

41

Brayton Manor was a stately home which comprised various conference rooms and the ballroom which today was transformed into a grand reception held by the Carrick Foundation for selected members of the local council and the mayor's office, the recipient homes with some of the children and the trustees, as well as all of the staff of Campbell Construction and, of course, the local press. Twenty-five tables were arranged before a stage, each with white tablecloths, fresh white flower arrangements arranged in the centre of each, and pink and blue balloons at the ends, to match the bunting overhead.

Caroline was looking at her watch. Where the hell was Julia? Steve had just said goodbye to his business associate who he'd had coffee with at the venue and was returning; Caroline could see him at the door talking to one of the resident staff. She had the coffee ready to give her and all she needed was the woman to get here so she could watch her lose her new-found confidence in spectacular fashion. Caroline couldn't wait to see the woman degraded. The side door opened and Caroline looked over, thinking this had to be her, but it was the florist. No worry, she was just a bit late – it was always expected with her. She sent a text to her anyway just to hurry her up: *Where are you?*

"I've just texted her," she said to Steve, at the same time tapping the flask sticking out of her bag.

Steve nodded. "Good. When she arrives, we'll have our little meeting and at the start you offer to make us all a cup straightaway. I want to be sure it has time to kick in."

He looked around at how fresh and smart the room looked and at the pink and blue banner stretching across the stage, a long, white, flower-laden table below it.

"Looks good in here. Not sure about the pink but the girls will like it." He checked his watch just as Caroline's phone alerted an incoming message.

Caroline's face was a picture of contempt as she read out, "*I'm running behind. Should be there for twelve. Sorry.*" She looked at him and didn't have to voice her opinion but said it anyway: "Typical!"

"There's still time," Steve said, but he was irritated.

Caroline knew he would start picking on everyone in his vicinity until his wife deigned to arrive. "I'm going to check on the caterers, Steve. I'll be in the kitchen. Text me when she gets here and I'll bring the drinks with me."

.

Julia stood in her kitchen looking for her bag. She'd just called Tom to make sure it had begun, but he'd only just arrived there. He assured her he would be starting the job she'd given him as soon as he'd unpacked the tools and had a quick cup of tea. Julia had squashed her frustration. Maybe she should have been there from the start. The quicker she got to Carrick the better; Tom was reliable but God he was slow.

She grabbed her bag and headed out to the car. She mused on the information she'd just received from Lucy at the office. Apparently, Amanda had been there asking about her yesterday. Why didn't she just call her? Julia hadn't heard a peep from her since Mattie's party. Was it an excuse just to see Steve? Was she the secret on his laptop? It wouldn't surprise her. Well, she was welcome to him!

She directed the remote at the car and pushed the button. The lights failed to flash. She grasped the handle and found it locked. Oh no, not again. She aimed the remote at the car door and pressed the button again. She'd had this problem a month ago and Steve had blamed her, saying she was doing something wrong. The locks had been replaced at huge expense in the end and now it was playing up again. She tried the door – nothing. Damn! She tried a different combination of buttons, but the locks held fast. Damn you! She beat her fist against the window. She tried once more, with no result. On her way back inside the house she took out her phone to call a taxi.

•

Luke sat staring at the clock. He'd left her a message this morning, as he'd done every day since the fight, but today he'd expected no reply. He knew she had to clear up this part of her life before she could move on with him. He thought about the way she'd felt in his arms. She didn't realise he would give anything to have her back. He wanted to offer his home for her and the girls, and he would when this was over. He wondered what she was planning today. Was she going to use the press there as a platform to reveal the story of Suzanne? He hoped not. She would fry herself. Steve would have her sectioned at Caroline's insistence and there'd be nobody to protect those little girls from whatever it was that Caroline was into. It beggared belief to think about the cruelty she and John had inflicted, and he didn't like to dwell on it. No, Julia wouldn't be that careless to stand there with her memories as her sole backup, accusing Caroline without proof. But she'd said there would be no children where Caroline was going. It could be one of two places: jail or the morgue. He wished she'd told him what she was up to so he could protect her.

•

"What county show? Haven't you put on extra cars?" Julia listened to the taxi driver's proposal. "I can't wait till one thirty! Don't worry, I'll try somewhere else."

Julia put the phone down as Steve's name came up on an incoming call. She watched the screen nervously as if Steve could see her through it. Two minutes past twelve. She let it ring. After the sixth ring it went to the messaging service.

Wait. Wait… five more minutes. She dialled another taxi service and got put in a queue. What the hell! She looked at her watch again. What if he decided to come right now to the house? He had time. She didn't feel strong enough to answer his questions.

She waited two more minutes then abandoned the taxi queue and walked to the hallway. The signal here was weak and it would help to break up the call which would make up for the lack of car and children sounds Steve would expect to hear. She rang him.

"Hi, Steve." She held the phone away as Steve yelled at her. "I'm sorry. I'm stuck in traffic; it's really bad. Hello? You there? I'm on the Belmont Road. Something must have happened because it's not moving here." She moved around the hall.

"Steve? You keep breaking up. What? I'm not making an excuse – why would I? It's probably an accident but I can't see anything at the moment." She listened to Steve moaning some more and tried to change the tone. "I'll be there soon, I promise. How's it going there anyway? Is everyone arriving? Yes, yes, I said I was sorry, oh, it's moving now! Listen, let me go – I shouldn't be too long."

He was so mad. She hoped the guests started arriving soon, then he would be captive for at least an hour or so more. That's all she needed. She just wished she could be at Carrick to make sure it was happening. She selected Wynchstead taxis again from her list of contacts and cursed as she was put into a queue once more. This was ridiculous.

.

He wasn't in the right frame of mind for this, Steve thought, forcing a smile and a cheery demeanour as the guests started to arrive. Julia was up to something. That call hadn't been made from inside a car; he couldn't hear the kids. Something was up, but he didn't know what. He wondered at that moment if she was coming at all. Perhaps she was moving her stuff out to move in with the loser. Or was she snooping round the house looking for things? Steve squirmed. He took out his phone and selected the GPS app. He'd set it up on their phones that morning while she was in the shower. He would have read her texts as well if he'd had time, but the tracker was the important thing. That was going to be very useful in the run-up to the divorce.

"Mr Campbell?"

Steve turned to see the sound technician he'd hired shifting from foot to foot, holding a black cable. "What is it, Brad?"

"I'm sorry, but there's a problem with the mic. Rob's gone to the van to look for another cable."

"Right!" Steve said, irritated. "What does this mean?"

"Well, you might have to speak very loudly." The young man grinned.

"I'm not in the mood for jokes," Steve spat.

"I'm ever so sorry, Mr Campbell, I…" He stopped, seeing his colleague returning with some wire.

"Well?"

Rob was stressed. "Sorry, Mr Campbell, but we don't have the cable we need—"

"For God's sake. This is not good enough! Think of a solution, and think of it quick. This is not some Mickey Mouse outfit here, pink balloons or otherwise…"

Brad piped up, "Hey, what about the venue's own PA system? They'll probably have the cable we need. Do you have the caretaker's number, Mr Campbell?"

"Aren't you supposed to have it?" Steve snarled.

Brad's lips twitched. "I do, in my file at home."

"What the hell good is it doing there?" Steve snapped. "Jesus! Caroline has it, she's… Come with me," Steve said, stalking towards the garden.

Julia's stomach was a bubbling cauldron and she had a headache. She took out a cigarette from the pack she'd bought for today, opened the door to the patio area and stepped out. The rain had stopped and the sun had come out again. It was cold but not too bad. She walked around the patio while she smoked, trying to ease her stiff neck and relax. The garden was starting to peel back its white mantle, the ice dripping off gutters behind her onto the paving and the grass poking up, stiff green shards through the melting snow. She calmed herself, reasoning that Steve and Caroline were occupied and her girls were faraway and safe. Unexpected, but she'd begun to feel empowered like never before. Still, it didn't stop the worry that she might fail. She was about to ring Tom to find out how he was doing when a text came through.

It was Luke. He was begging her not to make any public declarations, listing all the worst outcomes that would result from it. He apologised if she felt he was interfering and told her how much he loved her, ending with a *Be careful.*

As she went to reply, another text came through from him: *Are you digging?*

She smiled and answered it: *Yes, Tom's on it.*

His call came through. "Julia, are you at Carrick House or the event?"

"Neither, I'm stuck at home because the immobiliser's locked me out of my car. I'm trying to get a taxi to Carrick."

"I'll come and get you."

"No, Luke, I don't want you seen here."

"Then walk down the road or something, I'll pick you up."

"Don't worry, I'll get a taxi soon. They said they were booked up but I'm phoning round."

"OK. I'll go straight to Carrick, Julia."

"Luke, stay out of this. Please."

"Let me help you. I can be there by one. Where is he digging?"

"The rockery, by the swing. It was put in by my father the year I arrived, the year she went missing."

"What if you're wrong?"

"I can't be wrong. This is the only chance I have to put this right."

·

Steve was livid. The lying bitch! His tracker showed she was still at home. What was she playing at? Was she nosing around his stuff? Christ, he had to go there right now! He wasn't even sure he'd left everything secure like he usually did.

He was about to call her when he saw Junayd Patel approaching him in the foyer. He was the Labour MP for the Highton constituency and Steve needed to win him round for a new development he'd planned of twenty flats in an already built-up area. He'd invited him for this sole purpose. Damn. He summoned his best smile, put his phone in his pocket and moved towards Junayd with his hand outstretched.

42

Caroline sat next to the mayor at the table on the stage, half listening to Steve explaining the origins of the Carrick Foundation to the seated audience. She was thinking about Julia and her absence. What was she up to? She'd remembered her past, but what could she do about it? They'd been very careful cleaning that mess up all those years ago.

Still, Caroline felt uncomfortable. The mayor was due to speak in about five minutes and she herself had a speech to make after him. Nothing to do but wait this out. She reversed the frown that kept settling on her face. She was going to damage that woman to the point of no return when she got the chance.

·

Get out of the way! Luke cursed at the driver in front of him. Why the hell was he driving at twenty? In exasperation he pulled out to overtake but had to pull back in again seeing a truck coming over the rise ahead.

He was finally able to get past the old driver and turned into the narrow lane a little too fast. There was still a fair amount of compacted ice there with it being in permanent shade and he just managed to keep control as the vehicle skid towards the bank. The wheels found traction and he pulled the car back to the centre of the lane where other cars had dug tracks and he accelerated again. The silver birch trees gleaming in the sun gave way to the heavier rhododendron shrubberies and pine trees as he neared Carrick. This part of town would soon be history for Julia. He had a distinct feeling that things were coming to a close one way or another, and new pathways, he hoped, were opening up for both of them. He had to make sure it was a good path.

As he pulled into the drive, he was surprised to see a couple of young guys sitting in a landscaper's truck in the driveway and an older, silver-haired man at the front door peering in through the letterbox as if they'd just arrived. The older man turned around as the car pulled up abreast of the front porch.

Luke took his time getting out and strolled up to him, arm outstretched. "Hi, I'm Luke. Julia... Mrs Campbell sent me – to see how you were getting on."

Tom looked bewildered and glanced back at the door before shaking Luke's hand. "Hello... er, Luke. We've finished the job."

"Oh! Really? Can you show me, please?" Luke was thrown by this development but also by the older man's strange behaviour; he kept looking back at the door and seemed unwilling to leave the porch. Perhaps they'd found something and didn't know what to do about it.

"Is everything alright?" He watched the old man's clear blue eyes for his response, which was slow.

"Well..." Tom looked back over at the dining-room window now he'd stepped down onto the drive. "We finished some time ago and we were just getting ready to leave when I happened to glance in my side mirror and caught sight of a young girl at this window here – banging on the glass in a panic. It was a real fright she gave me, but I've been standing here these last five minutes knocking at the door and nobody's answering." He glanced up at the upper storey then back at Luke. "Mrs Campbell didn't say there was someone in today."

Luke was staring at him and Tom shifted.

"Is Mrs Campbell coming or did she give you a key?" He glanced at the front window again. "That girl looked very upset."

"Er… no." Luke chose his words. "She is coming down, though, so maybe we should just wait around for her. As far as I know, the house is supposed to be empty. Shall we try knocking again?"

"Well, yes, I don't know who she is – not one of Mrs Campbell's daughters, that's for sure. She seemed older. A teenager, maybe."

Tom's son had joined them. "Dad? Thought we were going to the Bull?"

"Yes, in a minute. Frank, why don't you take… Luke around the back and show him the place we cleared so he can let Mrs Campbell know while I try knocking again."

Frank shook his head and strode ahead like Luke was a major inconvenience. Luke slowed his walk. If he was to have any authority here, he would have to be steady and sure. He slowly rounded the corner and saw the wide strip of exposed earth where Tom and his team had removed the rockery.

"Oh!" he said.

"Oh what?" Frank retorted, then added, "What's wrong?"

"Well, actually Mrs Campbell wanted the area hollowed out."

"Hollowed out?" Frank looked at him and at the flattened bed, which was about eight foot long and five foot wide. "Why?"

"She wanted to create an interesting feature here… a… a pond!"

Tom came round the corner holding his phone. He held it out for Luke to take.

"I called Mrs Campbell and she understood the house to be empty. She's going to come down soon with the key. She'd like to talk to you."

Luke took the phone. "Hi, Julia, it's Luke. I came like you asked me to. Good job too because it's not quite as you wanted it…" He paused, nodding. "Yes, they've cleared the rocks but they haven't dug out the pond – they haven't dug deep enough… yeah… I'm on it, that's fine…"

There was a pause while Tom peered into the sitting-room window, clearly confused by his experience, and his son looked on, arms folded across his chest.

"Yes, OK," Luke said. "No problem. I'll put you back on to Tom."

Luke handed back the phone to the old guy. He took out his cigarettes and walked back to the van to tell the other lad they weren't finished yet. He heard cursing behind him and knew Frank was not happy. Tough shit! He turned around and offered himself up to help. "If you've an extra shovel?" he asked.

He would dig her out himself if he had to.

43

The magician that had been arranged to keep the children occupied was well into his act now and enthralling his juvenile audience and some of the adults too. Caroline had just finished her speech and posed for photographs with the mayor and Steve. Now she caught his sleeve as he passed her.

"Have you heard from her?"

"Yes, a text to say the car was overheating in the traffic jam so she turned round and went back home – a load of shit basically. She'd told me she was at the Belmont Road just before quarter past but I tracked her back to the house right after that so she's been lying to me."

"You're kidding! What the hell is she doing?"

"I don't know, but I need to go home. I think she's poking around my stuff."

"Steve, I need to tell you something. I think she's remembered some of her past. Do you remember… I told you."

"About her father?"

"Well, yes, but there's something else…" She looked around. "We should go somewhere private… Oh, hello, Mrs Cawthwaite! Excuse me, Steven," she said as Mrs Cawthwaite took her arm to show her something on one of the boards erected at the back of the room.

Steve hurried towards the exit, hoping he wouldn't be accosted by another guest. His gut told him forces were amassing against him.

He checked her position again as he approached his car. Still at home. Once outside the manor, he rang her and was surprised when she picked up straightaway.

"What the hell are you up to, Julia? And don't give me that shit that you had to turn back because of traffic—"

Julia's reply was stronger than he'd expected. "Traffic was hell so I came back home!"

"You went home! Today? You went back home? Listen to me, you bitch! I tracked you an hour ago and you were still at home. You never left, did you? Is he there?"

"What? Who are—" The phone went dead.

"God dammit!" Steve almost smashed his iPhone onto the drive. She was infuriating. He tried to call her back, but it went straight to the network answer service telling him it hadn't been possible to connect his call. He bleeped the locks and climbed into his car. If that bastard was in his house, he would kill him this time.

.

Julia cursed. She'd had so much to think about she hadn't made sure her phone was charged. Damn! She had to call Steve back to stop him from coming over, but she couldn't even use the landline as she didn't know his new number off by heart. The only record of it was on her mobile. She stood up on shaky legs. She needed the charger. She hadn't heard back from Luke yet so she knew it was too soon to tell Steve anything. If Steve dragged the story out of her now he would stop the dig and the chance to expose Caroline would be lost.

Where was that bloody thing? She always left it in the kitchen, but it wasn't there. Steve must have borrowed it. He had the same model phone and often took the charger into his study. What did Steve mean – is he there? Oh God, he must think Luke was with her. She feared nothing she could say would stop him coming home now, but she had to try.

Julia hurried into the study which was in darkness. Her husband never opened the curtains and she couldn't stand it. She drew them back and opened a window. God, it was messy. This was so out of character, she thought, looking at the sprawl of papers around his laptop. No charger there. Perhaps it was on one of the many bookshelves lining the back of the room? A quick glance confirmed not.

She moved behind his desk and was rummaging around the wires and files cluttering the floor when a faint ping caught her attention. The laptop was on. Her moving things around must have activated the screen. The password screen beckoned her and Julia stared at it. Unable to stop herself, she sat down before it, as if this was the real reason she was in there now with Steve absent and her life and all she'd known as Julia Allbright or Mrs Julia Campbell about to go up in smoke. She may as well go one step further.

Her hands moved to the keyboard. The password. She knew it now. It was 'angels'. Had to be. This is what Suzanne had been telling her through Mattie. She typed it in. She would learn now who Steve was seeing. All his unexplained absences from golf, his late nights in the study and the reason for his coldness to her would be revealed. She knew such information could only help support her in the divorce proceedings.

The screen opened and she clicked on the mail icon. She scanned the inbox but knew all the names in there: Martin, Bob, Caroline... She clicked onto Caroline's. It was a business email. She exited and scanned further... Amanda. Ah. She clicked it. Amanda had asked if Steve wanted to meet for a coffee, four days ago. So it was her. The two-faced cow! She checked his sent box for a response to her but there was none.

Julia's eyes flicked to the folders, one in particular labelled 'Fun'. There were emails from senders she didn't recognise in this one. She clicked the first one.

She stared, unmoving. As in a nightmare, she scrolled down through the minimum text and the photographs as her teeth began to chatter and heart began to hammer. She exited from the email and selected the next one: the same unbearable, despicable content. Unbelieving, she clicked onto the next and could fight the nausea no longer; she threw up into the waste bin, some of the vomit spilling onto the smooth oak flooring.

She wiped her mouth on her sleeve and returned to the keyboard. This was why. Why Suzanne had visited her in this home, drawing her to the study, why she'd manipulated Mattie – why the car wouldn't start. Like a demon she clicked the next email in the folder and forced herself to look at the defenceless children, victims that people like her husband and Caroline had preyed on. She was thankful that she didn't recognise any of them; some of their faces were obscured but the ones she could see were dazed or terrified. Her trembling fingers swarmed over the keyboard, like flies over shit. She scrolled down through the file names, one in the name of Bakersdozen with contributions – could that be Caroline? Yes. Another file labelled Shaz had photos sent just yesterday. Steve was in these; she could see his wedding ring in one shot. Julia's stomach turned again as she viewed the pictures of her husband with the doped-up teenager. And dear God, one email was from his own father, who hadn't even used another email address. Had he also been involved in Suzanne's abduction and death? Julia's whole body shook, the enormity of what she saw spreading like an oil slick through already muddied waters. She didn't know how long she sat there, immobile, until the papers on the table stirred and she heard tyres crunching the drive.

44

"There's some sort of plastic cover here," Dylan said. He was about three feet down at the centre. "Uncle Tom! There's some plastic here..." he shouted over to the old man who was transporting the excavated soil by barrow to the bushes.

Tom glanced over. "Probably old foundations. Don't worry, I'll have a look."

"That will have to come out, Dylan," said Luke in a low voice. "Mrs Campbell said to clear all debris away. How far along does the plastic go?"

"Am not sure," panted the lad, his face red. "Jeez, I deserve a pint after this." He scraped away the soil as far as he could, exposing more of the dull, grimy covering.

"Let me help you." Luke rushed to uncover what appeared to be an oval-shaped mound, the sweat running down his chest under his jersey.

"It finishes here," Dylan said. "It's not very long."

Luke had uncovered another two feet. He knew he had to act before the old man came back. "Grab the end, will you, and I'll get this one – let's lift it out onto the top."

Frank had come to stand at the head of the depression, his eyes drawn to the plastic mound; his hand smoothing his hair suddenly paused.

"Hey, hang on a minute," he said. "I don't—"

Luke interjected, "God, I need a drink right now. Let's get this finished, Dylan, and we can go, alright?" He eyed Tom returning from the other side of the lawn. "Let's just get this out, grab the end on one, two—"

Frank's voice rose an octave. "Dad!"

45

"Julia?" Steve threw his keys down onto the mantle in the hallway. "Julia?" Louder this time, the demand bouncing off the bare walls and closed doors. He listened for any activity in the kitchen and, hearing nothing, walked to the sitting room. He could see the open study door across the room and the daylight streaming out of it. He walked over and stood at the doorway looking in.

His wife sat at the desk, facing his laptop. Her elbows were on the table, head in her hands, her hair plastered over her forehead and wet cheeks. Eyes red from crying bore into him as more tears fell.

He looked at her, taking in the situation, walked over to the window and closed it. He pulled the curtains to and picked up the paperweight on the desk, looking at it. "You're much happier when you're drunk, Julia."

Her eyes blazed with hatred as she stammered, "Y-y-you!" It was a groan of anguish.

"Me? What? What now, Julia?" He tossed the paperweight from one hand to the other. "You look like you've seen a ghost. Oh no, we did that one already, didn't we!" He put it back on the desk.

"You... are s-sick, Steven. You... monster!"

"Am I? Well, you should know all about monsters."

Julia shook her head and stood up, her hands clutched for support on the edge of the desk. "My father? You know about S..."

"Apparently you didn't take too well to it the first time. Fought him like he was the bogey man? Caroline told me. Not very nice when your daddy was only trying to teach you something."

"What…? No – San!" Her voice ran hoarse as her mind began to whirl.

"Dear deluded Julia. You must try to remember… when you were twelve and after that…" He laughed. "You really have been successful at blotting it all out. Or did you invent someone in your little brain, someone to offload *all that suffering* on? You have to know, you're just part of a process, as they all are. As I was." He gestured towards the laptop. "It's an exclusive club. An alternate lifestyle, if you will. You don't look so well, darling – come to Daddy for a hug. That's what I say to all my angels. How did you guess my password, by the way?"

Julia pulled herself up to standing, staring at her husband before her, his arms spread wide in a mock gesture of welcome. Her shoulders jerked back in a desperate attempt to reassert herself, trying to find a way to reverse what she'd just heard. She was struggling to breathe, heart pounding so hard she could hear it in her ears. The room spun around her as she tried to think. What was he saying? That she was the prisoner? Had she invented Suzanne somehow? No, she recalled the silver necklace she'd held that morning, the silver 'S' like a snake. Was she Suzanne? Had they changed her name? Her life see-sawed around her in flashing images. Steve was lying – he had to be. She couldn't focus on him for the darkening in the room. Her panic choked her. She was there again, in the black space, the thick smell of sandalwood enveloping everything. She tried to reason with each laboured breath. They'd found the necklace. She'd seen San. Her photograph was in the paper. Suzanne was real, but the pressure on her chest was crushing her and the dark around her told her she was in the box with its pain and fear. And now she remembered. Her father's rasp in the dark as he lay on top of her: "Be an angel… lie still…"

She was in her bed. No. The box: where she told herself to go whenever it happened. Where it was dark and she could feel nothing but the hard wooden sides. The box had to protect her because there was no-one to help her. She remembered mustering a call for help, but her father had put his hand over her mouth and nose, cutting off her air supply. She thought then she would die as the lack of oxygen brought her to the edge of consciousness while a pain sliced up into her abdomen and sheer terror engulfed her.

Julia gasped now, longing for release. Wishing for death rather than face this. As her hand fell away from her mouth and she started to scream in horror, Steve leaped around the table and punched her deep into her guts, taking the wind out of her. Julia dropped to the floor.

"You fucking whore! Do you think you're going to wreck my life? The only time you were ever any use was for a good shagging. You're pathetic. You can't even be a proper mother! Forcing me to hire nannies while you sit doing nothing all day. I am as tired being with you as you are with me, Julia." He turned back around to the laptop, leaving his wife crumpled on the floor. "I'm going for custody of the girls, and I will win; you don't have a chance."

Julia tried to regain her breath, making tiny wheezing noises while she struggled to get up onto her hands and knees.

"And if you don't like it, there's the door. And don't even think of going…" Steve went quiet as he stared at the screen. "What have you done?" he whispered. He began to tap the keys, his eyes darting about in the light from the screen. "What have you done?" he yelled.

While her heart screamed in torment and despair, the oxygen seeped past her contorted lips and the room came back into focus as she pulled herself into a crawling position. Her voice was hoarse but determined: "D-did you think I would let you just carry on, Steve? Let you hide the laptop away somewhere, rub me out and take the girls?"

She staggered to her feet, her voice getting stronger. "Carry on your… disgusting habits with that bitch who dared take my family's name? You're the scum of the earth, Steve – you, Caroline, your father; you are all going down. I sent those emails to the *Herald*…" She rejoiced at his flushed and sweating face as he tapped wildly on the keyboard, his eyes wide, mouth open.

"Don't bother trying to retrieve them. In the time it took you to get out of your car and walk in here, Mike already replied to the first one. It's you who has no chance. Right now, the garden is being dug up at Carrick House. They killed a girl! After they used her – but you know, of course… all these disgusting things you consider normal." She registered his shock but didn't stop. "It's over. For all of you, you sick bastard!" She gulped back tears. "My girls will be protected. You're going to jail, you filthy pervert!"

Julia had begun to stumble away, but Steve roared and, rising out of his seat, grabbed her by the neck and shoved her against the wall.

•

"Three!"

Between them the plastic package came up with a sudden release and they dumped it onto the edge of the bed they'd dug out.

"What the hell?" exclaimed Tom, rushing the last few steps.

"It's the plastic. I just told you." Dylan looked back at the hole. "Is that deep enough? Can we go now?" Nobody answered and he turned to see the three men staring at the long black shape lying before them. "What's up with you lot?"

"I hope that's a dog, but I sure don't like the look of it." Tom grimaced.

"Me neither," Luke said, but deep down he felt relieved for Julia. If this was poor Suzanne then uncovering her skeleton would free both of them. He hunkered down and his hands went towards the plastic.

"Are you crazy, lad?" the old man said. "You and I both know what that could be." His eyes narrowed. "Did you know it was there all along?"

"No."

"Shit, I was right!" Frank's acid voice cut through. "Have you just used us to dig up a body? Doesn't that make us… an accessory or something?"

"No way," Luke said, holding his hands up. "Calm down. I don't know what this is. That's what we're going to find out."

"Here," Tom said, handing Luke his gardening gloves. "Put these on…"

Luke could see the logic in that.

"Thanks."

46

Julia stared into eyes that blazed with hatred as Steve's hands tightened around her throat. Lights flashed in front of her and her husband's face blurred. Her hands beat against his chest and pushed against him, but he didn't even feel it. She struggled to think as the panic and lack of air began to take over. Her hands came up and she clawed the side of his face, but he just tightened his grip on her. She remembered her knee and brought it up as hard as she could into his groin and it was his turn to double over.

She staggered to the side towards the door, but he stuck out his leg, tripping her up. As he moved past the desk, he grabbed something off it before lunging onto her. She twisted round to fight him off, but he pinned her down at her midriff. He held the short, spiked chrome letter opener to her throat. Julia closed her eyes for a moment and reopened them, staring straight at him.

"I am your children's mother," she said through gritted teeth. "You have to stop."

"You can't be their mother when you're dead—" he began but stopped, stunned, as a book crashed into his forehead.

Julia saw from her place on the floor, pieces of paper rising into the air from the desk and moving across the ceiling. There was a bang as another book flew overhead and hit the desk. More books began to hurtle from the shelves across the room, their pages being torn from them as they flew. As Steve staggered up, ducking and batting at the missiles as they came towards him, she scrambled to the space under the desk between the pedestals.

"What the fuck is this?" Steve looked mesmerised at all the pages and books which began to move faster and faster around the room in random directions. He dodged the paperweight that flew past and thudded into the wall against which he'd just tried to strangle his wife. He watched, stupefied, as the heavy glass orb rushed past him again to the other side of the room.

He began to edge towards the door, but it slammed shut and he saw the pens, pencils, staplers from the desk all rise and join the debris now moving clockwise round the room; the papers and books continued to be shredded as they flew. The air was full and he could no longer see the door, just a mass of moving junk. Steve's terror grew as he watched the bulk of it narrow into a cylindrical shape in front of him while a wind howled around it. He took a step towards where he knew the door to be but stopped horrified when a grey shape emerged out of the swirling detritus, a thing that was here and not here. The air chilled and the stink of decay filled the room.

Julia watched as her husband's eyes widened, his hand outstretched to ward Suzanne off. She heard him gasp.

"Julia, stop!"

He moved back as Suzanne advanced until he was against the wall, moaning like a baby. He realised he still held the letter opener and began to slash at her as she moved into arm's length, but the blade only dulled as it travelled through her grey form and out again and he whimpered as she came ever closer.

"No! No! Please! Please, Julia!"

Julia was unable to look away as the rushing wind stopped and the miasma of junk hung suspended in the centre of the room. She shivered as she heard the small figure implore, *"I'm your angel, Stephen. Come to me."*

Steve began to shriek in despair and Julia crouched, transfixed. She could see Suzanne was right up to him now; her slender arms seemed to be controlling his as she brought his hand holding the letter opener up to his face.

He was crying like a baby now and, even knowing what he was, Julia still felt some pity for him. She had to stop this.

"San!"

As she spoke she saw the quick jab of his hand to his own face. At once everything that had been airborne fell to the floor. Her husband stood alone, staring ahead at nothing, his fist held to his brow obscuring his left eye, the blood pouring down his face and neck like a deep red sash. He took a step before his body pitched forward and a piercing scream sliced through Julia's paralysis. She shrunk back under the desk as Caroline ran to where Steve fell, face down, further embedding the blade into his eye socket.

"Oh my God, Steve. Steve!" Caroline tried to turn Steve over. "Steve! Talk to me... Don't leave me. Oh, God, no!"

Julia wanted to tell Caroline of Suzanne approaching her from the shadows. She would have called out to her, but the words stuck in her throat. She watched as Caroline saw the two grey feet streaked with filth and congealed black blood advancing towards her. The woman whined like an animal and thrust herself backwards, hitting her head on the corner of the desk as the flotsam and jetsam of the study again took flight and whirled around the room in a howling wind. Caroline's head twitched right and left, trying to absorb what she was seeing, but always came back to Suzanne standing above Steve, arms outstretched, her eyes luminous with an unholy light and her lips drawn back in a snarl. Caroline dragged herself up and lunged for the door, but Suzanne was there before her, blocking her escape, and it seemed the speed of the flying missiles in the room increased. A book hit Caroline on the shoulder and her face was obscured by loose pages whipping around her. She pulled at them as she backed up.

The curtains tore from the rail and shredded, adding to the swirling wreckage. The sunlight flooding into the room gave depth to the spectre's pallid limbs and illuminated her ravaged face, full of rancour and revenge. The wind howled and screeched as it blasted the wreckage of the room about her as weapons. The laptop which had been jumping around on the desk pulled from its cable and hurtled into Caroline, catching her on the hip before crashing into the wall. She yelled in pain and spun round in confusion.

As Caroline made for the window Julia took a chance and ran for the door. She held her hands up as protection but the paperweight smashed into her forehead. She fell to the floor next to her husband, her vision blurring and darkening. She heard Caroline's piercing screams for mercy muffled now through the roaring wind that was Suzanne's wrath. Julia grasped at Steve's shirt, her waning consciousness still reaching out to the one person she'd believed for so long was in control. She slumped onto him, whispering, "Steve…" Pain and dizziness overtook her and she fell back, staring at the whirling wreckage above her.

From far away she registered the sound of the window shattering. In her dazed state she saw tiny glass crystals, like sprays of diamonds, shoot across the room. Weaker now, she registered a flash of hot, stinging punctures into the flesh of her hand and cheek as she closed her eyes.

·

Luke pulled back the encrusted tarpaulin. The remains of Suzanne Moore were a pathetic sight. Her tiny skeleton, still partly clad in the remnants of a dress or nightgown, lay facing one side, the limbs sprawled out of alignment; next to her was an indestructible teddy, its typical shape just discernible under the slime.

Tom choked back outrage. "Oh, God bless us! Oh my Lord—"

"Jesus, it's a kid!" Frank said, fascinated.

"You made me touch that!" Dylan said, staring at his hands.

"I'll call the police." Luke sighed and got to his feet. His relief at finding what they were looking for had dissolved into sadness for the victim and the pitiful end to her short, unacknowledged life. He took out his phone.

"Julie, come…"

The menacing voice pulled at her consciousness.

"Come with me now…"

Unwilling but unable to stop them, Julia's one eyelid flickered open and the other, hampered by the trail of gelling blood, pulled back to reveal Suzanne towering above her.

Her peripheral vision took in the moving walls of debris that had once been their study, encircling them.

I… can't, San. Julia's own voice seemed to float somewhere above them both.

"Together… now."

Julia tried to raise her arms in protestation but they were as heavy as lead.

My girls… they need me… She tried to move her head, but it stayed fast, as if held in a vice. Her own voice sounded weak or faraway; she could not decide.

"Friends forever, Julie." The soft words floated down to her from lips that didn't move but held a half smile.

No, San… please…

The eyes glowed. "I protected you."

I remember… you stopped him… Julia felt herself sob, or maybe she was dreaming. The tears spilled out and splashed onto her cupped hands in huge sparkling drops, but she knew that wasn't possible because her hands were trapped at her sides. *I think he saw you…*

The tears flowed fast now and she cried for the innocent she had been and the ultimate betrayal from her father; for Suzanne, cruelly denied a life, love or dignity; and the children she'd witnessed who had been used by vile creatures who were nothing more than parasites sucking life and hope from the helpless. Her cries melded with other times when she'd wept and there'd been a friend to comfort her and times when they'd made friends in a song. When her crying had become muted as if it was in another room, she felt herself smile.

Thank you, San… for being my friend. I'm sorry I forgot you…

"Friends always, Julie."

Yes…

San smiled and her eyes glinted.

Julia felt herself spiralling upward to *her* waiting at the top of the swirling, grey funnel. It was not unpleasant and she felt at peace as she moved closer and closer to her friend. It felt like floating in the water and she remembered her mother holding her in the sea, teaching her to swim, the salt on her lips and the sound of seagulls on the sea breeze; the breeze in her hair when Luke took her to Brighton on the back of his bike below the white popsicle clouds in the cornflower sky; Steve clowning around on the top of a float at the student rally and him holding her hand in front of the vicar with the promise of everlasting love and happiness. And her children; such gifts they brought to her life: joy and beauty, pain and meaning. She felt her heart clench. *Mattie, Grace, forgive me…*

The smell of the grave invaded her nostrils as San's mouth slowly lowered to hers. A wrench from her heart shook her now and she cried out, "Luke!" Her plea seemed to resonate all around her and faded, like a lost echo in a cave so deep and forgotten that time itself could not find it.

PART TWO

47

Once the police had confirmed the child's grave at Carrick House, they'd sent a unit to the Campbells' family home. Luke had been standing at the dig with two of the response unit when the message came through of a dead body found at Fir Close. He'd made an excuse and slipped out to the road where he'd moved his car and headed over to Julia's house as fast as he could.

At the gate, he'd joined the small crowd of neighbours and a couple of journalists hoping to get the scoop. One dead, one injured, he heard, and one missing. Speculation was soaring; wasn't this the home seat of the Carrick Foundation and Campbell Construction? Hadn't there been an event that very day hosted by the charity?

Luke only cared about Julia.

He tried to enter but was stopped by the policeman on the gate, another joining him for support.

"Officer. I am a close friend of the family. Please let me through."

The officer shook his head. "We must ask you to stay back, please, Sir, while we conduct our search. It's for everyone's protection."

"Can you tell me then, is Julia Campbell alright? Is she alive?" Luke tried to keep the panic out of his voice.

"I cannot confirm any information at this point, Sir. Please move back." The other officer shouted at the journalists who were trying to photograph the house.

Luke started to assess the border of the property to see if he could sneak in some way when he felt someone touch his arm. He turned to see a worried-looking older lady with white hair retracting her hand in embarrassment.

"Do you know Julia?" she asked quietly.

When Luke hesitated, she continued, "I'm looking after her children, I—"

"Are you Rowena?"

She looked relieved. "Yes."

"I'm Luke, an old friend. Julia contacted me recently to help her. Do you know what's happened?"

Row shook her head. "Something terrible. That's Steve's car and Caroline's over there, so they were all inside, I think…"

A flurry from the journalists alerted Luke to activity at the front door. A body bag with its occupant was being brought out on a stretcher.

"Oh my goodness!" said Row, stifling a sob.

Luke put his arm around her. "Don't worry, that's not her, she's much smaller than that." Luke squeezed Row's shoulder to reassure her.

"I shouldn't have left her today, but she wanted the children out of the way. She wouldn't say why – I should have pressed her." She sniffed. "Do you think they've been burgled, or maybe they had a row?"

"I would say they've most likely had a row," said Luke. "Was her husband a violent man?"

"Good heavens, no. I didn't like him, but he was a well-respected, upstanding member of the community. I doubt he would ever lift a finger against any woman."

Luke reserved judgement.

A sudden surge forward of the journalists took their attention. The cameras flashed while Luke saw Julia being led out of the house by a female officer. She was leaning heavily on the officer's arm. He could see saw a massive cut on her forehead, blood on her hands and blouse. She was so pale and her wide, staring eyes were red-rimmed.

Her hair looked scraggy and dishevelled. She stared straight ahead and didn't notice her sleeve snagging on a rose bush as the officer walked her to the police car.

"Julia!"

The policeman at the gate snapped to attention. "Right, Sir, just stay back, please. Everyone, move back from the gate. Let the team do their job."

"Julia!" Luke shouted again.

The female officer supporting Julia looked over at him, but Julia did not even flinch. The officer was still looking at him as she helped Julia into the car.

48

The light bounced off the tiles in the sparse room like mini searchlights.

She touched the steri-strips on her forehead, wincing a little as she did so. Elizabeth Strawson, sitting next to her, noticed the move but said nothing.

DCI Devon scowled at her. "You expect us to believe that your struggles caused that mess back there? There isn't a book that hasn't been torn to shreds."

She looked at the table, impassive.

"Where's Caroline Allbright?" Devon continued. "Why would she leave her car on the drive if she was making a getaway? Mrs Campbell?"

"I don't know."

"Did you do it together?" he persisted.

DS Blakely looked up from her note-taking.

"You see, I don't understand how someone can fall onto a knife in a way that so conveniently hits the mark," he said.

Strawson interjected, "I must remind you my client herself has suffered an attack in this incident, Inspector."

"And I must remind you to be quiet, Ms Strawson. How do you know so much about the child found at Carrick House, Julia?"

He looked at Blakely and she began reading from her notes. "Er, thirteen-year-old daughter of Sheila Moore, 29 Raffles Road, Brinnington, abducted during a day out in Blackpool on September the fifth, 1977, by Micah Wozniak in league with the Allbrights…"

Devon tapped his pen rapidly on the table. "Micah Wozniak, recently deceased, in a car crash involving you, Mrs Campbell."

She said nothing and Devon continued, "You couldn't possibly know these details unless such information was shared with you by the Allbrights. How long have you known?"

He paused as she continued to stare at the table.

"No comment," she mumbled.

"I don't know about you, but I'm tired of this, Mrs Campbell—"

"I don't feel well," she said as she began to slide off her chair.

Strawson caught her around the shoulders. "Inspector, as you can see, my client needs a break. She's been here the best part of nine hours. Perhaps you could allow her to stay with her children? She's clearly not capable of going anywhere. Unless you're going to charge her…?"

Devon blanked her as he stood up. "Blakely…"

The two left the room as Strawson made her charge sip some water.

Minutes later Blakely returned. "Mrs Campbell can go to Rowena Silver's house but she's not allowed to leave there until she is collected tomorrow morning. In the meantime, she can pick up her things at the desk."

"Come on," Strawson urged as she stood up. "Before he changes his mind."

She rose with care, steadying herself with a hand on the table. She was so very tired. Her brain felt like sludge. She couldn't remember anything, just noise and screams and the terrible mess, then nothing. Now she was here, being asked questions she didn't know how to answer. She felt like she'd lost something important and she should be looking for it. At the same time, she just wanted to sleep.

At the counter she was given the handbag. She began to check inside.

"What is it, Julia?"

"I… I can't find it."

"If it's your phone, the police will keep it while they continue their investigations. I warned you of this," Strawson said.

"No, it's… they… don't need it." She was dumping the purse, lipsticks and keys onto the counter along with receipts and a bottle of perfume, a small hairbrush which dropped to the floor.

"What's missing?"

"They don't need it."

Strawson watched, interested, as did the policeman opposite.

When she stopped looking, Strawson helped her put the items back into the bag. "I think we need to get you to Mrs Silver's," she said.

She looked around her, bemused. She felt Strawson staring at her.

"Row Silver?" Strawson reiterated.

She closed her eyes for a moment, trying to clear her head. "Yes, Row," she said.

She started to rifle through the bag again, but Strawson took it from her.

"Come along now. Thank you, Officer," she said as they left the police station.

Strawson's patience gave way in the car as they pulled up outside Row's house and her charge had emptied the contents of the bag onto her lap and was scratching at the lining.

"Dammit, Julia! You'd better tell me what this is about or I won't be representing you."

She stopped. She looked at the woman who'd helped the Campbell family out of so many scrapes. "I'm sorry… Helen. I don't know what's wrong with me. I just feel so tired and strung out."

Strawson put her hand on the woman's arm. "Listen, your kids are most likely in bed, but Row is expecting you. I called her when you went to the ladies'. Go get some sleep, for God's sake, and I'll call you in the morning. We need to talk."

"Thank you, Helen. You've been so good to me tonight. So kind."

"Just doing my job, Julia," Strawson said, a quizzical look on her face.

Again, Strawson helped her put everything back into the bag and watched the dazed woman slowly open the door and drag herself up out of the seat. Row Silver was there to lead her into the house.

49

In the hallway she submitted to Row's tight hug.

"Julia, you poor thing. What on earth has happened?"

Her arms came up to embrace the older lady. She felt Row rubbing her back.

"My God, was it necessary for them to keep you so long? You're exhausted! Let me see you…"

Row tucked back the long hair that threatened to obscure Julia's pale face.

"You need some hot food and drink, my dear. Come into the sitting room, it's nice and warm there. Goodness, your hands are cold! Those bloody police! Never there when you need them and all over you when you don't! Come on in here… sit down. Pull that blanket over you, love. I'm going to heat up some tomato soup for you. It will warm you up nicely."

"No! I don't like that," she said. Her own voice sounded small and tinny. "I… Do you have any hot chocolate?"

"It's the same soup we make every year, love…"

Row didn't receive a response to this, only a smile.

"Of course, hot chocolate it is. I'll be back in two ticks," Row said.

She watched Row hurry out of the room then she looked down at her red chapped hands, or were those red stains? No, they'd let her wash her hands after they'd swabbed her. Once they had all their samples and had taken her blood-soaked top, they'd let her freshen up, but it had taken hours. Hours of questions and prodding and poking, and now, here in this house, more questions. She could see them behind the old woman's eyes: who was dead? Why was Caroline's car on the drive and where was she?

She didn't want to answer any more questions and didn't even care. She picked up the handbag and emptied it out onto the carpet, then she scoured the inside, scraping it with her nails to see if this bag had a hole in the lining or one of those secret inner pockets.

Row returned with the hot drink. She put it down on the table and put her hand on the younger woman's knee.

"What have you lost, dear? Can I help you?"

"My necklace…"

Failing to find anything in the bag, she threw it down, distraught.

"Don't worry, dear. What does it look like?" Row started to put all the bits and pieces back into the bag.

She stared at the muted TV till she realised she'd been asked another question. Her eyes came back to Row, who was handing her the drink.

Row sat opposite, her hands clasped together on her lap.

"There was a man asking after you… at your house. His name was Mr Crawford?"

She heard the words as if from far away.

"Luke? Luke Crawford? He said you were old friends – I think he must be the Luke you spoke about so often to me, I—"

"What did he want?"

"Well… what we all want… to know you're OK. Perhaps you'd like to call him just to let him know? I did take his number and I gave him this address. I hope I didn't do wrong?"

After a pause Row pressed on. "What happened, Julia? I saw Caroline's c—"

"I want that fucking bitch sorted!" She saw Row's stunned expression and realised she'd yelled. She noticed she was sitting forward in her seat, every muscle clenched as if she was about to hit somebody. She breathed out and sat back a little.

Row was upset. She put down her own drink and reached for a tissue from a box on the table.

"Julia, my love! You've spilled..." Row dabbed at the liquid chocolate soaking into the sleeve of the cheap fleece the officer had given her to wear. "Something awful has happened, hasn't it? Please tell me. I know you hated Caroline. Has she done something? I hate to see you so upset—"

"Steve's dead."

Row nodded. "I'm so sorry, my dear. He was a... good father, a—"

"No, he wasn't." She'd stood up. "I think I'll take the hot chocolate upstairs, if you don't mind. I want to lie down."

"Of course, love."

She felt the older woman hovering behind her as she headed for the stairs; fussing and fawning, she was, and telling her to get some rest.

"It's my room," Row said. "The second bedroom on the left. I've put you in with your girls."

"That's fine. I just need to close my eyes, I think." She looked back, saw the older woman's worried expression and smiled. "I'll be right as rain tomorrow."

Row had stopped at the foot of the stairway looking like she might reply then her arms came up to cross her chest and she rubbed her upper arms as if to ward off the cold.

50

Inside the bedroom she stood over the sleeping child, watching the rise and fall of her small chest. Her hands reached out to the young girl's neck.

She peeled back the nightgown collar. A smile broke through, dissolving the rigid scowl she'd held all day.

There it was! It hadn't been in the bag because it had been given to the child. The silver 'S' beckoned and she reached down and undid the clasp. As she pulled it from around the child's throat Mattie stirred, turning over in the bed, her little hand slipping through the crook of Julia's arm. The chain now loose and in her possession, she shrugged off the child's hand and walked to the mirror to fix it around her own throat.

Her eyes shone as she rubbed the silver 'S' with her thumb. Then she turned and walked to the corner of the room, picked up a travel bag hanging on an old rocking chair and proceeded to fill it with leggings and socks from the chest of drawers.

·

She slept four hours. On waking, she lay there, making plans. Once accustomed to the dark, she rose and pulled on the socks, jeans and jersey she'd left out then took the daisy chain from the bag and wrapped it around the bottom of her plaited hair. She emptied the purse into her pocket and without a glance at the two children sleeping in the little camp-bed she left the room and crept down the stairs.

In the cloakroom she was going to put on the same light shoes she'd arrived in, but seeing some hardy-looking walking boots she picked one up to investigate. It looked about the same size as her own shoe, but these would keep her feet far warmer, she thought. She put the boots on, double-tying the laces. She took down a hefty winter coat and put it on, checking the pockets for money without success. After shoving some mittens into the travel bag, she searched the rest of the coats for cash and, finding none, moved to the sitting room to Row's handbag tucked between the side of the chair and the wall. The purse held sixty-five pounds in notes and three pounds in coins. She took it all and added it to the ten pounds from her own purse. A creak on the floor above her caused her to pause. Had she been too noisy? She held her ground until no further sounds emanated from the floor above before moving as quiet as a shadow to the kitchen.

She went straight for the breadbin and grabbed two rolls, which she sliced open and filled with some ham and tomato from the fridge, foregoing the butter. She shoved the rolls loose into a plastic bag with a whole packet of biscuits, cleaned the small kitchen knife she'd used and placed it in an inner pocket of the travel bag, all the while listening for more creaks overhead. She left the house via the back door, closing it softly behind her.

51

Luke blew on his hands some more, the sun through the windscreen bringing no warmth at all and the old heater taking time to warm up now the engine was running. He had a crick in his neck from his sleeping position in the front seat. Well, sleeping was a strong word; he'd dozed on and off through the cold night, snuggling deeper and deeper into his sleeping bag – grateful he always kept one in the car for dawn photoshoots but even though he'd been warm enough he just couldn't stop thinking about her and what she must be going through.

He'd established Steve was dead. It was handy being an ex-journalist – you still had your contacts. The details of how were sketchy, though. Stabbed, he'd been told. By who? Julia surely wasn't capable of that. Caroline then? What the hell had happened? No doubt they would be questioning Julia as the main suspect, but perhaps they'd let her out last night? He fished for his phone and dialled the number he'd entered only yesterday at the gate to her house. He realised how early it was and was about to ring off when someone picked up.

"Hello, Rowena Silver."

"Mrs Silver. Hi, I'm sorry to bother you at the crack of dawn. It's Luke here, Luke Crawford. We met yesterday at the… at her house."

"Oh! Er… Mr Crawford, I did tell Julia about you, but she was very, tired. Exhausted, in fact."

"So she's there? Can I speak to her, please? I mean, if she's up."

"Oh! Mr Crawford…"

Row's voice broke and Luke waited while she composed herself. He heard her blowing her nose.

"Mrs Silver, are you OK? Is Julia alright? Look, I'm sorry for intruding, but I just need to know she's alright."

"She's not here."

"What do you mean? Did she stay with you last night?"

"Yes," said Row. "But she must have risen early and I didn't hear her. We went to bed late and I slept right through. I was hoping she'd just gone for a walk or even met you somewhere. I hope she will turn up soon because… well, what will the police say? They're coming to pick her up this morning!" Row's last words ended in a sob. "It's all my fault. I was looking after her."

"Wait a minute, it's not your fault at all. Can I come over, Mrs Silver?"

Row gulped her tears down. "Yes, do come round."

"OK, I'll be there soon. Don't worry. She's probably not far."

Luke closed the screen and looked out at the silvery sunlight spreading over the lawns. He hoped he was right.

The First Ride

The driver of the blue Renault had a voice like an electric saw; every word uttered chafed my brain.

"So I just stood there, yeah! Like a bleedin' idiot. Couldn't believe what I was seein', like! You effin' bastard, I screamed at him, and she just turned round and smiled at me! She didn't even try to cover up or nuffink!"

She was in her element describing her fight with her boyfriend, rolling her eyes at me every now and then while she drove. She had been going on about it for at least half an hour and I was bored.

"What did he do?" I asked her.

"Eh?"

"What did he do next?" She was one sandwich short of a picnic, this one.

"Oh, he just started chattin' shit, like, oh, babe, she don't mean nuffink, y'know! I swear I just lost it, y'know! I picked up the first thing – a photo of us in Brighton – and I just threw it at 'em. So the corner of it caught the tart on the arse – drew blood as well. There was a lot of yelling then, I can tell yer. Wiped that smug smile right off her weasely face."

She looked at me for a reaction but was disappointed.

"That ever 'appen to you?"

I really didn't want to talk about me. I shook my head and replied, "I don't have a boyfriend or a husband."

I felt a throbbing in my head and I think I spent some time checking out my steri-strips in the mirror in the visor. Isn't the body amazing with its constant attention-seeking, announcing what it wants and feels every minute – like a spoiled child.

More than the throbbing head, though, was a gnawing hunger. I had the rolls I'd robbed from Row's, but I wanted something hot to eat – and a drink. God, I was thirsty.

She asked me what had happened to my head, but I just gave her a look.

She was offended. "Just checkin' you're alright," she said.

"I'm fine," I said, and smiled. "If I were you, I would have killed her."

The driver laughed. "What?"

I faced her then. "That girl you found shagging your husband."

"Yeah right! I felt like it!"

"I would have smashed her head in with that door stop you always trip over."

She shot me a look, her mouth hanging open. I tried not to laugh as she turned her attention back to the road, clearly uncomfortable. What would she say now, I wondered?

"How do you…?" she asked me.

"Just a lucky guess," I said. "I would have smashed her head till it was jam."

My driver was worried now. After a silent moment or five, she reached forward and put the radio on. When she found her voice again it was brief and exactly what I wanted to hear.

"I'm starvin'. I think we'll stop at the next services."

52

Luke shifted from foot to foot on Row Silver's doorstep trying to keep warm. The door opened to the old friend of Julia's looking more troubled than yesterday. She was frowning at him.

"My goodness, that was quick!"

"Yeah, well… I phoned you from my car, Mrs Silver – in the next street," Luke said, almost embarrassed.

Row took in the hair sticking out here and there and the unshaven jaw. "Oh my! You'll be chittered!"

They both looked back at the police car at the gate and the young officer inside who was sleeping through his shift.

"Come in quickly, and do just call me Row."

Luke hung his coat and pulled off his shoes in the cloakroom before following her, past the sitting room from where the sound of cartoons and a child's singing emanated.

Row was putting the kettle on in the bright kitchen. "Sit down, Luke. She's still not back."

"What time did you discover she'd gone?"

"Around seven thirty. Last night, when she came back from the police station, she was in shock. You would expect that after such a horrific incident. Her husband was killed."

"I know. Do they think Julia did it?"

"They questioned her. It must have been gruelling. It was very late when the family solicitor brought her back here – Strawson, her name is. She phoned here this morning wanting to speak to her. I had to lie – to Helen. I said she was still sleeping. Now I think that wasn't such a good idea. Oh, goodness, I'm being so rude, sorry, would you like some toast or something to drink?"

"No toast – but tea will be great, thanks. That explains why I haven't heard from her. The police have likely taken her phone and I doubt she can remember my number." He paused. "There's more to this, I'm afraid. But I think Julia should tell you. So you don't think she's just gone for a walk then?"

"I'm not sure, Luke – may I call you Luke?"

"Sure."

"She's taken money from my purse. I don't know why she would do that – she has access to much more than I. She didn't take my debit card, though, even with the pin number tucked behind it. I know I shouldn't do that, but I just can't remember all these silly codes and passwords."

Row retrieved the milk from the fridge and put it on the table.

"If she really needed money, she could have just asked – she didn't even leave me a note. Not one word to say I've just borrowed some money, Row, but will pay you back soon, that type of thing. It's not like her – she knows I would give her anything she asked of me. She's also taken my coat and a couple of jerseys – I only noticed because she left a drawer open, and she might have taken my travel bag. I'm sure I left it in the wardrobe, but when I saw how she'd helped herself to my clothes I checked and I can't find it—"

"She never said anything last night about how she was feeling or what she intended to do?"

"She said very little, but she did vent her anger over Caroline, rather crudely, in fact. It was so awful to see her in such a state."

Luke took a breath. "I think I should tell you then… It's not good news, Row… They found a body at Carrick House – of a child."

Row was ashen. "A child? Who? Who is it?"

Luke moved to Row, taking the cup out of her hand. "Here, why don't I do that and you sit down?"

Row walked to the chair and sat, plainly glad for the support it afforded.

"Who's that, Aunty Row?"

Row and Luke turned to the door. Mattie stood there, one hand on the door handle, the other pulling at her hair. She was staring at Luke, wary.

"Mattie, dear, this is Mr Crawford, a friend of your mummy's."

"Hello, Mr Crawford."

Luke stared at her. "Hello, Mattie," he said after some time.

"What is it, dear?" asked Row.

"Can we have some biscuits, please?"

Row smiled. "I don't think your mummy would allow that so early, but I do have some fruity yoghurts. Would you like one of those?"

"Yes, please," Mattie said, walking self-consciously to the fridge.

"They're on the top shelf. Just one each, mind. Luke, would you give Mattie two teaspoons from the drawer, please?"

They watched as the child, shy and reserved, took the teaspoons from Luke and skipped out of the kitchen, hugging the goodies to her chest.

"She looks like her mother, doesn't she?"

"So much," said Luke.

"I can't believe what you're telling me, Luke," she said sadly.

Luke poured the water into the mugs and faced her, his voice soft as he continued, "It was the body of an abducted girl. It appears John Allbright, Caroline and the grandmother were all involved—"

"Old Annie Allbright? Surely not. Oh my goodness. This cannot be…"

Luke put the mugs and sugar bowl down before her and patted her shoulder before sitting opposite.

"Oh, dear Lord!" Row continued. "Oh my…! Poor darling. The shock of it all, no wonder – what can we do to help her, Luke?"

"Right now, you're doing the best thing to help her by looking after her kids. If you can keep doing that, I know she'll be so grateful. She'll just want them to be safe."

"Of course – but will the police allow me to?"

"I don't know – you should deny any connection to Annie,

Caroline or John Allbright if they ask you. Did she take her handbag then?"

Row shook her head. "No, and her keys are still here, but she couldn't get to her house or car anyway, there's a policeman outside the property – I phoned her neighbour. That's the advantage of living here so long. I have everyone's number…"

"What will you tell the police when they arrive?"

"I… I'll have to tell them the truth."

Luke finished making the tea.

"Put two sugars in mine, please, Luke."

"It's OK. You must. You don't want to appear to be abetting a possible criminal. It's imperative you prioritise the children."

"Those poor little mites…"

"Listen, Row, you must be strong and adamant about your innocence. Call Strawson back and tell her Julia's gone, but give it an hour or so. Tell her everything you know if they question you – you can't hurt Julia by doing that. If they want to search the house, let them. They'll want to make sure you're a safe house for the children."

Row's hand wobbled as she lifted her cup. She put it down quick as the tea spilled onto the table. "I'll do everything I can to hold on to those little girls."

Luke gulped his drink, savouring the warmth coursing through his thawing body. "Let me know if she returns or you get any update from the police. I imagine they'll put out a search for her if she doesn't show up soon," Luke said. He put a hand on hers. "Try not to worry."

Row smiled back at him but looked like she would dissolve into tears. They sat in silence. Row took some deep breaths.

Luke finished his tea. "I'm going to drive around. Perhaps she's heading to Carrick…"

"Why would she go there?"

"She is drawn to that place and I can't think where else she would go. Don't get up, I'll let myself out. I'll get her back, I promise."

Row could only nod her head in response.

There was an officer leaning against his car at the scene of the crime; the house remained cordoned off. All three cars of the family were still in the drive. The policeman cast a cursory glance as Luke drove past him in as relaxed a fashion as he could muster and headed towards Carrick House. His eyes sought every bus stop and sidewalk, looking for her familiar dark hair and slight frame. If she reached Carrick she would probably be arrested. He'd heard one of the police team at the scene yesterday suggesting the whole lawn might have to be dug up in case there were other bodies. This was so much bigger than they'd anticipated. He could imagine the tabloids would be full of it soon: 'Charity Bosses and the House of Hell', 'Murder at Home Seats of Children's Charity Perverts' – Luke felt a pang of dread for Julia, knowing she would take the brunt of this. When would it be over for her? It would take years – even if she moved away and changed her name. And what about the mental scars? How do you forgive your father when you find out he was a perverted murderer? His resolve to help her strengthened, but first he had to find her.

Burger and Chips

It was around nine thirty when we pulled into the parking area of the Watford Gap Service Station.

My driver practically jumped out of the car like she hadn't eaten in days.

I felt stiff all over as I got out; it was wonderful to stretch and breathe the cold fresh air after the stifling dog smell in her car. I took my coat and travel bag with me and followed her in through the big glass doors.

She asked me if I needed the lav. I didn't. The smell of the café drew me to it as she went to the ladies', the plan being to meet back in the foyer in ten minutes.

I had just walked into the café when who do you think I saw through the window getting into her car? That's right – she of the chainsaw voice. So, there'd be no meeting her in ten minutes then. I knew it anyway, but it was disappointing that she lived up to my expectations, reversing out of the parking bay as fast as she could.

Typical of such a spineless slag. Stupid cow!

I walked right up to the window to get a better view. The Renault paused at the exit of the car park as I concentrated. It just needed the right amount of focus to hold her there. It took a while for the HGV to show up, like a graceful mammoth, and I released her to it. As in a gruesome pas de deux she pulled out to greet the huge thing. The truck scooped up the tiny Renault and shoved it into the bank, mashing it against the concrete retainer.

It wasn't that I thought she was evil or that she deserved it for ditching me – it was more that she irritated me shitless and my hunger was making me disagreeable.

The bang from the collision easily reached the patrons of the Burger King. Some of them stood up, craning their heads to see what had happened, their meals forgotten on the table and some left the queue. I took the opportunity to move nearer to the front. While I waited, I watched a young girl next to me playing on a small TV screen.

"Put that phone away," her mother said to her, but the child ignored her, of course.

I think I was as entranced with the little coloured jewels as she was.

The manager of the takeaway took charge of his team, chivvying them on with cautions of targets to meet and promises of bonuses.

Soon it was my turn. My belly was rumbling.

"Can I have a burger with cheese, please?" I asked the spotty attendant.

"Do you want chips with that?" he intoned.

"Yes, please... and a Coke."

"Large or medium?"

"Large."

"To eat in or take away?"

"Yes, to eat in here."

The tray was clattered down onto the counter and a burger grabbed from a heated shelf behind slapped down onto it. The youth strolled over to the large vat, where some fresh, fried chips had been deposited, scooped a portion and dropped them into a pre-made carton on the side. A person on the drinks machine leaned over and put a Coke in a huge cardboard cup onto the same tray.

"Do you want ketchup?"

"Er, yes."

"Two ninety-nine, please," he said, dropping a couple of sachets next to the chips.

It took me a while to work out the shiny smaller coins were one-pound ones – very strange. I wondered where Row had got them, but I counted out the right amount and put it in his hand. I thanked him as he deposited it into the till, but he ignored me.

I chose a seat by the window so I could see what was happening. I could hear sirens from emergency services in the distance now as I opened the burger wrapper with anticipation. The smell was fantastic and my mouth was watering. The first bite of it was a moment in heaven: salts and sugars of the rich meat juices triggering multiple sensations in my mouth and brain; I almost groaned out loud. I shoved another bite in my mouth while I emptied salt all over the chips till they were dressed in a fine white blanket. It was so good – like the best burger I ever tasted. The chips went down well too, the salt crackling on my taste buds as I rolled them round my mouth before biting down with pleasure into soft potato explosion.

An old man sitting on the table next to me smiled, but I didn't smile back.

I watched the emergency crew assemble their machinery, ready to cut the driver out of the Renault. The car park was filling up with people either watching the rescue or coming in for breakfast: tired parents and energetic kids, salesmen on their way to their next pitch, truck drivers, moving down the car park lanes like tributaries from a river, filtering into the complex entrance, looking forward to a break from the road.

I pushed the straw into the beaker and took a big sip, gasping as the bubbles seemed to get up my nose and the sugar excited my blood. There's nothing better when you're enjoying a meal and you still have plenty of it. I can still remember that salty grease on my lips now – in fact, I bet I could eat another one and it was only two hours ago.

When it was finished, I grabbed my bag and tray of remains and headed out. At the exit, a TV screen caught my attention: a man leaving an official-looking building and getting into a taxi. The words below said: Mark Cavendish, sixty-two-year-old caretaker released on bail after being charged with twenty-nine alleged counts of sexual abuse on underage residents at Marsden Centre.

I watched the close-up of the man. He looked so like someone I'd come to hate but rougher, more twisted… the same name, Mark Cavendish, the same children's home.

The screen had moved on to the next headline. I looked around, but nobody was watching me. Feeling a bit sick now, I put my wrappers in the bin and moved into the foyer. I had to take a few minutes' rest against the wall, watching the travellers pass by.

Everyone looked so different in this town. Clothes seemed brighter and more interesting. Some people had wires about their necks or headphones on; even some of the children and many of the adults had their own phones. Shop windows were full of stuff I hadn't seen before. There was so much to take in. My curiosity got the better of me and I strolled over to a general supplies shop which had a colourful display of teddies at the entrance.

I picked up a pink one. It was so soft, like Kas's cheek. I knew she would love it. I held on to it and wandered further into the store entranced by the huge selection of sweets in bright, vivid wrappers.

I love chocolate. Some names I recognised, but they had a big selection and there was a lot of stuff that was new to me. I took some Mars Bars, Cadbury's Flake, a packet of Buttons and a Twix. I grabbed a packet of Oreo biscuits as well plus two packets of crisps and two cans of Coke. I nearly bought a glossy magazine, but it was too expensive. I remembered in time that I have to be careful with money. I chose a cheaper magazine instead but was still shocked when the till lady asked for fifteen pounds forty. I didn't want to put anything back, though, least of all the teddy. I paid the money and put all the gear in the travel bag.

I was going to the ladies' toilet at the back of the complex when I came to an arcade full of noisy, colourful slot machines. I found myself standing by two teenage boys playing on a bike-riding game. The smaller of the two was sitting on a copy of a bike which rocked back and forth and side to side, and I could see its movement was linked up to the screen. It was fantastic and I got all fired up watching the boy struggling to stay on track while increasing his speed.

Before I could stop myself I asked him if I could have a go.

Then the bigger boy said a really weird thing. He sneered at me and said, "You're too big for it, you daft cow."

I don't know why he said such a thing because he was the same height *as me. I remember thinking, you cheeky little shit, but then I caught sight of my reflection in the black glass case of the game next to it. I think it was my coat that made me look so bulky, but what was really scary was my face. It was blurred, and when I moved, the blurred face stayed with me.*

I hurried to the toilet after that. I didn't even wash my hands afterwards. Couldn't wait to get out of there...

53

Luke stood hidden in a shop doorway. From there he could see the entrance to his flat and the two police cars parked outside. He took out his phone and called Row.

"Hello, Row. It's Luke."

"Have you found her?"

"No. She can't be at Carrick because I can't get near it. It's covered in white coats, inside and out. They're digging up the entire garden at Carrick."

"Oh, Luke, I'm getting in such a muddle. I had to tell Mrs Strawson that Julia was not here and she said when the police find out she's gone they're likely to question the children. I'm so afraid I might lose them. She was so unkind. That woman is as hard as nails."

"Don't let her bully you, Row. Just tell everyone she's been gone since early morning."

"She said the longer Julia is absent the more her actions implicate her – and she's right!"

Luke sighed. "I know, but if you can mitigate it somehow…"

"I'm so worried they will think she's lost her mind and then the children really will be in danger of being put into care."

"That's where you can help. Tell them she was just tired and assure them she's just out for a walk. If they question why you waited to tell them, say you expected her back by now. Play dumb if needs be, whatever it takes."

"I could suggest her aunt's, in the Lakes, if they ask me... what do you think?"

"Do you think that's where she's gone?"

"No, Julia told me years ago she didn't know where the woman lived."

"Maybe. If they continue to hassle you, tell them you can't imagine her going anywhere but the one possible place is her aunt's; let them spend the time following it up. It will give us more time, I hope."

"I can't stop worrying about her. She was just not herself. She didn't like her favourite soup... she didn't even recognise your name..."

"Well, we agreed she was probably in a state of shock..."

"Yes, but she didn't even ask about her girls. Surely they would have been her first priority after losing her husband and suffering such shocking revelations? The only thing she was worried about was that necklace that—"

"What?" Luke interrupted.

"A necklace. She and Mattie, both of them very upset about it. Mattie said she'd gone to bed wearing it but it was nowhere to be found this morning. She and Grace were yelling their heads off and that's what woke me. I do wonder if it's the same one that Julia was distressed about... I didn't notice Mattie wearing it when she went to bed – she must have hidden it from me. It's not safe to—"

"A silver necklace with an 'S' on it?"

"Er... well, Mattie said it was silver—"

"And you say Julia was upset?"

"Yes, near to tears."

"What were her exact words, Row?"

Row tried to remember. "Er, I said, what have you lost and she said, a necklace – well, my necklace, she said—"

"She said '*my* necklace'?"

"Yes. She was definitely acting like it was special to her. Is it important?"

"I think it is… Listen, I have to get rid of this phone. The police are outside my flat. I think they may want to invite me for lunch. They haven't seen me so I'm going to a friend's now, but they'll put a trace on my phone, so I won't be able to use it."

Row sounded panicky. "How will I reach you?"

"I've got your number, so I'll call you back from another when it's safe. I better warn you they'll see we've been in contact so there will be questions about what we've discussed. I've got an idea where she might have gone, Row."

"Please help her, Luke."

"Remember, tell them it's possible she's gone to her aunt's. Don't mention the necklace. Keep it together."

"I will."

Luke clicked off. He couldn't get near his car with the copper standing next to it. He was going to need cash first and foremost. He looked back up the high street from where he'd come. The majority of shops and cafés were only just opening up and more people were milling about. There was a taxi hire at the far end of the street. That would do. He pulled up his collar, waited for a couple of ladies to reach the doorway he stood at then joined them on their way up the high street, giving them a winning smile while he asked them the time.

Whatever it takes, he thought.

A Happy Family

It's half an hour ago since the family picked me up.

It wasn't that I hated them. It was more like, a little bit of jealousy. I mean, why do some people have it all and some have nothing? Nothing!

They picked me up on the slip road: Jack and Beth, a young couple. They were very encouraging and it had started to rain. As much as I was enjoying the raindrops on my face and the rainbow in front of me, they were going my way and I had to get on.

It was a silver Volvo. Jack smiled at me, said they were going to Manchester, M6 all the way – was that good for me? His wife waved at me from inside, so I knew it was safe.

Beth insisted I sit in the front. She wanted to shake my hand as part of the introduction, but I just smiled at her.

"Suzanne... just call me San."

"OK, do you want to put your bag in the boot or keep it with you, San?"

"I'll keep it."

"Have you been waiting long?" Jack asked.

I pulled the belt over my coat, trying to fix it into the socket. "About half an hour."

"Well, I think you're just in time..." He nodded his head to the windscreen where the fat splats of rain landed, the sky dimming as the clouds took over.

"Where you going?" asked Jack.

"Brinnington. But I think I can get a bus from anywhere near Stockport if you're going that way."

"I can take you close to there." He pulled onto the motorway as the rain lashed down onto the tarmac.

"We can take her on to Brinnies, love. It's only a couple of miles or so…" Beth smiled at me. "Providing Shauna behaves!"

I stretched round and saw their baby, fast asleep in a little baby car seat. Her round cheeks were flushed red, but even in sleep she was a beautiful child with soft brown downy hair and long black curling lashes.

"She's lovely."

Beth was bursting with pride, of course.

"Thanks, but she has her moments. She's teething right now and she can be a right little whiner."

"I remember… when my sister Kas was teething, her cheeks were red like that."

Beth looked at me, a frown on her face. "Yes… well, she's exhausted at the moment, we all are! Can't get a full night's sleep for love nor money, can we, Jack?"

Jack laughed and I thought at the time, obviously the lack of sleep hadn't affected his good nature.

"It's not her fault," he said. "Are you visiting someone in Brinnington, San, or is that home?"

"I don't live there anymore. I'm going to get Kas," I said.

"Forgive me for saying it, but you're not the usual type of hitchhiker."

"Jack…" Beth put a hand on his shoulder.

"Sorry, I just say it like it is. It's your shoes."

I looked at the old lady's expensive walking boots at the end of my legs. "I… my lift let me down and I have to get there today."

"Where have you hitched from?"

"Jack! Give it up, please. Just ignore him, San. Anything we can do to help. That's nice… seeing your sister. Has it been a long time since you saw her?"

"About two years."

"Oh yes, that's quite a while. I see my brother every week. Ooh, look who's waking up!"

I had to twist round again to see the baby opening her eyes. Beth took the child's tiny fist in her hand and started talking in a softer, higher voice. "Hey, sweetie, did you have a nice sleep?"

The baby's large eyes turned to me and I gave her a little wave. Shauna smiled at me and I felt a pain in my heart.

Beth was reaching into her bag and brought out a bottle of milk. "She likes you, San." Then she asked me a weird question. "Do you have kids?"

I just stared at her. Her smile was infuriating – like she was trying to catch me out. I just wanted her to shut up then, the nosy bitch. I looked past her, trying to erase her question in my head. I realised she was still yakking.

"She's our first… I found it all a bit harder than I expected, the motherhood thing, but my mum's helped us, hasn't she, Jack?"

Yak, yak, yak! I didn't want to listen to it. I thought for a moment I should maybe walk the rest of the way – even if it was in the rain. I twisted back around in my seat and stared out of the window. Fucking happy families all around me all going back to their fucking happy homes. Dimly I heard Jack speaking.

"She's been great. Family comes first, that's her motto… she's done so much for us."

Family comes first… family comes first.

I felt a sudden heaviness sweep over my eyes. I closed them.

"Are you alright, San?"

Over the rush of voices echoing in my brain I heard my own: nervous and high-pitched. "I… I'll have a sleep, I think." I could hear the unease in Beth's voice as exhaustion enveloped me.

"…Sure… I hope Shauna doesn't start creating… You rest up, San, and we…"

I'd fallen into a dark place.

54

Julia knew there was something important she'd forgotten but she couldn't remember what? Had she given the girls their dinner?

Had she cleared those leaves on the lawn? Steve got so mad when it looked messy – she didn't want to annoy him!

And the house! She had to finish packing up the house! It had to go on the market. Tom said he would only be two weeks. How long had it been?

Did she get that chicken out of the freezer for tonight?

Why couldn't she remember to do things? She was a rubbish wife. Steve expected his dinner ready when he came home.

Family comes first, that's what he'd said – and he was right! That's what makes us so strong, you see.

What did she have to do today? Something important…

They'd had an argument, she and Steve. Something about the children – she missed them so! But it was OK, Mum was looking after them.

This place was a mess… rubbish everywhere and so dark. Robot parts lying everywhere amongst the leaves… on the wooden floor…

She saw the back of the woman sweeping in the corner.

"Mum? What's happened? My little bots! Have they been fighting? Oh! Look at the tiny bits. This is my fault isn't it, this… wreckage… Oh God! I just forgot about them… I was busy. I forgot you too, Mum. I don't deserve you.

"A trail of waste wherever I go! Steve's right, I am a useless mother. What can I do to make it right? Help me make it right, Mum! Let's put them together again – our little bots! Look, here's an arm, and here's a hand. If we join them up – don't you see? We can fix them... so they won't be afraid anymore... wait! That's a headlight...?

"Mum? Where are you going? Please don't leave me, Mum – I have to put all these cars together. You have to help me, Mum, there's too many of them... We've got to do it – before the hurting starts..."

55

"Mum!" She jerked awake with such force the seatbelt tightened, pulling her back sharply.

Jack glanced at her but quickly resumed his focus on the road through the rain-soaked window.

"You alright? You went out like a light."

He glanced back at his dazed passenger as she wiped tears from her cheeks, looked at her wet palms and then at the window. So much water was being thrown up by all the cars and trucks, visibility was near zero.

"Stop the car," she said.

"What?"

"Stop the car now!"

"Right! OK, OK... Beth, can I go?"

Beth twisted round. "Wait! Not yet... there's no gap. San, I can give you a bag if you're going to be..."

"You've got to pull over now!" she shouted.

Beth twisted round. "Alright!" She tried to assess the traffic. Panic edging her voice, she shouted above her daughter's cries, "Wait, Jack... there's a space coming up, but you'll have to move fast. Get ready... now!"

Jack swung the car over. "Check again, Beth. I can't see a bloody thing." He glanced at San, who was staring out of the window, her eyes bulging in concentration. He looked away quickly.

"Go now, Jack, it's clear. Shush, sweetie – it's alright!" Beth wiped Shauna's face with a tissue and cooed at her to calm her down.

Jack pulled the car to a stop on the hard shoulder and put the hazards on. "I don't like this – it's bloody dangerous, San… San?"

She was staring out of the window still, like she was mesmerised by the swishing of the wipers as they tried in vain to clear water from the screen.

Jack's mouth twitched now in irritation. "Well, do you need to be sick or…"

Her gaze shifted to him and Jack would recount later to the police that for a millisecond he felt she was looking into his very soul before she said in a strange, child-like voice, "*Why've you stopped?*"

A massive bang erupted somewhere ahead of them then a squeal of brakes and a further bang.

"Christ almighty!" Jack's head jerked round and he peered through the waterfall rushing down the window.

Horns and alarms started to blare and cars zoomed by into what was fast becoming a collection of hazard lights in the thundering rain ahead. Two more bangs, then a third.

Jack's stare darted to his left. "Beth, get Shauna. We have to get out." Jack undid his belt as did San and checked in his side mirror before he opened his door. Whipped by the wind, he rushed round to the other side to help his wife and baby from the car. Beth was crying and Shauna was screaming at the top of her lungs. The shocking bangs and sickening crunches continued as more cars joined the pileup. Seizing the coats from the back shelf, he proceeded to push Beth up the hill, the two of them slipping and stumbling in their haste.

"Don't worry, you're OK up here." He helped his wife put Shauna's coat on her even while they kept moving. The rain, driven horizontal by the vicious wind, pelted them, getting in their eyes and plastering their hair to their faces. He helped his wife into her coat, tucking the baby inside.

"Keep going up," he said as he turned from her.

"Where're you going?" Beth grabbed Jack's arm.

"I'm going to warn them—"

"No, Jack, stay with us!"

"I've got to try and help somehow."

"*Here!*"

Jack half turned. San had his coat for him. She'd pulled up her own hood against the driving rain, her travel bag hung from her shoulder.

"Thanks." Jack donned the garment as quick as he could. "You stay here, San." He started to move down the slope amidst his wife's tearful protests and saw San following him. He shook his head at her, but she looked away and continued.

They had a good view of what was happening from there and could see the carnage at the centre of the northbound lanes which was spreading over the roadway like a hulking, black monster, securing its prey as more cars skid into the twisted metal hell with a hopeless screech of brakes and a deathly thud.

Jack whispered, "Oh my God, we would have been in that…" He rounded on San. "You knew, didn't you! You knew it was going to happen."

San stepped back from him, her eyes not leaving his.

"How?" he said.

An almighty squeal of brakes followed by a bone-scraping screech as a car collided with the central barrier galvanised Jack. He half slid down the hill and hit the tarmac, running away from the accident, towards the oncoming traffic. He waved his arms, trying to get the drivers' attention. The sudden appearance of him in the rain must have slowed many of the motorists if the look of panic on his face didn't. Jack yelled, gesturing frantically. Some of the cars put on their hazards and although the sickening bangs and crunches continued from those he'd been too late to warn, the cars ahead of Jack did start to slow down.

That's when Jack realised San was no longer with him. He turned to look for her but couldn't see her down the straight or up the hill. He saw Beth, alone up on the hillside, and turned tail suddenly, heading back.

56

DC Blakely couldn't understand it; Julia Campbell didn't look the type to run. She was learning to trust her hunches and she was usually right. This woman could not be a murderer, so why disappear? Blakely had felt sure she wouldn't leave her kids. So had Devon. Now they had to find her before the press got wind of it – and the super.

Blakely had an update ready for the chief, but he wasn't going to like it. She knocked on his door and entered.

Devon was terse. "OK, let's hear it."

Blakely eyed her boss, trying to assess how bad his mood was. She stood in front of his desk rather than taking a seat.

"She's not at either house. Our forensics teams are combing both sites and she's not been seen, although the boyfriend has been to Row Silver's between eight thirty and nine today. He left alone. So, confirming with our man on the gate and after our initial recce at Silver's residence, it looks like Campbell left there through the back door; it was unlocked and there was a piece of fabric, the colour of Mrs Silver's missing coat, caught on the fencing on the back border of the property. Er…" She scrolled down her notes on her clipboard. "Silver says it was a knee-length, green Barbour padded coat and a brown pair of Berghaus walking boots – those are the missing items – and Julia was possibly carrying a British Airways travel bag. Also, she took some money from Silver's purse…"

"How much?" Devon was tapping a speedy rhythm on the desk with his pen.

"About sixty pounds. We don't know when she absconded. Could have been any time between twelve thirty and seven thirty. The roads flanking the fields behind the house are Baileys Lane and Long Lane. Neither of these have CCTV until the junction on Mears Street and Bailey Lane, but that camera is not working. Long Lane has no cameras at all until Chipford. That's as far as we've gotten with the network – until we can determine which direction she took, we've held off the search."

"Damn!" Devon threw down the pen. "So she could have been picked up by any vehicle on that road… What about ANPR on the boyfriend's car since Silver's?"

"A surveillance point showed the car returned to his house this morning at 10.05."

"Did you question him?"

Blakely shifted on her feet. "He went for a walk before we got there and hasn't yet come back."

"Bloody fantastic. Well, I'm sure he'll let us know when he's back home if you leave him a nice message!" His voice rose louder, "And you've put a trace on his phone, right?" Devon turned his hands palms up in irritation at Blakely's silence, his eyebrows almost disappearing into his hairline.

"We're doing that now, Sir."

"Have you got anything substantial on Campbell at all? What's her reason for running? What did Silver say?"

"Chief, she said Mrs Campbell was very out of sorts, not at all herself."

"So a possible EDP… who could do herself harm or hurt someone else." Devon paused. "Did you just say you've held off a search on those fields?"

Blakely blinked. "We… er… we were waiting for the OK from—"

"This woman is possibly deranged from shock – we need to get some officers out there."

"Shall we pull the first team off Carrick House, Sir?"

"Why is that team still there?"

"We… there was a large group of reporters there this morning."

"I don't care if you've a swarm of tabloids to deal with, you don't need a team!"

"No, Sir."

"Who ordered that?"

"Fielding, Chief."

"Fielding, again!" Devon's mouth set in a grim line.

Blakely smirked. Nobody liked Fielding.

"Did you ask Silver about family members or friends? What about Campbell's laptop?"

"There's no immediate family, only an aunt in the Lake District, but Silver didn't know her name or address. We're going through Campbell's phone and her laptop, Sir, and the contacts we've picked up so far are…" Blakely referred back to her clipboard. "Amanda Beaton, Sarah Miller, Mrs Silver and the boyfriend, Luke Crawford. Campbell doesn't do Facebook or any other social media, but there are a few one-off contacts, and her tennis friends, which we're currently following up. Er, she'd also recently called Micah Wozniak."

Devon's eyebrows lifted again. "Why am I not surprised?"

"That's right, Sir, we're looking into it. Er, none of the people we've interviewed so far could suggest where Campbell might be, except Silver, who said she may have gone to the aunt's house. I guess she might do something like that if she were traumatised, Sir…"

"I take it you've found the aunt?"

"Er, yes – Sarah Boothe, based in Kendal."

"I think we should stay local for now but get on to the Cumbria force and see if they can send someone down to Boothe's to put an eye on the place – keeping it soft…"

"Alright, Sir."

"In the meantime, I want all eyes on surveillance points covering the main roads out of Little Wynchstead and on to the bypass."

"Of course." Blakely turned to leave. "Any update on the murder weapon yet, Sir?"

"Not yet, but while we're waiting, let's get a warrant to search

Crawford's place. I've a feeling he's with her or at least trying to find her. I need his contacts and we have to get his prints. We can't rule him out until we have those. But let's find him and bring him in."

"Right, Chief."

"And Blakely?"

"Yes, Sir?"

"Send in Fielding."

57

Luke stood some distance from Robert Shaker's semi, watching for activity of any kind which might reveal the police had got there first. He was in Bedford.

It was doubtful they'd track him to this place. Luke had left no details of the guy back at his flat: no photos, numbers or contact info. Shakes was a very old friend and the type you didn't advertise. He wasn't a grass, but he did know a lot of people in the underworld. Luke had committed the guy's address and number to memory since their last contact a year ago. His surveillance now of the place was a habit borne of his reporting days.

After seeing the police outside his own home and updating Row, he'd turned about and walked to the taxi rank at the end of the high street then took a cab out of there to Ridgley.

Ridgley had been a sleepy village up till recently, but a new train link had elevated its status to an up-and-coming, expanding town. He could use the new cash points there on the main thoroughfare, but he was more interested in the Ridgley market, which he'd known was on today.

Before he'd left the taxi he'd found out the driver's next pick-up was two towns along at Flatbridge, a further thirty minutes' drive. After making a note of some of the numbers on his phone, he'd left it in the back pocket of the seat in front of him: anything to throw the police off the scent, even if it gave him thirty minutes.

Business was in full swing among the stalls set up along the main road when he'd got there. He'd selected the largest of them, big enough to walk into. From the back wall inside, he'd selected a large navy-blue hoodie, a pair of navy jogging bottoms and some black trainers. After paying the cashier he'd had the items put into a thick white plastic bag before continuing on down the high street to a cash point. He drew three hundred pounds from one account and two hundred from another, stopped to purchase a coffee and a toasted ham and cheese as well as a bottle of water and a couple of snack bars as he didn't know how long it would take him to get to Shakes' place.

Turning off the high street, Luke had chosen a pathway he knew led onto a maze of small streets. As a teenager he and his friends had explored their hometown on their bicycles and this part of it hadn't changed much. It used to be a working-class area but now a lot of the houses had been done up and had extensions put on. Judging by the cars on the drives, the residents here were doing alright for themselves. He'd checked out the exteriors, noting at least two with cameras outside their frontage, but he wasn't worried because he knew these houses stretched over to a wood through which he could access a main road out of the area. There would be no footage of him from there onwards.

The wood glowed in the amber and golds of the season and he'd found himself breathing easier as he walked through the trees. After scanning the area for onlookers and finding none, he'd changed into his tracksuit and trainers between a huge tree and some holly bushes and shoved his old clothes into the plastic bag, placing it under his hoodie to bulk him out a bit before emerging from the bushes onto the path again.

He'd thought about Julia and her fretting about the necklace. San's necklace. Why should she be so bothered? Except for the fact San's pitiful corpse should be buried with it? The truth was, her demeanour as she'd been led out of her home by the policewoman had unsettled him. She hadn't responded to his call at all. It was like she wasn't present. Row's account too of how strange she acted last night was worrying. Discounting shock, what did that leave? Insanity? No way.

He was sure of one thing, though: if the necklace had become a priority she wasn't thinking of her own needs; she was thinking of Suzanne's and Suzanne's past was in the north. If he was to help her at all, he would need transport.

He'd pulled his hood up against the rain which was just starting as he neared the edge of the wood and the road. It was a main through-road but with a sudden shock he registered the lack of usual traffic ahead of him. He'd forgotten it was a Sunday. A sudden panic arose that he wouldn't get picked up before a police car arrived. He'd be no good to Jules stuck in a police station answering questions. A white Ford Transit had crested the hill within minutes and he'd crossed his fingers on one hand while he stuck out his thumb on the other. He was thankful it had pulled over.

The guy that had stopped for him dropped him off at a crossroads thirty minutes later just outside Long Buckby, a small village his parents had frequented decades ago to lunch at their favourite pub.

He'd cut across a field, seeing nobody, and, once into the residential area, ducked his head all the way to the station, making sure his hood hid his face. He had a skinny teenager buy him a train ticket at the unmanned machine just in case there was a camera on it and paid him twenty pounds for his trouble and, with any luck, his silence. From there it had been a short wait for the train to Bedford.

As much as he'd tried to appear casual and used his newspaper, pretending to read to keep his head down – even while walking – he'd gained a crick in his neck from all the tension. He hadn't noticed it until he'd made it to his friend's road and was trying to ease his muscles now, rolling his shoulders and moving his chin from left to right while he surveyed Shakes' place.

It looked OK. There were no cars outside, only a motorbike, which he assumed belonged to his mate's collection. He hoped he still had a couple more in his garage as he used to – in fact, he was counting on it. The curtains were drawn on every window despite it being well after lunch. He approached slowly.

Coventry Station

So here I am, halfway home. I can see the pileup on the tarmac below and I feel calmer now. I move away from the scene as the police cars draw near, finding a lane just over the fence. I walk in the direction parallel to the motorway and stick out my thumb, knowing it won't be long.

A truck comes to a stop beyond me within minutes.

I check out the driver, looking for clues in his face as to his intentions, the tell-tale signs like the constant smile, the ruthless checking me over or the standard, "What's a little beauty like you doing hitch-hiking?"

This one, however, is grumpy as hell. A Scottish man, fifty-something, bald and grizzled. He isn't even looking at me as he shouts above the rumble of the engine, "Where're ye going?"

"Manchester."

"I can drop y' in Coventry."

"Is that on the way?"

Now he is looking at me.

"Aye."

I think he's alright.

It's not easy climbing up into the lorry but I'm glad once I'm in to have somewhere to dry off. After a long silence I ask the moody Scot if he thinks I could get a train from Coventry to Manchester.

He nods.

And how much does he think it would cost?

"More than it would to fly, that's for sure!"

I'm confused by this response but figure it's a joke.

"Nah, it'll be 'bout twenty to thirty, I should think," he continues.

"Thirty pounds?"

"Aye, it's a wee bit more expensive than hitchhikin'."

"I know that – I'm not a divvie, it's just more than I expected…"

The man's face breaks into a grin. "Did you say divvie? I haven't heard that expression in years." His attention's back on the traffic now and he suddenly blasts his horn at an opportunistic Mercedes.

"Ah, ye wanker." He blares the horn again. "I'll burst ye," he yells at the windscreen. He glances back at me. "Sorry. I've nay patience wi' these assholes."

I smile at him and resume my assessment of my finances and the dismal weather, watching the spots of rain just starting up again, splatting against the window. My coat is soaked almost through and I don't want to stand in another downpour; hopefully I can make my money stretch somehow. And this rain can't go on for ever. Can it?

·

The truck driver drops me at Coventry main station with a, "Take care, lassie." I watch him leave, slightly bemused and grateful I'd not had to pay in any way.

Now I'm at the main ticket office observing the closed kiosk and the two attendants standing near the barriers. I follow a young girl to a ticket machine in the wall and watch her while she purchases a ticket. The girl orders a single to Manchester. Her fingers fly over the buttons too fast for me to follow, but I can see she's paid half price.

My turn at the keyboard and I'm not sure of the cut-off age for a child's fare, but I'm selecting exactly that for a single to Manchester for twelve pounds, twenty pence.

"Is this going to take long?"

I swivel round to see an old woman, smaller than me and hunched over, like she's carrying a huge pack on her back. Her eyes are stony and they narrow as they focus on me. I turn back to the machine to pay for my ticket.

"Where are you going?"

My gaze shifts round a little towards the cracked, deep voice, but I keep on putting in the coins, no longer paying attention to which coins I'm choosing. Finally, the machine delivers the ticket and I turn to leave.

"You have no face," her voice rings out.

I look around and see the attendants watching us, but they can't hear me. I put my hand affectionately on her arm and she jumps like I burned her.

I smile my biggest smile as I assure her, "You don't know shit, old hag."

The old woman starts to pant. As I move away towards the barrier, the old bat drags her twisted body around, extending her arm and finger towards me and tries to speak, "Sh... sh... she is..."

I approach the men at the barrier. "I think there's something wrong with that poor old lady over there," I say, and I turn back round to the woman and smile again. Her face fills with horror and her gnarled hands suddenly clutch her chest as she falls and the two men start running to her.

I take the opportunity to use my ticket in the machine and the barrier opens, showing up as 'child' as I pass through, scooping it up on the way. I turn to look back at the little scene, and although the two men's hulking figures mostly obscure the tiny figure on the floor, I can see the old busybody's wide-eyed face twisting and straining to find me, the whites of her eyes standing out until her small chest arches from the agony of an exploding heart.

The men shout instructions to the spectators. I make my way to the platform.

58

DS Blakely hovered behind her colleague, Benson, as he checked his screen.

"What you got?"

"Well, markers at Bifford Park Rise, 10.53; Flatbridge Tower, 11.15, to this point here just outside Little Seething at 11.31, where it's been for fifteen minutes."

Blakely looked at the cell site map reflecting Luke Crawford's phone. Where was he going? What's there? At Little Seething?"

"Car park."

Blakely nodded. "Send a man out there now. Whoever's nearest… and get some footage of every high street on that route in the meantime, including his own town's. If he hasn't picked up a ride from a friend, he's taken a taxi."

"Yes, Sarge."

"In the meantime, I'm going to call Silver again and try to get some more info on this guy."

Blakely drifted over to her desk, looking at her notes. Crawford was an old boyfriend of ten years from when he and Julia were both in uni. Julia Allbright had married Stephen Campbell soon after that love affair had ended. Rebound? The Campbells hadn't seemed unhappy all these years from what she knew about them; however, she could see how his recently revealed habits would have been a deal-breaker. Creep! She looked further down her page. According to Silver, Luke had told her they'd only renewed their friendship that week. Yet he was the one who'd called in the Carrick corpse – as Bennie had named it. And he'd been instrumental in digging it up, according to the gardener – as if he'd known it was there. All of this done under the instruction of his ex? How had they known about it? Had she found something that led to the tragic discovery? Julia had revealed little of herself at the interview but knew a lot about the deceased... She turned her page. Suzanne Moore, a misper case run cold from the seventies. Reported to have run away from a juvenile's home in Marsden – *the* home, she mused – that was a regular item on the news at the moment. Coincidence? Had she known all along about the buried girl in her family home? Had the footage on the news pricked her conscience or sparked her memory somehow? Yet Julia had given the exact address of the mother of the deceased and said the child had been lured from the Blackpool trip by a man who frequented Marsden in an unofficial capacity. How could she have known that? She would have been a child herself at the time. They needed to get her in. The chief sure regretted letting her go more each minute that passed. They had to come up with something concrete soon... She started to dial Row Silver's home, but her radio pinged. It was the search party.

"Blakely... any update? Over... Nothing? What about Caroline Allbright? Over... Hmm... OK, complete to the perimeter then come in. Call us if you have anything... anything at all. Over and out." She clicked off, frustrated.

"Boss!"

Blakely returned to Benson, who looked like a kiddie that just found the cookie jar.

"There he is." He pointed to the paused footage of a tall man with wavy dark hair getting into a taxi. "This is his high street."

"What's the rank's name?"

Benson clicked onto Google Earth on another screen to get a full view of the shop front where the taxi was parked. "Blue Dollar Taxis."

"Can you get that reg?"

"Uh-uh, camera angle's not right – maybe at the end of the road." They watched as the car neared the camera on the playback and the registration came into view.

"OK, so that's ten forty-three pick up on that reg." She assumed he was going to Little Seething since that's where his phone was, but she wanted to be sure. "Get the destination of the ride." She stood, impatient, as Benson made the call. Judging by the look on Crawford's face when he'd seen Julia yesterday, Blakely guessed he was on a mission for her. Like a lovesick puppy. Catch one of them and they'd get the other. But Caroline Allbright? No sign of her anywhere. Like she'd disappeared into thin air.

God, she was hungry. She checked her watch. Almost lunchtime. She'd been in so early this morning and hadn't even had her customary Danish with her coffee.

Benson's voice broke her thoughts. "They took him to Ridgley."

"What about Little Seething?"

"No, that was another pick-up."

"Boss?"

Blakely turned to a young PC.

"I've got DS Carver on the line at Little Seething; our target is not there."

"Bloody hell!" said Blakely. "Tell Carver to check the taxi – he'll find Crawford's mobile in there somewhere."

She turned back to Bennie. "Check out the high street footage at Ridgley. This guy's got us on a goose chase."

She picked up her phone.

59

"Fok, china, you come in here and just tune me, hey!"

Luke laughed, as he usually did at his friend's South Africanisms. It was like Robert Shaker had just stepped off the boat when in fact he'd lived in Bedford now for twenty-four years, courtesy of his mother's British citizenship. He went back to Cape Town every now and then, and every time he returned his accent was full-on, like now.

Shakes laughed with him. "What! You take the piss, man… first a bike, then a laptop, hey. Now you want my phone!" He drew on his stub of a cigarette from the side of his mouth before removing it with his thumb and forefinger. He flicked it round and crushed it once into the ashtray, leaving it to smoulder.

He loped to an Ikea dresser in his loose-limbed way that belied his ferreting mind and nervy disposition. He opened the cupboard door and at least two phones fell out onto the carpet.

"Shit." He picked them up and chucked them to the back, taking out another from the front. "Here!" He threw it towards Luke, who caught it deftly.

"Thanks, mate." He took the battery and sim Shakes was offering him and went to insert the battery first.

"No, no! I don't want this one being picked up here, hey! It's a burner but still gives out a signal. Fok, bru, you need to stay sharp. Wait till you're on the road, china – and don't hold on to it too long afterwards."

Luke put the battery and sim into his pocket and returned to the laptop. "Just a bit paranoid."

"When you've been hassled as much as I have, you think differently, man. Have you found anything yet?"

"Got the mother's name from an old newspaper article, just looking now on the electoral roll." Luke continued scrolling.

"Ja, but if she's a junkie she's not gonna be on that list, man."

"It's all I've got. Anyway, there's a chance that in one of her drugged-out states she might have figured why the hell not when the census came to call... Right, I've got two Sheila Moores and one is in Brinnington, listed since the eighties though – so not far back enough."

"I've never been on that fuckin' list."

Luke smiled. "Yeah, well, it's not exactly your style, is it! You're the proverbial termite." He was writing down the two addresses. "I may as well try these."

"So you think your girl's on some mission, for a dead kid or what...?"

"It's the only thing I can think of. I think she's gone to find the sister – perhaps to give her the necklace we found – I don't know. What I do know is, she's torn up by what her family did and she'll be wanting to put this right." He sighed. "Maybe it's what she needs after finding out so much that was wrong—"

"Ja, hey. She's probably all gefok finding out her pa's a nonce. World's full of shit, man."

Luke put the laptop aside. "Thanks so much for this, mate. Have you got those helmets for me? I think I should get going."

"You don't wanna stop a while? I was enjoying your company." Shakes laughed at him. "Ag, I know that look. Come on."

He led Luke through a door to his bike collection and switched on the light. Unlike the cupboard he'd opened in the sitting room, the double garage was well organised. Three bikes stood gleaming, tilted all the same direction on their stands, and down the one side was a collection of bike parts and wheels neatly stacked with some large parts hooked onto the wall and hung above their heads on racks. A bench ran the length of the wall to their left and even the top of it was clear with a plethora of tools fixed to racks above. Shakes went to a large plastic tub at the side and pulled out some black leathers, handing them to Luke.

"Good job you're the same size as me, bru. Grab two helmets off the shelf there."

Luke was gawping at the Ducati as he took possession of the biking gear and moved to his bike of choice.

"It's kiff, hey! But you're having the Honda." Shakes smirked. "Think about it. Ducati draws too much notice, especially that one…"

Luke stroked the gleaming tank with his finger. "Oh, man!"

"That's a beauty Hannah did on the tank, right!"

Hannah was his wife, a fantasy artist who loved to paint cars and bikes, which was a huge turn-on to his friend when he'd met her. Anybody that loved bikes was worthy of attention according to Shakes. She was out with Shakes' son right now, which Luke was grateful for. He didn't want to involve her in this if he could help it.

"The Honda is reliable and fast enough. You said you wanted to make up some time…"

"No, you're right. The Honda's good."

"So how long is it since you rode a bike, bru?"

"Ninety-nine."

"Fok, man! I want this back in one piece – even if you're not."

Luke laughed. "Thanks for this, Shakes…"

"Nooit, hey! I owe you, man. Saving me from that junk big time…"

Luke clapped his back. "I think this makes us even…"

"Ja, but if that bike's not in one piece when you get back, you gonna be in shit, hey."

60

"I've got three mispers, two dead bodies and no answers!" Devon was yelling. "We're a laughing stock!" He stood, glaring at his team from the doorway to his office, focusing on each team member till they squirmed. "The tabloids are screaming for a press conference and I've got nothing to tell them!"

No-one dared respond to him when he was like this. Blakely stared at her feet urging herself to wait a few minutes; speaking up now would only get herself shot down.

"I'd better have something on each of the three within the hour or there's going to be some transfers made." He turned and went back into his office, slamming his door.

"Jesus Christ!" Benson announced, turning back to his screen. "Friggin' starving. How 'bout some pizza round here?" Nervous laughter erupted from some of the team.

Blakely picked up her phone and dialled the local pizza delivery. It was past lunchtime, but nobody had left the station. "Hiya, Sharon, it's Denise here. We're all famished. We need three margheritas, two Hawaiian and three pepperoni? Yeah, all twelve-inch. Super, put it on the tab, please. Thanks." She replaced her handset. "Fifteen minutes. Hang in there, Bennie!"

Perhaps she should wait until the boss had eaten before she tried to update him? No, best to put him in a good mood before his digestion was called to action. She grabbed her notepad and proceeded to his office.

"What?" he shouted at her knock.

She took a breath and went in. "I've good news, Sir, we located Crawford at Ridgley where he drew five hundred pounds, purchased some clothes and some food off the high street…"

"And?" Devon looked at her, expectant.

"Then, er, private footage showed him entering Ridgley Woods. We think he's either meeting someone in the woods or he's picking up transport on the other side. I think he's following Campbell, Sir. I have Benson monitoring Ridgley High Street in case he returns there and we've extended our camera search to all bus and train stations within a twenty-mile radius, and that includes relevant bus cams as well."

"So you've lost him again?"

"I've sent a car down to Ridgley Woods to check it out, but in the meantime, we've had a report back on those blood samples from the back of the Campbell house. They were neither Stephen Campbell's nor Julia's."

"Caroline Allbright's?"

"Could be. We're going to get some dogs in and see if we can pick up a trail. It's a long shot but better than doing nothing."

Devon's lip curled but he didn't respond.

The door burst open and Benson's head appeared. "Chief, come and see this…"

Devon and Blakely followed the sergeant back to the screen in the corner of the office, where the picture had been frozen.

"Don't keep me waiting," Devon growled, but Benson couldn't stop smiling; he pressed play and the scene of a motorway accident was revealed.

"This happened earlier this morning, Sir, on the M6 northbound, just before Coventry."

"Yes, we all know about that, Sergeant – what are we meant to see here?"

"Her!" Benson was triumphant and grinning from ear to ear.

Just past the hideous sprawl of mashed steel and glass which was the nineteen-car pileup was a lone woman, heading away from the accident up the grassy slope to the left.

"Rewind it! …Stop."

They watched the scene from behind the woman who picked her way through the debris of steel compacted on steel, torn-open boxes and cases, and walked up to a mangled, yellow Mini Cooper, the driver of which was waving his arms. The walker appeared to be talking to the driver through the window. After a couple minutes the woman walked on, the driver continuing to stare after her as she left.

"Did she just leave that poor bugger to die alone?"

"Looks like it, Chief."

"Can you zoom in?"

"I can't get any closer, Sir, but look at the bag she's carrying…"

The British Airways carry-on bag was clear to see and the coat was a dark colour, and padded.

"What are the chances, Chief? Do you think it's her?"

The lines on Devon's face had eased. "Could be, could be… What was the exact time of the accident?"

"Ten fifty-five, the first call-in, Sir."

"Wouldn't Julia be way past this point by that time, if she was on her way to the Lakes?"

Blakely interjected, "Would all depend on the previous lift: how far it took her, whether she loitered at the services."

"Get me footage inside and outside the previous two service stops, including from the top of that hill and a radius of two miles. We need confirmation that it's Julia before we act on this."

"Right.

"And let's get her face up on tonight's news…" He looked at the screen again. "Even if that's not her. She's missing. I'll take the responsibility."

Blakely looked surprised. It was unusual to put a misper's face on the news before twenty-four hours were up. It could have been regarded as wasteful by the super.

"Sir, the mugshot was—"

"Get one from the house and make sure it's nationwide. Right now we look like a gaggle of bloody geese in a farmyard."

Home

I'd always remembered my home as a dump and now, standing at the gate, I can see nothing's changed. The remaining light of the day reveals the long grass of the front garden as it always was, peppered with litter right up to the base of the hedge borders and plastic bags lying abandoned here and there, their contents spilling out like bad language. The house itself looks no different, just like the ones either side, but right now ours has a long crack across the front window which has been covered with black tape. The curtains, as always, have been badly hung and the stops have come off so one droops down at the end. The whole place is in darkness.

The gate looks older than I recall: coked brown with rust instead of green and one of the hinges broken, launching the thing onto the path. It looks like it hasn't been moved from its crooked position in years. I can just get through without having to move it and I pick my way round the side of the house onto the small drive, through trails of cigarette butts, empty beer cans and bottles to the kitchen door. It's ajar despite the cold and the oncoming dark.

Inside is so still, I wonder if someone has gone out and forgotten to close up.

I call hello as I push through into a much more modern kitchen than I recall, though it has the same mess about it. I remember my efforts to keep it clean all those years ago, but it had been too much for me. Now the huge sprawl of dirty dishes and takeaway boxes with mould on them piled around the empty bottles and cans barely encourage a second glance.

I can see the gloom of the living room through the half-open door. "Mum?" I call as I push it open.

The glimmer of light through the dirty windows reveals bare walls with two mattresses on the floor against them, a large grey sofa on the other side and a low table in the middle, again covered in the remains and litter of several meals. The air is thick with a distillation of sweat, rotting food and pot. A flat-screen TV on a stand in the corner plays the end titles of an old movie in silence, the flickering light revealing the baggies and plastic injectors discarded across the floor. The only occupant, a bony body dressed in jeans and a skinny rib jumper with an unpicked hem at the wrist, stirs on the mattress by the stairs and drags itself up to a slumped position. I almost recoil when I see the face, horribly shrunken and wrinkled.

"Mum?"

The woman on the bed looks dazed and reaches for a can of cider, from which she takes a swig. In that moment I think I'm wrong – this isn't her. I watch the woman as she shakes her head, trying to clear the fog.

"I don't deal anymore. You've got the wrong 'ouse."

I cringe at the sound of the voice I know so well. I can see the scrawny physique, the dyed auburn hair with the inch of grey roots, and cannot think of a response. The voice is lower and rougher, but it still sounds like the woman who'd made the barest effort to bring me up. I have to make sure. "Sheila Moore?"

"What do you want?" Some of her drink has dribbled down onto her top, which she doesn't seem bothered about.

What do I want?

What do I want from this human being that revolts and devastates me in equal measure? Want or need? All those years ago? I'd needed to be cuddled as any baby would. Certainly as a young kid I'd wanted to be treasured, like I saw some kids were at school, or cared for at least, with clean clothes and proper food. Yes, kids need all of those things, to survive. At the bare minimum, I'd wanted to be wanted, like Shauna was to Jack and Beth, not left to scrabble and flounder and deal with all the evil shit *out there, alone. But now I wanted nothing that Sheila Moore could give. I would just take instead.*

"I've come for Kas. I'm going to look after her now."

The woman's head snaps up. "You what?" She staggers to her feet, breathing heavily, and lurches over the table as she tries to regain her balance. "Who the fuck are you? If you don't get outta here, I'm gonna call the police."

She looks even smaller standing upright, her head too big for her torso and her arms like thin pieces of twine gesticulating now before me. Yes, it is my mum, but it's like her whole body has shrivelled through some process, sucking in the cheeks and the eyes to the back of the head, leaving behind a creepy version of the person I'd known. I walk to the foot of the stairs.

"Kas! Kas! It's me—"

Sheila Moore launches herself at me, grabbing my arm and pulling me. "You get out of here, you fuckin' retard. I've got a friend next door who'll beat the shit outta you if I ask him to—"

"Don't you ever touch me!" I yell, shoving her.

Sheila's leg connects with the table and she almost falls. Her face contorts to even deeper ruts and fissures, and her eyes dart towards her phone on the far end of the table. I follow her stare and focus on it. The phone flies off and hits the wall on the other side of the room, breaking into at least three pieces. Sheila gawps, trying to work out what just happened.

"Kas!" I shout again.

Sheila looks at me with a mix of contempt and something close to sympathy. "You rattlin' or what? If you're looking for my daughter, she doesn't live here anymore – she's long dead."

I stop on the bottom stair and turn to her. "Dead?"

Sheila's face twists. "Yeah, she's fuckin' dead – from an overdose. Nine years ago – so you need to get the fuck outta here."

The word swirls around my brain. Dead. Dead. Dead.

I can still hear my mum's continuing rant. What's it to you? Who are you? Who do you think you are, just walking in like that?

It all feels like a strange dream where the stupidest things happen and things don't make sense but you know you're in a dream and you're going to wake up so it doesn't matter. Only this time I'm not waking up.

Sheila is shouting now. "You ain't getting sorted here, OK? I said – get the fuck outta my house!"

I look around again. Where's the cabinet that has all the ornaments on it? Where is the big blue carpet where Kas and I had practised gymnastics? I look again at my mum's aged face and now I know. Time has slipped away somehow. I'd felt something wrong between me and the others: the kids at the game machine, the way Beth had looked at me.

That's why the gate is rusted.

How many years? How many years lost? My heart is breaking. My sweet little sis, lying somewhere, choking on her own vomit, or her heart exploding from the sorrow of it all. Because I hadn't been there to look after her.

Her name slips from my lips. "Kas…"

How had she died? What had happened to her since that day she'd been dragged from me, as I myself was dragged many times, to places and people I did not want to see, to do things I didn't want to do. I'd been used – then discarded, like the dishes and empty cartons on this table, still covered with the shit from the user. I was nothing more than a vessel, but I'd known that for a long time. It was Kas that had kept me going, sustained me in my worst times…

A howl rises, magma-like, from the depths of my body, and as it grows louder, the room shakes and the pieces on the table are whipped away to hit the walls and ceiling, leaving Sheila Moore staring wide-eyed at me. Yet, through the fear, she sees something, someone familiar.

She murmurs, "S… Suzy?", not daring to believe what her brain is suggesting.

I throw out my arm and Sheila's feet leave the ground so fast she doesn't realise what's happening till the wall stops her flight with a sudden and unforgiving snapping sound in her shoulder blade. She screams and slides down, half onto the mattress and half onto the floor. While she clutches her shoulder to stem the agony, she cannot take her eyes off me and I know she can see me, her daughter, fourteen years old in the blue cotton dress she'd bought for me after she'd got clean that one time. Her own Suzy, standing here trembling with hatred.

It's Only Me

"Suzy!" she shrieks. "Oh my God, Suzanne, is that you, babe? Oh, jeez! Uh, this is one fuckin' bad trip. Is that really you? Aw... my babe! Help me, darlin'..."

"Help you!" I scream at her. "It was always you. You never thought about us for one second as you were bringing in those perverts and they were looking at me like I was meat, and at Kas too! I couldn't wait to get out of here – away from you – our own mother!

"All that Kas and I had was lost. Such a short time together that was good – but it couldn't last for us because I'm part of you and I am cursed. You are the dirt under the shoe, Mum, the scum in the drain, and so am I. Kas was the only pure thing in my life and she mattered to me; she was part of me and she was ripped from me...

"Don't you see how you ruined us? The hell I've suffered – the hell she must have gone through? This is yours to bear now."

I kick the dirty knife with the burnt edge towards her.

"Do it, Mum. Do it for Kas and me, your darling little girls that you treated like shit."

Her cowering, scrawny being revolts me and I turn away from her whining. I look at the screen on the television and I can see Mark Cavendish on the news again with his wife, making a statement before they turn and go through their front door.

I know that house.

I look back at my whimpering mother on the mattress.

"Everybody's going to pay, Mum."

It's like I'm on a stage playing to the world. I see my hand reach down into the travel bag and pull out the fluffy pink teddy bear and place it on the coffee table. As I leave the room my mum pleads, "Don't – Suzy! Come back to me!"

Her voice rises to a shriek. "Suzanne! Please! I'm sorry, babe..." and dissolves into sobs.

I feel myself becoming calm as I leave, her voice already fading into memory.

61

Caroline sat in the car she'd borrowed watching Julia leave the Moore's house. Her gut contracted seeing the person who'd destroyed all she and Steve had worked so hard for. She'd hardly believed it when the bitch's face had come on the news that afternoon as a missing person of interest in the murder inquiry, but Caroline had known straightaway that she would come here, given her new-found bent for interfering in the past. It felt like destiny when Caroline discovered from a local news report that she herself was staying just minutes away from Suzanne's family home and she'd driven into Brinnington as fast as she could. A few discreet and well-paid-for enquiries had directed her here.

How quickly a life can be ruined. Yesterday she was a respected CEO of a major company and a valued benefactor of the village she lived in, and now she was a fugitive and Steve was dead. Yet this feeling was familiar. Every time she built herself up, something came along and tore it down.

She recalled how she'd run in panic from Steve's house and struggled across the field to her friend's, her face bleeding and her clothes torn. She wondered why she hadn't thought to run round to the drive where her car was parked. Obviously in shock. When she'd arrived at her friend's she'd been unable to speak coherently and he'd had to take her into the kitchen and give her a whiskey. She'd calmed down and told him what happened. He was quick to point out her error in running away from a murder scene and how dare she come to his house? Caroline had begged him to let her stay and he relented, on the proviso she left in the morning and went to the police with some explanation that would extricate her from the mess.

It had all gone up in smoke in the morning when the news revealed the find at Carrick House and her friend received a call to say police were closing on the circuit.

Julia had inflicted more harm than she'd believed possible. Her friend, now worried about his connection to her, had arranged a car and insisted she get out of town. It was over.

She would be traced here to Manchester, she knew. Maybe her friend would dob her to the cops to keep them from looking into his private life or maybe he wouldn't, fearing she'd shop him in retaliation. Still it would only be a matter of time once Steve's emails were fully investigated before each addressee would be arrested and would reveal their wider circles.

In Manchester she'd had some time to think. She'd planned to go on to a contact in Scotland and from there fly to Norway, but seeing that murderess was on the run and knowing she would come here was irresistible.

She followed Julia, keeping a fair distance behind, stopping when her enemy reached the corner and crossed over to the motley selection of boarded-up shop fronts defaced with the words 'bleedin' shitter' by some local disenchanted; the neglect and despair evident around her reminded her of her own charming hometown. She watched Julia peer into a telephone box then go in and pick up the phone.

The streetlight revealed the little red scabs on her own hands which rested on the wheel and Caroline recalled the awful sight of Steve, standing rigid before her with the knife embedded in his eye and his wife standing there, throwing things round the room like a mad person. Then the window crashing from one of her missiles; strange how the glass had flown inwards, she thought, eyeing her face in the rear-view mirror. Thank God, the shards had missed her eyes. She turned her face to the side to view the full damage, noting some deep cuts. If they scarred, she might have to have plastic surgery. Or maybe she would leave the scars to remind her to hate Julia Campbell every day, even once she was dead – which she soon would be. If Micah had removed her as they'd planned, Steve would still be alive, she thought for the umpteenth time that day. Hell, so would Micah.

That bitch had taken everything from her. Everything. Caroline stared at her adversary, who was examining the adverts inside the phone box. She felt her hate for the woman boiling over. Her one consolation was that Julia had flipped; her discovery of Steve's other life had obviously turned her mind, driving her to murder. Life would never be the same for her either, what little life was left; Julia's double strike of exposing the ring as well as the dead child at Carrick was impressive, but she would rue the day she dared to take them all on.

Here, in front of her now, was the chance to get even. She considered ramming her when she came out of the telephone box but quickly discarded the idea. Her sole advantage on the police was them not knowing where she was, and she didn't want to stick her head up at this stage. Later then, she thought, looking round at all the houses. When there weren't so many potential witnesses. It was worth the wait, if it meant getting the pleasure of choking the life out of that bitch before she left the country. She watched her strolling up and down along the pavement now, obviously waiting for a lift.

Where's the whore going now?

Caroline waited.

62

A good distance behind the taxi, Caroline pulled over. She watched as the taxi left and Julia, now on foot, turned down the lane. So she was going to Marsden. Caroline couldn't believe it. Why? What did she want there? Was she going to confront Cavendish? As far as she knew, he still lived on the site in the caretaker's house. She had recognised the building behind him on the recent news footage and was surprised that he hadn't distanced himself from that place by now like she had. Or thought she had. It was ironic she was back here now and all because of this conniving witch. Was Julia intending to wrench some confession out of him about the Moore girl? What the hell!

Still, what did she care about Julia's plans? It was nice and quiet out here and no-one about… a perfect opportunity to conduct her own business. A simple hit-and-run with no witnesses. She checked her rear-view mirror for oncoming cars, but the entire road was dark now except for her own headlights. Caroline geared up and pulled back onto the tarmac. She drove up to the junction and followed Julia's route into Marsden Lane. She expected to see her walking up to the gate which lay halfway up the road, but there was no sign of her.

She pulled over to the left and peered into the trees which aligned the property. Apart from the meagre light from her headlamps reflecting off the nearest trees, the woods were pitch black inside.

A shiver ran through her and she switched the locks on the doors. What on earth was wrong with her? Julia was just a slip of a thing. But Caroline, for all her usual pragmatism, felt like she was being watched. She pulled out a cigarette packet from her bag and lit one up, drawing on it to calm her nerves.

63

DS Blakely stared at the stills Benson had prepared for her: numerous shots of a woman carrying a British Airways travel bag, getting out of a blue Renault, standing at the entrance of a shop holding a pink teddy bear, walking to the on ramp at Watford Gap. All of these photographs clear enough, except for the face in each one, which was no more than a blur. For Christ's sake! Blakely shook her head, moving on to the next set of pictures near a roundabout where she'd hitched a lift from a truck driver. Blurred faces, all of them.

"What the bloody hell is going on, boss?" Benson looked at her for an answer.

"Haven't got a clue... when her mugshot turned out like that, I assumed it was a quirk – a fault of the camera or something, but this... is..."

"But it's definitely her, right?"

"Got to be. These could never be used in court, though..."

"Can we get a positive ID from the Renault driver?

Blakely was irritated. "What do you think? She drove straight into a truck; she's in a coma."

The phone rang on Blakely's desk. She walked over and picked up. "DS Blakely... Right... Name and number?" She sat down and began to write.

Benson looked back at the photos. He re-ran the footage of the first sighting; everything was perfect of the Renault coming into view, parking up. The driver got out of the car first and she could clearly be identified. The passenger alighted, but her face was not… 'set' was the word to use. That part of the image moved and twitched, and when he froze it; it blurred.

He shook his head. "Freaky."

"We've got something," Blakely shouted. "Heads up, all. Just in from a member of the public. He confirmed he picked up someone matching Campbell's photo at Watford Gap Service Station around ten thirty. This ties in with our sighting of her heading towards the slip road at ten. He said it was definitely her, but he claims she left them at the accident – as we know from Bennie's stills and the crash footage – and she'd said to him she was going to Brinnington, Manchester, to see her sister. She said her name was Suzanne."

There was a murmur round the room. "OK, everyone, this woman is obviously in shock and needs our help. I'm going to send a team round to the mother's house, but in the meantime, we need to switch our focus on the immediate area there. All cameras in the area from Percy Road, Brinnington, five-miles span, now. Let's bring this woman home."

A voice piped up from the back. "Sarge, what can we say at this stage about the two car crashes connected to Mrs Campbell?"

"What are you suggesting?" Blakely tried to see who'd asked and identified an older member of the team with known contacts with the press. "This is a vulnerable person already and she'll be in further shock after experiencing that accident, making it all the more important we find her, and soon."

Blakely was relieved to have something concrete at last. The search for Caroline had run to the edge of Barter Wood and the residents at a house there were being interviewed, but the trail had stopped there for now. Still no trace of Luke, but Blakely wasn't worried. Wherever Julia was, Luke would not be far behind.

Marsden

I stand in the kitchen of Marsden Centre and I'm trembling. It's very dark but I'm not scared. It's the memories that are flooding back of this greedy monster of a house that swallows you whole and digests your puny life; once again, I am that helpless no-hoper, left to rot at the mercy of people that have no soul.

Through the dusty gloom I can see the corridor where the pot wash guy had given me the message. It had been a sunny day when he'd pulled me aside.

"He'll meet you at the foot of the pier at eleven," he'd whispered. "By the hotdog stand. He said to bring what matters – you won't be coming back."

For a split second, I'd believed it. Believed that life could be different for me. That someone cared. I should have known better.

They have soul-stripped me and now, just a shadow of my former self, I return to these dark corridors of cruelty beyond imagining. I don't hear my footsteps as I cross the hallway. I hear the whimpers of the girls lying in their beds as they are violated and the screams for help or raucous laughter in the night from far-off rooms.

And Cavendish's cruel, reedy voice. "Nice little artist, aren't ya! Mind you, I don't think the missus'd like this picture of her. Ha ha. I'll take this to show Larson, though, he'll love it – put your pants back on, love. Yeah, I really like these. You've got me – you really 'ave."

As I climb the stairs, I hear other voices.

"Get outta my seat, Moore, or you'll get another beating."

"Yeah, Moore, you want your other eye blackened?"

And the cronies of Cavendish and his wife as they came to prey on us, returning again and again, like vultures picking on the bones of little birds.

I'm on the fifth floor now of the airless prison. A light shines from a room down on the left and I see myself being dragged down the corridor by Micah that night long ago, the sound of Micah's trainers squeaking on the lino, the only accompaniment to my pathetic pleas. He's pushing open the door to the lit room and, terrified, I see a huge man sitting on a bed wearing only his underpants. He pats the mattress next to him as I'm presented. The revulsion and horror of that moment resurges now and I recall how his fat rippled as he pat-patted the bed: his enormous sweating chest, his thick wet lips. I remember how my insides loosened and the piss trickled down my legs.

Oh boy, did he swear and throw his arms about! Micah got it full force.

"Who do you think I am? I pay good money to this hovel and you bring me this! How dare you? How many times do I have to tell you? Bring me someone who knows. Bring me Elaine… or Mary! Is that beyond your abilities, man?"

He'd looked like those giant, inflatable men flapping their arms about that you see at fairgrounds or festivals, and I would have laughed if I hadn't been so petrified.

Micah had dragged me out again while the inflatable continued his shrieking behind us.

"And bring a towel to clean this frightful mess up!"

Micah hauled me to the bathroom on that floor and told me to clean myself up. He'd asked if this was my first time and I'd lied and said yes. He'd nodded, as if he knew that. As I'd dried myself he'd said I reminded him of his sister who was dead now. He'd said I was prettier than her and that I shouldn't be in this situation.

That was when he made the promise. He wanted to help me. In memory of his sister, he said. I believed him. My natural cynicism had given way to that treacherous bitch, hope.

He would help me escape and he'd find me a flat. Together we'd find Kas and bring her home. Foster homes don't keep them long, he'd said. She was maybe even back home with Mum by now; it would be easy to take her.

I remember lying in bed that night, holding the 'S' on my chain close to my heart with joy surging through me. Finally, I would get out of here and I'd rescue Kas and we could have a proper life…

I stand now looking into the room where it happened. The soft light from the dwindling day reveals the old iron bed and peeling wallpaper — like shredded skin from the husk of the house. A smell of mildew and decay and fear prevails.

I walk to the window and look down on the caretaker's house. There's a light on.

I sit down against a wall and focus on the un-shaded bulb hanging from the ceiling. It sways. It begins to flash on and off.

64

Christmas come early, Luke thought, standing some distance from the blue flashing lights, winking indicators and white flashes from cameras outside Sheila Moore's house.

Suicide, a neighbour had said as they'd watched the local police and paramedics swarming the property. She was enthusiastic in her description.

"I always pop in, you know, every evening… to make sure she's eaten. There she was, on the floor. Blood everywhere, sprayed up the walls and the table – her eyes just starin'…." The woman shuddered. "She'd sliced both wrists – really deep. I don't know how she did that, high on that stuff, no doubt! To be honest, I'm amazed old Sheila lasted this long. I thought she would overdose long before now with the amount of junk she did."

Two policemen were questioning neighbours and passers-by at the gate. Luke saw them taking notes between cursory scans of the crowd. He realised he would look conspicuous, standing there with his helmet still on.

"She lost both daughters, you know – the first one went missing and the youngest one overdosed… must have been about ten years ago now – just tragic."

Luke saw the taller of the two cops eyeing him while his partner questioned a young man.

He had to be quick. "How do you know it was a suicide?"

The woman couldn't wait to describe it. "She'd scrawled a message in her own blood – can you believe it! 'Suzanne, forgive me', it said. She was her eldest, you see... So sad!"

"Did you see anybody visiting her today?"

"What? No, she never has visitors! Well, not friends as such. I think she has business callers sometimes – you know what I mean. But I didn't see anyone today. She was more miserable than usual with all this news about Marsden and the awful things that went on there. It must have got to her, though she wouldn't talk about—"

"Marsden? The care home on the news?"

"Yeah, that's where Suzanne disappeared from – in the seventies. So long ago, but it never gets easier for parents, something like—"

"That's the one in Stockport, isn't it?"

"Just south of here... on the M60 – hey! Did you know the family?"

Luke heard her voice rise behind him as he strode off to his bike. He curbed his impulse to run in case the police were watching him. He'd taken a chance going into the thick of it, but he needed a lead and now he thought he knew. Julia had come to the house here to give the sister the necklace, or just to talk to her, perhaps, and now, finding she'd died, there'd be just one place left to go. He didn't know why Julia would feel the need to retrace Suzanne's steps to this extent, but guilt was a strange thing – perhaps this was a sort of pilgrimage for her, an exorcising of the whole terrifying experience she'd gone through in the cellar and the deception and betrayal of her own family. He mounted the bike and set the Satnav for Marsden. He pulled off. He sure as hell hoped Julia hadn't been seen if she'd been here today. It just wouldn't look good, the mother dying soon after...

He turned onto the main road, geared up and opened up the throttle, heading south.

65

Caroline hadn't seen the light flashing on the fifth floor because she was already inside the building. After talking herself out of her nervous state, she'd approached the old mansion from the rear, just in time to see Julia climbing in through a small window. Now she crept as quietly as the old structure would allow, along the corridor, listening past the creaks of her own footfalls to pinpoint where Julia might be. She was on the second floor when she heard footsteps on the stairs below and somebody muttering in a low voice. She darted into one of the rooms, just off the stairwell.

"I don't bleedin' know! It could be a squatter or something…"

Caroline heard the woman pause on the stairs while she continued her phone conversation.

"I know there's no electricity – maybe it's torchlight. Well, how long are you gonna be? It's probably just kids – or maybe it's one of them reporters snooping around. What? Oh, alright. Keep your damn hair on. I'll wait. Yeah… fifth floor. OK, OK, I said I'd wait."

The woman's footsteps continued up the stairs, and after a couple of minutes, Caroline crept out and followed her. After the fifth flight, the woman ahead stopped and sat down on the top stair.

Caroline pulled up at the bottom of the flight. From her vantage point in the shadows she could just make out the woman's face illuminated from the phone screen she was staring at. Caroline recognised her. Rachel Cavendish. What the hell was Julia's game, luring this woman up here? Did she plan to blackmail her and her husband? Did she plan to secretly record them? More fool her if that was the case. Caroline had known Cavendish when he was a gangster on his home estate in his teens. To outward appearances, he'd turned over a new leaf when he went into the social services, but she knew his ulterior motives for changing profession. He was a mean old bastard who was reputed to have bitten someone's ear off once. A little middle-class bitch was not going to scare him.

She wondered if she should approach his wife. They weren't acquainted, as Caroline had already moved down south before Cavendish had married. No, it was a bit weird to introduce herself here. It would be best to wait for Cavendish to arrive then they could all go and have a little chat with Julia together.

Caroline thought again of Steve, all beautiful six foot of him lying stretched out with a dagger in his eye due to that crazy bitch.

I'll do her for you, Steve. Her lips pursed and her fists clenched.

A faint cry issued from the floor above. Her head snapped up and she strained to hear. She peered up the flight to see if Cavendish's wife had heard it. The woman was sitting upright, her head cocked at an angle.

A moan wound its way through the rafters, but it sounded like a moan of pleasure. Caroline watched the woman get to her feet and creep down the corridor. She followed her.

As Caroline approached the top of the stairs and eased her head around the corner to peer down the dark passage. Cavendish's wife, now reflected in the sporadic light from the open door, was peering through the crack at what sounded like a couple in the throes of noisy sex. This was some weird shit and no way was Julia making out with someone in there. Unless it was the boyfriend? No, it was just too crazy! Even if the boyfriend was here, they wouldn't be screwing here when they could hire a hotel room. Unless they were into kinky stuff and creepy locations? But why attract attention by putting a light on? No, that was to lure them up here, Caroline was sure of it. Julia was still on the rampage; that temper she'd witnessed wouldn't just dissipate. It needed something to work on. Maybe she should warn the woman... Caroline hesitated.

As the moaning got louder, along with an accompanying banging – was that a headboard? – she watched the woman crane her head around the door. At which point the moaning and banging stopped.

Caroline held her breath as the woman stood there for what seemed like five minutes before she walked into the room, out of sight.

Caroline waited, ears straining for sound: a voice, a plea, a shout. Anything. The air hung, soundless and still. The light flickered on and off.

She inched nearer, intrigued, in spite of a gnarly feeling in the pit of her stomach which began to tug at her subconscious. Why no sound? Nothing? Like the woman had walked into a black hole. Caroline felt guilty for not stopping her now. The woman had come up here thinking it was some kids from the neighbourhood – she wasn't to know it was some psychotic whore out for revenge. She should have warned her.

The thought occurred to her that this may not be Julia at all but could be one of Cavendish's previous victims from the home. There would be a lot of them. Maybe he should find some other occupation from now on, she thought as she moved closer, till she was just outside the inconstant splash of light. She could only hear her own breathing. She eased up to the doorway, peering first through the crack of the hinge. She could see a bed in the corner, covered by a sheet. She moved to peer round the door. Nobody, just a tall cupboard built into the wall, a bulb that fizzed and hissed as it spat out its dim light in yellowy spurts onto what appeared to be someone lying there, covered up on the bed. Unmoving.

The dread growing in her gut twisted and turned as she approached the bed, and she heard her own voice croak, "Mrs Cavendish?" Her hand shook as she reached out to the sheet and pulled it back. Her feet slid on something which she knew right away to be blood and she slammed backwards onto the floor. She couldn't tear her eyes away from the eyes that, minutes before, had been staring through the crack in the door but now leered, sightless, at her with a mouth pulled into a snarling rictus. A knife stuck out of the neck and thick, dark fluid oozed and coagulated around it and down the side of the mattress. Caroline heard the door behind her moving and she lunged up for the knife, pulling it out with a sickening sucking sound and spun round to face the killer.

Mark Cavendish stood, stupefied at the sight of his dead wife, his mouth hung open, and as he flicked his torch beam to Caroline, a deranged roar emitted from him. He charged at her, his arms outstretched.

"Wait!" She struggled to her feet as best she could on the blood-soaked floor as he came at her. She was forced to duck and side-step, slashing wide as she did so. He yelled in pain and, dropping his torch, grabbed at his upper arm. He turned towards Caroline again, his anger undimmed.

"Mark! Stop, it's me, Caroline… Caroline Allbright, remember? The parlour at Hewitt Street? I didn't kill her, Mark. It was Julia – she did this."

Mark peered at her, trying to make out her features in the intermittent light.

"I didn't kill her, Mark, I swear. Why would I?" Caroline saw him looking at the knife. She lowered her hand. "I'm sorry, Mark. I thought you were… Listen, to me, there's someone else here… she's…"

Mark had turned from her and dropped down next to his dead wife. "Rach!"

She watched him stroke his wife's hair back off her forehead and felt the guilt again.

"You'd better explain what you're doing here, Baker," he rasped. "Who did this?"

"She's deranged, Mark, I followed her here – my stepdaughter… she did this, Mark… she…" Caroline froze as the door of the cupboard slowly opened. The wavering light played tricks on her mind, making it look like Julia was gliding towards them.

Caroline shook her head in an effort to clear the illusion. Her voice was weak: "Mark, get up!"

She heard him shuffle to his feet and his exclamation. "What the...?"

She roused herself and took a breath. "You mad bitch! Did you think you could get away with this? And what you did to Steve?"

Julia stopped halfway and said nothing. Caroline couldn't see her face for the light flashing behind her.

Caroline was not afraid of her stepdaughter, no matter how insane she'd become. Her voice strengthened. "You thought he deserved it, didn't you! And Micah. This is not justice, Julia. There is no justice for you – not for any of us. This..." she gestured to the dead woman, "is nothing but sport. You've made a big fucking mistake coming here..."

Before Caroline could move, Mark ran at Julia, but her hand flew up and the old man was propelled back into the wall. He yelped as his sliced arm was squashed between it and the weight of his body. He slid down into the pool of his wife's blood.

Caroline tried to make sense of what just happened and took a step back, holding the knife up in front of her. "Don't come any closer..."

Julia laughed as the bulb behind her began to sway, tossing the light from one corner to the next. What started as a low chuckle gained strength and volume, even after she'd closed her mouth. The laugh reverberated around the room and Caroline, now confused, started yelling.

"Stop it!"

Caroline's body suddenly jerked to the left and her face slammed into the wall. The knife dropped from her hand and she felt a hot fluid flow down her neck as she reeled back, her hand going to her benumbed face. She tried to speak but her mouth was full of blood and broken teeth and the room had blurred. With a violent twist, her body was jerked upwards till it hit the ceiling, where it hung suspended. Mark's horrified gasp below brought her round to stare down at him, her eyes struggling to gain a perspective. She felt the blood leaving her mouth, dripping onto the floor below. She tried to clear her brain and speak aloud but heard only a whimpering of terror from a voice that didn't sound like her.

·

As Luke approached the door, he heard a man's terrified voice.

"Fuckin' hell, what the fuck?"

The swinging light revealed Mark Cavendish, the man from the news, scrabbling away from Caroline.

Cavendish saw Luke at the doorway and started to whine. "Help me, mate! For Christ's sake!"

"Oh my God!" Luke said, staring at the sight of Caroline pinned to the ceiling. "Jules?" He turned to the woman, who didn't even stir at the sound of her name. He raised his voice as he stepped inside.

"San, you don't have to do this."

Luke was thrown backwards to the floor. He gasped in shock.

"Get us out of here," Cavendish pleaded, his voice ragged.

Luke's eyes flicked to Cavendish cowering in the corner and the dead woman in the bed. He looked back at the one who held all in thrall. His voice trembled: "Julia, it's me, Luke, remember...? Come back to me... you've done all you had to. Julia!" Julia's eyes flickered yet she stood, transfixed, the moment interrupted by the sound of Caroline's lighter falling from her pocket and bouncing off the floor below, coming to rest next to the bloodied knife.

"Please, Jules..."

Without warning, Luke was wrenched from the floor and propelled towards the window. He threw out his arms at the last second before he smashed into the left side of the pane, the glass shattering, the frame splintering but holding. He fell back; his arms, held up around his head, had protected his face, but a piece of glass had sliced into his leg. He yelled in agony. Through the haze of pain he saw Julia plunge towards him, dropping to her knees, tears streaming down her face. He saw the silver chain snap and fall from her neck and heard Caroline plummet to the floor, where she lay groaning.

"Luke!" Julia whispered, tears streaming down her face as she kissed him. "I'm sorry... so sorry!"

Luke clutched at her and at the same time wrenched the glass out of his flesh as the light started swinging again and Cavendish's gibbering in the corner ramped up to shrieks. Julia twisted round to see Suzanne, who stood in the centre of the room in a towering rage.

"S... stand up, Luke," she urged, watching Suzanne. "Hurry."

She helped him stagger to his feet as Cavendish began to inch towards the door.

"Remember me, Mr Cavendish?" The words floated, hollow and child-like around them all as Suzanne extended her arms.

Cavendish froze and his head sunk lower.

"Come on, Sir, you remember, I'm your little artist—"

The bed lifted up in the air and slammed into him, catching him on the side of his head before his wife fell from it on top of him. He screamed and shook her off, scrambling back into the corner. The room began to shake and dust fell from the ceiling. The light swung round and round, and Suzanne laughed. Cavendish was picked up and thrown to the other side of the room, connecting with his leg first, which snapped on impact.

Julia screamed, "San, don't! Not this way!"

San turned to her and rasped, "Go now, Julie!"

Julia pleaded, "There'll be no rest..." Her words could not be heard over the agonised screams from Cavendish.

The door flew open and San shrieked so loud the rafters shook.

"*Get out.*"

Julia dragged Luke out as fast as she could muster and looked back once.

San half-smiled and the door slammed between them.

Music

I watch the Controller as she tries to sit up. Each groan and whimper she utters sends a thrill through me; each utterance of pain eases my own, if only for the moment. It is a joy to see her so helpless.

I see the slow recognition in her eyes as she focuses on me and then, the terror. She's saying something. Silent words spill from her bloody mouth and now her eyes are pleading. I feel stronger than ever; the air crackles with my rage.

The lighter explodes and covers the Controller's upper body and face in flames. She screams and writhes, trying to put out the fire, but this fire is mine. It is the fire of my life's own breath, my footprint, my legacy. Her agony exceeds my expectations.

I am euphoric.

Cavendish is petrified. He's crawling to the door. I lift him up. His arms are flapping, his feet pedalling. He is my puppet, I his master. Terror overwhelms him and he begins to cry. I am deaf to his incoherent pleas.

Now there are others here in the room – boys and girls, pale in the orange glow of the flames licking the walls: lost souls who once had dreams and two feet on the ground. They seek their old tormentor, who writhes from their outstretched hands.

Caroline's screams are waning, her bluckened body curling in on itself.

"You're going to stay with us now, Mr Cavendish," I say.

My brothers and sisters of the long-forgotten reach out to him to take a piece. He shrieks and contorts his body – away from the victims of his own depraved appetite.

The room trembles and the ceiling flexes. The flames swell upwards and across.

Cavendish is splayed now, mid-air, his face an agonised snarl, eyes rolling back as my ravenous friends rive at him. His mouth is open, but I can't hear him. I can only hear music. The music grows louder. This is for you, Kas.

66

The door slammed, rendering Julia blind in the sudden blackout. She could hear jangling as Luke turned on the mini Maglite on his keyring then pulled her from the door, limping ahead.

"This way," he was saying, his voice weak, his body stooped in pain.

Behind them Caroline's pleas turned to screams of agony. Cavendish was begging for mercy.

Julia stopped. "We should help them," she said.

A tremor rippled through the roof above, scattering dust everywhere.

"We have to go," Luke gasped, pulling her again.

"I can't leave her, Luke."

"You have to! Think of your girls."

They were at the top of some stairs now. Luke winced as he took the first step down and Julia grasped his arm to take the pressure off his bad side, encouraging him as they descended.

The banister rattled beneath Luke's hand.

"How did I get here, Luke?"

"I don't know," he panted, his voice hard in the dark. "Suzanne used you, Jules."

A deep rumble vibrated through the floor and great cracking sounds from the roof set off a shower of dust and plaster all over them. They coughed and spluttered through the haze. Luke groaned with the pain.

Julia took the Maglite from him and hooked her shoulder under his oxter to enable them to move faster. With her outside hand she cast the thin beam of light through the dusty white haze before them.

They stumbled down the first level of the fourth flight. The grumbling from the bowels of the house swelled around them, pulsing in every part of the stairwell and through their bodies. Thumps and bangs sounded from far-off corners of the old mansion. Windows were shattering above and below with sporadic roars of masonry ripping through floors. Julia felt a jolt beneath her and her hand flew out to steady herself on the wall, the light from the torch zig-zagging, the stairwell flexing and bowing around them like some great galleon rolling on the waves. She fought the disorientation and brought the beam back to the steps below, concentrating on the small circle of light ahead of them.

"We're doing good, Luke—"

An explosion overhead sent a shockwave through the ceiling, raining chunks of mortar about them and thickening the air with more dust. Julia felt herself sway and then Luke was pulling her in front of him, urging her to grab the banister. They clung to the metal rail on each step down, shouting to each other through the cacophony. Then a tremendous bang rocked the stairwell, propelling Julia forward. She fell, half-jumped the last few steps to the landing, her head bashing into the back wall. She sank down, stunned.

She heard her name called through the clamour around her. She tried to move, but pain seared through her head.

"Jules! Answer me!"

She opened her eyes that were caked. Her face was pressed against the damp, peeling wall. Her hand rose to her forehead, where she encountered steri-strips and something wet.

A spasm flowed through the wall and she watched, fascinated, as a crack followed, winding its way upward, fissuring out like tributaries, bits of plaster falling from it on top of her.

Luke!

She twisted round, groaning with the sudden movement. She

was on the midway landing and Luke was sprawled on the stairs where she'd left him, clinging to the steel spokes of the banister. He looked like a ghost under the shaft of light she held up. Between them was a massive hole.

"Are you OK?" he shouted above the groaning and whining of the dying house.

"I… think so."

Luke appeared to relax and lay back against the stairs.

"Luke?" Julia panicked. She struggled up and shone the beam on his face. "Can you stand up?"

"Yeah, in a minute."

"We haven't got a minute. Luke, we have to keep moving."

He looked over and laughed at the gaping hole with nothing but a flimsy, foot-wide platform on the wall-side linking his flight to the landing. Something had torn through from above, severing the banister and taking out the bottom stairs.

"Luke, get up. You're not a quitter."

He heard the panic in her voice, took some breaths and coughed again. He dragged himself up using the part of the banister still moored to the floor. Where the hole was, the banister, still attached to its wooden feet, had been launched, suspended over the gap between the flights.

"You remember how to ride a bike?" he shouted, looking down over the handrail.

"Why?"

"You've got the keys for the bike I came on. It's in the woods at the back of this place."

"I'm not going anywhere without you." Her voice rose. "You're coming with me, Luke!"

He took a laboured breath and looked back up the stairs. "Maybe I should find another way down."

Crashes and bangs cascaded from the upper floor and something else – smoke, swirling down like a treacherous snake.

"No way," Julia shouted. "We're staying together!"

She moved the beam over the aperture. "Use the banister, Luke. You've got to get across somehow."

"As easy as that, huh!"

A splitting sound spread across the ceiling and they both looked up. She looked back at him, saw the blood still seeping from his wound in his leg, his deathly pale face, his hunched shoulders.

"You can do this."

Luke turned round to face the arching framework. Forcing himself not to look down into the pitch-black void below him, he stretched his bad leg down to the almost horizontal rod while keeping hold of the one still moored into the staircase. Julia kept the light on it so he could see what he was doing.

"If this doesn't work, you get yourself out of here," he yelled.

"You're coming with me, Luke," she countered.

"Here goes," he muttered.

He eased his weight over onto the makeshift ladder, still holding on above him.

Plaster burst from the walls behind him. He ducked instinctively and the twisted frame bobbed down but held. The coils of smoke wrapped around them, making it harder to see, and they were both coughing.

He let go and carefully lowered his upper body down to grasp the cool rods that had formerly held up the handrail. He began to traverse the frame with shaky steps. It bounced slightly as he moved over the yawning maw beneath him.

"Keep going, Luke – that's it."

Luke paused. He wiped his blood from the rods he'd already stepped on so he could grip them.

Julia watched him, holding her breath, the broken banister bowing a little lower with each rung he crossed, sinking closer to her. She could see the sweat on his brow caking the dust there. The smoke was stinging her eyes and she was coughing more, as he was. The din above was so loud now and larger chunks of mortar were falling in bursts from the roof, miraculously missing Luke as he drew nearer to her.

She stepped down two steps, placing the torch on the top one to project the light through the veil of dust and smoke. With a clang the ladder suddenly dropped, taking Luke lower than they wanted. He stopped. He was a metre or so from her outstretched hand. He pulled the zip down on his leather.

He shrugged out of the jacket, keeping one hand on the frame and using his knee to pin the garment between him and the frame so he didn't drop it. He took hold of one sleeve and swung it towards her. She caught the other sleeve and began to slowly pull him to her, the buoyant frame obliging, moved upwards with him, closer to her outstretched hand.

A sudden grating noise, as the upper rod broke free of the base and the ladder dropped slightly, pulling him away from her again. The jacket slipped from her grasp.

"Oh God," she whispered.

"I'm OK," he shouted, peering down. "I should maybe… drop down lower and swing through onto the stairwell."

Julia grabbed the torch and shone it down and back again. "I don't think…"

The ladder jerked as another rod popped free.

"Oh Christ, Luke…" she choked, as much on the words as on the cloying smoke and dust.

She shone the torch full on his face in her anguish and he blinked in the glare. He smiled at her. She saw him mouth the words, "It's OK."

A rending sound and the ladder dropped away, taking Luke with it in a tangle of metal and wood.

"No!" Julia screamed. "No! Oh my God!"

She ran downstairs as fast as she could, tears blinding her vision, past buckling skirting and splitting walls, keeping the small circle of light in front of her.

"Please, no, please, no! Luke?" she shouted. "Luke!" The crashing din drowned out her pleas.

On the flight below, she came to a huge block of concrete at the end of a beam that had caused the hole above. It had wedged into the stairs, but the beam sticking out had stopped it falling further. She inched around it all the while coughing and calling his name. Once past it, she hurtled down the flights, flicking her light before her then out into the space between the stairs, trusting her feet to find the steps that would take her to him.

At the first floor she saw the broken banister had caught across the aperture and fell no further. Luke was not on it.

She cried out in anguish.

"You're not having him!" she screamed to the pall of dust and smoke.

Debris fell from the roof, urging her to go faster, and a wall imploded behind her, throwing bricks over the rail to plummet below.

At the bottom she found him curled up on the floor, a pool of blood around his head.

"Oh my God, please, no, please, please, Oh God…"

Julia knelt beside him, her tears splashing onto his shoulder while her shaking hand reached out and she gently turned him onto his back.

"Luke…" she said.

His eyes were closed.

He half-smiled, half-grimaced. "What a ride."

"Oh, Luke!" She laughed in relief, wanting to hit him at the same time.

A gash on the side of his skull oozed dark, sticky liquid. It was more of a scrape than a cut, but it was nasty all the same. She kissed his forehead.

The smoke was descending all around them now and a table-sized piece of wood fell with hefty chunks of mortar from the ceiling, landing feet from them.

"Can you stand?"

He nodded. She helped him to his feet. He groaned aloud when he put weight on his leg.

"I think you're driving," he said.

The hallway rumbled and rocked, crashed and shattered around them as they stumbled back to the kitchen and the way out.

•

Luke directed her through the trees to where he'd left the bike. They could hear police sirens now as they stumbled through the wood. There was a sudden concussive boom from the house that almost knocked them over. It sounded like the roof had caved in; Julia pulled Luke on. They were nearing the road now and the bike was in sight. Luke stopped when he saw the travel bag in a hollow to their right.

"Grab that, Ju."

Julia did as she was asked, thinking it was familiar, but she couldn't work out why. They struggled on.

He took the bag from her once they were at the parked bike, opened the top box and stuffed it inside.

"Take off your coat, Jules," he said. "Ju?"

She was looking back in the direction of the house.

She turned towards him. "This is Marsden."

He nodded. "It was."

The sirens were pretty loud now, and he took her coat and gave her the leather jacket, which looked worse for wear. She zipped it up then donned the helmet, clicking the strap closed.

She helped him ease his helmet over his head wound then held his arm while he swung his bad leg over the seat. She straddled the bike then and instructed him to hold on. She heard him laugh and twisted round.

"What?"

"Nothing. Stay off the main roads where you can and don't speed." He put his hands round her middle and squeezed her. "You OK?"

"I'm OK." She squeezed his hand tight so he knew.

She approached the road with the lights off till she was sure the oncoming police cars wouldn't see them leaving the property then pulled off as gently as she could in the opposite direction before speeding up. She sped away, checking in the wing mirror, waiting for the police to come into view, but they still hadn't appeared by the time she took the bend.

.

Five miles on and Julia pulled over. She let Luke dismount. She was trembling all over. She put the stand out and dismounted on shaky legs. Luke was flagging. They were heading to Shakes' house, but she just needed a minute. She was crying as they pulled off their helmets.

He pulled her close. "It's alright, Ju."

"I remember holding a knife… someone crying, begging, I think I—"

"It wasn't you, Jules, I saw it all. It was Caroline."

Julia searched his face, desperate to recall what had happened.

"Steve died, Luke… it was…" She shook her head. "And I can't remember what happened after that. I was lost, but I heard your voice. I followed your voice. You pulled me back from… I don't know where." She buried her face on his chest.

"It's OK," he said. "We'll work it all out."

For a while they didn't speak. He hugged her tight as her shuddering body calmed, then she looked up at Luke. She felt a surge of hope. Hope of a good life: one with good memories, one built on the present. One she could share with him and her children.

She managed a smile and looked over his shoulder towards Manchester, expecting to see an angry burning sky, but all was calm.

The wind blew softly around them, stirring the petals on the daisy chain in her hair as she kissed him.

Acknowledgements

Thank you to Chloe May and Liberty Woodward and the designers at the Book Guild for their expert advice and infinite patience with a complete novice and for helping me at every stage of this exciting journey.

Thank you also to my sister Carla for being a very early reader and later a proof reader and for her encouragement with my endeavour.

And to Isabel and Evalyn, a massive thanks for your time on the photo shoot for the cover; Isabel for being a patient and enigmatic model and Evalyn for all the work you did on the photo afterwards capturing that moody, malevolent moment!

And thank you Luke and Maja for helping us that day and ensuring it ran smoothly.